Hidden By Moonlight

Hidden By Moonlight

Embahra Maat

32nd Dynasty Publications

ISBN-13: 978-0-9962750-2-6
ISBN-10: 0-9962750-2-9

© 2015 by 32nd Dynasty Publications

Printed in 2015 in the United States of America

Cover design by Sa-Nekhet en Asut Menta of Konscious Creations
http://www.konsciouscreations.com/

For Olivia

"It is not just disbelief that is the problem, but also, fear of the responsibility of believing. There is inherent cultural power in myths. Discarding myths to avoid being judged for believing in them, and ignoring their wisdom because of what they ask us to do, give, and be, causes us to lose access to an important source of spiritual power and cultural pride."

-- Hem NTR Naswt Biti Ra Sankhu Kheper

I was born on the fifth and final day.

When I was born, my great grandfather's warmth beamed down upon me, my mother wrapped me with stars, and my father gave me his side to rest upon. I looked out and saw my siblings, all of us together, as we had been in the womb of our mother. We were young, but we were not babies. We were children of the cosmos.

Being youngest has its perks; being last has its consequences. Despite, and because of, what has happened, I strive to tell my story, my truth. That will not always be easy, but as I've learned, the most difficult things tend to be the most important.

SEMA – UNION

I held the small mirror in place while my sister affixed the final lotus flower to her crown. She frowned while adjusting it, creasing her brows and chin with small lines of worry. I smiled to myself, happy to see her anxious for once. She finally stood, straight and tall, completely finished.

We were identical in many ways, my sister and I. We both had smooth auburn skin, unblemished and softly reddened from loving kisses of the sun. We wore our hair long, and it puffed around our faces like soft, wavy halos. We had large, bright eyes that shone like stars, and happy smiles that never seemed to fade from our cheeks. At least, this is what our father always says, and his opinion would be a bit biased, of course. Our resemblance was such that, in the beginning, it was decided that we would distinguish ourselves; yet somehow, our mother always knew how to tell us apart, and I loved her all the more for it.

Geb, our father, peeked into the dressing room from the hallway. "Are the two of you ready, or should we hold up the entire universe so you can finish preparing?" he scolded playfully, the twinkle in his dark brown eyes matching the gleam of his bald head. I glanced up at him with a knowing smile. Even though he had been gentle, he was telling Auset to speed it along. Good luck with that, I thought to myself, knowing if I said it aloud, he'd be the only one to find it amusing.

Auset sighed. "I think I'm ready, but **Yit**, is it okay?"

She turned and faced the door at the same moment a soft

gust of wind flew in through the window. The silken fabric of her gown swayed; it was the deep hue of lapis lazuli that she loved so much. She looked beautiful, and our father looked genuinely happy. He opened his arms and she slowly walked over to him.

Grasping her by the shoulders, he looked her square in the eye. "Beloved one, you are a queen today. You look lovely."

Auset smiled brightly and hugged him tightly. "Thanks Yit. I am ready."

"How about you, my young lady? Are you ready?" Yit asked me after letting her go.

I picked up the hand mirror once more and gave myself a quick glance, smiling as I examined the round ball of hair that had accumulated at the back of my head. On the top, my thick tresses had been slicked down to make room for my crown, which was firmly affixed into place. Whereas Auset wore the infinite blue of our mother, I wore the fertile green of our father, and the hue glittered on me like emeralds. It was the easiest decision to make when figuring out how to distinguish ourselves. We quickly gravitated to our respective shades, and never begrudged the other her choice.

I sighed, knowing that this was the moment I could stall no longer.

"As ready as I can be." I placed the mirror down on the wooden bench, stood, and smiled. Yit took long strides into the room to hug me, knowing I would never bound into his arms like Auset. She was the affectionate one, always smothering our brothers with hugs and kisses. I am reserved, not secretive as some might think, simply thoughtful and contained.

It wasn't strange for me to be this way, or at least it should not have been. My name, Nebt-Het, means she who masters the house. Djehuty, our tutor, often reminded me that before one can be master of a domain, she must first be master of herself.

This name was given to remind me that, even though I am the youngest, I still have a duty and purpose in this world just as my siblings do, and my place is no less significant than theirs.

So I am reserved, careful in my movements and words, purposely attempting to be masterful. Sometimes it is real, and sometimes it is a charade. What can I say? I am not perfect, but I am perfecting.

Yit let me go and stepped back. "Let's get you two married."

Out in the hall, our mother Nut was pacing slowly near the entrance of the hall. When she was in this form, her gown changed color depending on how the light reflected off of it. When I first laid eyes on her, one side appeared as a sky silvery blue, and the other a nighttime blue black. It was impossible for anyone to keep their eyes off her, and yet today was supposed to be about us.

Nut stopped moving when she saw us, standing directly in the light, her long black hair bouncing upon her shoulders, her dress bright silver. The look on her face was a priceless grin of pride and love. She hesitated in moving towards us, but I could tell she ached to put her arms around us in a loving hold.

Auset reached her first, naturally walking faster. She couldn't help but to want the affection our mother's face promised. The hug between them looked so tight that I was worried one might stop breathing before it ended, but soon enough it was my turn.

"**Mwt**, you don't have to sit still during the entire ceremony," I assured her. I wasn't particularly happy about this in the first place, so I wasn't about to object to the possibility that she might draw the attention on to her and away from me.

She shook her head soundly. "Nonsense; I won't be the one to disrupt this occasion." Her arms wrapped around me with a tender amount of distance. I smiled and placed my head on her shoulder. I never told her I didn't care for the affection, but she knew, as she did most things. Mwt hugged me differently than she hugged my sister. She hugged me like I was me.

I pulled away after a minute and looked up in her eyes, a mischievous grin spreading over my face. "If you're ready," I said, "we can all go in and get this over with."

She smiled down at me with the same grin. "Yes. I'm ready."

We turned and entered the hall, our mother on my right, my sister on my left, and our father on her left. The four of us strode completely in step with one another. As we neared the front, Mwt noticed a spot in the room with deep shadows and moved into it, the absence of light darkening her dress so it would stand out much less. Yit joined her and it was just Auset and I.

At the front were our betrothed, waiting for what we'd all known was inevitable. Our eldest brother, Ausar, stood to the far left, waiting for Auset, anxious to marry her. He cleared his throat and stuck out his chest, broadening his shoulders and standing as straight as possible. I glanced over at Auset and she was blushing like a girl in love.

I looked up to my betrothed, Setesh. He was born third, squarely in the middle. As much as I disliked being born last, I was thankful to not have come in the middle. Setesh carried himself with a certain petulance that made him difficult at best, unbearable at worst. Not that I didn't understand his turmoil, but I wished he would find a way to accept his lot in life, as we all had.

But, that was not his way, and he was to be my husband. I smiled at him and he nodded at me in approval. At least he does care for me, I thought to myself, even if I am the consolation prize.

My brothers were wearing white vests with loose white pants beneath them and sashes bound around their waists. Ausar preferred a sash of the darkest black; Setesh wore a red rich as blood. Clasped at the neck were the broad collars of royalty and their wrists were bound with cuffs of solid gold. Their heads were covered with the **Nemmes** crown that matched their respective sashes perfectly.

Despite being dressed so similarly, they couldn't look or be more different. Ausar was a finger's length taller, with the sepia toned skin of our mother and the slender build of one destined for priesthood. He kept his hair cut low, not bald as our father, but closely shaved. Setesh was broader and muscular, having quickly taken to warrior training; his skin darker, the color of cocoa, like our father's, and the tight coils of his hair wound into slender ropes that skimmed the tops of his shoulders. He carried a constant scowl upon his countenance, a look which had only the slightest of variations, an expression that you'd never find on his older brother. Ausar had moments of seriousness, but they were backed with gentle love and inner peace. Mostly, he captivated with his joy, and today would be no different. He grinned at Auset like he was the luckiest man at the ball, and no one thought he wasn't.

Ausar reached out for her hand, and she gave it quickly. I looked back to Setesh, and he reached out his hand as well. I placed mine into his gently, with what I'd hoped was grace. He used it to pull me in a bit closer to him, turning to face **Seba** Djehuty, as our teacher was presiding over the ceremony. I tried to keep my face calm, impenetrable, but Setesh squeezed my hand, so I must have been frowning, anxious. I looked over at him and he was looking straight ahead, scowling in the way that meant he was content.

I took one last look over at Auset and Ausar, holding each other's hands tightly. They were staring into each other's faces, beaming, grinning. They couldn't keep their eyes off one another. I was certain they wouldn't hear a word anyone said. I sighed and looked to the front, past Djehuty, out through the hall, into the edge of the universe.

5

Heru-Ur dropped the last of my things into the doorway of the sitting room and knocked on the frame. "Are you sure this is enough room for you?" he asked sarcastically. "Because I get the feeling this apartment isn't quite large enough."

I grabbed the nearest headrest and made to throw it at him, causing him to feign ducking. He smiled and shook his head. "Where in this house would we find a smaller space?" I asked jokingly with a hint of realism. "Everything in here is monstrous."

He sauntered into the room and stopped just short of where I was standing, keeping little space between us. I looked up at him, happy that he was here but disappointed that he was leaving so soon. It felt like we'd just gotten here, and yet there he was, about to take his leave and head to the countryside.

We'd moved out of our home in the skies and down to our new home on the riverbank of the great **Hapi** in **Kemet**. Here, Ausar would take his place as the first king and leader, and teach the people the way of **Maat**. Heru-Ur was set to begin the work of identifying sacred ground for temples and holy sites. His mission would start just north of here, and as he made his way up the Hapi, he would oversee each building's construction to ensure the physical alignment with the spiritual goals of each house.

Heru-Ur leaned down and kissed me on the forehead, square in the center. "You know I shall miss you the most, dearest sister."

I abandoned my rule about affection and hugged him closely. "You shouldn't be the one leaving here today." I meant it to sound as pouty as it did.

He wrapped his arms around me, welcoming the hug.

"Actually, I'm exactly who is supposed to leave." Heru-Ur sighed, then pulled away, turning his back to me. Heru-Ur was built like Setesh, broad and warrior-like, but his features resembled Ausar, except for the dark mane that sprang from his head and reached for the heavens. When the three stood together, their masculine presence commanded attention, and received it.

I watched him pace for a moment, then tried to turn my attention back to the boxes on the ground. I sighed and looked around at the work I had before me. "We are all in the right place at the right time, as they say." I sounded more sarcastic than enthusiastic, which wasn't my intent, but the natural result of my present emotions.

Heru-Ur leaned against the frame of the door, turning back to face me, his dark brown eyes glimmering with love. His facial expression was serious, and he took a deep breath. "You may not yet understand the wisdom of it all, but you will, in time. When you're ready to."

I nodded in acceptance, wanting to roll my eyes at words we all knew so well, choosing instead to avert my eyes to the ground. I wanted to plead with him, ask him not to go, but I didn't, knowing nothing I said would matter. "We'll celebrate tonight, and say our goodbyes," I said, looking back at him and trying to smile. "You will face the world with all of our support."

Heru-Ur nodded. "I'll need it." He turned as if to go, hesitated, then turned back to me once more. "Is there anything else you need? Can I help with anything?"

"No, I just," I started, looking around, exasperated. "I just need to not feel so overwhelmed, is all." I looked up at him. "I already know what I should do for that." We both smiled.

"Nebt-Het," he stepped back into the room tentatively, "I know I said so already, but I am sorry, you know, the way everything went before, it wasn't, I didn't mean for it to be that way." His arm twitched, as though he wanted to reach out for my hand, but he didn't. "I'm sorry, you know."

I took his hand, not caring about who might see. "I'm sorry too, I really am. I never meant for any of this, and I wish, I wish -"

He pulled his hand from mine, stopping my words. "There's no point in doing that," he responded, turning away. "We can't change anything now."

My shoulders slumped. "We never could."

"We shouldn't want to." Heru-Ur started out of the door, ready to take his leave. "All will go on as it is meant to, and you will be who you are meant to."

I nodded without adding another word, and he left. I sighed again. "Whoever that is," I whispered, low enough that no one in the hall could hear, but out loud, so I could feel rebellious. In this moment, I was dissatisfied, and it was hard to contain such a strong and confusing emotion.

The problem was, everyone had their assignment. Even my husband knew what he was here to accomplish, what his work would be. He was to serve at the right hand of the king, as commander of the warrior corps. We all anticipated this being a difficult arrangement, for Setesh and Ausar opposed one another on every topic. The idea that Setesh argued just for the sake of being antagonistic crossed my mind enough times to be more than coincidence. Djehuty insisted that Ausar would need people around him who are not going to say yes to his every whim; as king, he would need advisors who are not afraid to make him think about the large and small of leadership. Challenging Ausar was something I knew my husband could do very well.

Everyone had an assignment. Everyone except me. Auset was queen and Ausar was king. Heru-Ur was head priest and

Setesh was war chief. I was their baby sister. What was my place in this world? What would my contribution be? I hadn't figured it out yet and I felt as though no one else had either. Or, if they had, they hadn't explained it to me yet.

It was immature, I know, but it was how I felt, and it caused me to struggle on that first day moving in, and for many days after. But I am getting ahead of myself.

After a few hours of unpacking, our mini apartment on the west wing was nearly set. There was an oversized sitting room with wooden armchairs and stools, the feet on all seats clawed. The armchairs were covered from top to bottom in gold leaf, while the stools were mostly black with little accents of gold. On the arms, our names had been carved and the stools had papyrus reeds and lotus flowers painted onto each leg in gold. The square seats of the stools were covered with dark leather to make them a bit more comfortable than the rigid wooden frame would allow.

The sitting room opened to our magnificent bedroom, with a large wooden bed frame in the center, covered with mats of woven papyrus reeds which smelled sweet and fresh. Like the seats, the legs of the bed looked like those of a lion, and the corners at the foot of the bed were designed to look like the face of a lioness so that she would protect us while we slept. The lioness' face shone with gold plate, and her eyes glared of the darkest onyx. There were two more armchairs in this room which matched the armchairs in the sitting room, and several small chests that sat upon the floor where we could store our things.

The bedroom opened to a small courtyard where we could sit and watch the sunset every night. It was here that a small pool had been built, to siphon water from the river so that we could bathe and swim with complete privacy. The courtyard itself was surrounded by low walls of red mud, which were made beautiful by the overgrown water lilies and papyrus plants that seemed to stretch to the heavens. The fragrance was delicious, and I wondered what occasion would cause me to ever want to keep those doors closed.

I allowed the wind to blow directly into the room, cooling myself and the space almost immediately. It was relaxing and I laid down, thinking I might take a quick nap while I had some time to myself.

Alas, it was not to be. I could hear my husband sternly barking orders to an unfortunate attendee as he approached our bedroom, the boom of his voice nearly shaking the walls. I sat up and gathered myself, hoping to meet him at the door of the apartment.

We stepped into the sitting room at the same time, and upon catching my eye he stopped in his tracks. He was sweaty and dirty, which told me he had been outside in this dreadful weather, probably engaging in a friendly wrestling match with our brothers. I smiled at him and tilted my head. The frown on his face changed from the look of defeat to a scowl of appreciation. Heru-Ur must have bested him in their last match or he wouldn't be so dour, I thought to myself.

"Well?" he asked without moving. "Aren't you going to say something?"

My smile widened. "And risk being your next victim? No thank you."

He began walking over to me, peeling off his garments one at a time until he stood directly in front of me, completely naked. My breath hitched at the sight of him, and my nostrils curled at the smell.

I took one large step backwards. "If I'm to give you what you want, you're to give me what I want," I demanded, looking him squarely in the eye.

"And what's that?" he asked, moving in closer than he was before.

"Cleanliness."

His mouth and cheeks barely twitched, but his deep set eyes laughed loudly. They were my favorite feature about him, how expressive they were. "I request your assistance," he stated, clearly not a request. I grabbed him by the hand and took him to the outdoor pool, and as he stepped into the lukewarm water I undressed myself and slid in next to him.

"Everything looks good in there," he said, the best compliment he could muster. I smiled, because if he'd bothered to say anything he must really be impressed.

"Thanks," I whispered shyly. "I've been putting things in order since the morning."

Setesh nodded, leaning back on the edge of the pool, the water lapping around the sides of his neck. "Did you have any help, or you did it all by yourself?"

I didn't want him to know of Heru-Ur's involvement, but I didn't want to lie completely. I moved over to the other side so I could look him in the eye while we talked. "I had an attendee come help me with some heavy things, but mostly I did it myself." After a brief pause I asked, "what were you yelling about before you came in?"

He smirked. "I wasn't quite *yelling*, more like, *instructing*. I don't want anyone around who can't manage to use his own mind, is all."

"Instructing about what, if I may?"

He hesitated. "Asking where things should be placed. Clearly things related to the throne should go into the throne room." He glanced at me quickly, checking to see if I was judging him harshly, then looked away, across the courtyard, towards the horizon. "Some of those questions should have been directed at Ausar, but the attendees are too nervous to ask the great and powerful king," he said with a hint of sarcasm added to the end.

I chose my next words carefully. "Today has been a long and difficult day. Everyone is figuring things out." I reached out and took his hand. "Things will run smoother tomorrow."

He pulled his hand away unconsciously and ran his fingers through his thick mane. "It will help when Heru-Ur is gone. When he's not here, everyone will have to learn to manage themselves." He looked back at me, coming out of his short contemplation. "Don't get me wrong, I will miss him too. But he always acts like a buffer and it is hard to manage things when he is constantly interfering. Apologizing for me, like I don't know what I'm saying or doing, treating me like he's tired of cleaning up my messes."

Setesh came closer to me, taking my hands into his. "I just want the chance to be who I know I can be, who I am meant to be. I feel like they are just holding me back, you know?"

I touched my hand to the side of his face lightly. "If there was any doubt about you being ready to do this, we wouldn't be here. You will make an excellent general... the best this land has ever seen."

He looked at me, slightly puzzled. "I am the first general this land has ever seen."

"Well... that makes it easier for you to be the best, then."

He snickered, appreciative of my joke, moving to sit next to me and pulling me into his lap. Setesh then wrapped his arms around my waist and clasped his fingers near my navel. This was uncharacteristically warm of him, and I was growing to enjoy these moments. He was my husband, after all, and in the month since our wedding we'd had a chance to figure each other out. It was an adventure and one I was glad for.

"I didn't mean to pull away before," he whispered into my

ear, "I am just frustrated is all. I want everything to go well just as much as everyone else, and I keep feeling like -"

"Shhhh," I cut him off, nestling into him and touching his chin with my forehead. "Just focus on the fact that we all want the same thing, and the only way for us to get there is together."

We were both quiet for a few minutes, not speaking and not moving. I closed my eyes, feeling once more like I could drift off to sleep, realizing how badly I wanted to.

Again my nap was interrupted by a loud throat clearing. My eyes opened to find our tutor, Djehuty, standing awkwardly at the opposite edge of the pool as if he wished he hadn't found us bathing together.

I tried to pull away, but Setesh tightened his grip around me. "I assume you didn't just walk in on us for no reason?" he snarked at Djehuty, causing our tutor to raise his eyebrows. I nudged Setesh in the ribs gently, hoping Djehuty wouldn't notice. He cleared his throat. "I mean, is it something that can wait until we're done?" Setesh added, changing his tone slightly.

Djehuty took a deep breath, shifting his weight from one leg to the other. "Unfortunately, no." He looked Setesh directly in the eyes. It caused my husband to loosen his grip on my waist momentarily. "Ra is here, and he'd like to talk to all of us. We're meeting in the great hall for dinner in an hour. You both need to be there," he stressed, looking at me for a moment and then shifting his stare back to Setesh.

We finally unattached from one another completely, and I slid away from him, looking for the nearest cloth to cover myself with. It wasn't close enough to grab without getting out, so I looked up at Djehuty, eyebrows arched.

"Of course," he said, getting the hint. He usually did. "If you want to see me before the dinner, I'll be down in the throne room finalizing the details for tomorrow's festival." Djehuty gave a slight bow, which caused his dark brown locks to fall across his face. He brushed them out of the way before quickly marching out of the courtyard, through the bedroom, and into the sitting room, closing the bedroom door behind him.

Setesh sighed, wordlessly standing and climbing out of the pool. He nudged the fabric closer to me, and walked naked across to the courtyard doors, apparently choosing to air dry.

I climbed out of the pool and grabbed the cloth, wrapping it around myself so that only my arms and legs were showing. I stood there for a few minutes, not wanting to go inside, until finally resigning myself to fate.

Setesh was halfway dressed when I entered the bedroom, and he glanced up at me. "I can't believe he came in here when we were bathing," he grumbled, pacing the room in his white lapa and red sash, having not yet put on his shirt nor any other adornments.

I wanted to laugh. What a silly thing to be upset about, I thought. "He probably knocked and we didn't hear it. I'll ask him about it later."

My husband nodded. "I wonder what this meeting's going to be about." He looked me straight in the eyes, and I looked away.

"As do I," I added, shrugging my shoulders. "I suppose we'll find out soon enough."

He stood, walked over to me and took my face in his hands, forcing me to look him directly in the face. "I wasn't finished with you."

"Nor I with you."

His lips twitched, and I began to smile, placing my hands at his waist. He kissed my nose, then my forehead, then pulled away quickly, without lingering. Turning his back to me, he asked me quietly, "I'm going to take a walk before the meeting - I'll meet you there?"

"Yes, of course," I whispered in response, and he left without looking back. I took a deep breath and folded my hands behind my back. So many things have changed, I thought, such good things.

The heavy wood doors to the great hall were open when I arrived for dinner. In my anxiety, I had dressed in one of my fancier outfits; a sheer green loose-fitting gown that covered everything from my wrists to my ankles, and shimmered when I walked. I knew it would leave nothing to the imagination if not for the plain linen dress that I wore underneath. Setesh and Heru-Ur were already there, and neither had shared my inclinations, for they were both bare-chested, and had decided against wearing the Nemmes to dinner. The identical white lapas they wore which spanned from belly to knee were accented only by the sashes they tied at their waists; Heru-Ur choosing his sash in gold, and Setesh donning his patented red.

Both turned and looked at me when they sensed me approaching. I nodded at Heru-Ur and sat between them, taking my husband's hand in mine. Setesh pulled it to his lips and kissed my knuckles gently. Heru-Ur looked away.

Djehuty came sweeping into the room on a heavy gust of wind, the hem of his thick purple robe floating behind him. "I am glad to see you three are here and ready to begin. Has anyone seen Ausar and Auset?" he asked before realizing that we could hear them coming up the hallway. They practically sprinted through the doors and stopped short at the look of impatience on Djehuty's face. Ausar gathered himself quickly and gave all of us a somber nod, while Auset suppressed her giggles and grabbed his hand. They too were dressed casually, with Ausar in an outfit that matched his brothers and Auset in a plain sky blue linen dress. They walked together to the table and sat down across from the three of us, still glowing with the distinct look of young love.

I wanted to roll my eyes, but I stopped myself. Instead I took my hand away from Setesh and clasped mine in front of me on the table, straightening my back and looking straight towards the doors where I expected Ra to enter. Setesh followed suit and did the same, and after a few moments, so did the others, except Djehuty, who was standing behind Ausar and Auset, arms tightly wound around scrolls of papyrus, as they usually were.

A bright light went off outside the doors, blinding us all momentarily, and when we got our bearings back, we could see Ra, our great-grandfather, standing there in a bright gold lapa and darker gold sash that were almost entirely concealed by the heavy gold and white robe that would have consumed a lesser being by its extravagance. We immediately stood to show him the honor and respect he deserved, and remained standing as he moved through the room, the cuffs on his wrists and ankles creating a soft clatter with every step, and the metal of his **usekh**, the broad collar worn by royalty, shooting out blinding rays of light.

Ra pushed his hair off his shoulders, long and heavy ropes that made my husband's appear childish by comparison, and took his place at the head of the table. The grain of the thick wooden planks that made up the table's surface swirled to life, straining to get close to his light. Behind him, the view of the east framed his form with a soft, reverent glow. Djehuty sat next, at the foot of the table, and the five of us sat simultaneously. Still no one spoke. I kept my head down, looking into my lap, nervous about what this dinner meant for us.

"My darling girl," Ra started slowly, his voice deep and resonant. Heru-Ur tapped me on the shoulder, causing me to look up. The Great Father was speaking to me, and I tried to meet his stare with a smile. He smiled back. "There is no need to be nervous, Nebt-Het. I am only here to share a few words and celebrate your successful transition to your new home."

I smiled, relieved. "Dua, **Yit-Eah**. I am thankful we can share this moment with you."

Ra chuckled, sitting back in his seat comfortably. Attendees approached the table and began to pour water into our cups and setting down platters of odd looking objects, which I knew was likely the food that was indigenous to this region. Back home, food is not a concern, but being here makes us more susceptible to the needs of the flesh. I realized I was famished, but waited to see if Ra would eat first.

Ra waved his hands as if to give us permission to indulge, which we did slowly at first, increasing with speed as our shyness melted away.

"Seba, are you going to have so little?" Ausar asked our teacher after seeing the small amount of food he'd taken. Setesh and Heru-Ur were hoarding food as though they might not have another chance.

Djehuty smiled and nodded. "For clear thinking here, in our new home, it is important that we keep our bodies light. We mustn't weigh ourselves down with heavy meals."

Ausar looked down at his portion, which had been growing in size. He contemplated it for a moment, then sat back from the table, following the example of Djehuty. I looked over at Ra, who had also been watching Ausar, and he smiled, glad to see that even though he was to be king, Ausar was humble enough to listen to wise counsel.

"Were all of you able to finish getting your rooms in order today?" Djehuty asked, glancing around the table to see who would answer first.

I swallowed quickly and frowned. "Our space is completed,

Seba. We got everything in order and found that there was nothing missing aesthetically or functionally. Please give Ptah and Seshat our deepest gratitude," I added. Seshat had chosen which spaces would appeal to which couple, and Ptah crafted the furniture pieces for our rooms, as well as the first set of royal ornaments to be used during the upcoming coronation.

Our teacher smiled subtly, then turned his attention to Auset. "How about you? How are you getting along with setting up your rooms?"

Auset glanced up at him shyly. "We still have a lot left. The apartment is spacious and there is much to be done. I don't think I properly assessed how much."

Ausar nodded, also looking slightly bashful. Heru-Ur nudged me under the table; I looked up at him and he raised his eyes at me suggestively.

"We did get a lot done Seba," Ausar added, "but not what we'd hoped we would." He looked down at his plate for a second, then out of the corner of his eye to his wife, who was now blushing deeply. I smiled, glad that someone had enjoyed their first day in this beautiful home.

Even Ra was smiling, the look on his face one of amusement. There was a brief moment of silence, and Ra took this occasion to call the attendees over to clear the table. All of us cleared our throats almost simultaneously, and I straightened my back to prepare for whatever was coming next. I looked towards our great-grandfather, whose tall and imposing figure seemed to hover over the entire room. He didn't seem to be preparing for something devastating, so I kept my breathing steady and deep. Finally, after what seemed like an appropriate anticipatory pause, Ra began to speak.

"I had always known that your birth would lead to my departure from this realm, and although I was against making this change, I have come to accept that change is both necessary and healthy," he began, reminding us of the story of our birth. "When our circumstances transform, it creates the opportunity for us to transform. What we become, what we change into, well, that is up to us," he said with a slight chuckle, sitting back in his seat.

He turned to the eldest of us. "Ausar, you have learned enough to be ready to lead. I would not leave this world in your command if I did not see the potential of all you can and will become. Yet, you are young still. You will see your beliefs change. Who you think you will be and what you think you will do will change in time. You must remain flexible to allow it to. Your charge will be to make adjustments when things do not go as planned. Infuse new life into projects, plans, and expectations. Seek alternative perspectives and consider the counsel of others. Be open to transformation, because it is coming whether you are ready for it or not."

Ausar nodded without speaking. Ra turned his attention to Heru-Ur. "Your journey will take you away from here, and it may be a very long time before you are able to return. You will constantly ask yourself why. Why it must be you, why it must be this way" He paused and took a sip of water, the first time he'd touched anything on the table since dinner began. "As we introduce the people to the way of Maat, they will need inspiration, and motivation, and it is your light that will give it to them. They will need you to be a close and constant reminder. Should you need your own, turn your face to the sky and allow the light to be your guide."

Looking past me to Setesh, Ra hesitated before speaking. "No one understands you, do they, Setesh?" he asked rhetorically, choosing to lighten the mood first. "It is not your imagination - it is true. You believe in the rules, and you believe in what is right. That is not the popular way, but it is your way. Your firmness will challenge others to the very core. They will see things in a light they never considered before, and it will be because of you. Yours will be a thankless job. There will be very few people who will appreciate you, and if you are not careful, this will cause you to experience great disappointment and resentment. Do not allow those emotions to fester, and stay focused on the goal, not the process."

Setesh looked down at his hands, twisting his fingers on the table in front of him. Ra looked over at Auset, who was sitting up straight, as though she couldn't wait to hear his message to her.

Ra took another sip, purposely to make my anxious sister wait a bit longer. I wanted to smile, but restrained myself.

"Today, you are a girl. Tomorrow, you will be a woman. You will be queen. You will be admired and respected and you must earn this distinction by standing for something." Ra leaned in closer to Auset and lowered his voice. "What do you stand for? What is most important to you?"

Auset's eyes grew large. "Maat," she whispered, more like a question than a statement.

Ra leaned back. "Then, you must live accordingly. You must choose accordingly. You must do more than say what is right. Remember what is most important, and allow these things to guide your steps day in and day out. If you are true to what is most important to you, you will be someone who all others strive to emulate."

Auset's face reddened and she looked away, face pained with discomfort. Ra finally turned his attention to me. I cleared my throat, even though I had no plans to speak.

"It has been hard for you, feeling as though you are in the background while everyone else is in the forefront. Wondering what your purpose is, why you are here. You must always remember that you are not just wife, or sister, or friend. You are not meant to fade quietly into the background of someone else's story. You are here for a purpose, and yours is no less significant than anyone else's here. Do not let yourself think that because your role is less distinct that it is less important. That is your challenge, to constantly affirm and be secure in your own worth."

I didn't speak, and I quickly looked away. I hated that all of my insecurities had just been spoken about, in front of everyone. I took a deep breath and looked around. Everyone seemed to be thinking about their own stuff, as if they'd stopped listening once they heard what concerned them. I sighed, relieved by the thought that no one had heard a thing he'd said about me.

Djehuty stood and tapped the table sharply, pulling everyone out of their meditation. We looked down to the other end of the table and Ra was gone, nothing left in his space but a soft golden mist that was quickly dispersing. I sighed again.

"Is that it, then?" Setesh asked. "Are we dismissed?"

Djehuty nodded. "These words are meant to be remembered. They came directly from the mouth of the Great Father. Do not take them lightly."

We all nodded in acquiescence, and took our leave. I linked my arm into my husband's and together we strolled slowly back to our apartment in silence. Ausar and Auset continued holding each other's hands and rushed back to their rooms, to be alone once more. Heru-Ur went outside under the moonlight, at the time I thought to take a contemplative stroll in the outer courtyard.

Once we were back in the front room of our apartment, I let go of his arm and sat upright on the nearest stool. Setesh stayed standing, not pacing or moving about nervously, just standing in one spot, arms behind his back, staring at the wall in front of him. I looked down at the floor, not sure if I should interrupt his thoughts but knowing I wanted to.

"Did you say something earlier, about not knowing your place in this world?" he asked me without looking over towards me. I took a deep breath. He had heard everything.

"I did, I mean," I started, twisting my hands in my lap. "I mumbled something when I thought no one was listening." I stopped talking for a moment and smiled. "I should know better. Someone is always listening."

Setesh nodded. "I mumbled something earlier about not being understood, or appreciated, or both, during one of my disagreements with Heru-Ur." He finally relaxed and sat on the stool opposite mine, facing me from the other side of the room. "I suppose with the coronation tomorrow, he couldn't allow us to continue having these types of thoughts."

"No, I suppose not, although Djehuty is probably right and we will need to hear these words again."

"And when that time comes, we will need to repeat them to ourselves," Setesh finished, looking me straight in the eye, firmly.

I nodded, agreeing. "If it at all helps, I will do my best to understand and appreciate you."

Setesh's eyes smirked at me. "Yours will never be a small part in my story."

I grinned, and with that, we resumed what had earlier been interrupted.

I slipped out of bed early in the morning, before the sun had begun peeking over the horizon. Covered to my ankles in a pale green silk robe, I exited our apartment and walked into the hallway. It was quiet, as none of the day's bustling had yet begun, which was exactly what I'd hoped to find by waking so early. I yawned and stretched quietly while tiptoeing towards the outer courtyard.

I approached the front door and noticed a slip of papyrus tucked into the corner of the door frame. It almost looked as if it had blown there accidentally and gotten caught, but I pulled it out and opened it, reading its contents quickly.

"Dearest sister,

Are you taking your walk, meditating in the silence of the morning? I thought about waiting long enough to see you one last time. I wish I was there to say goodbye properly, but I knew if I stayed I would never leave. I wish my mission didn't take me away from here. But all of you depend on me, and I don't want to let any of you down. I wish this didn't have to be, but it did. Promise me that you'll forgive me and understand why it had to be this way. Tell Ausar and Setesh that I will see them again soon, and tell Auset that I know she'll be beautiful today. I love you all, and you especially.

Shem e em htp,

Heru-Ur"

My eyes teared up, and I clutched the letter closely to my chest. Then, I wondered how long it could have been tucked there, and I flung one of the heavy doors open and stepped out boldly into the cold morning. I wouldn't be able to see him anyway, I realized, as the estate faces south and Heru-Ur is planning to travel north. I walked closer to the river's edge to see if I could peek around the side of the building. There was a tiny boat moving slowly from the rear of the estate, having traveled only a short distance as if it had just disembarked a few moments before.

I wrapped my arms around myself and said a quick prayer for my brother's success and safety. At the same time that I completed my prayer, the first rays of sunrise warmed my cheek. I sighed deeply and wiped my tears from my face, turning to find Djehuty standing a few feet away, waiting quietly, his simple white garb beginning to shimmer under the glow of sunrise.

"**E em htp** Seba," I greeted him, assuming he had been waiting for me. "Today will be a long and glorious day."

"As they all are," my teacher responded. He took a step towards me, keeping his hands clasped behind his back. "Is everything alright? I thought I might find you out here."

I waved the note around, not wanting him to read the contents. "Heru-Ur left a little while ago. I was watching his ship sail away."

He nodded, looking out towards the eastern horizon. "Seshat and I have just arrived and will need most of the morning to prepare. Will you be with your sister? She will need you."

"Yes, of course," I answered hastily, knowing that today was to be all about Ausar and Auset. "I assume I should head down to her rooms now?"

Djehuty nodded again. "We will be in the great hall and throne room, should we be needed." He bowed royally and stepped back into the estate, not waiting for me to follow.

I stepped inside and looked around, immediately getting distracted by the bustle that appeared to have come out of nowhere. People were rushing around, some carrying things off to their respective destinations, others cleaning and decorating for the day's events. I stood there momentarily, in the threshold between the outer sanctum and the inner, and breathed it all in. Then, I smiled, steeling myself to take on my mission for the day.

The last major occasion had been our joint wedding. This,

Ausar and Auset would do without me. They were to be crowned today as king and queen, formally introduced as the **Naswt Biti** and **Hmt Naswu** of **Ta Meri**.

I started walking down towards Auset's rooms before realizing that I needed to get dressed - I was still in my robe. I turned on my heels and began walking back to my apartment to prepare for the day.

I knocked on the outer door of Auset and Ausar's chambers and walked in without waiting for anyone to answer. I was right to assume no one had heard the knock; Auset was outside in the garden area, and Ausar was not in the apartment at all.

I stood at the threshold of the garden, looking at my sister, who was sitting on the ground, staring pensively out into the deep waters of the Hapi. Her suite faced east, and since it was still early in the day the sun bore down upon us heavily. She was not dressed; covered only in a short robe of blue and silver that barely disguised anything underneath. Auset had no reason to be modest, since it was only me who had entered, but I wondered how she would have felt if it had been someone else.

I put that thought out of my mind quickly - there was no one else who would bother her today. Everyone on the grounds right now was running around getting things in order, and attending to Auset was my duty. I took a deep breath and stepped out into the thick burn of the morning.

"Is everything ok?" I asked her, not knowing how else to break her spell. She didn't move, and had she not taken a loud breath, I would have thought she hadn't heard me either.

"I am a bit nervous today, is all," she admitted loudly, not bothering to hide her feelings. After the conversation we'd had with Ra last night, it was no use pretending that we could escape his presence. "It is just all so much."

I smiled and took another step towards her. "It is different now, that it's here? Different because thinking you're ready and being ready are not at all the same."

She glanced back at me over her shoulder quickly, not wanting to take her eyes off the beautiful river. "Yes, that's exactly it." After a few moments of silence Auset turned her entire body around so that she could face me, and I could see the worry in her eyes. "I know it was my actions that got us to this place, and I can't help but be angry at myself for setting something in motion that I cannot change."

I shook my head and frowned. "It was our birthright, our **MesKhenet** that we would eventually come to Kemet and rule. You know that. You didn't make anything happen that wasn't going to happen anyway."

Auset shook her head at me in returned and looked off into the distance. "No, but I made it happen sooner than it should have. And today is the day I formally accept the consequences of my actions."

"You don't know that, sister. Perhaps you did exactly what you were meant to."

She shook her head, still looking away from me. "There is no way that what I did was... right. There had to be another way."

I rolled my eyes, a gesture she couldn't see, frustrated by the sincerity of her self-deprecation. "You don't know that." I sighed and sat down on the ground, taking the risk that I might stain my linen dress so that I could look into the eyes of my twin. "This is our place and we were going to take it, so honestly, what is the difference between today and tomorrow? There is nothing we can do about it now, Auset, except to embrace it. We each reap the harvest of our choices."

"Oh, Nebt-Het, you sound just like Seba. Can't you just tell me it's not fair and I shouldn't have to do it?" Auset pretended to whine while smiling, teasing me for being myself. I smiled back and looked down at the ground, taking a small blade of grass between my fingers. I didn't really know what to say that would make her feel better, but I knew lecturing her wasn't helping.

I shook my head and looked back to her. She was looking at me as though she needed to say something to make me feel better. That was the way things worked between us; I always knew the words to appeal to the head, and Auset always knew the words to appeal to the heart. I stood and held my hand down to her to pull her upright.

"Come, we must get you dressed and ready," I ordered rather than asked, choosing to demonstrate my strength rather than run from it. "Being late would be a terrible way to start your reign."

Auset giggled, and I smiled. She reached up, grabbing my hand and I hoisted her up to her feet. Once standing, she squeezed my hand, and we turned and walked back into the apartment.

"Are you sure everything is okay out there?" Auset asked louder than necessary. I was standing right at the entrance of her chambers, and she was shouting like I was at the other end of the estate.

I looked out into the hallway briefly, finding it completely empty. "When last I checked, everything was in place. Djehuty was double-checking everything, and Seshat said we would begin shortly."

Auset sighed and smoothed out the sides of her dress. It was plain, suffering from a lack of jewels and adornments. It hung limply down the sides of her body, barely touching her hips or breasts at all. The fabric was soft and cooling, but humble. It was distinct only by the richness of Auset's blue hue. The adornments would come later, as part of the ceremony. Auset would enter as one of the people, to be elevated by the people, so that she may, in turn, serve the people.

I looked over at my sister, who was sitting, then standing, pacing, then sitting again. No longer nervous, she was now anxious to get the ceremony underway. I frowned.

"Auset, sit down, take a few deep breaths," I told her, closing the door to the hallway so that we couldn't hear the sounds. "Try to relax a bit. You'll want to enter the room as if you are in complete command of everything that happens."

She looked at me as if I were speaking gibberish, but sat down anyway. After a few deep, difficult breaths, Auset began to calm down. I knelt on the floor before her, covering her hands with my own.

"This one day cannot overwhelm you," I whispered to her fervently, searching her face, demanding her eyes meet mine. When she finally looked at me, I continued. "This is only the first step you must take in becoming who you are meant to be."

Auset took another deep breath, smiled and nodded. "I can only do this with you on my side," she responded softly, and I knew she meant it.

I stood. "You will never find me absent from it."

She stood and nodded again. I turned and opened the door, walking just two steps ahead of her as we entered the hallway.

There was not a sound coming from the great room as we approached, and yet with the large doors set open, I could see that it was filled to the brim. I couldn't see the dais clearly from so far back, but I knew Ausar had not yet taken his place.

I walked in first, which was the signal for everyone in the room to stand and face the aisle. I turned to Auset, who had stopped right in the threshold to gaze wide-eyed at the spectacle. She was right to stare, for the room was beautiful, covered in lotus flowers with soft fabrics of blue and white draped upon the walls and around the windows. There was a lovely breeze coming in from the Hapi and the fabrics didn't stop the sun from shining into the room, giving one side of the room a bright glow and the other side a soft shadow. The gold thrones upon the dais glittered brightly, like an invitation to be sat upon. Everyone in the room appeared to be dressed in their finest clothing and jewels, and as she began to walk up the aisle they began to bow, one by one, acknowledging our Queen for the very first time.

Seshat stood to the left of the dais, and Djehuty on the right; she in a slim fitting white gown with a short leopard skin cape draped over her shoulders, and he in the same white outfit that I had seen him in earlier, but Djehuty had draped a purple sash over his shoulder and across his body, making him appear more in command than usual. There was an attendant behind each of them, holding the trays that carried adornments for Ausar and Auset. When Auset reached the front, she knelt before the dais, resting her knees on the dried skin of a leopard. She outstretched her hands before her, palms facing upward to the heavens, and appeared to look straight ahead. I imagined how nervous she must be, and prayed momentarily under my breath.

I didn't move further into the room, yet I could see everything once everyone sat. However, I couldn't hear what was being said, which was of no consequence, since I knew what the ceremony was to entail. Djehuty opened the sacred text and began to read from it, causing the people's eyes to grow with wonder. After each question, Auset would make a pledge to live up to the responsibilities of that charge. Seshat then leaned over and added something to her garment as a symbol of that specific commitment.

When the cuffs were tightened around her wrists, I knew she'd promised that her hands will do great work on behalf of the people. The dark red knot they fastened at her waist bound her to be devoted to her charge. The earrings of amethyst that hung from her ears kept them open to words of right and truth. Seshat fastened the usekh around her neck, reminding Auset to hold her head high, never to act in a way that would bring shame or embarrassment. When the ostrich feather of Maat was placed in her left hand, she was charged to uphold the virtues of righteousness, and when she wrapped her right hand around the golden **Ankh** that glimmered the color of sunset, she was to be the giver and maintainer of life.

Finally, they placed the crown around her head, the **Urat** snake protruding from her forehead, as a reminder to have foresight and insight, not just hindsight. I took a deep breath and smiled. Auset stood and faced the crowd. They stood and cheered loudly, clapping and shaking rattles, dancing in celebration as she walked, step by step, up the dais and to her throne. When she sat, the room erupted in climax, and her cheeks reddened deeply as she closed her eyes and smiled.

After several minutes of celebration, the noise began to calm down and the people took their seats again. I felt a hand on my shoulder and turned sharply. Setesh had come in behind me, with Ausar hovering outside the threshold of the throne room, draped in white linen. Ausar had a look of determination and steadiness on his face which surprised me. I thought he'd be as nervous as Auset, but somehow he'd found a way to steel himself, and looked uncommonly regal in the process.

The room was finally silent. Setesh cleared his throat, and the people turned to see Ausar enter and make his way up the aisle. They stood and bowed to our King, one by one, row by row. His walk was deliberate, each step seeming heavy and purposeful. He knelt on the same leopard skin at the front of the room, and Seshat and Djehuty moved closer to him to begin his portion of the ceremony.

Setesh took my hand and together we stood at the back of the room, watching the ceremony behind the last row. I didn't have the desire to move closer to the front, but I wondered if anyone would think my decision to stay at the rear was a sign of displeasure. I for one was happy to see my brother and sister take their rightful places. I didn't want their place; I wanted my own.

There were cuffs tightened around Ausar's wrists, thick and gold, bigger than Auset's, and around his biceps, as he was the protector and defender of the realm. The sash tied around his waist was the same dark red as Auset's knot, yet Ausar's represented a willingness to shed blood on behalf of our way of life. The usekh was fastened around his neck, this one larger and bolder than his wife's. In his right hand the **Heq** was placed, the crook a symbol of his authority and dominion; and in his left hand, the **Naqqaqa**, the flail which represented his tireless commitment, as a King's work is never done. On his head he first received the **Hedjet**, white crown, as ruler of the southern lands. Around it, Djehuty slid the **Deshret**, red crown, to represent the northern lands. Having now received the two crowns together, Ausar was officially Naswt Biti, unifier of the two lands.

The crowd began to dance and chant again, not waiting for Ausar to stand, and it seemed that the room erupted louder than it had for Auset. When he turned to face the people, he threw his fists into the air above him, clutching tightly at the Heq and Naqqaqa, the muscles in his arms taut. Dozens of fists flew into the air after his, the men stomping and the women wailing in celebration. Every sistrum in the room seemed to be chiming at the same melody, even though there was no official song or tune, somehow everyone found themselves on the same accord. Ausar ascended the dais and took his place before his throne, and before sitting, he stretched his arms out before him, signaling the crowd to become quiet again.

Setesh squeezed my hand and released it. "Are you okay back here?" he asked me, looking back at me quickly, knowing he only had a moment to make his way to the front. I nodded and pushed him along. Appointing Setesh as war commander was Ausar's first act of authority, allowing Ausar to demonstrate fairness, confidence, and wisdom. Setesh's acceptance was to demonstrate respect and loyalty towards Naswt Biti and duty for the kingdom. He wasn't going to get the reception that Ausar and Auset received, but the idea of seeing him up there made me grin with pride.

Setesh walked up to the front purposefully, confidently, head held high and shoulders back. He was wearing his bright red Nemmes, with a white lapa and red sash, but no other adornments, I assume to minimize the attention he pulled away from the royal couple. I found myself taking three nervous steps up the aisle, wanting to hear but knowing I would have to go at least halfway into the room for that, and if I did at this point, it would draw attention to me, which I was avoiding. I shrank back a bit, embracing the shadows but still able to see everything.

From the ground in front of the dais, Setesh bowed to Naswt Biti, the first time that Ausar would receive the **Nedj Hra Heberber**, the royal salutation. A few people in the front rows mimicked his movements, having never seen this bow before, while others appeared to be in awe, watching contemplatively. Ausar said a few words to the people, then looked down at Setesh, who was standing before the platform. Setesh then knelt before the dais on one knee and bent his head to Naswt Biti and although I couldn't hear what he was saying, I assumed he was, in that moment, pledging to serve the King and the kingdom in accordance with the will of **NTR**.

Ausar turned to his throne, and when he faced the people again, he had put down his heq and naqqaqa and was holding an Ankh, the same size as Auset's, but bronze instead of gold. Setesh stood and accepted the Ankh from Ausar, then turned to face the people, giving a rallying war cry in the process. Every man in the room responded in kind, and they went back and forth several times, with Setesh initiating the cry and the men matching his loud and determined intensity. Even the young boys were crying out, trying to do what they saw their fathers do, and some of the fathers responded to this by hoisting the boys onto their shoulders. The women chimed in by shaking sistrums and clapping. I felt like dancing myself, but instead I just fidgeted soundlessly, grinning even larger than before.

Setesh took his place behind the throne of Ausar, then Djehuty and Seshat turned to the crowd. Djehuty stepped out into the aisle so that his voice would carry better than it had during the ritual as he gave the closing **Dwa**. Before he began, he noticed me hiding and raised an eyebrow. I didn't move from my place, but lowered my head in respect.

"Praise be to **Amen Ra**. I make hymns in His name; I give Him praise to the heights of heaven and to the ends of the earth. I tell of His majesty and might to those who sail downstream and those who sail upstream. Stand in awe of Him. Declare Him to your son and daughter, to the great and the small. Declare Him to generation after generation who are not yet born. Declare Him to the fish in the deep and to the birds in the sky. Declare Him to the ignorant and to the wise. Stand in awe of Him."

No one spoke for several minutes. Many had turned their faces to the heavens, keeping their hands outstretched to the sun, the symbol of Ra's power and dominion. A few had fallen to their knees, pressing their foreheads to the sand. I was in awe of their reverence, which surprised me, at the time not realizing how much the people of Kemet knew of us, the **Neteru**. The sentimentality of the prayer warmed me, and I breathed deeply, inhaling the essence of these moments so that I could hold them forever.

"I found Amen Ra came when I called to Him," Djehuty spoke again, breaking the silence for the final time. "He gave me His hand and I found my heart strong and full of joy. And all I did succeeded."

Amen Maat, I whispered, then crossed my arms over my chest. I exhaled deeply, thankful that we had gotten through today, and painfully aware of the many days before us that remained.

DJED - STABILITY

"You *don't* know what you're talking about," I mumbled, not wanting him to see my face wet or hear my voice crack.

"Whatever, *dearest sister*," Setesh spat out, mocking the name that Heru-Ur had given to me. "I DO know - everyone knows. It is only you who is still pretending."

He was gone, and I cried openly then. It was the third fight we'd had since learning we were to be married, but each time his anger escalated and the words became more destructive. I wiped my tears from my face, trying to stop them from falling, but after a brief reprise they began to flow once more, freer and heavier than before.

Suddenly my sister's hands were on my shoulders, as if she had been sitting there the entire time. I turned into her body and wept uncontrollably, for what seemed like a lifetime. She didn't say or do anything but wrap her arms around me, rocking our bodies back and forth, attempting to soothe my frustration. I hated that she saw me so miserable when I knew that she couldn't be happier.

Auset cleared her throat. "Did you tell him the truth?"

I pulled my head back from her shoulder and wiped my face again with the palms of my hands. "I tried, harder this time than before. I don't think he wants to hear it."

She frowned. "He does. He just thinks the truth is going to be unpleasant."

"He won't believe it."

Auset shook her head. "Just tell him you're being **maakheru**. He'll have to believe you if you insist that you speak true."

I glared at her. "Setesh doesn't *have* to do anything," I mumbled, using a softer version of his mocking tone. "You would think he would be over this foolishness by now."

"It hasn't been that long." She shrugged and sighed. "I guess he needs more time."

"What I don't understand is why this is happening so suddenly," I said purposely, knowing that Auset knew the answer, hoping she would finally share it with me. "Not long ago they were telling us we had all the time in the world, and now, all of a sudden, we are to be married, immediately. I don't understand it." I stressed each syllable, looking into her eyes pointedly, expecting an explanation.

Once more she fidgeted uncomfortably, wanting to escape my gaze without telling me anything. "Nebt-Het, **ab en NTR**. It's not up to us to know why and it's not important for us to understand. It is Maat, the Divine will. We have to do it."

I pulled away from her entirely, sorrow abandoned. "See, that is how I know you're hiding something."

"What?" Auset said, feigning surprise. She turned away from me, continuing to avoid my eyes.

"Those are my words; that is my sensibility. You are not being yourself, Auset. You think I don't know when you're hiding something? We all know you are, just tell us."

"I can't" Auset whispered, lowering her eyes to the ground. "I, I know why this is happening, and I'm sorry, I really am, but I can't tell you what happened, I'm sorry."

"Sure you are," I said, ending our conversation. She was gone in a flash, and I rolled my eyes to her absence. I hated not knowing why our timeline had changed so drastically, especially since the suddenness of this was part of why Setesh was so hostile towards me.

Our first fight began the very night we learned we were to be married. Ra called us to him unexpectedly and told us the news, just the five of us, giving us the opportunity to process, not as if we had a say in the matter. I remember my eyes falling on Heru-Ur as soon as I heard that it was time for us to make the big move, the move to Kemet that we'd anticipated since our birth. We all knew the Great Father never wanted to relinquish his place in the physical world, but here he was, putting the realm in our hands. Heru-Ur smiled at me before turning his attention back to Ra, and I diverted my gaze downward, so focused on the idea that Ra had somehow come around that I barely heard him say that I was betrothed to Setesh.

I looked up quickly, my eyebrows rising later, when Ra had already moved on to talk about something else. I could not bring myself to interrupt him, so instead I looked across the room to where Setesh sat on the far end. He appeared to be simmering on the inside, his facial expression even but his eyes red, his jaw tight. I looked away before he noticed me staring at him, trying to focus once more on what Ra was telling us.

Ra stood and excused us, and Setesh came over to me, his expression unchanged. "Should we talk?"

I nodded. "Yes." Neither of us spoke. "You want to talk here?" I asked him, my tone indicating that I did not.

"Where would you want to talk?" Setesh asked, and I hesitated, not knowing what to say, apparently taking too long to answer. He shifted his weight, annoyed. "Why don't you take me where you'd like to go." Setesh reached out his hand to me and I took it, deciding to make the descent to the spot where our father Geb had first made contact with our mother Nut, at the opening of the Hapi River. We were so seldom seen without one or all of our siblings, and I thought traveling together to this sacred place would help us to start in harmonious accord.

Setesh was distant from me the moment we arrived, standing at attention as though he was there for business rather than to discuss a marriage. I didn't know what to think of this. Ausar was always so tender with Auset, and Setesh was being cold and standoffish. At the time, I decided he must be unhappy with the idea that he would not get to be king; disheartened by the idea that I was an unwanted consolation prize. After many moments of complete silence between us, I thought it was best to confront this head on.

"I know you must be disappointed that you aren't marrying Auset," I began slowly, trying to choose my words carefully. Even with much thought, I still did not succeed in this goal.

"What makes you think I care about marrying Auset?" he responded, almost disgusted that I thought this was his issue. His tone utterly surprised me, and I almost didn't know how to respond.

"Well, I, I mean" I stammered, "I know that who marries her will become Naswt Biti, so I assumed that your disappointment is that you will not be Naswt Biti after all."

"You should not *assume* anything."

My shoulders dropped, and I sighed in frustration. "You're right. May I ask what is wrong with you then?"

He turned to me, a look of righteous indignation firing up his eyes. "What is wrong with ME?"

I shook my head, beginning to lose my patience. "I thought we were going to talk, and then we come here, and you say nothing. You don't look at me, you don't tell me what you're thinking. You just stand there like you'd rather be anywhere else than with me. What am I supposed to think?"

Setesh rolled his eyes. "Think whatever you want." He was gone.

It annoyed me primarily that he had not actually told me anything, and yet he seemed to be angry with me. For what I couldn't deduce, and I hated that he'd left me to try to figure it out on my own. I laid down to think, trying to figure out how things had gone so wrong so quickly, and when I didn't return with Setesh, my sister came to find me. I looked up, the dark blue flash that announced her arrival surprising and yet expected. When I forced myself to smile, she sat beside me on the grassy mound and did not speak; Auset took my hand in hers and cradled it in her lap, letting me decide when to break the silence.

When I was ready, I sat up to face her and confess my concerns. How I hoped he'd learn to love me even though he wouldn't get to be king like he truly wanted. How he'd reacted as though I had done some unforgivable wrong towards him. How I hoped we could resolve these discrepancies before the wedding was to take place. Auset listened patiently, awkwardly and deliberately choosing not to look at my face, attentively distracted.

I sighed, realizing how selfish I was being. "What's wrong, Auset?" I asked, assuming that hearing about me and Setesh was causing her to want to share a secret concern that she had about her engagement to Ausar.

She finally glanced at me, then quickly smiled, a fake smile that hid nothing from me, her mirror image. "I guess I'm just nervous, is all. You're right, it is very fast, and I wish we knew why this was happening. I guess we just have to deal with our feelings about it, and you know how Setesh is about his emotions."

She turned the conversation back to our brother, and I quickly dismissed my thoughts about her troubles to focus on his. "Yes, you're right. He does avoid dealing with his feelings, despite being the most emotional of us all," I said with a joking tone to my voice. Auset smiled for real this time, nodding in agreement. "He is probably just overwhelmed with the quickness of it all," I added, trying to convince myself that this was nothing serious.

Auset looked relieved, probably that I had not continued to

drill her for information. "I bet you're right," she assured me, placing her hand on my arm. "You understand him better than us all. You are the right person to be his wife."

I nodded and smiled, not saying out loud my next thought. I understood Setesh better than she did, but that didn't mean I wanted to be married to him. I had always assumed I would marry Heru-Ur, who was born second, but suddenly, with this announcement, he was to take no wife at all and I was betrothed to Setesh. It was a lot to accept all at once. Still, I wasn't ready to share that thought with Auset, and I didn't want anyone to overhear. If Setesh thought I preferred Heru-Ur over him, we would be doomed to have a miserable life together.

After this, Setesh and I didn't speak again until our second fight. We didn't see each other between our lessons at all, which were meant to prepare us for the move and the work that we would be doing once there.

It was weird being home during those two days, because things had changed in our sibling dynamic. Watching Ausar take the opportunity to cozy up to his future wife was uncomfortable at best, nauseating at worse. They were holding hands, whispering and laughing at each other's awful jokes. Truthfully, they always had eyes for each other, but now that the wedding was confirmed, the affection had doubled to obnoxious levels. In retrospect, I was probably just jealous. I could barely have a conversation with my betrothed, and Auset could not get hers to stay away for a moment.

Unfortunately, I had no idea where Heru-Ur or Setesh were during that time. I sought them both out once or twice, to no avail. I wasn't sure if they were engaged in warrior training, or just taking space for themselves, but being left alone with the lovebirds was less than appealing.

Home is a beautiful place though, and even though we took

very frequent trips to Earth back then, I loved it there, this home of ours which transcended reason. Home is a dynamic place, a divine blend of infinite potentiality and prodigious realization. It resonates with a warmth that holds you as though you are still gestating in the womb, like the entire universe is conspiring to keep you safe, and what you want or need it to be, it becomes, with only a thought. Being at home is like living in a constant retreat from anything that might disturb your peace; like living in the veil between night and day, light and dark.

Home is like becoming one with everything that ever existed. It's a reflection of your true self, a vision that is simultaneously empowering and diminishing. Later, when we lived in Ta Meri full time, I craved the empty fullness of home.

The next time I saw Setesh was at our next class. I got the sense that he wanted to talk to me when I walked in, but I wasn't sure I was up for it. I decided to escape as soon as we were dismissed, but right as I made to leave, it was Heru-Ur who grabbed me by the wrist.

"Hey you," he said, grinning. I grinned back. "Where are you in a rush to?"

I shook my head. "Just wanting to go somewhere to think, is all. Why, what's up?"

Heru-Ur released his grip on my arm and looked down to his feet. "I've barely had a minute to touch base with you, since, you know, since all of this. We should talk," he told me, looking at me, still smiling, but smaller, with a bit of seriousness to it.

I nodded and took his hand. Heru-Ur preferred windy climates, so he took me to the top of the highest mountain in the area called Kush. It was one of his favorite spots, because it allowed him to feel close to everything that was important to us - our parents and grandparents, even **Aten**, the sun, felt so close from so high.

Heru-Ur was still holding my hand, and we sat near the edge of a cliff, completely at ease. "The group seemed focused today," I started, easing into our conversation slowly.

He nodded and shrugged. "It's a lot. There's so much that we need to go over before the move."

"It's not like we're learning all this for the first time; it's really more like a review," I said, eyebrows scrunched.

"No, I know, I know," he quickly responded, frowning. Then he smiled again. "I just mean, I feel like it took us by surprise, you know?"

The memory of our sister's discomfort came back to me, and I thought about asking Heru-Ur what he knew, but if Auset had not told me, she definitely hadn't told him. If anyone knew, it was Ausar, and he'd never say a word.

I let go of his hand and turned so we could face each other easier. "I'm sorry we haven't talked for a few days. I don't want you to think I was avoiding you."

"No, I didn't think that," he said, looking down at the ground, pretending to examine a rock. "I feel like I should give you space to figure things out with Setesh."

"That doesn't mean we should stop talking. You're still my brother. This doesn't change anything," I emphasized, trying to sound convincing.

Heru-Ur looked right at me. "It changes everything. Your... your husband will feel antagonized if you are closer to me than you are to him."

I rolled my eyes. "That's silly jealousy, and he'll just have to get over that. He can't be that unfair."

"You can't act like his feelings don't matter."

We were both silent for a moment, with me staring off in the direction of the setting sun, and Heru-Ur continuing to examine each stone on the ground as if fascinated by them. "He thinks you're disappointed, you know."

I looked back at him. "What?"

Heru-Ur looked up at me. "He thinks you would rather be married to me," he mumbled.

My eyebrows shot up in a look of surprise. "Why, what makes him think that?" I stammered, trying to sound like the idea was unbelievable.

My brother looked at me as though I should stop my act. "Why do you think? It's no secret how close we are."

I shook my head and found myself looking down, examining the same rocks. "Well, that doesn't have anything to do with getting married," I mumbled quickly. The truth was, our relationship wasn't romantic or intimate; we weren't courting and hadn't discussed the idea of being husband and wife. We were close, almost as close as I was with Auset. The biggest problem was I didn't feel that way about Setesh.

Heru-Ur didn't respond. I looked up and away, over his shoulder. "So fine, I was surprised that I wasn't going to marry you. But that doesn't mean I'm... *disappointed* about marrying Setesh. I just have to get used to the idea, is all."

"Can't you see how that might make him feel?" Heru-Ur whispered pointedly, speaking in a soft tone to not offend my emotions too deeply. "That you need time to adjust, rather than just being happy about it?"

I stood up and turned my back to my brother. "Can't he understand how I feel? Preparing all this time for something only to find out I'm getting something else. This isn't fair and you know it."

"You say that like somehow you knew of the plan before any of us. We all just learned this plan at the same time. How could you have been preparing for something that you didn't know anything about?"

I sighed. "I guess I just assumed, is all," I mumbled again.

"Right," Heru-Ur said, standing up and coming around to the front of me so he could look me in the eye. "You *assumed*, and now you aren't getting what you want and you're hurt. And Setesh, who already feels like, less than, because he's the youngest brother and all, now he gets to feel even worse."

"Well fine," I answered, "but what about him wanting to marry Auset, wanting to be king? How am I supposed to feel knowing that I'm not *his* first choice?"

Heru-Ur chuckled softly. "Setesh does want to be king but he's not interested in Auset. If marrying Auset will make him king, he will marry her, but that's not what he wants. He *wants* to be king."

I was still staring off into the distance. "Still, that means he isn't quite happy with the life he's getting either and that includes me. That means he's not happy with me."

"Which is why I am trying to give you two space. Because clearly, you need to talk," Heru-Ur concluded, walking back to our original spot and taking his seat again.

I hesitated briefly, then turned to face him, still standing. "Are you disappointed?" I asked in a quiet voice.

This time it was him looking past me, into the horizon. "Yeah, I guess I am. I guess, I think I also assumed that you and I..." his voice trailed off, and his eyes fell once more to the ground.

I turned away again, wrapping my arms around myself, not for warmth, but for comfort. This was all confusing, and too much. I had no idea how this was supposed to get resolved between me and Setesh, and whether we resolved it or not, we were getting married.

It felt like time was standing still, while we were sitting there, not saying anything. Finally, he spoke. "I'm sorry there isn't anything we can do about it, dearest sister. But I know this must be for the best, or else -"

"Don't say that," I cut him off, not wanting to hear him say something true. "Just, please, I can't hear that right now."

He was silent again for a moment. "After you move, I will be gone for a long time. I don't even know what it will be like to be away like that."

I turned back to him and looked down, just as he was looking up at me. I held his gaze for a moment, then looked away. "I will talk to Setesh and make peace with our betrothal, and I will reassure him that he doesn't need to be jealous of you."

Heru-Ur nodded. "I think that's best."

I sat once more and took his hands into mine. "I feel like I miss you already."

He smiled. "I miss you too."

We sat there for a few minutes longer, until the light was completely gone from the sky, then returned home. Setesh was in the same place he'd been during our tutelage, sitting cross-legged, as if meditating. His eyes opened as soon as we came in, and his frown deepened. Heru-Ur and I dropped hands and he left quickly, without a word.

"I was just looking for you," I started, taking a bold step towards my betrothed.

Setesh stood. "Really? That's *exactly* what it looked like to me too," he threw at me, sarcastically.

I took a deep breath. "Don't do that, please. Heru-Ur and I needed to talk, and now, you and I need to talk."

"I am not interested in talking to you," he told me stiffly, straightening his back and taking a deep, angry breath. "If you'll excuse me -"

I grabbed his arm before he could leave. "No, I don't excuse you. You don't even know what I'm going to say. Now who is making assumptions?"

He rolled his eyes, but didn't try to pull away from my grasp.

I used my grip to guide him back to the spot of our first spat, hoping that maybe this time we could make a positive memory here. I didn't want to always think of the mouth of the Hapi as our fighting grounds.

Setesh sat down formally, facing the water, choosing not to look at me at all. When I didn't speak right away, he sighed loudly, exasperated. "Well? I thought you had something to say."

"I do." I thought about standing in his eyesight and forcing him to look at me, but decided that was probably too confrontational. Instead I sat next to him, looking at the side of his face. "I apologize for what happened the first time we talked. I wasn't being thoughtful of you at all."

After a long silence, he sighed. "I apologize too," he responded, softening his posture a bit, although his expression didn't change at all, and he didn't look at me. "I was angry before we even started talking. I should have been more open."

I smiled, feeling like we were getting somewhere. "I would like to hear what it is you have to say about this whole thing."

He hesitated. "I'm just, frustrated. I wish this wasn't happening, is all." He stopped for a second, then furrowed his brow. "Do you get the sense that Auset knows something about all this? Today during the lesson, she had this curious look on her face."

I practically jumped. "Yes! I asked her once, and she dismissed me. I'm going to ask her again, because I am having a hard time dealing with all of this."

He grimaced. "You're not the only one, you know. You say that like you're the only one who got bad news."

"I, umm, that's not what I meant," I stammered. "I mean, Ausar and Auset are totally excited to get married, but the rest of us, we all got news that surprised us."

He stood and turned his back to me completely. "Well, if it

makes you feel any better, I'm not happy to be the one standing between you and him. If it were up to me, I would stand down and let you have what you want."

My eyebrows shot up in surprise. "That's not, you don't have to do that."

"But you want me to."

"No," I answered tentatively. "You're still assuming that I'm unhappy about the idea of being your wife. You haven't asked me if that's how I feel at all."

He turned back to face me, a slant of curiosity having taken over his eyes. "Fine. How *do* you feel about being my wife?"

I did not want to lie. "I feel like this is sudden and we only have a little bit of time to get used to the idea. I feel like I want us both to be okay with this."

"But not happy."

I stood up, realizing I was probably backing myself into a corner. "Well, yes, I want us to be happy, but -"

"But you're not happy right now. It's fine, I get it." He shrugged and turned away again. This time I walked around to his front, forcing him to look at me.

"Stop putting words in my mouth," I demanded, starting to lose my patience. "I feel a lot of things and it is really hard to put them into words without making you feel bad."

He scoffed. "Oh, so I'm so sensitive you can't even say what you want to say without hurting my delicate feelings?" He laughed and shook his head. "Just say what you have to say. I can handle it, believe me."

I rolled my eyes. "I know you can handle it, Setesh, but that doesn't mean I should be insensitive with my words - look, we are getting off track here. Why don't we back up and try this over again?"

"Just answer one question for me, Nebt-Het. Would you feel so confused if you had been told you were engaged to Heru-Ur?

Would that have produced feelings that you needed to sort through, or would your feelings have been just as straightforward as Auset's feelings for Ausar?"

My eyes widened, and I scoffed before looking away; the words I sought were entirely unavailable to me.

"Okay then." He left without another word.

This time, no one came to find me. I stayed there as long as I reasonably could, and when I finally returned, I found that my siblings were, for the most part, avoiding me. Heru-Ur was spending additional time with Djehuty, reviewing the details of his journey across Kemet. Ausar and Auset were wrapped up in each other, and when I did see Auset alone, I could see the guilt as she made desperate excuses to avoid me. I had no idea what Setesh was doing, but he certainly wasn't making himself accessible. I didn't know where he liked to go to be alone or what he did when he was away from us, so I didn't even know where to begin to look for him.

After a little while of being ignored, I needed some grounding. I went back to the mountaintop where Heru-Ur and I had last spoken, and sat facing east. It wasn't long before Setesh surprised me by sitting next to me.

"What are you doing?" he asked, his tone casual, neutral. I wanted to roll my eyes.

"The same thing you're doing, watching the sunrise."

Setesh nodded, still refusing to look at me. "I guess I should apologize for walking out of our conversation before."

I looked at him incredulously. "You *guess*?"

"What do you want me to say, Nebt-Het?" he asked me, sounding almost like a plea. "You practically tell me you wish you didn't have to marry me -"

"I never said that," I stopped him, refusing to acknowledge the truth in his words. "Again you are putting words in my mouth."

He looked at me with a suspicious scowl. "Actually, I gave you a chance to tell me how you felt and you didn't say anything at all. In this instance I think your silence speaks volumes."

I shook my head and looked away. "I am trying to make peace between us, I am trying, and you are... avoiding me and ignoring me every chance you get."

"If you wanted to speak with me," he said carefully, "you could have asked me to give you another chance to explain."

"Give me another chance," I mumbled, smiling out of pure disbelief. I couldn't believe he was trying to make me feel bad for being honest, and I didn't think it was fair that he was angry at me for having a close relationship with our brother.

"I don't know what it is you want me to say," I finally said out loud, figuring we should at least try to finish the conversation, since neither of us had left by this point.

"I don't want you to say anything, just, forget it."

"No, Setesh, I can't," I told him, practically pleading. "We're supposed to be husband and wife, we need time to figure this out."

He stood. "I just realized I'm not up for this right now." He took a few steps away from me, then turned back, as if furious. "I really don't understand why you need so much time. Why is this so hard to accept? Having me for a husband is that bad?"

"Setesh, this is not about you in the way you think it is."

"And that's my problem, Nebt-Het," he said, finally throwing it all on me. "You aren't thinking of me. You're focused on what you're losing, not what you've gained. You don't think I'm as good as Heru-Ur. You don't care about me like you care about him, and you never will. You approach this like you're settling for me. I am not a consolation prize."

Neither am I, I thought to myself, taken aback by the use of my own thoughts against me. "Don't say I don't care about you,

I care about you."

"You *love* him."

"He's my brother, you're both my brothers, I love you both." I stopped, closing my eyes to get my thoughts straight. "What are you even saying right now? Stop making this about him."

Setesh pointed down at me. "YOU made this about him. You could have said 'I am happy about this unexpected development and I am ready to face it with you' and instead you said you want us to work on being okay. How do you think that makes me feel? You sound like you're crying every night just thinking of the miserable life you'll have with me."

My eyes began to tear up. "I said that because I figured you needed time to deal with *your* feelings about this."

"Don't project your feelings onto me, I never said that."

I looked up at him from the ground. "So you're saying you are totally okay with marrying me?"

He hesitated. "How honest do you want me to be here?"

I rolled my eyes and mumbled his words back at him. "Just say what you have to say, I can take it."

Setesh shrugged his shoulders. "I wasn't actually, at first. To come in now after you and him spent all that time courting -"

"We *weren't* courting," I cut him off quick, shaking my head.

"*Seriously?*" There was no chance he could disguise the disbelief in his voice or on his face. "All that time you two spent together, and you expect me to believe there was nothing romantic going on between you?"

"There wasn't," I whispered, which I knew was only half true. Nothing happened, but we'd both admitted that we wanted it to. Perhaps all that time together wasn't so innocent. Perhaps we were purposely growing close so that one day something could happen. Perhaps I was more disappointed than I wanted to admit.

"Right." His voice brought me back to the present. Setesh

was done listening. "I am asking you to be honest with me so we can put that stuff to rest and move forward and here you are trying to tell me I don't know what I'm talking about."

"You *don't* know what you're talking about," I mumbled, battling with my feelings.

"Whatever, *dearest sister.*"

At this point, we'd perfected the art of avoiding each other between classes. When I arrived, the tension in the air was distinct. Heru-Ur and Setesh were sitting on exact opposite sides, with Ausar and Auset squarely in the middle, clearly trying to appear neutral.

I had no such luxury. I took a deep breath and sat right next to Setesh, staring straight ahead, not looking at my other siblings. He didn't acknowledge my presence at all, just continued his aimless scowling.

Djehuty took one look at us and arched his eyebrows, then cleared his throat, deciding to begin without confronting what was going on.

"Humility is a greater virtue than defying death," Djehuty began, pacing the room, arms clasped behind his back, "it triumphs over vanity and conceit." He stopped dramatically in the center, taking a moment to look us each in the eye before finishing. "Conquer them in yourself first."

Behind him, against the backdrop of darkness, the words he spoke appeared in the glyphs of Medu NTR, glowing brightly like the stars in the night sky. He did not turn to face them, but instead resumed pacing, looking downward as we waited for him to continue. "You must be neither above those whom you serve nor their equals. They must see you in themselves, yet unable to see you as themselves." Djehuty stopped pacing once more, this time not in the center, but standing right in front of Heru-Ur. Turning, he faced our brother and looked at Heru-Ur directly. "This requires a most delicate balance."

Heru-Ur cleared his throat, taking Djehuty's position as his cue to state the obvious. "You're reminding us to be humble; aware of our divinity without being full of it."

Djehuty nodded. "**Tu.**" He turned away from Heru-Ur without walking further into the room. "This is one of the most important attributes that you must demonstrate."

"That should be simple, then," Ausar jumped in, eager to push along the discussion. "We just have to be regular; dress like one of the people, walk around amongst the people - we shouldn't stand out, we should appear to be like one of them."

Setesh sighed loudly, never missing an opportunity to voice his disagreement. "That would be stupid. If we are the same as everyone else, then anyone can be king." He turned and looked directly at Ausar, silently issuing a challenge. I looked away.

Djehuty hesitated, seeming to take note of the tension. "Despite his hostile approach, Setesh does have a point. Can you be the same as everyone and still expect them to accept your rule?"

"Not all of us are going to Kemet to rule," Heru-Ur started, then hesitated, as if seeking the right words. He was usually thoughtful in that way. "We will not be rulers in that sense."

"Tem," I started slowly, "but we will be teachers." Setesh scoffed loudly. I looked at him and continued carefully. "We have knowledge which they do not possess. They are not our equals."

Djehuty walked over to stand directly before Setesh. "Something to add?" he asked pointedly.

"Did someone say something?" Setesh responded, equally as pointedly, without budging. I looked up at his face, hoping he would meet my gaze, to no avail.

"Are you seriously just going to ignore her?" Heru-Ur defended me, making matters worse. "Whatever your issue, you shouldn't behave with such insolence."

Setesh refused to look at him either. "And what," he asked, sarcasm dripping from every word, "is it you who is going to teach me to act with honor?"

I turned my gaze to Djehuty, praying he would take this opportunity to stop them. He didn't.

"I don't know what that's supposed to mean," Heru-Ur mumbled. Setesh shrugged, apparently choosing not to respond to either of us now.

Auset cleared her throat. "We should get back to the lesson at hand," she calmly instructed in her nurturing voice. "I think we have established that each of us will hold some measure of authority that we must strive to maintain."

Djehuty continued to survey the room without moving from his spot, right in front of Setesh and I. "Have we all agreed upon this point?" he asked. "I am not sure we have agreed upon anything at all."

"I agree with Nebt-Het; they are not our equals. Seba, you said this yourself as well," Heru-Ur asserted, wanting to get things back on track.

Ausar nodded. "I agree with this as well, but the other portion of the riddle required that we be neither their equals nor their betters. We cannot be beneath them, if they are to accept us as figures of authority."

Djehuty smiled. "That appears to be the conundrum." He began to pace once more, nodding his head as if in deep contemplation. "I would have expected this to be much easier to comprehend than you have found it to be. Perhaps you are all distracted by other things?"

Everyone looked around with a bit of discomfort, except Setesh, who sat with a straight back, looking forward as if he believed himself to be just. I realized no one else would speak. "We have come here with clear minds and clear hearts, ready to receive, Seba," I told him firmly, hoping the other three would back me up. They did quickly, sitting up straighter and nodding.

Djehuty nodded, accepting their agreement. "Very well then." The words quickly faded from the background, and others took their place. "Auset, please read these words aloud."

"If you are a powerful person, gain respect through knowledge and gentleness of speech and conduct." She hesitated, glancing over at Setesh, before looking back to the board.

"Have you something to say, sister?" Setesh spat out, not letting her hesitation go unnoticed. "I couldn't help but notice your eyes peeking over in my direction." His tone was light, almost joking, but we all knew he wasn't trying to make us laugh.

Auset swallowed. "I was only thinking of your hostile tone, brother," she answered measuredly, keeping her composure for the moment. "Perhaps it would be wise to mind your approach in the future."

Setesh nodded. "I accept the critique and offer one of my own." He turned to look at her better. "As one who is destined for the throne, there will be times when your docility might be seen as weakness. You would be wise to seek balance; demonstrate a firm hand on occasion."

Auset tried not to appear unnerved. "I accept your critique in return." She turned to face forward, not wanting to continue looking Setesh in the eye. "I believe this is the humility Seba is asking us to cultivate, that we grow into strong and enduring leaders."

"I find that if you say you're being humble, you are actually not being humble at all," Setesh told her, still looking at the side of her face. "That's actually a very *conceited* thing to do."

Ausar turned to face Setesh, clearly annoyed. "Why are you picking on her, Setesh? She's not the one you're angry with, leave her be."

"No, I am the one he's angry with," I whispered, "and he should take it out on only me."

"He should put his anger in its place and take it out on no one," Heru-Ur jumped in, again my unsolicited defender. "I don't see why we are entertaining his outbursts at all."

Setesh turned to face forward. "I am not going to alter myself to suit you, *dearest brother*," he said icily. "If you cannot handle my simple discourse, then what are you going to do when faced with the petitions of the people?"

Heru-Ur scoffed. "The people will bring their justified concerns to us, seeking resolution. You are doing none of the above."

"You don't think my concerns are justified?" Setesh asked, his anger rising. "Or is it that you don't think I desire resolution?"

"Neither," Heru-Ur told him before waiting for the sentence to complete itself fully. "I don't know what you think gives you the right to carry such anger -"

Setesh stood and looked him dead in the eye. "You know *exactly* why," he hissed, poison in every word. I reached out for his arm, grabbing him by the wrist, but he ripped it away immediately, looking down at me with the fieriest glare he could muster, before disappearing into thin air.

I looked to Heru-Ur, surprised and apologetic. Djehuty cleared his throat. I held my breath.

"After that spectacle, I believe it best that we conclude for now. You are all dismissed," Djehuty began, stepping forward, arms behind his back as they were at the start of class.

I exhaled, grateful, thinking it would end there. "Not you,

Nebt-Het. I'd like to have a word with you." Djehuty's penetrating stare made it clear he hadn't misspoke. I sighed, frustrated; why did I have to stay when I wasn't the one fighting? Auset looked at me with pity and departed quickly, our brothers following her wordlessly, leaving me alone with Seba.

"May I ask what is going on?" he asked softly, being direct as ever.

I swallowed. "It's nothing really, just -"

Djehuty held up his hand to stop me. "It's clearly something."

"Well yes, but I don't want to make a big deal out of it."

"It's interrupting our progress, so it's already a big deal," he answered. I sighed.

"Setesh and I, we've argued a few times, and I think Heru-Ur feels badly, because, well, he's part of the reason why we've argued."

Djehuty nodded, a look of clarity coming across his face. "Yes. This is about the impending nuptials." I nodded in confirmation.

He cleared his throat, thinking for a moment before speaking again. "Heru-Ur is not the reason you and Setesh argued. To put him in the middle is to confuse the issue and stop you from connecting with your future husband. It doesn't serve either of you, and it isn't true."

Djehuty touched my chin lightly, forcing my eyes to meet his. "What did *you* do to create or escalate the tension between you and Setesh?"

"What did I do? Why do I have to be the bad guy?" I spat out, annoyed at this turn of events. "You should be asking what he did."

Djehuty took a step back and looked around. "Perhaps, but he is not here. So I am asking you what you did."

"I didn't do, I wasn't... I wasn't trying to create a problem. I just wanted us to be okay," I mumbled, the answer flooding over me but my reluctance to admit it stopping the words from coming forth.

"You may not have meant to," Djehuty said, stressing his words, "but how did you create or contribute to it?"

My eyes started to tear up again, a familiar feeling. I wanted to run, to be anywhere but there. "I, I... I wasn't totally honest with myself... which meant, I couldn't, I wasn't totally honest with him either." I looked down again, wanting to run, but didn't. "I just want us to be close."

"Did you ask Setesh what he wanted?"

I nodded. "He said he wanted me to be honest."

Djehuty hesitated. "No, I don't mean what he wants you to do now. Do you know what he wants out of your relationship?"

"He said," I started, searching my thoughts for an answer. "He said he wanted me to be happy to be his wife."

"He wants you to be happy and you will be happy if you feel close to him." He stopped, so I nodded in agreement. "Do you want him to be happy?"

"Of course."

"What does he need to be happy?"

I frowned. "I don't think I know the answer to that."

Djehuty smiled and patted my arm in a patronizing gesture. "Learn the answer next time you speak. I believe you will find the tensions between you begin to ease."

I waited for him to say something else, and when he didn't, I grimaced. "That's it?"

"It does not take many words to speak the truth."

Some of the tension had relieved itself by our next class, even though Setesh and I still hadn't spoken. He and Heru-Ur must have talked, since the wide chasm between them seemed to be repaired. They were chatting casually when I walked in, not in heated, angry tones. I still chose to sit close to Setesh and away from Heru-Ur, opting not to do anything to revive any ill feelings. Auset smiled at me with compassion, as though she wished that this will work out but didn't believe it would. I was starting to agree with her.

I couldn't let this go on any longer and wanted to give Djehuty's advice a chance. After class I tapped the shoulder of my betrothed before he had a chance to leave. "I am planning to visit the mountain range in the eastern valley," I told him, practically whispering, "right between the sacred peaks." I looked up at Setesh, hoping that my eyes echoed my sentiment. "I hope you'll come, if you're ready to talk."

I left quickly, not waiting for him to reply. The air was moving quickly, carrying a chill that was more perceptible the longer I waited. I watched the sun set and the moon make its journey across the sky before he showed up, carrying a white bundle of fabric for me to use as a shawl. I stood and let him wrap it around me, and as I pulled it in close, he dropped his hands to his side but didn't put any space between us.

"I apologize for what happened last time we talked." Setesh looked at me, his scowl stiff and his eyes soft. "I wasn't listening to you, and I should have. I said I would be open, and I wasn't. I was wrong."

I hoped this was the last conversation we'd have to begin with an apology. I sighed. "I apologize too. I said some hurtful things, even though I didn't mean to."

"You didn't answer my question," he said tentatively, realizing this was a delicate subject. "I really want to know if you are incredibly unhappy with this."

I shook my head emphatically. "I'm not incredibly unhappy, I'm surprised. But that doesn't mean I hate this outcome. I don't," I stressed, hoping he would get it. "I am willing to make the best of this, with you."

He nodded. "I was surprised too. I thought I would be the unmarried one. I was kind of looking forward to that."

I didn't really know how to respond to that, so I just looked down, not wanting to make a big deal of it and get us arguing all over again. Setesh lifted my chin with his thumb. "I don't hate this outcome. I am willing to make the best of this too, with you."

I nodded, looking back at him, then looking away, over his shoulder. "I didn't realize this would be so hard."

"Me either."

I smiled; his scowl softened to a frown. I put one of my hands on his. "I appreciate that you are being honest with me, about how you feel. I don't want you to pretend to be okay if you're not okay."

Setesh sighed. "I am okay, I just didn't expect this. I think it's harder on you than it is on me."

I frowned. "Why would you think that?"

He shook his head. "Because you're losing so much. I can imagine that you're miserable."

I shook my head. "I'm not miserable, Setesh, not at all. Let's put that in the past and focus on the future, okay?"

He nodded. "You're right. I apologize."

I smiled and pulled away, turning to look at the great mountain before us. "It was good that we had a bit of space to put things into perspective."

"And?"

I inhaled sharply. "And I think... I was wrong for having expectations or assuming I knew what would happen. I accept this turn of events. I'm happy with it, happier than I thought I would be."

Setesh paused before responding. "I too accept our charge. I believe we have what it takes to make the best of this."

I exhaled in relief, turning to face him once more. "I do too." We didn't speak for a moment. I took that as my opportunity to ask him what Djehuty had charged me with discovering. "What is it, I mean, is there something that will make you happy?"

He looked as though I had surprised him with the question, but that expression passed quickly. "Yes, I suppose there is," he answered, searching for the right words, hesitant to be vulnerable. "I have spent a lot of time feeling underappreciated, misunderstood. Maybe even a bit unloved," he said, mumbling the last part. "I guess I feel like, if we're really going to do this, that what would make me happy is having a partner, you know, someone who always understands and who always gets me, no matter what." He looked at me, frowning, but with bashful, embarrassed eyes. "That might sound silly, but -"

"It doesn't sound silly at all," I whispered, finally seeing him. "I think I can do that. I want to try."

He nodded and his face went as close to a smile as I've ever seen. "That means a lot to me. **Dua**."

I wanted to kiss him, but instead I took his hand and pulled him down so we were both sitting, next to one another. He didn't say anything for a minute, but eventually, with a puzzled sound in his voice, he asked, "Why did you pick this spot, if you don't mind me asking."

I breathed deeply. "I don't mind at all," I told him, squeezing his hand. "When I sit here, it's like taking a cleansing breath. It's like that in-between space, like at home, but different, in a way. It's daunting, grounding, and encouraging, but scary, expansive. And it's beautiful, so beautiful, to be here, now."

Setesh nodded. "Sounds like a metaphor."

I giggled. "Yes it does."

"We have to get back soon."

My smile faded fast. "Yes we do."

Setesh stood without releasing my hand, pulling me up with him. "Can we walk in together, just like this?"

I smiled, shyly. "I would like that."

A few more days passed before Auset and I spoke again. I was anxious to share my new, hopeful perspective with her, but she was still avoiding me when she could and using Ausar as a buffer when she couldn't. I stopped trying for a while, giving her space and deciding instead to focus on building my relationship with Setesh. I saw Heru-Ur around every once in a while, but I didn't think enough time had passed for he and I to spend time together without things being awkward.

Soon enough, the time had come for me to face my sister. We were very close to the appointed day of our wedding, and I didn't want to avoid the discussion any longer.

"We will have the first rehearsal for the wedding ceremony tomorrow afternoon," Djehuty announced to us at the end of class with an unnecessarily stern tone. "Until then you should busy yourself with other preparations. You are dismissed"

Setesh and I had taken to holding hands throughout every lesson; I felt he wanted to test my resolve, and I wasn't about to show weakness or give his anger any reason to relapse. Now that class was over, he turned to me and nodded. "I am to engage in training with our brothers," he informed me, as if needing to let me know of his whereabouts. "I will seek you out when we're done."

I nodded, and he let go of my hand, turning to face Ausar and Heru-Ur.

"Ready?" Ausar asked, grinning excitedly. Being the slimmest, Ausar was always striving to prove his might when given the chance. Heru-Ur would go easy on our eldest brother, but Ausar was no match for Setesh, who had quickly taken to the artistry of combat and would never ease up. Setesh needed to be better than his brothers at one thing, and fighting was it, and he reminded them of it every chance he got.

Setesh stood and nodded. The three took off together in a bright white flash.

I looked over to where Djehuty had last stood to find that he too, had left. Auset was still sitting in the center of the room, crossing her legs as if planning to go into meditation.

"Sister, perhaps we should spend some time together," I said, breaking her concentration. "It's been so long since we've had a chance to speak."

Auset looked down, avoiding my gaze. "You're right, we should talk. Would you like to talk here, or elsewhere?"

I frowned. Even after all this time she still looked as if she wished I wouldn't talk to her at all. "Here is fine," I told her, trying to use a reassuring tone. "Unless you'd like another location."

"Here is fine," she repeated, partially mumbling. She finally looked up at me and tried to smile. I didn't want to take it personally, but I was running out of alternative explanations.

I sat down in front of her and took her hands in mine. "What's *wrong*, Auset? As of late you have been acting so strangely."

Auset sighed deeply, as though a heavy weight was upon her chest and shoulders, keeping her from breathing. Without letting go of my hands, her gaze crossed the entire room, which changed the landscape immediately, shrouding us in complete darkness. I couldn't even see her sitting in front of me, and would have thought she left if we weren't still hand in hand.

"Close your eyes," she instructed me, and I did. In the darkness I could see a door, light flooding through the frame of the wood. I opened it and stepped into a space that appeared to be made of nothing but light. Auset was inside, standing; she had invited me into her consciousness.

She smiled at me, for real this time. "I didn't want to have a verbal conversation," she explained. "I hope this is okay."

I smiled back at her. "We haven't talked this way in ages, sister. This is perfect."

We hugged, then sat in the room of her mind, facing each other, holding hands, exactly as we were. "I have a bit of a story to tell you, Nebt-Het. Please don't say anything until I've finished," she pleaded with me, asking for my forgiveness with her eyes.

I nodded, choosing to begin my silence right then.

"A few weeks ago, I was walking alone in the upper forest, and I saw Yit-Eah approaching, walking slowly, without purpose. He didn't see me and for some reason I decided to hide, I didn't want him to see me, so I ducked beneath a few overgrown bushes and watched him as he relaxed. He sat for a while on a huge boulder and it was a while before he left, I almost thought maybe he was waiting for me to reveal myself, but then he spat on the ground and walked away; he never even said anything, never indicated that he knew I was there."

"Why did you hide?" I asked skeptically, already breaking my promise.

She sighed loudly. "I don't know why, it was silly of me. I don't even know what I was thinking at the time... but please, let me finish, **senet**. Please."

I nodded again, hoping this time I could keep quiet while she finished her story. "Well, I saw the spit on the ground, and I just, I used it to soften the dirt into mud, and used the mud to fashion a figure, a snake. A tiny snake, very small, but I decided to make him venomous, deadly. I guess I just, wanted to see if I could," she tried to explain, clearly still beating herself up about whatever had transpired. My eyebrows furrowed but I didn't say anything, hoping not to seem too judgmental.

"The snake is beautiful too, sister, you should see him... but that is not the point. The point is, not long after I made the snake, Ra returned, and I realized..." her voice trailed off and she hung her head with shame. I waited a few moments, still hoping not to break my promise, and she took a deep breath, resolved to finish her story without any prodding. "I realized I could use my snake to learn... his secret name."

I let go of her hands. "You did *what*??"

"Nebt-Het!" Her eyes started tearing up a bit, begging me not to be angry with her. I wasn't sure I could stop myself, but I decided to let her finish her story. I took a deep breath to gain my composure, then took her hands again.

"I, well, I willed the snake to bite the Great Father," she started, looking up at me only occasionally to gauge my response, "and when he began to get sick I, I told him I would only give him the remedy if he told me his secret name."

"Why would you do such a thing?!" I asked in a most incredulous tone. I could barely believe what she was telling me, and yet by her fidgeting and tears, I knew it was true. "What if he hadn't told you - what if you had killed our great-grandfather??"

"I needed to know!" Auset insisted, pulling her hands from mine, running them across the top of her head as she ranted manically. "I have studied the processes and principles of alchemy and magick, light and dark and gray, and I knew, I just knew there was something I wasn't seeing, something I wasn't getting. It was driving me crazy! And I needed to know, I just needed to master it." She could not look at me as she tried to convince us both that her actions had been justified. "I needed to know everything."

I sighed, not understanding how this obsession could have driven her to such lengths. "You didn't *need* to know, though," I pointed out softly, trying not to sound condescending. "You *wanted* to know, and you were willing to risk way too much just to get what you wanted."

Auset started crying, weeping really, and I wasn't sure I wanted to comfort her, but I knew I had to. "You had to know that you'd gone too far," I whispered, taking her into my lap and arms.

"I didn't realize it until he was really sick, until he almost died," she mumbled through her tears. "I was going to give him the cure, even without learning his name, but he gave in before I did. Then he told me he would never come back to Earth, and we must move to Kemet immediately. He said now it was time we took over."

So that was why she felt responsible, I finally understood, rocking her back and forth. Well, she was right, I reasoned, but I had to believe that she had done nothing more than fulfill her destiny. How could she have tricked Ra? Was there any chance he knew about her little snake, and allowed it to happen anyway?

The only way to get the answer to that was to ask Ra, and I wasn't about to do that. I sighed deeply once more and pulled Auset out of my lap so I could look her in the eye. "Have you told anyone else about this?" I asked her quietly, figuring we weren't the only ones who knew, but that she might feel better if she thought we were.

She shook her head. "No, not even Ausar. It was killing me not to say anything, but I couldn't bear to see the look of disapproval in all of your faces."

"It is not us you should worry about," I reminded her, taking her by the hand once more. "You have to live with yourself and what you did for every moment. You have to live knowing that you put your thirst for magical power ahead of the life of our patriarch."

Auset couldn't steady her breath. "I will never forgive myself, never."

I smiled. "You will. You have learned what you are capable of, and you have learned who you do not want to be." I grabbed her shoulders and shook her gently. "You will be better than this, you will never make this mistake again, or any one like it."

"What am I to do about all of this knowledge swirling around my mind?" she asked me between her sniffles. "Now that I have his secret name, my mind is never quiet; there are all these pulses running through me, and I can hear everything whispering in my head all at once, it's too much. Every place I go is so loud, I need peace and silence and I can never find it."

WHOSE FAULT IS THAT, my thoughts shouted at her impulsively, but I went for a gentler response. "You know what Seba would say if he were here," I teased her, letting go of her shoulders. "Tell me, sister, I know you know."

She smiled, letting me ease her away from her heavy burden of guilt. "He would say, first control my breath, then control my thoughts."

I smiled broader. "See, you know what you must do."

Auset sighed deeply, her shoulders moving with her breath, finally light. "Yes, I do. I wish I hadn't brought this on myself, though. Sometimes I feel like, like how could I do something so awful and get rewarded? I'm going to be queen soon, Nebt-Het." She looked at me, shaking her head in disbelief. "I can't believe that I'm not being punished, banished or demoted or something."

I looked away from her then, trying to gaze into the brightness that surrounded us. Thinking of that moment now makes me realize how naive we were, how we should have known better than to think that being saddled with such heavy responsibility was a reward. I didn't see it back then. It took a long time before either of us realized that we had not escaped the consequences of our choices, and never would.

I looked back to Auset and squeezed her hands. "I think your guilt is punishment enough. Come now, let's begin to move forward together." We stood and hugged tightly, binding our arms around each other with a sense of relief and need. "Promise me something, sister?" I asked her quietly, causing her to let me go and look at me with concern.

"Anything, Nebt-Het. What is it?"

I sighed. "Promise me you won't keep something like this from me again, ever."

Auset smiled. "That's an easy promise to make, as I have no plans of doing anything like this ever again."

I dropped her hand and turned away, walked back through the door and closed it to find myself shrouded once more in darkness. In moments the darkness faded, and I could see my sister, still sitting, looking up at me. Her tears had been real, and the relief and anguish was visible through her expression. She stood and we fell once more into a tight, loving hug: Auset beginning the process of forgiving herself, and I hoping to reassure her that everything would be alright.

Nefer - Beauty

Mwt hugged us one last time, looking at our faces with a glow and warmth that could only come from a mother. I felt a bit bashful; for the first time, she was seeing me as a married woman.

"Will you check in with me before the move?" she asked softly, pulling away from me and wrapping her arms around herself, for comfort. Setesh reached up and pushed a few strands of hair off her forehead, his form of assurance. I smiled.

"We won't be on land the whole time, Mwt," I told her, looking back and forth between her and my new husband. "We'll be home some of the time."

She nodded. "Don't spend too much time away from me. Have a good time," she added, like an afterthought. I knew she meant it, but she was prone to worry. Our mother's place was in the heavens, holding the universe in place, which kept her away from us, physically at least. When we were home, she could speak to us without having to leave her place in the sky, so she preferred us to stay close. I knew Mwt wasn't looking forward to our move, but being in Kemet would put us in constant contact with our father, and she could take comfort knowing that he was always there.

Mwt moved on to say a few words to Ausar and Auset, and Yit took her place. He wordlessly shook Setesh's hand, firmly testing his grip and nodding, as if satisfied. Then, he turned to me, smiling and opening his arms wide, letting me decide when to step into them. If it had been up to me, I would have preferred the handshake - I felt all hugged out for the day. But I obliged him this one last affection, sliding into his bearish grip.

Yit squeezed me tight, whispering into my ear, "I'm proud of you, Nebt-Het. I'm proud and so happy for you."

The hug felt stifling, and much too long. I tried to pull out of his arms gently, with no success. "Dua, Yit. I'm really happy too."

Setesh cleared his throat, which caused our father to loosen up. I made a mental note to thank him later. "Yit, if it's alright with you I'm ready to take my wife away from here," Setesh told him cautiously, as though he was hesitant to be authoritative. Yit nodded and stepped back, taking in the sight of us with pleasure.

"Will you let me know when you've finalized your plans for the move?" Yit directed the question to Setesh, addressing him like an equal, which, from the way he straightened his posture, I could tell he appreciated. Setesh nodded his consent. Yit looked back at me again, sighed, and turned to find our mother.

"Ready to go?" Setesh mumbled, taking my hand in his once more. I looked up at him, and nodded nervously. "Where are we going first?" I asked, looking forward to the first of several surprises.

"Close your eyes," he whispered, moving in closely so only my ears would hear. I did, and felt the energy around us dispersing and gathering again, a sign that we had left home and arrived at our first stop. I heard the heavy wave crash before feeling its gentle counterpart tickle my feet; we were on a beach.

I opened my eyes when Setesh dropped my hand, and the view caused me to smile. Before me was nothing but water, the bright, vibrant blue of the sea becoming one with the sky at the edge of the world. I turned to face the other way, seeing trees different from those I'd seen anywhere in Kemet or Kush. They appeared to shoot up to the sky, determined to touch the sun with their leaves, creating a beautiful canopy of needed shade.

I'd never ventured to this particular place before, and I couldn't help but feel amazed by the beauty of it. I looked to my husband, whose eyes were twinkling; he was proud of the effect his surprise had on me.

I smiled and touched his arm. "You did good."

He nodded, looking out to the sea contemplatively before grabbing me around my waist and hoisting me over his shoulder. I screamed, mostly of surprise, as he ran out towards the ocean, throwing himself into its tide with abandon.

"Don't throw me down," I pleaded with him, watching the water climb up the back of his legs until it pooled around his midsection. "Setesh, did you hear me? I said don't -"

My cry was in vain; before I finished my sentence, I was flying through the air, and an instant later brine and kelp were invading my taste buds, my wedding dress ruined. I felt my limbs flailing with alarm, just long enough to remind me that the water was shallow, and when I stood, I was greeted by my husband's boisterous laughter, surging from his belly, causing him to double over.

I grinned in spite of my annoyance, unable to remember the last time he'd laughed like that. "I am so glad my pain was able to amuse you," I told him sarcastically, rolling my eyes. "You could have at least given me a warning."

Setesh walked closer to me, still laughing. "You knew it was coming as soon as I picked you up."

"No I did not," I protested, pretending to pull away from him. He caught me again, this time wrapping his arms around my shoulders. I landed a few playful punches on his stomach, which he didn't attempt to block. "I didn't think you would really *throw* me."

He looked at me, trying to see if my anger was real. I couldn't hide my amusement, and soon we were doubled over once more. After a moment, Setesh kissed my nose, then let go of me and flung himself under water. I watched him as he swam away from me, further into the depths of the sea, to the point where he could no longer stand. When he emerged and looked back at me, it was as if his head and torso were floating above the water. The vest he wore for the ceremony was gone and his legs were hidden by the deep blue.

"Are you coming?" Setesh called out, the sound echoing against the open space, booming happily. I snapped my fingers and my dress fell away, disintegrating in a shimmer of white light. Freshly unencumbered, I swam out to meet him, and when I got there, he took my hand and under we went, down to the ocean floor.

We lost all track of time down there, dancing with the creatures of the sea, and when we finally came up, the sun was rising again in the east and it was a new day. We crawled out from the ocean and found shade under the nearest tree, curling up next to one another and drifting to sleep without a word. I'd hoped we would go home, where exhaustion would quickly escape us, but instead I found myself lulled to rest by the gentle crash of the waves whispering a lullaby each time they hit the golden hued sand.

It was a few hours later when I woke, the sun past its midday point in the sky, its heat blocked by the heavy canopy of leaves that stretched above me. Setesh was no longer at my side, and I immediately wondered where he'd gone. I stood and, realizing I was barely dressed, summoned a dark green light to materialize as fabric, which I wrapped around my breast and allowed to fall loosely to my knees. My first inclination was to take a few steps out towards the water, but I quickly turned my attention inland, wanting to explore a bit of this forest, and feeling excited about what I might find there.

I only traveled a few yards before I could see him, practicing warrior forms, unable to relax even in this immensely serene place. I got a bit closer and hid behind a tree, watching his face contort as he summoned more force into each stroke, pushing himself to the limit. Setesh repeated his movements, over and over, attempting to best the previous round, wordlessly acknowledging that each new personal best wasn't good enough.

I watched my husband for quite some time, not knowing if he knew I was there, not wanting to disturb him either way. I was fascinated by his ambition and ability to challenge himself, yet astonished that he never seemed satisfied by his effort. In my estimation, his mastery of the forms was excellent, but I knew that my words would never satisfy his standard. If nothing else, Setesh was not one to settle.

Finally he ended his competition with himself, panting loudly, trying to catch his breath. I walked out from behind the trees and made my presence known, noticing a quick look of surprise pass over his face before it disappeared behind his usual scowl.

"How long were you watching?" Setesh asked, his tone even and inquisitive.

I shrugged, glancing up at the sky but finding my view of the sun obscured. "For a while, actually. I was starting to think perhaps I should go off on my own and leave you to your workout."

He nodded and looked away. "I didn't mean to make you feel neglected or anything. I just don't feel like myself if I haven't done my training for the day."

"No, I didn't feel that way," I said, trying to reassure him. "I didn't mind watching."

He nodded again. "Was there anything in particular you wanted to do today?"

I wasn't expecting this question, so I shrugged again. "I was going to explore the woods a bit. If you want to stay behind, I should be okay on my own."

"No, I'm happy to come with you," Setesh insisted, taking my hand. He pulled me to the left, and I followed him into the deep.

As lovely as I'd found this paradise, I only needed a few short days to tire of it. I sighed loudly enough to Setesh and he whisked me away to his favorite spot, a location previously kept hidden from all of us. When we arrived, I had my eyes closed, and he set me down softly on the ground, which felt dry and rough, quite unlike the sand on the beach we'd just left.

"Okay, you can open your eyes now," he told me, taking his hands from my back and letting me go. I quickly looked around, excited to discover this surprise, only to have my expectations shattered.

We were in the desert.

Setesh came from behind me, face lined with tiny beads of sweat that only complemented his radiant expression. He was happy, in a way I don't think I'd ever seen before and I know I haven't seen since. I smiled immediately to keep him from noticing my disappointment. He beamed.

"You asked me once where I hide when I want to be alone, well, this is it," he said, gesturing out across the landscape so I could take in the sight of the monotonous ground stretching for miles before us. The sun was beating across my face and there wasn't an inch of shade before me. I sighed, the smile forcibly pasted on.

Convinced, my husband grabbed my hand and began to show me the sights. I was surprised at how many things lived here; in this barren space, they managed to thrive. I looked up at Setesh; for once he was at peace.

"Have you done your daily workout?" I asked him, reaching out to touch a cactus with unusually colorful flowers, still trying to appreciate his choice of locale.

Setesh shrugged. "No, not yet. I was planning to work out as soon as we got here."

I hesitated. "Can I work out with you?"

This caught him by surprise, but he tried not to show it. "Sure, if you want. Have you learned any of the forms?"

I smiled, a real one this time. "Of course not. Don't you want to run or something first, to warm up? Maybe we can race or something."

Setesh grinned; I had brought out his competitive side. "I don't think it would be fair to race. I train all the time. I would have an unfair advantage."

"Says who?" I asked, my hand shooting to my hip in offense. I scoffed and broadened my shoulders. "Just because I don't train as often doesn't mean the victory should be given to you before you've even won."

He laughed. "Bragging, are we?"

I shrugged and began securing the fabric around my neck and torso, for security and flexibility. "Well, I would hate to see you lose but I would love to beat you."

"You're on." He turned and scanned the horizon, pointing when he'd found the perfect destination. "Do you think you can manage to make it to the base of that rock formation there?"

As soon as I realized that he was speaking of a mountain range as if it were an anthill, I wanted to call off the race. But when I looked back at him, all I could see was anticipation and I nodded in agreement. Still smiling, he tightened the waist on his wedding pants and got into position. I sighed and scrunched up my face, no longer finding any of this amusing.

"Begin!" Setesh shouted, and we both took off, running side by side.

I glanced over at him. "Don't hold back," I shouted, pushing myself. "You better give it your all if you want to win." I picked up my pace and found myself in the lead, which gave me a moment to breathe. I was enjoying this, in spite of my hesitation. There was something meditative about the run and the constancy of our surroundings. I focused my attention forward, hoping to make it to the mountain first.

Unfortunately, I had not considered the need for endurance. Since we'd already been earthbound for several days, my body was no longer infinitely energized. After a while I found myself panting and slowing, which gave Setesh the opening he needed to push past me, the winner.

I caught up to him a few minutes later and sank into a sweaty heap at the base of the mountain. "That was quite a run," I said, my way of congratulating him.

"I hope you don't take this as criticism," he began, then hesitated. "It's just that, I found this place because I knew that one day we would need to live here, full time, and we would change, because earth is so different from home. I wanted to become accustomed to living here for long periods of time, so that it wouldn't drain me." Setesh glanced down at me, trying to gauge my response. "This is what we'll feel like after we've been away from home for many months, you know."

He was right, I knew, and even though we'd all known, I had to admit that I hadn't actually prepared for the shift. I just figured I would rush home whenever my body felt weighed down or I needed to re-energize. I had no idea how often those opportunities would arise, or how often we would want to take them, and here I was, faced with the lack of evidence of my preparedness.

"That was good of you to think ahead," I told him, wishing I had thought of it first. "Especially for you, since you will certainly need the physical strength in your position." I sighed and lay back onto the ground, wishing the ocean was nearby so we could take a soothing dip. "Are you looking forward to the move?"

"It's not so much about looking forward to it. I'm prepared, if that's what you mean."

I frowned. "I mean, what are your feelings about it? Are you... looking forward to living here, full time?"

He sighed. "I am trying not to have feelings about it. We have to do it so I will do it. Just that simple. It's duty for me."

I didn't know how to respond to that, so I sat up and faced him. "It's duty for all of us, but that doesn't mean we can't be happy about it. We can embrace it and look forward to fulfilling our purpose."

Setesh paused. "I suppose it is no secret that this isn't quite the assignment that I was hoping for, so I guess I find it a bit harder to be happy about it. But I have embraced it and I am going to fulfill my charge."

"But have you made peace with it?" I asked him, trying unsuccessfully to force him to meet my gaze. "I'm sure you have to understand why you are so well suited to be war commander."

He shrugged. "I also think I am well suited for other things, but I suppose the Great Father didn't agree."

"Everyone can't be king, Setesh. There really is no one else who could be our general." When he didn't respond I continued. "Just think about what you told me today. You began preparing for this move before any of us did. You used the dynamics of the desert to test your physical abilities. You push yourself and train harder than any of us, and that makes you the most qualified to train others." I looked around, shaking my head. "Our warriors will be unmatched, second to none. There is no way Ausar could train warriors the way you can, you have to know that."

Setesh hesitated. "Heru-Ur could have. I could have been Naswt Biti and Heru-Ur our general and Ausar could have done... something else." He looked at me and sighed. "I don't mean to sound so petulant."

I smiled. "You do, but that's okay. You are supposed to be free to express your truth with me."

He stood and focused his attention downward, kicking around a few loose stones. "I hate that I'm the one dissatisfied. I already have this reputation of being a contrarian, and now here I am, predictably causing trouble." Setesh sat back down, looking away from me, sullenly staring at the horizon.

"You haven't caused any trouble. All you did was share how you feel."

My husband didn't respond, so I focused on the monstrosity he was sitting on. It wasn't very tall, all rock and gravel, as if no plant had found it a fitting place to make roots. I stood and began to climb, getting to the top quickly and assuming a meditative posture. With most of the ground below being level, I could see far off into the distance, this desert that seemed to stretch out into forever. I took a deep breath and closed my eyes.

The sun had begun to set before I felt my husband's hand on my shoulder. "It will get cold here soon; we should find a place to rest."

I stood and brushed off the back of my legs. "Is there anywhere around here we might be able to take a bath?" I asked, again wishing desperately for the ocean.

"Tomorrow, first thing in the morning. For now, rest."

I didn't argue, and took his hand, letting him lead me once more, away from the mountain into the bleak wilderness. We walked silently until we found a cavern large enough for us to crawl into. Setesh gathered some dry brush and blew on it, lighting it on fire. He placed the fire on the ground to allow it to grow, then sat down and gestured to me. I nestled between his legs and leaned back against him.

"You're right, you know."

I hesitated. "What do you mean?"

Setesh shifted behind me. "I mean, about what you said earlier." He paused, and I wanted to push him to keep talking, but I waited, hoping he would keep going on his own. He did. "I haven't looked at it that way because it's not really what I wanted. But, you're right, I know you're right. I was choosing not to adjust my perspective, but if I do, perhaps I can make peace with everything."

I pulled away from him so I could turn and look at him. "I understand if you feel like, like it was unfair all of this was decided FOR us. We didn't even get a say in any of this."

He scoffed. "Yes, I do feel a bit of that, of course."

"But," I insisted, "we do get to decide how we respond to it. And I really think you have an amazing opportunity and I really hope you find a way to be excited to take on the challenge."

He nodded. "I appreciate everything you said today. You sound like you truly believe in me."

"I truly do." I turned around and resumed leaning into him, and we slipped back into silence, this one more comfortable than the last. He took my hand and kissed the knuckles, and I fell asleep listening to his heartbeat.

He was no longer behind me when I woke, but was only standing a few feet away, practicing a warrior form vigorously. I watched him for a moment before crawling out of our cavern and stretching my limbs, experiencing tightness in my legs for the first time. Life will be much different down here, I thought to myself.

"If you want to take off for a bit, so you can bathe, I'll stay here and wait for you," Setesh said as he transitioned into the next posture. "Or if you want me to join you, where do you think you'll be?"

I thought for a second. "I will head to Kemet to bathe, but I don't want to stay there. There is a place I want to show you, if you don't mind. I can come back here and get you before I go."

Setesh held this position longer than the others. "No, I will come to the Hapi and clean up too before we go. Wait there for me, I promise I won't be long."

I nodded before departing, not mentioning to him that I would stop off at home first, needing a quick recharge from the density of the earth realm. Thankfully, my trip was without incident, and Setesh was still in the desert when I landed on the bank of the Hapi. Never so happy to see water before, I disrobed and submerged myself immediately and completely, taking advantage of the solitude of the moment.

I lazed about in the water for what felt like hours, before crawling out and resting on the riverbank, allowing the breeze to dry me off. When I woke, the sun was much lower in the sky and I was still alone. I didn't know what could be keeping Setesh, but I didn't want to be impatient. I sighed, wondering what I should do next.

I stood and decided to begin walking down river, but I didn't get very far before my husband appeared before me in such a bright red flash that it blinded me momentarily. I jumped back and blinked wildly. He grinned.

"What took you so long?" I asked, tilting my head and grimacing. I had intended to say that in an even tone, but this was one of those moments where my emotions got the best of me.

For some reason, that didn't appear to bother him at all. He stripped and kissed my nose. "I stopped off at the mountain to spar with Heru-Ur. I didn't mean to lose track of time; I hope you aren't too angry at me." Setesh jumped into the river without waiting for me to respond, and when he came out from under the water, he looked relieved and light-hearted. I sighed.

"I'm not angry at all, I just wish I had known. I guess I could have come back to look for you."

His smile faded. "No, I shouldn't have kept you waiting. But I appreciate how patient you were. I really needed that workout."

I smiled and sat down, pulling my legs into my chest. "I'm glad you feel better. So now I know where you go when you like to be alone, and I want to show you my place."

He nodded and looked around. "Do you want to go there now? It will be dark soon. We could stay here and go after first light."

I nodded, pulling my legs in tighter. "Yes, that's probably best. Do you want to go back to the desert and stay there? Or is here okay?"

Setesh looked at me and smiled. "We should stay here. I've had enough time in the desert." He looked around tentatively for a moment before asking, "what were you up to today?"

I hesitated. "I stopped off at home for a second, just to recharge, then I came here and I've been here ever since. I didn't do anything exceptional."

"Nothing wrong with that. This time is meant for us to relax. We will be plenty busy after the move."

I sighed and stretched my legs out on the muddy grass. "You will be plenty busy. I have no idea what I'm going to be doing."

Setesh had never heard me complain like this before, so he was completely caught by surprise. I didn't see this register on his face though; he must have needed a minute to think because he dove under water and stayed there until he could come up with a proper response.

"What is it you think your job should be? What is it you want to do?"

I looked at him suspiciously. No one ever really asked that question, because our lives were not about what we wanted. Everything was duty, charge, purpose. That's what made it so difficult, the fact that I didn't know what was expected of me. "I guess I have no idea. I just want to know that I am going to be useful, not just *there*."

He came out of the water and plopped down beside me, crossing his legs beneath him. "But since you don't have a direct charge, you get to decide what you want to do and who you want to be. Don't you find that liberating? Or exciting?"

"Well, I mean, I do have a charge," I said, "I am supposed to live up to the name I've been given."

Setesh rolled his eyes. "We ALL have to do that, and the rest of us have been told what we're supposed to do to assist us with fulfilling this responsibility. But you haven't been given the same specifics as the rest of us. You have more room to figure out who you are and who you want to be, on your own terms."

I was nervous about voicing my truth, but I decided to push ahead. This was my husband, after all, and I wanted to try to be honest with him, just as I had asked him to be honest with me. I looked down at the ground, avoiding his stare as he had avoided mine the day before. "Sometimes I just wish Djehuty or Ra had just *told* me what they want me to do. I am constantly concerned that I am going to be a disappointment, or that I'm not capable of much and that's why I haven't been assigned to anything."

He was silent again, this time longer than the first. I sighed after a while, realizing how ridiculous my complaints probably sounded to someone who wished he had the freedom to be who he thought he should be. Instead, he had been restricted and I had not.

"I think maybe your assignment is harder than ours," Setesh finally said, still looking up to the sky. "It's really easy to fall into the role that someone else has chosen for you, but you have to find yourself with much less direction. Maybe that means they believe you are capable of a lot."

I looked at him, and he looked at me, his scowl soft, eyebrows relaxed. He was really trying to make me feel better. "Maybe, I guess that's how I should see it. To be fair I haven't really thought of it that way."

Setesh stood. "Well, think of it that way, at least for a little while." He winked, and I couldn't help but to smile up at him before he ran back to the Hapi and jumped in without hesitation.

I watched him swim around until the light was completely gone from the sky. He glided across the bottom of the river as if he had not spent his entire day working out, as if he had enough energy for the rest of the night.

He was still in the water when I eventually drifted off to sleep, but when I woke he was behind me, his arms wrapped around me tightly. I sighed deeply, holding back my tears before rolling over to face him. I kissed his lips, causing him to stir and open his eyes.

"Did I wake you? I mumbled.

He smirked at me. "No, not at all," he answered, pulling away from me so he could lie on his back. I sat up and looked across the river to the other side.

"I need to get out of here," I whispered, trying to steady my voice.

Setesh took my hand. "Let's go, then."

I landed us in a thicket of papyrus, reeds, and rushes, our feet underwater, massaging mud between our toes. I looked up at Setesh, finding his trademark scowl betraying traces of confusion.

"You were dying to leave the Hapi to come to a swamp?"

I smiled. "You say swamp like it's a bad thing."

Setesh let go of my hand and took a few steps forward, choosing not to sink into the river but instead to hover above it. "I take it you don't agree."

I turned my back to him and faced the east, watching Aten begin its rise across the sky, taking a deep breath. "This is a place where two rivers meet, where they struggle to coexist, but somehow they find... resolution." I sighed deeply, turning around, finding him doing the same. We faced each other in silence, me completely aware of the emotions that my face betrayed. "Everything is so clear for me here, Setesh. If this can work," I whispered, glancing to my right, "so can anything; so can everything."

His expression softened, and he took my hand. "You're really bothered about the move, aren't you? More than you've said? It's like you don't want any of us to know."

I didn't want to answer. My natural impulse was to keep it to myself, to carry the burden alone. I looked away from him as the first tear made its way down my cheek, anxious to fix my gaze on anything but his face. "Yes, I am," I admitted, unable to muster any other words.

Setesh nodded. "Let's take a walk."

I let him lead me across terrain that found space in a senseless place, taking deep breaths the whole way, letting my thoughts go and finding silence. It helped that he didn't speak, and we walked slow, an even pace that didn't cause us to sweat or exert energy. I didn't know how long we were going to walk, but I was willing to follow him all day, to avoid talking about what I'd come here to discuss.

We reached a hilltop, and he stopped, sitting crosslegged and pulling me down beside him. From here we could look down onto the marshes and continue breathing the humid air that rose from the water. We were facing east, and the sun was at its midway point in the sky. I sighed again.

"How do you find your resolution?" Setesh asked.

I smiled. "I think I have to do what I told you to do. I'm just seeing this all wrong."

"Do you think it's more than that? Are you angry at Ra and Djehuty for making you feel neglected, or less important?"

I inhaled sharply. "I hadn't really thought about it like that."

I looked over at him, and he met my gaze. "Maybe you should," he answered, his expression blank.

I stood. "I don't really have a right to be angry at them, though. I am supposed to trust that they know best, so if they saw fit not to give me a charge, I'm supposed to be okay with that."

"But you're not."

I sighed again. "No, I'm not."

Setesh smiled for a second. "Now you see how I felt." He paused before continuing. "You were able to make me understand the wisdom that I wasn't able to see out of selfishness. What's stopping you from doing the same for yourself?"

I plopped back down on the grass, laying on my back, not wanting to admit that I was being a petulant child. "It just hurts, Setesh. It hurts to feel unnecessary. It hurts to feel forgotten." I closed my eyes, wanting to see, to feel, only darkness. "I just don't know who to blame. It's no one's fault really, and it would be easier to be angry if I could direct blame at someone. At least you can be angry at Ra for giving you the wrong assignment. But no one has actually *wronged* me, and yet I am carrying this heavy weight that is all on me, only me, and how is that right?"

We sat there in silence for a while, and I tried hard not to think. Setesh eventually cleared his throat. "What if you are not alone, though?" When I did not respond, he continued. "What if that is why we got pushed into marriage? What if they knew?"

I still did not speak, but I opened my eyes, and after a few more breaths, I rolled to my side and looked up at my husband.

"I asked you to be my partner, to work with me through everything, and you said you can do that for me." He hesitated. "You never asked me to be that for you. I didn't even think you needed me, but now I think, maybe you do, and maybe we need each other."

I blinked, unable to speak. He lay beside me and slid his arm beneath my shoulders, pulling me into him. I rested my head into the nook between his chest and his chin, allowing myself to be cradled.

He held me like that silently for a few minutes, before speaking again, whispering. "We are a lot more alike than I thought we were."

"So it seems," I whispered, closing my eyes once more.

Setesh took a deep breath. "I think I need you, and maybe that's your charge, and maybe that's enough."

I looked up at him, nervous to be so close to him but never wanting to be separated again. "It can be enough. We can make it enough," I said, desperately wanting that to be true.

"Are you sure?"

My answer came as a kiss, soft at first, then stronger, as everything I felt was poured into the moment. He matched my intensity, and I slid out of his arms and onto the ground beneath him. He was careful with me, at least this first time, considerate; and as our bodies merged I wondered if this is how Auset felt, to be loved the way she was, the way I thought I never would be.

Afterwards we lay there and looked up to the heavens, and I could not help but be amused by our surroundings. I had thought we would make love on the beach, which was perfect for romance, or even in the desert when my husband was most confident. Yet it was here, in the swamp, the senseless place that spoke only to me, and even in the midst of my vulnerability, it was enough.

I stepped out into the warm air of the afternoon, lifting my face up to greet the sun. I could hear the sound of laughter coming from the edge of the river, where the children were playing while their parents studied. I smiled and took a deep breath before turning my attention to the open courtyard where Ausar had assembled his group for class.

As hot as it was, Ausar was sitting before his students completely decked, wearing the double crown on his head and leopard skin draped over his shoulders. He'd apparently requested the attendees to bring the heavy, gold plated throne outdoors, and they'd placed several thick skins down so that the chair wouldn't touch the ground directly. In his right hand was the Ankh, gripped so tightly that his knuckles looked like they might produce their own sweat. If he was nervous, his facial expression didn't betray it.

I walked over to stand next to Auset, who was observing the class from the courtyard's edge, as she did for all his classes. It had only been a month since we'd moved in, and even though I didn't keep track of their activity on a daily basis, I wasn't confident that anyone here would be ready any time soon.

"What's he got them working on today?" I mumbled to Auset, leaning in so only she could hear. Back then the courtyard was barren as the desert, and I could tell my sister suffered under the relentless rays of Aten without any trees to offer her shade and comfort. Her shoulders tilted slightly forward and a soft mist of sweat lined her forehead. Auset had stopped wearing her adornments to classes and meetings, finding them heavy under the sun at midday, and chose instead to dress light in a loose, pale blue linen dress. Yet, with her lengthy hair coiled atop her head and her feet covered with gold trimmed sandals, there was no chance of mistaking her for a citizen.

She sighed, glancing at me quickly before responding. "The same thing they've been working on all month." Auset turned to face me, looking over my shoulder a few times to make sure no one else is in earshot. "He's getting concerned; he doesn't feel like they're connecting to the prayer like he expects them to. I'm sure he didn't think it would take this long."

I frowned. "Well, has he asked the council about it? They are here to advise him."

Auset gave me the look, raising her eyebrows and smirking. "Of course he hasn't. I understand why not, he doesn't want to feel like he needs them for everything, but remember Ra said he had to stay flexible, maybe switch things up if they aren't working." She turned away from me again, facing the lesson once more. "He'll figure it out eventually, he's still just trying to find his groove, as a teacher and as a King."

"Perhaps you could nudge him, remind him of the charge that Ra gave us?" I added, thinking maybe she already had. "I'm sure he would appreciate your support."

She shook her head. "I don't know, senet. I don't want him to feel like I'm telling him how to be a man." She looked down at me again. "How would you approach Setesh?"

That made me laugh. "Setesh and Ausar are two different men. I would approach my husband very differently than I think you should approach yours."

"Yes, you're right about that," Auset agreed, smiling. "I guess maybe I'm still getting into my groove too, as a wife."

"But you and Ausar are so good together, I'm sure you can approach him about anything."

She sighed, a look of worry crossing her face. "You are probably right but I just... I just feel like I should let him figure this out. I don't want to jump the gun and act out of turn."

I took her hand in mine and squeezed it. "You can't hesitate just because you're still feeling guilty about that other thing, you know. You still have your duty to live up to," I reminded her with what I hoped was a gentle whisper. To her, it probably sounded like genuine scolding, but if she had an idea that could help, and she didn't say anything, she'd be doing her husband a disservice.

Auset didn't respond, and we stood there watching class for a few moments longer before I decided to take my leave. I curtseyed to her, as was the custom, then began to head towards the field, to catch up with Setesh. Before long I could hear him shouting, pushing the men to their limits, scolding them if they fell short. His workouts were rigorous and demanding, and any warrior he trained would be completely prepared to protect and defend this nation, I felt absolutely sure of that.

By the time I reached the edge of the field, they were standing in formation, formally ending the training for the day. I stopped and watched as Setesh looked them over, making sure each and every one of them held their spot correctly. No one dared moved until they had been properly dismissed, but as soon as Setesh gave the word they collapsed to catch their breath. He turned and looked at me, looking rather pleased with himself. I grinned.

"What brings you all that way out here?" he asked, walking over to me as though the heat of the day didn't affect him at all, carrying the wooden training weapons as if they were deadly. Setesh almost never bothered with his ceremonial garb, and today he had been training shirtless, without his collar or cuffs. It was an enjoyable sight; he was sure to stay in excellent shape with this assignment.

I tilted my head and looked at him. "I thought I would meet you after training, I didn't want to wait to see you until dinner."

"Ah, so you missed me," he teased, putting down the training weapons. He picked up a cloth from the ground near my foot and used it to wipe down his face. As hot as it was, we would all need to bathe before dinner.

I turned to head back to the house, shrugging my shoulders nonchalantly. "I wouldn't say it like that," I said casually, smirking playfully.

Setesh came from behind me and walked in front of me, striding backwards so he could face me. "Really?" he asked, sarcastically. "And how would you put it?"

I giggled, then shrugged again. "I guess I just, felt sorry for you, stuck out here in this heat, all sweaty and hot." I looked into the distance for a moment, still smiling. "Just wanted to show you some mercy, is all."

When I looked back to him, he had stopped walking, forcing me to stop too, since he was right in front of me. Setesh raised an eyebrow. "So that's it?" he asked, eyes playful as ever, "I am so pitiful I deserve your mercy?"

"Well, I mean," I hesitated, "I guess I can be nice to you."

He smiled, grinned really, a quick flash of a smile that didn't last long, but was infectious enough. I grinned back at him, happy he was in such a good mood. "I appreciate your generosity," he told me, taking my hand so that we could walk side by side the rest of the way. It occurred to me that this was exactly the kind of cutesy thing that I'd once found annoying, but I chose to consider it as evidence of my personal evolution instead of a contradiction of my ideals. Besides, I thought to myself, we're married.

"Did you stop and check out Ausar's class too?" Setesh asked me as soon as we'd made it back to the apartment, dropping my hand so he could get what he needed for a bath.

I sighed. "I did, actually. I'm surprised he's still teaching out there with the throne and the double crown, everything," I told my husband, shaking my head. "I thought for sure by now he would have given all that up."

Setesh shrugged. "I suppose he can't afford to be casual; he doesn't want anyone taking advantage of him or disrespecting the throne."

"I know, I know, I just, it can't be comfortable like that."

Setesh was frowning again, this one a look of consideration. "Being Naswt Biti isn't a comfortable duty. Give him a chance to figure it out."

I looked up at him, somewhat surprised by his response. "You know, that's exactly what Auset said today, when I asked her about the lesson."

"Really? What did she say about his classes?" Setesh asked, opening our courtyard doors. I followed him outside so he could get into the water without breaking our conversation.

"Well," I hesitated slightly, "she said he was concerned that his students weren't catching on like he'd expected them to."

He tilted his head to the side and looked away contemplatively. "That seems odd. I can't see how anyone could engage in a group ritual and not connect to it, especially after doing it every day."

I hesitated again, sitting at the edge of the pool across from Setesh. "I don't think they're actually doing the ritual, I think they are just learning about it. You know, going over the mechanics of what, where, when, why, those types of things."

Setesh looked back at me with disbelief. "Well, that explains why they aren't catching on. You can't teach a feeling." He paused for a second, then asked, "Auset said she's going to just wait for him to figure that out on his own?"

"Maybe that's what we should do too," I said, not answering his question directly because I knew it wasn't a real one. "Maybe we have to be careful about how to approach him with our opinions."

"You're probably right," Setesh mumbled. "I don't want to undermine his confidence or authority."

I smiled. "Exactly," I said, standing and beginning to strip. I was tired of this heat, and this discussion. "Give him a bit longer and let him ask when he's ready. He'll be more likely to receive your advice if he asked for it."

Setesh looked at me, still thinking about Ausar. "You're probably right. Still, I hate the idea that all of this time might be lost while we protect his ego."

"You have a point, but since we're only a month in, we can afford for him to take his time, work out the kinks."

Setesh sighed. "I don't want to go over his head, but I feel compelled to ask Djehuty for his thoughts on this. What do you think?"

I slid into the water, letting my hair down and getting it wet. "That's safer than you just confronting Ausar head on."

"I'm not confrontational," he protested. I raised my eyebrows at him. "Well, I can speak to him without being confrontational," he compromised. I smiled.

"That's enough about Ausar." I glided over to his side of the pool. "What about me?"

"What about you?" Setesh asked, teasing me by pretending not to care.

I sat on his lap, facing him, tugging his locks with my fingers. "You really want to be talking about Ausar right now, while your wife is naked and sitting on your lap?"

He rewarded me with another smile, this one smaller than the last, but just as encouraging. "Another great point," he responded, wrapping his arms around my waist. "You are on a roll."

I was the first one to arrive in the great hall for dinner, which was usually the case. Right after the coronation, Seshat and I spent a great deal of time side by side, which gave me the opportunity to observe her as she kept the household running smoothly. Seshat introduced me to the people who kept mice and mosquitos out of the estate; the women who replaced the reeds on our beds every other day, to keep them fresh and sweet-smelling; the men who kept the water flowing in and out of our personal courtyards. She would occasionally monitor the attendees as they cleaned our chambers and make sure all the meals were served on time. Without her guidance I never would have considered the importance of managing such minor details, and while she never asked me to take over, after the first week I began to step in, eager to accept the responsibility as my own. It kept me busy during the day while the others taught classes and held council meetings, which I didn't, couldn't, attend, since I wasn't a member of the council.

Most evenings, while I was finalizing dinner, Setesh stayed behind in our room to cultivate a bit of stillness, his adrenaline constantly running with all of the warrior training . Today in particular I suspected he would reach out to Djehuty as he'd mentioned, but I didn't confirm. We all need a bit of alone time every now and again, and considering how easily he became agitated, this balance was even more important.

Auset entered the room first, just a few moments behind me. I had just checked on the food and learned that it would be ready for us soon. She looked up and down the table, as if checking for a flaw, then nodding, her expectations met.

"Isn't this something you could have one of the attendees handle?" she asked without looking in my direction.

I smiled. "What else am I doing that I can't manage this one little thing? Besides," I added with a hint of sarcasm, walking around the table towards my seat, "I would rather not leave the meals of Naswt Biti and Hmt Naswu in the hands of a mere mortal."

Auset tilted her head at me, smirking. She didn't think she was prudish, but I had a different opinion on the matter, and expected her to say something condescending in response. Instead, she silently walked around the table towards her seat, and stood in front of it for a second, looking down at the plate, the smirk fading into a frown. I stayed standing behind my seat, waiting patiently to see what she would do next.

Finally she looked up, an expression of sadness over her face. "I feel like everything's changed between us. I just don't like it," she whispered at me loudly from across the table, finally sitting with a flourish.

I sighed, following her lead and taking my seat. I did my best to act natural with my sister, but there was protocol to be followed. "Nothing's changed," I lied, whispering back with the same tone. "But we do have to keep up appearances."

I winked at her conspiratorially. She smiled and relaxed, just as our husbands entered the room, Setesh a respectable five steps behind Ausar. I stood immediately upon their entry, eliciting another sigh from Auset. It WAS annoying to have such strict rules with my own siblings, but the other option was to ignore the rules and undermine their authority. I might have resented my own lack of position, but I didn't have any intention of ruining theirs, or incurring the wrath of Ra.

Ausar took his seat at the head of the table, with Auset to his left and Setesh to his right. He took her hand and kissed her knuckles, causing her to blush. I motioned to the attendees to begin bringing everything to the table, the bowls of onions, chickpeas and lentils that we were all beginning to tire of.

Setesh cleared his throat. "Naswt, my wife told me that she stopped by your class earlier. How are things going?"

I glanced up at my husband warily, wondering where he was going with this, not that I could stop it, seeing as he'd already dove right in.

Ausar sat up straighter, appearing glad that someone had asked about his work. "I'm feeling very good about it," he began, fixing his usekh and pushing the cuffs back on his wrists. Despite how fidgety he looked, his voice sounded confident and assured. "I have two rather promising students, and I know it's early to think of this, but I suspect they will be the ones sent to the first **het NTR** after we receive word from Heru-Ur."

Setesh's eyebrows went up in surprise. "You've already chosen initiates to run the temple?"

"No, well I mean," Ausar responded, shaking his head, "I am keeping my eye on them, you know, they've already begun to distinguish themselves, so I'm just keeping track of who shows the greatest promise." He took a sip and pulled his seat in just a bit. "I want to nurture those with the greatest potential, if I can, so things can go quickly, smoothly."

Setesh nodded his head, impressed. "That sounds like a good strategy. Have you arranged for one-on-one time with them yet?"

Ausar shook his head, choosing to answer between bites. "Not yet, no. It's still much too early for that. But I am feeling optimistic about these two. They are incredibly bright."

Auset smiled, looking at the two men with a motherly warmth. "I've noticed it too, if we're talking about the same two students. That is a good group that you are working with, Ausar."

He smiled, glad to receive a compliment from his wife. "I think so too, dua. Did you spend any time today out in the fields?"

Auset shook her head and swallowed. "Not today, no. I will join you tomorrow while you show the farmers how to use the new harvesting equipment. Considering how difficult it is to find edible vegetation in this area, they are looking forward to increasing the food supply for their families."

The room got quiet for a moment before Ausar turned back to Setesh. "How was today's training?"

My husband's eyebrows went up once more. "Vigorous as usual, although I too believe I have a good group. They are fit and not afraid to work hard, and I find that they embrace the opportunity to properly protect and defend the realm." He stopped for a moment before continuing. "I was thinking, they may benefit from an opportunity to learn from you, Naswt, if perhaps you were open to switching classes for a week or two."

Ausar frowned. "That's an interesting proposition. Why do you think so?"

"Well," Setesh began, sitting up straighter, "the warriors will be better motivated if they understand more about what we're establishing, and getting an opportunity to hear directly from their King what their importance is to the realm can help to reinforce pride and duty. And," he added, "your priests shouldn't be completely unable to engage in physical defense. This could generate a level of mutual respect between both groups."

Ausar nodded without betraying his sentiment, taking a sip of water and sitting back from the table. "What you're suggesting makes sense, Setesh. We want all contributors to feel equally as necessary to the successful operation of the nation. Let me think it over and we can discuss it again in tomorrow's council meeting."

I smiled, seeing this as an acceptable response, and glanced up at my husband to gauge his response. His facial expression was even, but there was a simmer in his eyes, even as we continued our dinner in peace.

I closed the door behind me, tight, then followed Setesh into our bedroom, closing that door as well. It would be hard for someone to hear, especially if we kept our voices low, but I wanted to be as careful as possible.

"I was impressed by the way you spoke with Ausar tonight at dinner," I told my husband honestly, slowly beginning to disrobe and get prepared for bed. "The way you approached him, it was so thoughtful, so respectful."

He sighed, sitting with his back towards me, looking out into the courtyard. "You know I stayed behind to talk to Djehuty; he was the one who told me what to do."

"It was wise of you to seek guidance first," I told him, hoping to ease his mind.

"I tried to do what Djehuty advised me to do," Setesh told me, turning slightly so that he could look over his shoulder at me, "but I don't feel like Ausar heard me; he acts like listening to my perspective is optional."

I frowned. "It's not like he ignored you; I'm sure you'll discuss it at the meeting and the other council members will see the wisdom in your suggestion."

"Why couldn't he just accept it from me?" Setesh complained, slight annoyance sneaking into his voice. "He should be able to hear what I've said without having to hear everyone else's opinions on the matter."

"Don't worry about that," I said, sitting on the bed behind him, pulling my legs up so that I could face him fully. "We all agree that he's still getting his footing. I'm sure he appreciates your input. Give him time."

My husband stood and walked over to the open doors, silent for a few moments, his mind and heart heavy, his countenance dark. I watched him wordlessly, not knowing what to say to make him feel better.

Setesh signed. "You're probably right. He's probably just

being prudent. I should be more understanding."

I felt so relieved. I stood and walked up behind him, slipping my arms around his waist and touching my forehead to his back. "Don't worry about this all night. Come to bed."

He pulled away from me without looking back. "You go, I'll be in later. I'm just going to take a walk." Setesh exited without another word.

I watched him go, wrapping my arms around myself, hoping that he would find the peace he was seeking, and wishing he would find it here, with me.

It was a sight to behold, the divine blend of force, one subtle, the other assertive, demonstrating the harmonious balance of Maat. The subtle, led by Ausar, engaged in the flexible meditation postures meant to encourage the union of mind and spirit. The assertive, led by Setesh, channeled **sekhem,** personal power, with fists and kicks, rearranging the world around them energetically.

Auset and I sat on the field on stools brought out for us from the great room; far enough back that we could see both sides, close enough that we could appreciate the art. As wives we were proud of the progress our husbands had made in the last two years; as sisters we worried about the discord that was slowly developing between them. Each step that Ausar took towards being a strong and confident ruler added to the space between he and Setesh. It felt as if they could not agree on anything, and it strained all of our relationships.

Our outer courtyard had begun to change over this time, with Auset hiring gardeners to plant sycamore trees along the main path leading into the great house, and having the water workers divert a stream from the river to run along the far edge of the land. Along this stream, we'd planted rose bushes and chrysanthemum shrubs, and allowed a vine of grapes to wind along the short outer wall. It had achieved the task of causing the outer courtyard to feel like a welcoming place, and it made the **per eah** feel like a greater house than before.

The men ended their training sessions almost simultaneously, and the students disbanded and began to gather their things, ready to head home to their wives and children. Ausar approached Auset and I, and we both stood, following protocol. Setesh marched past us without a glance or a word.

"Were you to have seen this from our perspective, husband." Auset stood and wrapped her arms around Ausar's waist, not caring that he was sweaty, or that it was hot. "Both groups are coming along divinely. It was a true pleasure to watch."

Ausar kissed her nose. "Dua, my beloved. I'm glad you were able to join us." He glanced over and noticed my presence, probably for the first time. "Both of you," he added, not wanting me to feel left out. I smiled.

"I appreciate that, Naswt. I will go in ahead of you both and make sure the preparations have begun for dinner, if you will excuse me."

He nodded, and I took my leave, stopping first in the great room to give my attention to the many supervisors who sought approval from a member of the royal family. The overseer of the granary let me know that we were almost to capacity with our storage, and would have more than we needed to make it through the inundation and planting seasons. The overseer of the bees was concerned that the bees had not produced enough, news that I did not like, given my disposition towards honey cakes. The overseer of the vineyard asked how did Naswt Biti enjoy the quality of the previous night's wine, hoping to gain the King's favor. I gave time to each, but the truth was, the household had found a natural groove, and most days, there was nothing that disturbed it. It required little supervision from me, which meant I was back to searching out ways to keep myself busy during classes and council meetings.

Afterwards I sighed deeply and headed to our chambers, hoping for the best and preparing for the worst. Setesh was inside the sitting room, reviewing the very forms he'd taught today. I couldn't believe that he was still working out, but this was the best way for him to release aggression.

"It's me," I said, walking in tentatively. "I am going to take a bath before dinner. I'd love it if you would join me."

My husband didn't change his posture or his expression. "I will bathe as soon as you're finished. Let me know if you need me or something."

I smiled politely, not wanting to look disappointed, and continued to the back, stripping down and walking naked out into the patio. Once alone, I sighed again, thinking back to our honeymoon and those days when we'd never bathe alone.

Apparently Setesh had those same thoughts; he came out just a few minutes later. "I apologize for being so singular minded. The council meeting this morning did not go very well."

He slipped into the water on the opposite side. I didn't move towards him. "What happened, if you don't mind me asking."

He rolled his eyes before answering. "Just the same old thing. The first site has been cultivated and Heru-Ur reports that we should be ready to fully set up there in a year. But *Ausar* wants to take another five years to do something that he should have already done."

I hesitated. "Is it that the students aren't ready? What's the reason for the delay?"

"He just talks too much, you know? And then he doesn't have faith in the people around him because he doesn't lead as effectively as he should."

"He is definitely a different leader than you would be, but isn't it fair to say he's gotten better since he started? I mean, things are coming along much smoother than I expected them to."

Again Setesh rolled his eyes. "They aren't moving nearly as quickly as they could. The council gives him too much latitude. It's almost as if no one is willing to contradict him."

I tilted my head towards him. "Well, that's what you're for, right? At least they have you to offer an opposing view."

"Doesn't work if no one listens." Setesh dunked his entire head under water, staying there for far longer than I thought he should. None of us had been home in months and were more and more susceptible to the heaviness of this world. He came back up and continued his thought as if not a second had passed. "I find myself constantly frustrated about being ignored."

I slid over to him, sitting by his side, taking his hand in mine. "Perhaps he is learning from you in subtle ways. I think seeing how you push the warriors has encouraged him to be better, as a teacher. And today's session was exceptional. You have to know how impressed I was."

He pulled our hands out of the water and kissed my knuckles. "I am lucky to have you on my team."

I felt myself redden a bit. "They are all on your team, even when you don't feel like they are. We all want the same thing, Setesh. It helps to remember that."

He nodded, but didn't let go of me. That is a good sign, I thought to myself, stretching out a bit, wanting to dunk myself. Instead I nestled back into the edge of the pool, enjoying this quiet time before we had to join the others. Hopefully, by dinner, all would be resolved.

"You don't get it, you just don't get it." Setesh pushed his plate away, the roast duck that he favored barely touched. "Your way is not always the right way, Ausar."

Ausar nodded and reached for another cabbage leaf stuffed with onions and dried grapes. "No, but it is the way it will be done. I've said my peace, and it's final."

"How can it be final? You have a responsibility to listen to the guidance of the council, and I am a council member -"

"I've listened to you," Ausar interjected, annoyance creeping into his tone.

Setesh scowled. "How can you be listening when you keep cutting me off? You haven't allowed me an opportunity to complete my thought."

Ausar groaned. "This is the same thought you had earlier today, and you just won't let it go."

"You didn't listen to me then either."

"Setesh, enough." Ausar didn't bang on the table, or make any loud, dramatic noise, but the authority in his voice shook me to my core. I glanced up at Setesh, nostrils flared and eyes widened with anger. Still, he bit his tongue, attempting to respect the position of the King.

Ausar cleared his throat before continuing. "I know you think we should move faster, but we have an eternity to do our work here. I don't want to just do it. I want to do it right. We cannot build a foundation that is set to crumble as soon as we depart from this realm. The people here have to be equipped to continue forward without us, using what we've given them, and if we rush every step of the way, how will that happen?" Ausar stopped to take a sip of water, clearly not opening the floor for discussion. "What we have already begun here is not as strong as it could be nor as developed as it should be. It does not make sense to expand our efforts and stretch our attention when we have yet to excel at what we are already working on."

After a few moments, it was clear Ausar had finished speaking for good. Setesh took several deep breaths, clearly hoping to respond reasonably and with a clear mind. "I differ from you, Ausar, in that I believe that we can do it both right and quickly. I do not see the end of our time here coming soon. There will be many layers added to this foundation that will strengthen it over time. I do not understand the wisdom in focusing on one part, when this part cannot last if the other parts are not in their place."

Ausar did not respond, so Setesh continued, voice slightly raised. "We teach that all things are interconnected, which means that we should be able to improve upon all things simultaneously. I strongly feel that your approach neglects areas that are essential to our development as a unit, and we cannot stand with one broken leg."

Ausar nodded again, and did not speak for a time. I turned my attention to the food, choosing to avoid the looks of my sister and her husband, while he appeared to deliberate. I knew as soon as Setesh had finished speaking that Ausar was not really receptive to his message, but I wasn't going to be the one to say that. Apparently, neither was Ausar.

"Setesh, I have heard you, and instead of being rash or deciding quickly, I would like to meditate on your words for a bit longer." Ausar sat up in his seat, stretching his height another inch or two. "Tomorrow I will respond to you at the council meeting, and let you know if and how it has changed the way we will move forward, as a unit."

Setesh nodded and stood, taking his leave without another word. Auset looked across the table at me, then stood and looked down at Ausar.

"I think I am going to take my leave as well. I will see you when you return to our chambers," she told her husband, practically running out of the room.

I stared down, not wanting to run out right behind her, but feeling incredibly awkward in the settling silence. Finally I stood; ready to take my leave, but Ausar stopped me. "You didn't say much before. What do you think?"

I sat back down, not wanting to talk down to the King. "I suspect that you are both right, in your own way."

Ausar frowned. "How so?"

"Well," I started, taking a deep breath, "I understand your concern, not to pile so much on the students at one time, but I see the benefit of what Setesh is suggesting, in that perhaps they can grasp the materials better if they are challenged." I paused for a moment. "If they are charged with teaching what they know, it may be a demonstration of what they are retaining and what needs to be reinforced."

Ausar nodded, looking away from me, out the large doors into the hall. "You are saying that I should move them down to the new site and have them begin teaching new students? That sounds exactly like our brother's perspective."

"No, no," I said, shaking my head, "I am saying, perhaps it is time to take them to the next step." I leaned in closer to Ausar, taking my opportunity to stand up for both myself and my husband. "It does not need to be exactly the way Setesh suggested it, but to continue with things exactly as they are, it offers no opportunity for them to demonstrate growth. If they are to improve, if you are to gauge their improvement, they will need to be challenged. If you choose not to challenge them now, they will be unprepared to bear the pressure later."

He looked right at me from across the table, holding my gaze intently, as if studying me. Finally he cleared his throat and I looked away, focusing once more on how much of the meal had lingered behind.

"I will take that into consideration," Ausar said finally, after letting my words sink in. "In the meantime, I'd like to ask you to do something for me."

I nodded, refusing to look at him. "Of course, Naswt. What is it?"

"Please, Nebt-Het. I have asked you not to call me that," he said, sounding annoyed by the formality. "You are still my sister, we don't need to be so formal."

I shook my head. "Calling you anything else would be inappropriate and you know it."

He sighed. "How about we compromise; when we are with others, I am Naswt, and when we are alone, I am Ausar." I looked at him, prepared to object, but he lifted his hand to silence me. "I've spoken, Nebt-Het, and so shall it be."

Not wanting to be called the King, but still behaving like one, I thought with a smile. "Fine, as you wish." He smiled, pleased with his minor victory. "Now what is this assignment you are asking of me?"

"I'd like you to participate in our council meetings," he told me, not actually asking at all. "I'd like to hear your thoughts. You do a good job of seeing the common ground, and I'd like you to try to keep our debates from escalating like they did today."

I couldn't respond to this on the spot. This was a huge task he was asking of me, to represent the middle without making either party feel like I was speaking for them. The one who would feel betrayed by this was my husband, which made me immediately suspect that I should not accept this responsibility on any terms.

On the other hand, I would be refusing a direct charge from the King, and despite his insistence that our relationship be informal, I was uneasy about the precedent that might set.

I sighed, taking the only road I could at the time. "I

appreciate your faith in my ability," I told him, hoping that I sounded honored. "May I have a day to consider it? I just want to make sure it is something that will be beneficial to us all."

Ausar grinned and stood, making his way to exit. "See, that is why this is the best job for you. So diplomatic," he told me, gesturing for me to stand. We walked towards the door, me just two steps behind him. "Tomorrow, then, you'll let me know what you've decided," he acquiesced once we'd reached the door.

"Tomorrow," I agreed.

He hesitated, looking for the right way to say what was on his mind. "Heru-Ur asked about you, in his last message to me. I just, I thought you should know."

I inhaled sharply. "Please tell him I am glad to know he is well and everyone here misses him very much."

Ausar nodded wordlessly, appearing surprised that my reply was so short, or perhaps he'd expected me to inquire further. I quickly took my leave to dissuade further conversation about our brother, instead directing my thoughts to what Ausar had suggested, more like required, me to do. Having a charge was all I had wanted, and I was determined to find a way to accept without starting trouble in my marriage.

I entered our apartment and found the sitting room empty. I closed the door tightly behind me and moved into our bedroom, where Setesh was lying across the bed, the courtyard doors open wide, allowing a heavy breeze to burst in and consume the space. I closed the bedroom door just as tightly as I had the outside one, and pressed my back against it, looking down at Setesh, trying to gauge the temperature.

"Do you really think he's going to consider what I said?" he asked, acknowledging my presence. "Or you think he just said that to silence me?"

I paused before answering. "He is definitely going to

consider your suggestion. Are you going to be okay if he still doesn't concede to you?"

Setesh looked over at me, grimacing. "What, you think I'll only be happy if things go my way?"

"I didn't mean that," I said, shaking my head, moving closer to where he lay. "I just know how important it is to you to be heard, and I really think he listened."

"But he might not do what I want him to do." He averted his gaze from me back to the ceiling.

I sat on the edge, turning my body so I could look down at him. "Right. He might do something different. You can't take that to mean he didn't listen."

He sighed and shifted, turning on to his side, facing me. "I guess I can accept that. As long as he considered my suggestion. If he really doesn't want to do it, I won't have a choice."

I decided to dive right in. "He made a suggestion that I think might help. He asked me to join the council."

Setesh sat up, confusion crossing over his face. "Really? And why do you think that might help?"

"Well, we're a team, aren't we?" I asked, taking his hand. "Ausar thinks it would help to have me there, to help smooth out the communication between you two." I cleared my throat.

Setesh looked at me with a softer scowl. "He admitted that he has a hard time listening to me?"

I wasn't expecting that question. "Well, he didn't quite say that," I told him, truthfully. "Really, he thought it would help to have me there, as another... perspective."

Setesh nodded, looking away. "That's actually a great idea, the first idea of his I've completely agreed with. So did you accept?" he asked, looking to me once more, his eyes sparkling with anticipation.

"No. I asked him for a day to consider." I squeezed his hand. "I wanted to talk about it with you first, see if it was okay."

"Did you think it wouldn't be okay?"

I hesitated. "Well, I just... want to be sure that you are in agreement, is all."

He nodded. "Tomorrow you'll accept." I smiled at him, sighing in relief. I shifted towards him, wanting to lean into his frame, but he stood before I could and began to pace the room slowly. "I've been thinking of something else, although, it might seem sudden."

I perked up a bit. "What is it?"

"I was just wondering," Setesh turned to me, crossing his arms in front of his chest, "why haven't we talked about having a child together?"

I was unable to stop the surprise from registering on my face, or in my voice. "I don't know, I guess we just, haven't," I responded, taking a deep breath.

He nodded. "Well, do you want to? I mean, what are your feelings on the subject?"

I frowned. "Sure, I mean, I suppose so, at some point." He didn't respond right away, so after a moment I asked, "are you thinking about right now, because, I mean, I'm not anxious or anything."

"No, it's not that," he said, his voice incredibly calm and even. "No, I'm not asking because you did anything, or said anything..." he trailed off without finishing the thought.

"Don't you think it's too soon?" I objected nervously, my voice barely higher than a whisper.

Setesh looked disappointed, and he hesitated before responding. "Is it too soon?"

I took a deep breath. "We have classes, council meetings, the expansion. There is so much that needs to be done, and being with child will make me a burden." I looked down at my hands, feeling immensely selfish. "All I've wanted is to contribute, to *not* be a burden, and now I have my chance."

He walked over to sit next to me on the bed. "You will not be a burden to me. Our child will not be a burden to me. I don't even know how you can think that."

I looked at him. "I don't want your attention taken away from your work at a time when you're needed the most." We both looked away, and the silence returned. "Maybe we should think about this for a while," I said finally, wanting to put an end to this.

My husband wasn't ready to drop it. He looked back at me, scowling. "Are you certain your objection is about my attention, and not your own? That you aren't putting our family to the side so you can have what you've always wanted?"

I pulled away from him. "That's not fair," I whispered harshly, hoping to disguise my guilt. "You sprung this on me out of nowhere. I am simply suggesting that we give this proper consideration."

"Can we at least agree to consult Djehuty on the matter?" Setesh asked, determined. "Maybe you're right, and this is too soon, or maybe it's exactly what we should do."

My eyes widened, yet I managed a smile. "Yes, let's speak with him at the new moon." I hesitated before continuing, "Honestly, Setesh, where did all this come from?"

He hesitated before responded. "I thought of it tonight, after I left dinner."

"And you don't think that sounds rash?"

"Am I wrong for wanting more for me, for us?" He stood, turning his back to me once more, making his way to the courtyard so he could close the doors. "You're *my* wife, Nebt-Het," he responded, throwing the words over his shoulder like it wasn't a big deal.

So that's it, I thought to myself, confronted by the thought that he merely wanted something in his world that he could control, that even I had become a pawn. I shook my head in disbelief, debating what I should say or do to address my suspicion. Instead, I dropped it, confident that he'd follow **TepRa**, and equally confident that this ridiculous notion would be vetoed, and I wouldn't have to tell him how absurd he was being.

"Whatever the oracle says, we'll do."

I was nervous, walking in to my very first council meeting. I made sure to pull out all of my best finery, including a green dress that Auset had given as a gift right before the wedding. It rustled gently with every breeze, and covered my shoulders and my ankles expertly. I'd even asked one of the attendees to fasten my hair upon my head in braids with ribbons of papyrus. I was probably overdressed, but I wanted to make a good first impression.

Everyone else was in their most basic attire; Setesh and Djehuty in white pants with sashes in red and purple, respectively, and Ausar in black pants with a white sash and the Usekh draped across his shoulders, falling low down his chest. Ausar also wore a Nemmes instead of the crown, the only person in the room wearing one. The three of them were huddled in the corner, backs facing the door, unaware that I'd entered. Auset, sitting her in place at the table, was in dark blue linen, her locks falling down her back, unadorned save for one lotus tucked behind her left ear. Seshat was wearing a similar dress, made entirely of leopard skin. As Djehuty would naturally sit at the right hand of the King, Seshat had chosen to take the seat that would be at the right hand of her husband.

I had not expected to see our grandparents, Shu and Tefnut, with Shu positioned at the opposite head of the table, and Tefnut on his left. I knelt on the side of Auset, hoping to whisper without being heard. "Are they always here?"

She knew who I'd meant. "They started attending a year ago, after Djehuty proposed strengthening the council. They only come occasionally, whenever the council can't seem to agree." Auset glanced across the room at Setesh. Apparently they were here often. "They were the logical choice, really. You know how hard it is for our parents to be in physical form, and Ra..."

I nodded and stood, restoring the smile to my face, hoping it looked natural. I had not seen either of them since the wedding, not in their physical forms, at least. I stepped back from the table, not wanting to sit quite yet.

Ausar turned, the secret huddle finally coming to a close. He saw me and smiled. "Are we all ready to begin then, now that Nebt-Het is here?"

Everyone but Shu nodded their consent. "We are only waiting for you, Naswt Biti. We will begin when you are ready," he said. I looked across the room at my grandfather, sensing immediately why my husband found these meetings annoying.

Ausar took his seat, with Djehuty and Setesh sitting right after. I spotted the last open chair, directly across from my grandmother, on the other side of the table. I quickly walked over and slid into it, not wanting to hold up the proceedings any longer.

Ausar cleared his throat. "All of you have been informed that I've asked Nebt-Het to join the council in an advisory capacity, and she's accepted the responsibility. No objections were found and so she's starting today." He looked down the table at me, causing my cheeks to redden. "Senet, we are glad to have you as a contributor, to have your voice added for consideration. For now you will not have a vote, but your voice will be as important as all others to our deliberations."

I nodded in understanding, and Ausar looked to Setesh. "Last night, I had an opportunity to rethink the proposal brought to the council by our general. I was reluctant at first to integrate any of these ideas into our plan for expansion, but he convinced me to give it another thought, and I'm glad I did."

I breathed a sigh of relief, thankful that he didn't give me any credit for convincing him to think twice. I looked over at Setesh, who was sitting up straight, frowning, eyes dancing with pride.

"I want to propose what I think is the middle ground between our two ideas. I will travel to the first site with a select number of initiate candidates, two or three agriculturists, and a few warrior students as well. Heru-Ur and I will organize groups of warriors, initiates, and farmers, and let our current students demonstrate what they know to the new students."

Ausar looked back to Setesh. "Heru-Ur knows enough to make sure your current students are teaching correctly - at least long enough that we can get things stabilized there." Setesh nodded cautiously and Ausar continued, looking at each of us as he explained his vision. "The agriculturists can share what they know without supervision; we just need to make sure we can get equipment built for the new village. As far as the other two groups, Heru-Ur and I can gauge how well the current students are grasping the material and how ready they are for the next level, simultaneously preparing new groups for the expansion. When they are ready, Setesh can travel down to further the upper level training, and they can teach the lower level. In the beginning, I would prefer him to stay here and continue with his current group as well as confer with the council."

Shu cleared his throat. "And who is going to make sure the initiate candidates who are here will still be nurtured?"

"Djehuty can do that," Auset offered, looking across at our Seba. "I mean, he has the wisdom and the experience to take on the task in the absence of Naswt."

"It is my charge to take a behind-the-scenes role in your kingdom," Djehuty protested gently. "My responsibility is to advise and nurture the leadership. It would not be prudent for me to move into the foreground."

Seshat frowned and looked at Djehuty. "Why can't Auset teach if she has your supervision?"

All eyes fell on my sister, and she looked away. "I don't think it should be me," Auset mumbled, avoiding us.

The room grew silent. I cleared my throat, and everyone except Auset turned to me, causing me to gasp.

"Well it's just, I think Auset is the right person," I said, looking at her, even though she hadn't lifted her gaze from her lap. "She has the patience, and the knowledge. And Djehuty has the wisdom. She can do this."

"She doesn't seem to think she can," Tefnut whispered, glancing back at Auset before returning her stare to me.

I sighed. "She knows she can, she's just being cautious."

Ausar nodded. "Okay. You and Djehuty will talk it through with Auset and make it happen. Are there any other things that the plan has overlooked?"

Setesh cleared his throat. "What is the plan once I leave here and join you? My students will suffer if I abandon them."

"I am hoping by that time they will be ready to take on lower level students of their own, and protect our home and our wives," Ausar offered. "You can travel back and forth as needed, if you are unsure about leaving them alone."

"Do you think this means you both will be gone for a long time?" Auset asked timidly, looking up at her husband.

Ausar smiled. "I have no idea how long we'll be gone, but I want to strengthen the foundation and begin to build upon it. This seems to me like the best way to do both simultaneously."

Shu sighed heavily. "I'm not sure I agree with this plan. If you're not confident about your students, why entrust them to teach others?"

"They are my first students," Ausar conceded, looking at Setesh. "Perhaps I don't know how to tell if they are ready. Perhaps I need to see them in action, give them an opportunity to prove themselves."

"If we are wrong, and they are not ready, we can pull back, and this way we haven't risked too much," Setesh added, clearly on board. I smiled.

Tefnut coughed, letting everyone know she wanted to interject. "You are saying you haven't risked too much, but don't you think it's a bad idea to introduce new students to bad teachers? And what if you have to pull out, don't you think that would be damaging to the new site?"

No one responded right away, so I chose to speak. "We should also consider that Ausar and Heru-Ur will be there to make corrections and adjustments. Essentially, they will be teaching their students how to teach. That is bound to include some error; the only question is whether we are willing to experience this process now or later."

Ausar added on. "You're right Tefnut, it is much too soon to leave them unsupervised or let them figure it out on their own. Ideally, this is a process that will take years for them to master, yet in order to establish centers across the land, we need to have people who are ready to begin the work, even if their education is ongoing."

Tefnut inhaled. "You do realize that at some point you may be splitting your time between many different regions and sites. Is that what you want, to travel so often, to live always on the move?"

Ausar nodded. "It is my duty, as Naswt Biti. I will have to travel often, for morale, for celebration, for various reasons that have yet to be determined." He waved his hand around, brushing it off. "I will do what is needed."

Shu and Tefnut looked at each other, engaged in a conversation meant only for each other. I looked to my right and found Seshat consulting with her husband as well. I turned my eyes to my husband, his expression relaxed, knowing that his suggestion had been heeded. I smiled at him; he winked back, his lips twitching in the direction of a grin.

"We have no other objections," Shu finally announced, looking down the table to Ausar.

"Neither do we," Djehuty added, taking Seshat's hand.

Ausar exhaled loudly, relieved. "Do we need to take a vote or are we all in agreement?"

"As long as Nebt-Het is certain that Auset can take your place as Seba, we are in agreement."

I had forgotten about that one point, and everything we'd negotiated hinged upon it. I knew Auset was afraid about tapping into what she knew, since it had been ill-gotten, and I also knew if she didn't put it to use, setting right the balance she disturbed, she would never truly release her guilt.

"I am certain. She is equipped for the task."

"Then we have a plan. Let us move on to other business," Ausar said, closing the topic successfully. I admired the table fully for the first time, proud at how well my first council meeting was going, grateful to finally have a seat. I settled in and readied myself for the next subject.

Ausar sailed for the first site three weeks later, with Setesh following him after a season. Soon after, the warrior classes began to grow at an unexpected rate, and my husband spent more time away than we'd anticipated, satisfied with the vigorous training and constant physical stress that such work put him under.

After a few years, Setesh was splitting his time between four developing sites, while Ausar was based full time here, having relocated initiates here from across Kemet, which made ruling and teaching an easier task. Despite recruiting dozens of promising candidates over the years, and letting go of others who were not ready for the charge, the priesthood training had made no significant accomplishments; its primary success was that it had become the singular topic in council meetings.

"Maybe we should listen to Setesh on this," Ausar mumbled, shoulders slumped. "His techniques have been greatly successful in teaching combat and strategy."

Djehuty sighed. "Combat is an area where a firm hand is needed. One should not ask the hammer to do the feather's work."

Ausar was shaking his head in frustration. Auset reached over and took his hand. "You have always known this would be a process requiring patience. You are demanding too much of yourself."

"I am demanding myself to give my people what they deserve," Ausar answered pointedly, looking at his wife without pulling his hand away. "How are they to feel about their slow and inefficient King?"

Seshat leaned forward. "It is only you who are using the words 'slow' and 'inefficient'. All of our observation of the countryside shows that the people are satisfied with the progress made thus far. None of us thought we would be this far along after just a few years."

Ausar shook his head again. I glanced across the table at my husband who, while silent, was smirking with pleasure. I knew Setesh wasn't so much enjoying his brother's inner conflict as he was selfishly relishing his own moment of achievement. My husband was competitive to a fault, and right now, he felt like he was winning.

"Ausar is just trying to be flexible and make adjustments when something isn't working," Setesh offered, leaning back in his chair casually, hoping to sound nonchalant. "Isn't that what Ra has charged him to do, be open to transformation?"

Djehuty raised his eyebrows. "You are correct in principle, Setesh. In practice, Naswt Biti must know when to see things through. We cannot apply such advice uniformly; instead we must see each situation for the unique challenges it presents."

Setesh huffed and glanced down towards Seba. "But perhaps this is one situation where the principle should be the practice."

Ausar nodded emphatically, ready to follow the guidance of his more successful sibling. "Perhaps it should be."

"Can we identify specific areas that need improvement, instead of taking a broad approach and overhauling the entire process?" Shu asked, his voice causing a slight echo.

His wife nodded. "Yes, Naswt Biti," Tefnut agreed, "we should not change everything without knowing what needs to be changed."

"But what if it IS everything that needs to be changed?" Setesh argued, sitting up straighter. "If my way is working, and his way is not, perhaps he should adopt my approach wholly."

"And if that doesn't work?" Djehuty asked, asking in a genuine and even tone. "How does that affect the people, while we stumble around, blindly?"

The room fell momentarily quiet. "I think we should hear from everyone here before you decide, Naswt Biti," Auset spoke in a whispery tone. All of the eyes in the room seemed to turn to me right then, and I wished I could be in any other place.

"You have not spoken on this, Nebt-Het," Seshat told me when it was clear I would need prompting. "What do you think?"

I gulped while trying to seem unnerved. "I'm not sure yet," I started, "I mean, I recognize the validity of both positions..." I looked across to my husband, whose eyes were across the room, on Ausar. Setesh sat up straight as though he already knew this would go his way. I hesitated as long as I could.

"The truth is, I agree that it is unfair to expect the same level of progress, the same speed of progress, or the same results." I looked away from Setesh, knowing I would avoid his eyes for the rest of the meeting. "The goal of training warriors is having many men, thousands of men, prepared to defend and protect an increasing amount of land, an expanding number of villages and people. Are we expecting to need as many priests as we'll need warriors?"

Ausar tilted his head thoughtfully. "No, I suppose not."

"If the goals are different, then it makes sense for the approach to also be different." I shifted in my seat, emboldened. "The way to improve the initiation process for the priesthood is to examine the goals and ensure that our approach is addressing them. If not, we make adjustments or additions as needed. The warrior training has been successful because Setesh meets the demands of his charge, and we must do the same for the priesthood."

My grandparents were nodding emphatically, and Djehuty looked relieved. Seshat and Auset kept their eyes on Ausar, waiting to hear what he would say. For his part, he stayed silent for longer than I thought he would, a frown of consideration across his countenance. After a while, I found my attention focused on the table before me, pointedly ignoring the icy glare that my husband was directing at my forehead.

Finally Ausar responded, clearing his throat first. "Setesh has been successful, and I think it is important that we recognize that. But I am willing to discuss specific improvements rather than doing a full reconstruction." He looked at me directly and smiled. "I was feeling a bit impulsive before, out of frustration. I am willing to listen to reason."

Auset took his hand, beaming. "I'm glad to hear you say that. I really think this is the right course of action."

I looked around the room and welcomed the nods of all the other council members, except Setesh, whose dark stare was directed towards me still. I met his eye and tried to smile, but it changed nothing and I looked away, preparing myself for the discussion that would come later.

The meeting continued for several long hours as we hashed out as many details as we could, until we'd all tired of the discussion and agreed to handle the remaining subjects on the following day. The moment we adjourned, Setesh fled from the great hall, purposely striding long and fast to avoid my company. I held myself back from running, pretending not to chase him, pretending to walk casually, knowing that if I trailed him long enough, he would eventually turn and face me.

He surprised me by exiting the per eah and walking over to the river bank, taking a stance with his back to the setting sun. I stopped a few feet short of where he stood, realizing I wasn't sure of what I had chased him to say.

"I can't believe you sided with all of them against me, when you knew how important this was for me," Setesh began, the anger coming out as a gentle undertone.

I hesitated, taking another step closer to him. "You aren't being fair here."

He spun and faced me, eyes lit with fire. "*I'm not being fair*? Are you serious?"

"Did you think I would never have an opinion of my own; that I would only ever agree with you?" I asked him, digging my heels into the ground. "I have to think about what is in the best interests of the kingdom."

Setesh moved in closer, leaving no space between us. "We are supposed to be a team at all times. You promised me that.

You are supposed to be MY advocate."

I looked away and shook my head. "I am being your advocate when I remind you that it is our duty to stay aligned with the best interests of all." I stepped back and met his stare. "Ausar WAS listening to you, he didn't need a reminder to respect your opinion. You didn't need an advocate, the people did."

"So that's what you want me to believe? That you did this to me because it was the right thing?" He rolled his eyes and looked away, his arms tightly wound across his chest.

My eyes widened, and I practically shouted, shocked. "Yes! That's exactly why!" I moved closer to him once more, trying to force him to look at me. "All of us gain by Ausar being successful. He has seen what you can do, and he takes you very seriously, but he has to learn to take himself seriously too."

Setesh shook his head, still avoiding my eyes. "You really don't understand at all, do you?"

I shook my head. "Understand what, Setesh?" When he didn't answer, I grabbed his forearms, trying to force him to see me. "This doesn't change his respect for you; it doesn't in any way diminish your accomplishments. We have to go the way that ensures the best possible foundation for our future. This doesn't change your place in that at all."

He scoffed and pulled away from me. "This changes everything." Setesh was finally meeting my gaze, and there was no warmth there. "I *never* should have let you join the council."

I shivered without responding, and he stormed off. Wrapping my arms around myself, I sighed and settled onto the ground, crossing my legs beneath me and turning my face to the countenance of our mother. "You are the one who can touch the heart of her son," I mumbled, "please help him to understand."

A throat cleared behind me, and I turned to see Ausar waiting for me. "My apologies," I said, quickly standing, "I didn't see you there."

"It's okay," he said, motioning for me to stay seated. "I didn't mean to sneak up on you. I really came here to speak to Setesh and I found you two…"

I reddened. "Did you overhear?"

Ausar looked away. "A bit. I know I should not have eavesdropped, but I really wanted to make sure you were both okay."

"Well, I am, if a bit shaken," I said, sitting back down, prompting Ausar to sit across from me. "I feel as if I have done something wrong."

"Why would you think that?" he asked, frowning.

I laughed without smiling. "You saw his reaction. He believes so strongly that you must utilize what he has to offer and put him to greater use within the kingdom. I don't know, maybe we are being shortsighted not to have his vision," I shrugged, practically mumbling each word.

"Setesh is barely home as it is," Ausar said, immediately rejecting my suggestion. "I can't believe I was considering putting more on his plate. I am just so frustrated by my lack of progress that I was being impractical. I made the suggestion and he became attached to it; if I had been more thoughtful, this might not have happened anyway."

I shrugged again. "Frustration is only natural," I offered, "your people deserve more, and it is your burden to give it to them."

Ausar looked away. "Yes, it is I who must give it to them." I turned my attention to the ground before me, letting the space grow quiet. Finally, he spoke again. "I don't want you to take this as a sign that you should pull back from the council or from offering your opinions."

"I am afraid that I will never be able to say anything without considering how it will affect our marriage," I admitted, keeping my face turned away.

"Give our brother some credit," Ausar replied, "he may be hurt now, but in the long run, he will understand." He reached out and touched my knee, causing me to look back to him. "Setesh is not so shortsighted that he won't respect your vision."

I smiled, genuinely. "I hope not."

He stood and began to wipe the dust from his legs. "Having so many voices contributing at once seems like it would be a hindrance, but really, it helps me to remember that there are many sides to one issue, and I must consider them all." Ausar glanced back at the horizon before looking down at me once more. "If you cannot speak true, you will be of no service to the council."

His voice was gentle, but I knew it to be a charge. I stood and took a step back. "You are right. I have to believe that Setesh will understand."

Ausar smiled. "And he will."

KHEPER - TRANSFORMATION

My husband sighed loudly as he entered the great hall for dinner. I glanced up at him tentatively, quickly diverting my look back down to the table. His dissatisfaction was palpable, creating heaviness throughout the entire space. Ausar, already sitting at the head of the table, smiled at me and Auset as if nothing was wrong, apparently choosing to ignore Setesh.

I longed for the days when my biggest concern was whether or not the utensils had been properly cleaned before dinner. There had been too many arguments and fights thinly veiled as debates, mostly between Ausar and Setesh, although others were involved frequently enough. Even the number of conflicts between my husband and I had escalated to an unhealthy and uncomfortable level. I suppose centuries will do that to a marriage.

No, I shouldn't fool myself. Ausar and Auset did not fight nearly as often, and when they did, it included nothing like the hostility present in my arguments with Setesh. Auset had been dissatisfied during the years when her husband was traveling, whereas I found myself anticipating the opportunities to be away from my husband for long stretches of time.

At least progress had been made in substantial ways. The temples had been built and the priesthood established for several generations, performing annual ceremonies and teaching others how to pray and worship. New agricultural equipment increased productivity and irrigation mechanisms brought a needed surge of water to previously uncultivated land. These two developments led to greater stability, allowing the villages to grow significantly in population. The borders were protected by fearless warriors and the size of the kingdom had grown to its largest level. The people had experienced many years of prosperity because of the wise decisions of Naswt Biti. Ausar had become a great leader, loved by all but one.

I cleared my throat, looking over at my husband, who had moved his chair far down the table to sit apart from us. I wanted to ask if he was okay, but I knew he wasn't, and if I wasn't careful, the day's unpleasantries would recreate themselves at our dinner table. I decided against speaking at all and focused back on the stewed figs.

Auset chose differently. "Setesh," she started, sounding exasperated, "what's wrong, brother? You can't possibly still be upset about this afternoon."

My husband raised his eyebrow and glared at her. "I can and I am, and I would appreciate if you'd refrain from trying to cheer me up."

She tilted her head and smiled at him, choosing not to take his response seriously. "Come now, isn't there something that could make you feel better?"

"Leave him be, sister," I urged her quietly, looking across the table at her with wide-eyes. "Give him space. He's fine."

Setesh loudly cleared his throat, glancing at me and throwing Auset another dirty look before focusing his attention downwards. I looked back over to my sister, who was staring at him with a look of disbelief. I smiled at her awkwardly, making apologies for him in my head.

"Well fine," Auset finally acquiesced, waving away the hand of an errant attendee. "I just wanted to lighten the mood is all." No one responded, and we proceeded to eat during what felt like the longest silence ever.

Finally Ausar could take it no more. "Are you *really* going to sulk about all day?"

Setesh sighed, loudly, pushing his food away from him. "Do I need to ask for permission for my feelings, or am I still allowed the emotional responses of *my* choice?"

"You can do what you'd like," Ausar said, a hint of authority sneaking into his otherwise gentle tone, "but your behavior is unbecoming for a man of your stature."

"And what is that supposed to mean?" Setesh asked with a scoff.

Ausar shook his head and smirked. "It means, your emotional responses should reflect your position as head general and advisor to the King, instead of this rampant immaturity that we've had the pleasure of witnessing far too often."

Setesh shook his head emphatically. "You have no idea what it is to be a warrior, Ausar. You couldn't accomplish half of what I've contributed to building this nation and keeping things in order. Your people are protected because of me, and only me. I am certain that affords me the right to sulk every so often if I wish to do so."

"Now hold on a moment," Auset interjected, voice raised and nostrils flared. I sighed, wishing she would stay out of it and knowing she would not. "How dare you forget about the work that we've all put in here. The sacrifices all of us have been asked to make. You think you are the only one who has done anything of mention? There wouldn't be a kingdom to protect if it weren't for our King. You would be wise never to forget that."

Setesh rolled his eyes emphatically. "How exactly am I supposed to forget it when I have you here to remind me at every turn?"

Auset challenged him with her stare. "I would hope that you would not need my words to set your ego straight, brother."

"My *ego*?" Setesh said, his hands tightening into fists against the surface of the table. "It might be prudent to consider me arrogant if I was exaggerating, but we all know, I am not."

"That's *enough*, Setesh," Ausar said authoritatively.

"No, it's NOT enough," Setesh shouted, rattling the plates and utensils on the table in front of us. "I have spent way too long allowing you two to minimize my position. You've ignored me, disrespected me, cast me to the side like an inferior being."

Ausar looked around in disbelief. "You haven't *allowed* us to do anything, Setesh. You have fought with us every step of the way."

Setesh threw his head back and laughed. "These little spats can hardly be considered fights between MEN. We will have no real fight because you can't take me and you know it."

"Is that a challenge?"

"Ausar, please," Auset jumped in before Setesh could answer. "There is no need for you to entertain his arrogance."

Setesh shook his head. "Listen to your wife, Ausar. There is no shame in hiding behind her skirt."

Ausar was out of his chair before my husband finished his sentence. "That is the LAST time you address my wife like that," he growled, his countenance dark.

"So you accept my challenge then? Or is it you who is going to leave sulking and immature?"

Ausar breathed deeply, his arms trembling by his side, jaw clenched tight. It took everything he had, but he didn't attack Setesh, as I imagine he thought he would.

"You're wrong, brother," Ausar whispered, his voice soft and his tone filled with power. "I will leave this room just as I entered it, as Naswt Biti. There is no need to accept your challenge, when I already possess the prize."

He left, and Auset stood as if to follow him, but Setesh wouldn't allow her to leave quite yet.

"Your husband has the mistaken belief that he is somehow

proving himself my better by not accepting my challenge." He looked over to the window, still shaking his head. "You and I both know that he's wrong."

Auset took a deep breath. "Naswt Biti does not need to lower himself to your level, Setesh. He is the leader, OUR leader -"

"He is a *coward*," he snarled at her. "He is a weak man with a frightened girl for a wife."

I looked up at her, and she met my eyes, trying to muster up a response, not wanting him to have gotten the best of her. Unsuccessful, she fled the room without another word.

The room was finally still, and silent. I stared down at the plate before me, completely unable to ingest any of its contents. Finally I looked up at Setesh, his ugly words lingering in the dead air.

"You went too far."

He slammed his palms to the table and stood, pushing his seat back with such a force that it fell to the floor, cracking one of the legs. "Sure, right, defend *them*," he spat at me, beginning to pace the room with frustration. "You are always taking their side."

"That's not true! I am not on their side," I insisted, hearing the passion in my words. "This is not about taking sides. You went too far."

"He's my *brother*," Setesh hissed at me, still pacing, seething with anger. "You have to know how degrading it is that he thinks he can just talk down to me just because he's Naswt Biti."

I sighed. "You are not equals anymore."

"You don't get it," he said, dismissing me with a wave of his fist. "He will never be more than me; he will never be better than me." Setesh stopped pacing and stood in front of me, wide-eyed and nostrils flared. "He needs me to protect this nation. He needs me so he can be King. HE needs ME. We are equals, and he IS going to accept that. I will make him accept that."

I shook my head. "When will you learn that you will never get him to listen this way?"

Setesh scoffed. "What do you know anyway," he threw out there, not waiting for me to answer his question. "After five hundred years, you still don't even have a vote on the council. Your voice counts for nothing. You're just a wife."

"My voice counts in this marriage," I said, refusing to back down to him. "Are you really going to do to me what you've accused them of doing to you? Ignore me, talk down to me?"

"You want to talk to me about wife and husband things, fine, but keep your opinions on this matter to yourself." He turned and stormed out as loudly as he could, heading towards our apartment, which meant I would have to find somewhere else to decompress.

I took a minute to compose myself before standing. Picking up the chair that he'd broken, I signaled the attendee who had been hiding behind the main door, waiting in the hall for our fight to conclude. "Could you take this to the royal woodcarver, and have the leg repaired before tomorrow's morning meeting?" The attendee nodded and curtseyed, taking the chair and leaving without a word. I sighed and looked around before deciding to go find Auset. She had to be upset after the things Setesh said.

I walked down the hall towards the apartment that Auset shared with Ausar, passing attendees who were cowering in the corners, hoping I wouldn't take note of their presence. I smiled at all of them, which appeared to relax them. With each new group of attendees, we went to great lengths to earn their confidence, considering the very few places where we have absolute solitude and the reality that they must hear and know everything. I could only pray that our family disputes wouldn't feed the gossipy gatherings at the river.

I knocked on the outer door of the apartment, and when I didn't hear an answer, I entered the sitting room cautiously. "Auset, are you here?" I called out loudly, hoping that if she were in the bedroom or garden, she could signal her presence to me. After a few moments, I hadn't heard a response, but instead of turning away, I moved further into the apartment, not wanting to leave if there was a chance she was upset, and not wanting to go back to my apartment, where Setesh was likely fuming.

I finally knocked on the doors that separated the bedroom from the garden, and heard a muffled sound from the other side, so I pushed one of the doors open. Ausar looked as though he had expected it to be me at the door, but he was alone, no indication that Auset had ever been there.

"My apologies, I thought I'd find Auset here."

Ausar beckoned for me to step into the garden, welcoming my company. "No, I think she's taken an understandable trip home. She was plenty upset."

"I thought she might be." I hesitated before asking, "And you? Are you okay?"

He smiled. "I have become accustomed to his outbursts. I'm not sure if that's a good thing."

"I know what you mean." We smiled with mutual understanding. "I fear that our new attendees will be terrified of him for weeks after this outburst. They've only been with us for three months."

Ausar nodded, frowning. "At least half of that time we've spent arguing with Setesh, you more than any of us. How is that going, if I may ask? Are you two still sleeping separately?"

I hesitated. "I moved back in earlier this week, but after tonight... I may need to resume my tenure in one of the empty suites for a few nights."

"Are you sure you don't want to move in there

permanently?" he asked, each word emerging with care.

I smiled and sat on the ground at the edge of the pool, diverting my attention to the water. "No, I don't want him to feel like I've given up on him. It would only make things worse."

Ausar coughed. "At this point I fear that you are the only one who hasn't."

I shook my head. "I am his wife. He is my responsibility."

Ausar didn't respond right away, and we fell silent for a few minutes. Eventually I looked up at him; he was gazing upward, studying the night.

"The harvest festivals approach," I said, wanting to fill the space. "Are you and Auset planning to travel down river? It's been awhile since she's seen the lower lands."

He smiled without looking away from the face of our mother. "One thing I know is I cannot go without her. Her reaction to my extended visit to Khemenu is a sentiment we shall not revisit."

I watched him for a moment, then looked away. Selfishly I wished I still felt that way about my own husband, while simultaneously wanting to ask Ausar to take Setesh with them, an idea I knew he would compassionately reject.

"I have some things I'd like you to do in our absence," Ausar began, causing me to look back to him. This time, he had turned to face me, and met my gaze. "I have been thinking of having you lead the ceremony here, so that it does not go unattended."

I cleared my throat. "Don't you think Setesh should lead the ceremony? He is higher ranked, of course."

Ausar shook his head. "No, I am thinking of sending him down river as well, have him attend one of the festivals in a different center. Perhaps one of our major warrior stations, to allow him to boost morale and remind the people of our presence, all at once." He saw my expression and smiled. "It wouldn't be simply to give you two space, although I suppose that is one benefit."

"I appreciate that," I said, smiling in kind. "Only if it makes sense to separate us though; for the festivals, for the people. If not, you shouldn't do it. I would never ask you to."

"You didn't ask."

"Right," I nodded, looking away. "Just, only if it's prudent for all."

Ausar came around to my side of the pool and sat beside me, facing me. "I admire that about you, I always have."

"What?"

He inhaled sharply. "You never put your needs first. I know you need space, but you would never take it, you would never say so, because you want to do what's right for everyone else, even when no one else is doing right by you."

I rolled my eyes. "That hardly sounds like a quality to be admired."

"It is what's expected of us at all times, and yet, you find it easier to do than the rest of us." Ausar leaned back, resting on his forearms, his head dangling over the edge of the pool. "It does not come so naturally to me. "

I looked upward, facing my mother to avoid my brother. "Perhaps that's why you are Naswt Biti, to cultivate that quality in you, and I am not, because I have something else I need to become." I looked back to him, frowning. "We each have our place."

He nodded. I looked back up to the sky, wondering if Auset would return home soon, but not wanting to stay and wait. I sighed and stood.

"I am going to take my leave, so I can get myself situated down the hall. We have another meeting tomorrow, I believe?"

"Yes, we do," my brother mumbled. I nodded, and he waved his hand to signal that he consented to let me go. I didn't expect that he would have tried to stop me from leaving, as we were not subject and King, but sister and brother. Still, it was easier to maintain formalities in public if we did them habitually in private. I walked quickly through the bedroom, through the sitting room, stopping once I'd arrived in the empty hall. I looked towards our chambers, where Setesh was undoubtedly waiting for me, and headed in the opposite direction.

I woke to find Setesh sitting on the edge of the bed. "Why did you stay down here last night?"

I hated being caught unprepared like that. He was always ready for conflict, especially when I was avoiding it. "I thought you might need space," I mumbled, sitting up. "You were plenty upset last night."

"Still, you should have stayed in our apartment," he insisted, not looking at me. "You are sending the wrong message about our union."

I blinked. "*I'm* the one sending a message?"

Setesh scoffed. "I'm not the one running from you."

I sighed and shook my head. The sun was barely up. "I am not running from you either."

"Then why are you down here?"

"I told you, to give you space."

"Who said I needed space?" he asked, finally looking at me. "You should have asked me if that's what I needed."

I took a deep breath. "Actually, you told us all that you needed space when you sat at the other end of the table last night." I slipped my legs over the edge and stood, stretching my limbs. "I am not interested in pretending, Setesh."

He stood and faced me, angry and worn under the eyes, as if he hadn't slept. "You're assuming that I needed space from *you*. If you need space, you should say that, but do not make assumptions about my needs."

"Fine. I apologize for making that assumption."

He rolled his eyes. "But not that you stayed down here last night?"

I looked at him, searching myself for the capacity to apologize for not returning to our apartment. I didn't find it. "Do you want to talk, or do you just want to be angry with me?"

Setesh paced for a few moments without answering, keeping his eyes cast down, his expression unreadable. "I was dissatisfied with the way things were resolved last night."

I nodded and walked across the room to sit in one of the chairs against the opposite wall. Setesh continued pacing. "So was I."

He hesitated again, this time stopping his heavy march. "I am thinking of proposing that I stay in Inbu-Hedj for a time. At least through the harvest festivals, perhaps the entire season. I could return after the inundation. I am thinking of bringing it to the council today."

My eyebrows rose. "Are you *that* angry about me sleeping down here?" I surprised myself by sounding disappointed; just last night I was praying for distance, and now here it was. I cleared my throat. "I mean, why do you think such a long trip is necessary?"

Setesh sighed and sat in the chair opposite mine. His shoulders slumped as if releasing a heavy weight. It was then I realized how defeated he appeared.

"I am tired of fighting. I am tired and I am not winning." He stretched his legs out without straightening his back, and the back of his head touched the wall as he gazed at the ceiling. "I don't think there is any way to restore harmony in my relationship with Ausar, and I think I am dangerously close to ruining my relationship with you, and I don't want that."

I tried to smile. "I don't want that, either, but that shouldn't mean that you move away." We both fell silent for a moment. "You know this is not a competition, right?"

He closed his eyes. "What is that supposed to mean?"

"You said, you are tired of not winning. This isn't a competition."

Setesh barely twitched, but his darkened frown let me know he disagreed. "At least if you need distance from Ausar, I should go with you - we should go together," I insisted.

He sat up a bit, shaking his head emphatically. "No, you need to be here to cast my vote while absent. I just feel like it's something I must do. I've spent a lot of time thinking of it."

"All night?"

He nodded his assent and we fell back into silence. I couldn't help but regret seeing the manifestation of my wish before me. Considering how selfish I was to want it in the first place, it wasn't wise that we decide something like this on our own. There was one step we could take before bringing it before the council.

Without speaking I took his hand and sped us off towards home. It had been a long time since we had consulted Djehuty as husband and wife. Perhaps this visit would go better than the first.

Hundreds of years ago we'd made this trip on the new moon as we'd agreed. We arrived home to silence and solitude, and the space we landed in was shrouded in complete darkness. I remember looking to my right, looking to where Setesh was standing.

"We'll need to clear our expectations first," I reminded him then. I was still holding his hand tightly, our fingers entwined. "We'll only receive if we are ready to do whatever we're told, ab en NTR."

I heard his response, "I'm ready."

As he said that, a bright light appeared behind us, as if a

window had opened in the hollow. We turned to face it and found Seshat had been waiting for us. We could not see Djehuty as the light continued to flood the space. I held tighter to my husband's hand, closing my eyes to protect them, while the light permeated my consciousness, removing the shade and pushing the darkness out, completely.

"I am here to keep your words true," I heard Seshat say, her voice echoing through my being. "Tell us who you are. Ask us what you seek."

I found myself wanting to speak, but before I could get a word out, Setesh let go of my hand and confidently began his petition. "I am Setesh, son of Geb, protector of Ra, commander of the armies of Kemet. I am he who finds solace in the desert land; I am he who brings the storm. I stand at the right arm of Naswt Biti. I am his punisher." He hesitated before continuing, and the words that followed came nervously, less assured. "I am here to seek permission to start a family, bring forth children with my wife." I heard him swallow loudly, but he didn't continue, so I waited to see what would happen.

"Is that truly what you seek?" Seshat asked. Her question at this point was simply a formality; Seshat already knew if there was something that Setesh wasn't saying.

"Yes, it is," Setesh insisted, not backing down, yet his voice trembled. "That is what we have come here to learn."

A moment passed in silence before Djehuty spoke. "Setesh, you are one of great strength and power. There is strength in standing down. There is strength in following. There is strength in submission."

His response had not addressed our query, and yet it resonated with my husband, as it caused him to find his voice. "Seba," Setesh called out, "it is my nature to fight. It is my duty. I am a warrior."

"You can be more than one who makes war," Djehuty

responded, "if you are able to be one who makes peace."

Setesh took a deep breath. "Perhaps with fatherhood I can learn to be more than I am. I am here to learn if I am to be both warrior and father."

Silence again. "No, Setesh, you are not to be both."

"What are you saying?" Setesh asked, sounding anxious, angry even. "Are you saying I have to choose one or the other?"

Djehuty hesitated once more. "I am saying you have already chosen."

Our teacher was not one to beat around the bush; his delicate approach indicating that the answer he had to give was difficult. I became tense in the silence. This was the risk we took by coming here, the possibility that we would hear what we needed, and not what we wanted. I knew that Setesh had been completely sure that he would be told what he wanted to hear, and this wasn't it.

Setesh spoke once more, his voice steady and firm. "That is your answer, then; we cannot start a family?"

"You two will not ever have children together."

I had not expected Djehuty to respond so directly, but I was thankful that he did and left no room for interpretation. It was then that I heard Seshat speak out. "Djehuty is ready to speak to you, Nebt-Het, if you are ready to speak with him."

I felt my stomach tighten. I was unprepared to announce myself. Perhaps I didn't have to, since he'd requested to speak to me, and not the other way around? I took a step forward and took a deep breath, ready to figure it out no matter how wrong I got it.

Djehuty began, not waiting for me to fumble. "For now, embrace your role with the council, use your voice. Be wife, sister, friend. You will be many things before you learn who you are."

I blinked over and over again rapidly, wanting to thank him, simultaneously wanting to ask for further clarity. I sighed and nodded, knowing that he could see, if no one else could.

The light shrank away, until we were in a neutral space, able to see one another and our surroundings. Seshat was still there, waiting for our questions.

Setesh took a bold step towards her. "So that's it, then?"

Seshat looked at me nervously, knowing more than she was going to say. "Having children is not meant for you. It is wiser to renew your devotion to the sacred charge you have been called to."

Setesh looked at me, his eyes coldly blaming me. Once more he'd been denied what he wanted. I stepped towards him, then stopped, and simply held his gaze without touching him or moving closer to where he stood. Finally he sighed and released his rage. I took his hand once more.

"Before we pass judgment on this," I whispered, pulling my husband in closer to me, "let us take an opportunity to reflect upon it."

He'd kissed me then, and Seshat left us to our deliberations. I remember us staying there, in the ether, struggling to be okay with the direction we've been given. Talking to Setesh was easier back then. We behaved so passionately towards one another, and we were trying so hard. He's since left me on my own, or so I felt; I knew he believed it had been the other way around.

Later, Djehuty told him that he was infertile, when they were alone and he wouldn't have to receive that news in front of me. Setesh kept that information from me for decades, maybe even over a hundred years. Since that time, we'd consulted Djehuty separately, but never again together. I didn't think he would respond well to me bringing him here.

As before, Seshat was there to meet us. She took me by the hand and I held on to Setesh, who'd realized what I was up to.

He glared at me, but he didn't speak and he didn't leave, both of which were good signs. I squeezed his hand and light flooded the room. Djehuty joined us and I closed my eyes.

"I am here to keep your words true. Tell us who you are. Ask us what you seek."

Seshat's words hit my ears like a loud and breathy whisper. Without dropping her hand, or my husband's, I answered.

"I am Nebt-Het, daughter of Nut, wife of Setesh, our general, sister of Ausar, our King. I am here with my husband, who has proposed a temporary separation for the sake of our nation and our family. We want to know if this will contribute to the maintenance of Maat, or create further discord in our home."

There was a long silence, and I wondered if perhaps I should speak again. Just when I thought I would, Djehuty's voice rang out.

"His physical separation is no cause for concern. Setesh can take his proposal to the council, to see if there are any objections, but we have found none here."

I was taken aback. "None? No objections?"

"Do you have any objections, Nebt-Het?" Seshat asked pointedly, clearly aware that I did.

I dropped her hand. "Well, I... perhaps I should include that I would like to go with him, if he is to go. I think perhaps we should go together."

Djehuty answered quickly, "No, either he will go alone or he will not go at all. You must stay."

"But, why?" I asked, feeling somewhat desperate. "I don't see how this brings no cause for concern."

"Right now, you are needed where you are." Djehuty paused. "In the interest of Maat, you must stay where you are."

I shook my head. I couldn't believe that he was saying it was okay for us to be apart. I couldn't think of anything else to say, yet I wasn't done.

Apparently, however, Djehuty was done with me. The light escaped and we were once more left with Seshat. She looked at me, then Setesh, and left without a word, realizing that what had to be said did not require her presence.

"I need you to stay," I whispered, looking at my husband's face.

He was taken aback. "I honestly did not think you would care this much."

"Why wouldn't I?" I asked, moving closer to him. "I don't want to feel like we're just giving up."

Setesh stepped in to meet me, looking down with a gaze of pure resolve. "Then allow me to take this trip, or at least to bring it to the council. I need to figure some things out. I need you to let me do that."

I looked away and bit my lip. In that moment I was convinced that nothing good would come from this; I was filled with such dread that it frightened me. Yet all of the evidence pointed to the contrary, so there was nothing left to do but dismiss my feelings and be on his side.

"Yes, you're right," I told him, leaning into his chest. "I apologize for reacting so selfishly. I want you to do what is best for you; I will support you before the council."

Setesh sighed, relieved, and held me for a long time before taking us home, but I knew while I listened to the thumping in his chest that I was not finished with this. He jumped us home and I smiled up at him.

"Would you mind if I exit for a bit? I will meet you at the council meeting," I whispered before looking up at him.

Setesh pulled away and studied my features. "Is something wrong?"

"Not with us," I stressed, hoping to reassure him. I stepped back and took his hands in mind. "I just need to speak with the royal chefs about tonight's dinner." I hesitated before continuing. "I would like to... do something different."

I looked into his eyes, hoping he would think that I would plan something special, since he was so intent on leaving. Setesh nodded and his eyes softened, and I sighed, relieved. Without another word I let go of his fingers and left our apartment, heading straight for the kitchen; once there, I jumped into the sitting room of the suite that Ausar and Auset shared, glad that the door to the hall was closed and no one would see me enter.

I knocked loudly on the bedroom door, and Ausar flung it open quickly, with a bit of annoyance. "Nebt-Het," he said, clearly surprised, motioning for me to come in.

I looked around for a moment, then turned my attention to my elder brother. "You have to say he cannot go."

Ausar frowned. "What are you talking about?"

"Setesh," I clarified, taking a deep breath. "I changed my mind. I don't want him to go."

"You never said you wanted him to go in the first place," Ausar reminded me, taking a seat in one of the armchairs while watching me curiously.

I shook my head and turned away. "I know, I just..." I walked over to the courtyard doors and looked out at the bright sun of the early afternoon, my arms mindlessly reaching around themselves, wrapping me in an imaginary warmth. "I don't think he should go."

"Well, you must have a reason."

I closed my eyes. "No, I don't, I just think it's a bad idea."

Ausar cleared his throat softly. "Did you talk to Djehuty?"

I wanted to be dishonest, but I knew I could not. Instead, I mumbled, hoping he would not hear. "He said Setesh should go and I should stay here."

"Then it's settled already." I felt Ausar's hand rest unexpectedly on my shoulder, and I jumped before relaxing beneath his touch. "You know I cannot go against what has already been decreed."

I shook my head again. "I know. I apologize, I'm being silly."

Ausar gently turned my body around to face his. I still could not bear to look at him, but it was comforting to have his chest to lean my forehead against. "You are not usually this... unreasonable," he said warmly, his voice low and calm. "What's wrong?"

He did not push me to speak again, instead supporting me silently while I struggled to find my voice. Eventually I took a deep breath and pulled away, looking him in the eye and dropping my hands to my sides.

"Something bad is going to happen if he leaves. I just know it is."

Ausar tried not to react, but I could see the confusion pass across his features quickly, and I did not ignore it. "You think I'm being ridiculous," I pressed him, wanting to turn away again.

"I apologize," he said, which surprised me. "That was my first reaction, but in truth, if you feel so strongly about it, there must be a reason."

Again I shook my head, and my arms crossed once more. "But Djehuty said he can go. I don't know why I feel this way if everything will be fine."

Ausar hesitated. "Perhaps everything will not be fine."

"Don't say that," I whispered, tightening my fists.

"I don't mean..." Ausar looked down, trying not to upset me. "I just mean, perhaps you did not ask the right questions. Maybe you need to go back and speak with him alone. Or perhaps there are things that Djehuty cannot tell you. But that does not mean you are wrong. It just means you must..." he paused again, "make... peace. With it."

After a moment he looked up at me again, and the look on

my face caused him to open his arms to me. I did not resist for long, and fell gratefully into his embrace. Ausar held me silently for a few moments, and before he let me go I wrapped my arms around him in return. His chin fell gently onto my crown and I sighed deeply, listening to the soft rhythm of his heart.

A knock at the door pulled me from my trance, and I jumped back awkwardly. Ausar chuckled at my reaction before walking over to see who was in the sitting room. I could hear a man's voice there, and I was not sure if Ausar was planning to invite him in or not, so I jumped back to the kitchen to have the needed conversation with the chefs. There was only a short window left to make any changes to the meal, and I had to come up with something so that my lie to my husband would not seem egregious.

Setesh began preparing for his extended stay away from the great house. He was to leave in three days, and in the time since the council meeting, we'd barely spoken, choosing instead of pass each other in the hall with polite, painful smiles. Increasingly I felt my heart tugged to its maximum, but I could not let it show on my face, not wanting to be an obstacle to his journey. Instead I relinquished any illusion that the household needed my attention by promoting the head cook to steward of the royal household, placing him in charge of speaking with each of the individual overseers regularly and reporting to me only when trouble arose.

This meant I had more time to spend in the blossoming garden along the far wall of the outer courtyard, where the tiny stream had cut into the ground around it, forcing the rock to yield and make room for the demanding flow to expand. Now there were a host of frogs and fishes that called the stream home, and water lilies grew in abundance. Date palms had been planted throughout the courtyard as well, and the sycamore trees continued to grow stronger and taller each year.

Ausar had commissioned for pillars to be erected on either sides of the opening to the courtyard, hoping to stop the vegetation from completely claiming the space as its own, but I would have been completely satisfied if we had awoken to find ourselves consumed by greenery. It became the place where I regularly took my early morning walks, before the gardeners began their daily maintenance work, before Aten emerged over the eastern horizon.

As usual I headed straight for the rose bushes, getting close enough to the stream to lean over and let the water trickle through my fingers. I wanted to lie on my back and look up to the sky above, but I chose instead to stroll lazily from bush to bush, hoping the thick scent would rub off on my heart.

"I should have known you would be out here at this time," I heard Ausar whisper from behind me. I smiled and turned to face him. He was smiling and dressed in a long kilt and thin linen vest, not even wearing sandals. I glanced over his shoulder and, finding that he was alone, chose not to greet him in the customary fashion.

"What are you doing in the gardens so early?" I asked, even though I was happy to have some company, growing tired of my constant solitude.

Ausar shrugged. "I never get any time to myself," he admitted, looking around the garden casually, "so I thought I could come out here and be alone."

My eyebrows shot up. "Well, if you want I can find another place to wander and talk to myself," I joked, with a touch of sincerity.

Ausar shook his head emphatically. "No, I don't... please. I don't want you to leave." He paused, then looked at me. "If anything, I should offer to relocate. This is your time with the garden, everyone knows that."

I smiled. "I think we can share it."

He smiled, relieved, and joined me in the flower beds. "Is Setesh almost complete with his preparations for Inbu-Hedj?"

I hesitated. "I wouldn't know, actually," I admitted, turning away a bit to conceal my expression. "He has not spoken to me about it."

"At all?"

I shook my head no and looked back at my brother, who appeared surprised. "I apologize for asking, I know it is a sore spot," he said, looking at me directly, with eyes that pierced.

"It's not a sore spot," I started, stopping because that wasn't true. I took a deep breath. "You know how I feel, is all."

"You should go home tomorrow morning instead of coming out here to the garden, and find out what your concern is about."

It was sound advice, but I knew I would not take it. I ran my hand along the top of a rose bush as I began to move forward, pricking my finger on an errant thorn. "Clearly I am just being selfish. I am allowed to be every once in a while.

"Yes, you are," Ausar responded firmly, and I realized he was not following me. I turned to face him and the look on his face was one of admiration.

"What are you thinking?" I asked him, tilting my head in interest.

Ausar shook his head and looked away, beginning to stroll both closer and away from me, his steps following a crescent path. "I continue to be in awe of the capacity of your heart," he mumbled, staring down at the rocks beneath his feet.

His words took me aback, and I knew he was referring to my affection for Setesh, but I no longer wanted to discuss my husband with him. I took a step to the right and soon I was behind him on the curved path, watching him as he examined the garden, of which I knew every nook. Ausar appeared to be deep in thought and I wanted to hear every word of it, but I was afraid if I spoke, it would disturb the flow of his consciousness.

"I wonder, sometimes," Ausar began, "if I was not who I am, if I failed more often, or if I was immature and emotional and self-righteous... I wonder if Auset would still love me as much as you still love Setesh."

I frowned, and he looked up just in time to notice my disapproval. "Auset loves you better than any woman has ever loved a man," I reminded him sternly.

"I know, I know," he agreed, "it is true, but, it has never been tested. It is so strange that I feel this way but, sometimes I envy you and Setesh."

"That is ridiculous!" I exclaimed, barely able to keep down my voice.

Ausar turned to me and grinned. "No, hear me out," he said, and his face became somber again. "You fight for him, even when no one else will, even when no one else does."

"Auset will fight for you -" I started, but he stopped me.

"Even when he does not deserve you, you fight for him."

I stopped and looked at him, to see if he was serious, and he was. It caused me to look away. "That is no virtue, Ausar. That is nothing to envy."

"I envy it nonetheless."

I looked back at him, weary. "I used to envy you, the simplicity of your union, the seamless partnership between you and Auset. *Yours* is a love story for the ages."

Ausar smirked and looked away. "Our story is boring."

We would get nowhere with this subject, so I turned my back to him to wander back to the small wall along the far end of the courtyard's edge. I sat upon it and waited for him to join me there, for I knew he would, and he did.

Once at my side, I took his left hand in mine and looked down at his long, slender fingers. His hand was soft, not hardened by sparring matches and bruised by training weapons. It was the hand of a King, someone strong in decision making, wisdom, thought. Clarity.

Fixing my gaze upon our hands in my lap, I sighed. "Restlessness is the seed of isfet, and we must guard against Apep winding his darkness through the holes of our being." I looked into his face, confident that he understood my meaning. "Look with renewed eyes, and see with a renewed heart," I added emphatically, convincing myself most of all.

Ausar placed his right hand atop the delicate pile of fingers that I had created in my thoughtfulness. "You are ever true of voice. I am grateful to have stumbled upon you this morning."

I nodded without speaking, and a sharp ray of light pierced my vision quickly as Aten announced its arrival. I closed my eyes and released his hands, and before I could look again, Ausar had stood and walked away, or dispersed away, leaving me to the endless motion of my thoughts.

I stood on the shore, waving at my husband's ship as it departed from the port and headed north to the lower lands. I noticed a single hawk sailing in the heavens above the ship and the feeling of remembrance passed over me sharply, causing me to recall another departure from this dock many moons ago. In that moment I understood how I had grown to love Setesh. Not the passion that we'd felt in the beginning of our union, or the excitement of rediscovering one another; not the desire to consume the other or the stimulation of constant challenge.

Instead, he was a duty that I was charged to care for. He was my responsibility. He was the person who I had been bound to for lifetimes, and that meant something, but maybe not the right things. I loved him and I knew that I had loved him for as long as I could remember, and I would love him, always. But never the way he'd wanted to be loved. I had tried, and would continue to try, but he knew that I couldn't, and I finally did too.

I took a deep breath and the first tear slipped past, making its way down my face to drip from my chin to the ground. I had not asked him to stay for the right reasons, and so he was gone. I'd been immersed in dread since we first discussed this trip last week, and now, it felt heavier, ominous, but I hadn't taken any time to consider what it meant or seek counsel. Soon, Ausar and Auset would leave for the north, and then I would have nothing but time.

I thought I was the last one standing along the river's edge after his boat had departed, but when I turned I found my sister waiting for me, just a few feet away. I smiled, glad to have her with me, and walked over to meet her where she stood.

Setesh would arrive in Inbu-Hedj earlier than needed for the harvest festivals and stay until after the inundation. The council had overwhelming approved of his time away from our home base, primarily, I believed at the time, because they hoped he would come back a less contrary, mellower personality. I wasn't sure what I was hoping for; in retrospect I think I just wanted him to come back.

Auset took my hand. "Come now, senet, let's make our way inside." She pulled me towards her and began to head for the estate. I followed, although it felt like I was being dragged.

Once inside, Auset headed towards my apartment. Not another word passed between us until we were securely behind the heavy sitting room door.

"I can't believe you aren't jumping for joy to have him gone for so long," Auset finally let out in a breathy sigh of relief. She sank into one of the armchairs in a rather unladylike fashion.

I smiled at her and sat on a stool, facing her. Auset never allowed any of her girlish ways peek through in front of others; it was only with me that she would show remnants of her old self. I found myself both admiring and envying her growth, the journey that she had taken into becoming such a poised and graceful Queen.

Shaking my head, I answered, "I know what you mean, but soon I will be left by myself."

Auset sat up a bit. "I know, but it won't be for very long. We will only be gone for a few weeks. Besides," she added, her voice sounding excited, "you are only staying here so that you can govern the festivals in our absence."

I smiled again, but wasn't as excited as she. "Yes, that's true."

My sister frowned at me. "Are you saying you aren't looking forward to this? Or are you really wishing you could be in the lower lands?"

I hesitated. "I suppose I am not excited because it is a huge responsibility and I have to be sure I am ready for it."

Auset smiled again and fell back into the seat, completely relaxed. "You are."

"I appreciate your confidence in me."

"It's not just me, Nebt-Het. Ausar believes in you also. He would never leave you with such a duty if he wasn't sure you could handle it. He has been advocating for you to have a vote on the council practically since you joined."

My eyebrows shot up with this news. "Really? I had no idea."

Auset waved her hand around dismissively. "Since forever all he can do is talk about how smart he was to add you to the council. He really values your opinion." She looked at me with a raised eyebrow. "At least he got one thing right."

I smiled at her joke, but focused on the truth she'd revealed. Ausar had always said he appreciated me, but I thought he was just being generous, trying to keep me motivated. "So why haven't I been made a voting member?" I asked casually, or what I hoped sounded casual.

She hesitated and sat up a bit, straightening her posture to resemble more of the woman she was. "No one doubts your ability, Nebt-Het, we just had to consider what made sense." Auset paused for a moment before adding, "As much as Ausar listens to you, you should know that you've had an unofficial vote all along. I hope that is consolation. If I'd realized it would mean so much to you, I would have helped him push harder."

There was a knock at the door, and one of the attendees poked her head in. "Pardon me Hmt Naswu, **Seret**," she said, greeting both Auset and I in order. "Naswt Biti has asked about where you are, Hmt. He was looking for you."

Auset stood into her full stature, naturally regal. I quickly stood as well, following protocol. "Duty calls," she said, a soft smile creeping across her face. The attendee held open the door for her to pass through, then led her down the hall to where Ausar waited.

I sat back onto the stool and sighed before standing again and making my way out to the courtyard. To avoid making an unladylike scramble over the courtyard walls, I quickly dispersed my energy and landed roughly on the other side, in the open plain where I could walk and think freely. No one would look for me out here; in fact, I doubted anyone would look for me at all.

I found myself walking deep into the west, far from the town which sat on the east bank of the Hapi, away from where anyone else would be. I found a small patch of land and laid back upon it, looking up at the body of my mother, stars twinkling across her face. I sighed.

"What is going on with me?" I mumbled to myself. I settled in for a long night of staring. I would go home eventually, just not

yet. I needed time to prepare myself to face whatever it was
that I would learn from my visit, but I wasn't sure I would ever
be ready. The dread pulsed in my body, causing me to sigh
again, loudly.

I'm not sure when I dozed off, but when I next opened my
eyes, the sun had already risen and moved above the horizon. It
wasn't quite midday, but I was late. I got up and rushed back to
the estate as quickly as I could, mentally cursing my brother
and sister for not looking for me, and trying not to dwell on the
fact that this only happened because Setesh was gone.

"Are you nervous about the festival at all?" Ausar asked for
the hundredth time. I rolled my eyes.

"I'll be fine," I responded, yet again. "I am completely
prepared; you have told me more than I need to know. I can
handle this."

He nodded and looked down at the materials we'd been
going over, apparently needing to reassure himself. "I
apologize; I don't mean to make you feel like I don't trust you."

I shook my head, taking a step back from the table, not
wanting to be so close to him. "It's not that, I know it is my first
time and you are just being cautious. It's fine, I get it."

Ausar nodded and glanced over his shoulder, searching my
face for any sign that I was uncomfortable or unsure. When he
didn't find anything, he began rolling up the scrolls, putting
them away. "Did Auset tell you when we're leaving?"

"She didn't," I answered, "but one of the attendees said they
were preparing for your departure in four days. Is that still the
plan, or has it changed?"

"No, that's the plan." Ausar pulled out a chair and sat at the
table, his back to me. I started walking around to the other side

so I could sit across from him. "We will be back in five weeks, sooner if anything urgent comes up."

I sighed again, practically slumping into the chair. "I suppose I should ask you if you are nervous. You know, this isn't the first time I have been left here alone."

"I know, I know," Ausar protested gently. "This is just the first time during a festival, is all." He paused and looked down at his hands. "It should have been sooner; you could have handled this years ago."

"Then why wasn't it sooner?" I realized my delivery made the question sound impertinent, as if I had no need for tact. My own sense of right made me want to take it back, but if Ausar minded, or even noticed, he didn't mention it.

"Honestly?" Ausar looked up at me as if he couldn't believe I didn't know the reason. "Your husband has never quite appreciated that we placed you on the council. We were concerned that anything more would agitate him further."

I sat back in my seat, glad to have my suspicion confirmed. I wasn't the only one avoiding the landmines of his personality. I shook my head, almost wanting to cry. How many things had I been denied just so we could placate Setesh? I hated him for being oblivious to his own sensitivity.

"Is he the reason I never got a vote on the council?"

Ausar hesitated. "I wouldn't say that."

I closed my eyes. "Is he? Yes or no."

"It is more complicated than that."

So yes then. I wanted to jump from my seat and break chairs, throw things across the room, clear the table with one violent swipe, but I couldn't. My natural instinct was to hold back, to hold everything in, and I did the best I could, even though it hurt. Still, something peeked through, because after a moment Ausar was beside me, taking my hand in his, and a wayward tear snuck past my closed eyelid. I slowed my breath and unclenched my jaw.

"I appreciate you being honest with me, but as you can see, all of our attempts to keep him from blowing up at us have failed." I opened my eyes and looked at Ausar to my right. "Setesh is just as uncompromising as ever, so the only thing we accomplished by not standing up to him was not staying true to ourselves."

His eyebrows shot up. "Don't you think he would be worse, if we had not tried as hard as we did? Didn't we owe it to him, and ourselves, to at least make the effort?"

Ausar was probably right, but in my anger I couldn't verbalize agreement. I simply nodded and looked away, taking back the hand he'd borrowed.

"Are you still feeling that sense of dread you mentioned, about him leaving?"

I sighed. "Tu, more than ever. I haven't gone home yet to consult with Seba, but I know I must."

"What do you think it means?" he asked. "I mean, you must have some idea of where it comes from, what it forebodes."

I shook my head emphatically. "I truly wish I did. At first I thought maybe it was a sign that something bad would happen while he was gone, but when I saw the falcon, I knew that wasn't it. Then I thought, maybe I'm just nervous about the festival, but now I'm sure that everything will be okay, yet still I feel like something isn't right. I can't shake it."

I looked over to him, and Ausar was shaking his head in contemplation. "What has been your hesitation to hear what it means?"

I took a deep breath. I hated this part. "It's just, it fills me with such... *fear*, and I don't know why, and I don't know if there is anything that is going to make me feel safe." I paused and instinctively leaned my shoulder against his. "There was a time when Setesh gave me that, but now I just don't feel like I can turn to him, and that makes this even worse."

"You don't think he would understand? Or that he will be reasonable about it?"

"I don't want to be told that I'm being irrational." I slumped further against my brother's arm. "I *know* I am being irrational, but I don't want to hear him say it."

Ausar paused. "I don't think he would say that to you. It may be a long time since you've seen it, but Setesh has a soft spot for you."

Again I rolled my eyes, my soft spot for him having hardened a bit given the new information I'd learned. I didn't move or speak for a few minutes, and almost pulled away when I felt Ausar shifted in his seat, but when I tried to sit up straight, he threw his arm around me and pulled my body into his. I relaxed against him, thankful for the reprise.

"Auset told me that you've been my biggest advocate for a long time," I mumbled, finally sitting up straight. "I never knew that you felt so strongly about it."

Ausar straightened up as well, his eyes avoiding mine. "I've always told you how much I value your opinion and perspective; I've never been shy about my admiration for you."

I smiled. "No, I just mean, I had no idea that you really fought for me to have a vote. It really means a lot to me to know that you tried."

He nodded, still looking away. "I did try, many times. It just didn't work out."

"Dua."

Ausar finally looked at me, searching my face as if readying himself to ask me a very important question, but before he could get it out, his wife glided into the room as if carried by a gust of wind. "Are you two finished with this meeting?" she said sweetly, oblivious to the fact that we had long finished discussing the festival.

We both diverted our attention to her, fully pulling apart. "Which one of us were you looking for, senet?" I asked, trying to sound as normal as possible.

"Actually, I was looking for you," Auset answered, her eyes wide and bright as she sat in a chair on the opposite side of the table, "but since my husband is here I can just talk to you both."

Ausar cleared his throat. "No, I think I should give you two space. Seba should be here soon, as we have some things to discuss regarding our trip." He stood and began making his way to the door. It took me a minute to gather myself, and by the time I remembered to follow protocol, Ausar had already made his exit.

Auset adjusted her posture, appearing to be completely proud of herself. "I'm glad he's gone; I really only wanted to talk to you."

I shifted in my seat, a little uncomfortable. "Is everything okay?"

My sister smiled, attempting to ease my concern. "Of course," she told me, leaning into the table. "I wanted to talk to you about childbirthing. There are always other women present who assist the new mother with bringing her child forth, and I have been contemplating ways to improve that work, to make it easier on the woman in labor." Auset frowned, seeing me unresponsive. "I am hoping to have your involvement on this. What are you thinking, sister?"

I exhaled, and smiled. I had been wondering what Ausar was going to ask me before he'd left, going over various scenarios in my mind, but I needed to let it go in order to focus. "I was thinking, it is surprising that neither of us had thought of this sooner, actually." I leaned in to the table to appear excited. This was the first time she was inviting me on a project of this scope, and I could tell it would mean a lot to her. "What did you have in mind?"

I woke with a start, the acute sensation that I had experienced a night terror, and yet with no distinct recollection of any specific dream sequence. Dread had been haunting me for weeks, made heavier by my choice to ignore it. Waking in this fashion provided an opportunity for me to seek counsel, yet I still couldn't bring myself to go home.

Instead, I dressed myself, and ventured out into the night. The hallways were dark and empty, and the only sound was that of my feet sliding gently across the dirt floors. I thought I would sneak out into the fields and travel south along the edge of the Hapi, but before I could reach the door, I heard a voice behind me.

"Nebt-Het?" Ausar asked in a whisper. He had just returned home earlier today, and the month-long trip had so drained him and Auset that they'd retired to their rooms almost immediately after disembarking.

I turned to face him, surprised. "I hope I didn't wake you."

He shook his head emphatically. "No, not at all. Actually, I have rested plenty, and I am starving. I tried to convince myself that no one else would be up, but this IS the time when you take your walks." Ausar looked back towards the kitchen nervously. "I really want to get something to eat, but... do you mind? I will wake someone if you think that's best."

I tightened my robe around me. "No, I, I don't mind. I think I can rustle something up for you."

Ausar exhaled, relieved. I led the way back to the kitchen, but instead of waiting in the great hall, he followed me in and sat on one of the stools. I looked at him, eyebrow raised.

"What?" he asked innocently. "There is no need for me to behave formally for a midnight snack."

He had a point. I smiled and started gathering the figs, sweet breads, and jars of pickled fish that I knew wouldn't need to be cooked. Despite all that I knew about maintaining the household, I certainly was no culinary expert, and hauling the sheep dung needed to light the oven fires was not a task I was interested in.

"We received a hawk this morning as we were pulling into port," Ausar started, then stopped. He looked around nervously, as if perhaps he shouldn't mention it after all.

I looked at him and smirked. "You've already started your story, you may as well finish."

He smiled. "Setesh says he will be home in three weeks. He must be preparing to leave now, instead of staying until the inundation."

It was my turn to be relieved. "Dua for telling me that. I'm glad to hear it."

"Are you really?" Ausar asked cautiously. "I mean, did you ever find out why you were feeling so scared before?"

"No, I avoided it for as long as I could." I turned my back to him, pretending to look for something. "I was actually trying to muster the courage to go home now, before the day begins."

"So you've avoided it all this time?" I turned back to Ausar and found him looking puzzled. "I'm surprised Djehuty didn't come here and seek you out."

I nodded. "So am I, actually, and now that it's been so long, I can only expect that I will be thoroughly chastised upon my arrival." I shrugged and placed the bowl before him. "Not as if I don't deserve it, of course."

"I don't think it will be as bad as you think it will," he answered.

"Really? What makes you say that?"

Ausar had to pause for a moment to chew, and I found a second stool on the other side of the kitchen. I took that opportunity to pull it closer to where he was eating. "If it were that important, you would have been summoned." He motioned for a glass of water, and I got up to retrieve one for him. "Maybe you were nervous for nothing. Maybe you really were upset that Setesh left."

I put the cup down. "You say that as if you find it so incredibly hard to believe."

Ausar shrugged. "I do, actually. You are so reasonable and he is the exact opposite." He put down the bowl, taking a pause. "I used to think that maybe your temperance would rub off on him and he would mellow out a bit. Actually, at the very beginning, you were rubbing off on him and he was calmer because of you, but at some point, it just stopped working."

I sat back on the stool and looked away. "I don't know that it ever really worked. Sometimes I think he was pretending, and who he is now is who he has always been." I smiled, looking back to my brother. "Sometimes I think I was pretending that he wasn't always this person. That I refused to believe that he hadn't changed."

He nodded again before picking up the bowl. "It wasn't wrong for you to believe the best about your husband. That's what you were supposed to do."

I sighed again, done with this topic. "I hope the food was okay, I didn't want to have to light a fire or anything."

Ausar grinned. "This was perfect, actually. I would never have figured out where to find these figs without you."

I smiled and looked down. "You're welcome." I paused. "You haven't said a word about the festivals in Anu. How did everything go?"

"It was beautiful, Auset loved it, but honestly," Ausar fidgeted, keeping his eyes cast downward, "I would have preferred to be here, at home."

I frowned. "Why? I thought you enjoyed your travels."

He shrugged. "I used to, but it does eventually become too much. I would like to have the opportunity to settle down and stay still for a little while."

I shook my head. "You should know that settling down is not as much *fun* as I make it look."

Ausar snickered in between bites, shaking his head. "You only say that because you want the opportunity to roam the countryside. I have been everywhere, and I am ready to be right here, for good."

"But you can't, and you won't," I smiled, tilting my head at my brother. "Because the people need you, so you will go, for them."

Again he chuckled, this time with more of a frown than a smile. "Yes, I will. It seems that some of your altruism has rubbed off on me, dearest sister."

I blushed for a moment, averting my eyes. "No one has called me that in years," I said aloud, more to myself than to him. I looked back and Ausar had stopped eating and was sitting up straighter. His eyes came up to meet mine and the intensity in them connected to something smoldering within me. I cleared my throat. "If it's okay with you, I'm going to run home to see if I can't set things right with Djehuty."

"Of course, you should." Ausar put his bowl down once more, tenderly. "Will you keep me posted, let me know what happens? I am willing to help in any way I can."

"I know, and I appreciate it," I told him, nodding. "I will let you know." I left the kitchen, telling myself that I should change out of my night clothes first, as if what I was wearing on earth would make any difference. But once I got back to our chambers, I had changed my mind completely. I wasn't going home. I was going to bed.

I came into the sitting room just as Setesh was coming out of the bedroom. We smiled tentatively before approaching each other and hugging stiffly.

"I missed you," I mumbled into his shoulder, as his arms wrapped around me. "I missed you too," he mumbled back.

I pulled my head back so I could look into his face. "You look happy. I'm so glad your trip went well."

He nodded. "It went very well." Without letting me go, he frowned. "How did the festival go here? You didn't send word to me."

I tried to gauge if he was upset by this, but he only looked interested. I slipped out of his hug and took his hand into mine. "It went very well. I apologize for not writing to you. I have thought about you every single day."

Setesh clenched his jaw. I bit my lower lip and frowned. "Maybe I should give you some time to settle in? Do you want me to give you some time alone?"

"No, I have had plenty of time to get settled. Please, join me."

I smiled and followed him into the bedroom, still holding his hand. "Tell me about Inbu-Hedj, and the harvest. Was it bountiful? I heard this year was one of the best ever."

"I don't want to talk about the festival." Setesh sat on the bed, pulling me down beside him. "I suppose it would be unfair for me to be angry that you didn't write to me when I didn't write to you either."

I looked away. "I suppose that neither of us should have been so distant."

Setesh sighed again. "I apologize," he started, then stopped, standing and looking out into the courtyard. I watched his back until he was ready to speak again. "I do not expect things here to improve between us; between myself and Ausar, Auset and I, or even between you and I." He turned back to face me, determined and full of his power. Renewed. "I cannot stop challenging them, challenging myself. It is who I am and it is who I am meant to be."

I shook my head, not expecting that at all. I wished I could ask him to be kinder, nicer, or gentler about how he expressed himself, but I knew that he couldn't, or wouldn't, or both. "The truth is, there have been times when you were right, and having you around has made Ausar a better leader." I looked at him and tried to smile. "I think we all can acknowledge that."

"Do you?" he asked me, his question sincere. "I am ever frustrated by the same dilemma. If we can all acknowledge that, why do I end up feeling so misplaced?" He sat next to me and took my hand. "While I was gone I spent a lot of time recalling the message that Ra gave me back when we first moved here. He told me that I would be misunderstood and my contribution would be unappreciated. I needed to come to terms with that truth. Things would have been easier if I had accepted that years ago, but I kept hoping for something different."

I frowned and searched his face. "Perhaps we haven't appreciated you the way you wish we had, but that doesn't mean we don't see you, Setesh. It hasn't always been easy, but that is no reason for us to give up."

"I'm not asking you to," Setesh responded quickly, looking at me directly. "This isn't about you, any of you. I needed to accept that I am not meant to fit in. I just have to be who I am because it is best for us all. I will not intentionally create conflict but I cannot shy away from it either."

I looked down at our hands. We fidgeted gently, twisting our fingers around each other's. "I support that," I told him, my voice practically a whisper.

Setesh kissed my forehead, then stood once more. "I appreciate that you came here to greet me. I am going out to train. See you at dinner?"

I looked up at him and nodded. He disappeared in a flash, headed for his favorite spot in the world. I wished immediately that I had pushed him to say that he was done with our marriage – that we were done – but I had been too afraid to be so direct, to make it so final. I was not ready to admit that I was tired of fighting and tired of not knowing what I am fighting for.

I glanced around at my surroundings, never feeling so alone before, and realized it wasn't my sister I was longing for, but my brother, Ausar. Dearest sister, I thought to myself, before putting it out of my mind for what I hoped would be forever, but what I knew was just a moment. I could not feel immense sadness for an ending when something new was beginning.

I had just gotten out of the bath after attending another birthing with Auset, a project with incredible success thus far. We had spent the last four months showing women across the upper lands how to incorporate the new midwifery techniques, and the response to the improvements was overwhelmingly positive. Auset came home from each birthing glowing, ready to become a mother herself, wanting to talk about the magic of children for the rest of the night. It had the opposite effect on me; I was satisfied simply to be of assistance at a time when a woman is most in need of the strength of her sisters.

I was back to sleeping in one of the spare apartments towards the rear of the estate - not because Setesh and I were fighting, but because after these birthings, I wanted to be alone. I laid down to rest for a while before my early morning walk, my heart racing, knowing that I would run into Ausar, as I had on most mornings since he'd returned from Anu. We'd never agreed to meet at a specific time or made arrangements to run into each other, but every few days I would slip into the hall, and he would be there, sauntering, waiting.

After a few hours, I rose, slipped on something presentable yet casual, and opened the door to the sitting room. Ausar was standing on the other side of the door, causing me to gasp in surprise.

"What are you doing out there?" I whispered, looking behind him to make sure the door to the hallway was completely closed, which it was. I could only pray no one had seen him come inside the apartment.

"I was just checking to see if maybe you were already out walking or maybe you were sleeping," Ausar insisted, stepping back defensively. "I didn't expect to catch you coming out at that exact moment."

I grabbed his arm and pulled him inside. "You can't go back out through the door! What if someone sees you? No, you need to disperse. Just, I'll meet you in the front hall or something."

Ausar smirked and looked down at me, not moving. I sighed. "I don't mean to overreact. You just surprised me, is all."

I sat on the bed and Ausar sat in one of the armchairs across the room. "Auset was gushing about this birthing all night, said it went really well." He leaned forward, resting his elbows on his knees. "It sounds like they are all the same to me, but she talks about each one like it's a new experience."

I shrugged. "I want to know how dinner went without either of us there. I was surprised to learn that nothing was broken." We both smiled. "How was it though, was it uncomfortable?"

"Same old with Setesh, you know how it is." It was Ausar's turn to shrug. He changed the subject. "I did think perhaps you should join us when we travel to Waset next week. Whether Setesh comes or not, it would be a good opportunity for you and Auset to teach more women the things that you've learned."

My heart leapt. "Really? I would love that." My cheeks

burned with excitement, and I diverted my eyes to process the invitation. "Have you discussed it with Djehuty at all, or anyone?"

"I asked Setesh at dinner tonight what he thought." Ausar sat up again. "He seemed to think it was a good idea. In fact he suggested that the four of us make one long tour of the kingdom, together."

I clutched my hands to my chest. "I would love that," I whispered, looking at Ausar.

He grinned. "I thought you would." He came over and sat on the bed, reducing the space between us. "I'll bring it up at the next council meeting."

I nodded and looked away dreamily, wanting to bask in the possibilities, but it only took me a moment to realize something was unsaid. "You never did tell me why you were looking for me," I started, turning to face Ausar. "Is everything okay, did you want to talk about something?"

Ausar shook his head and moved to face me. "Mostly I just wanted to see your face when I told you about Waset. I honestly couldn't wait to tell you," he shared, his tone even, yet low. I looked into his eyes and caught his gaze. We should have looked away, but we didn't. "I'm glad I didn't," he uttered softly, his voice heavy.

I inhaled sharply. "I'm glad you didn't," I whispered, losing control of my breath.

We were sitting too close, much too close to one another, and I knew that what was happening should not be happening, that one of us should stop it. I pulled away and cast my eyes to the ground, catching myself before we'd gone too far.

I walked over to the door of the bedroom and glanced back at him. He wouldn't stop me; he knew we were wrong also. I looked out into the sitting room, which still empty, yet instead of exiting, I closed the bedroom door tight and turned back to face him.

He stood and removed his clothes. I removed mine.

He looked at me as if he'd never seen me before, as if my face and body were being discovered for the first time. His gaze made me uncomfortable; I wasn't used to being looked at in this way.

"Why look at me like that?" I asked. "I look just like Auset."

He lowered his eyes to the floor and began to walk over to me, one step at a time, slowly. "I used to think that," he started in a low, almost inaudible whisper, "but I've learned how wrong I was." He stopped, standing close enough that I could feel the energy radiating from his skin as he brought his eyes up to meet mine. "You don't look anything like her."

I took a deeply appreciative breath without breaking our gaze. Ausar wrapped his arms around my waist and lifted me, and I responded by wrapping my legs around him. He carried me back to the bed, inhaling my every breath, pressing his forehead to mine as if separating would cause great agony.

He was not like Setesh, whose passion and fire was consuming and overwhelming; who had a ravenous appetite and pushed me to my every physical limit. Ausar opened me, emotionally, causing feelings of vulnerability to wash over me repeatedly, which he soothed with his attentiveness and intensity. When I looked at him, he was seeing me, and it made me feel like no one had ever really seen me before. I didn't want it to end, and it felt like it never would.

After, we laid there for a few minutes, looking up at the ceiling. I wished I knew what he was thinking, but I know now that it was similar to my own thoughts. The moment of lovemaking had passed and we'd moved immediately into experiencing regret. I couldn't imagine how we would share this news with our mates. I didn't want to. I hoped that if neither of us got out of this bed, we wouldn't have to.

Eventually, Ausar sat up fully, placing his feet on the ground, his back facing me. "I'm sorry," he started, then stopped.

I sat up, keeping my legs outstretched on the bed. *"I'm sorry."*

He dropped his head. "I will never, we'll never do this again." I nodded, even though he wasn't looking in my direction. I couldn't imagine that he thought I would disagree.

He turned and faced me, a look of worry in his eyes. "You can't tell Setesh. He'll never forgive either of us. I won't tell Auset either, please. Let's just leave what happened here, in this room."

I took a deep breath and curled my legs under me. Keeping this between us had not occurred to me; the Great Father knew everything, and if Auset could learn Ra's secret name, someone would find out about this. But even if others knew - even if everyone else knew - he was right that we couldn't tell Setesh what he'd done. What we'd done.

I looked back at Ausar and nodded. "I won't tell either of them. I swear."

THET - FERTILITY

I began to understand why Ausar longed for the constancy of home. It was two months into our tour of Kemet and already I was tired of this ship.

Auset sat next to me, holding a fan of ostrich feathers in one hand, using it to direct a breeze of fresh air towards us. "I am thinking of heading to the per eah, taking the jump, resting up and coming back in a day or two. You would be alright here, if I left you with our brothers?"

I gripped her arm to keep from retching openly. I made daily retreats from my private space below to the upper deck, where I would be less affected by the unfortunate combination of unclean bodies and spoiled grain. "It is not being alone that would bother me," I mumbled, "but I would be jealous that you were on solid ground while my insides are being tossed around by the fickle waves of the Hapi."

"If you feel so strongly about it, perhaps we should both head home," my sister suggested casually, her look one of concern. "We can ask Ausar tonight if we can miss a couple of days, rearrange the schedule. It can work, I think."

I sat up straighter, immensely motivated by any suggestion that I might be freed from this experience. "If you think he will be amenable, and it won't cause too big a dilemma."

"What dilemma?" Ausar's voice chimed in from over my shoulder, causing me to practically jump out of my skin. I stood to face and greet him, and Auset shifted on the bench to look up at our King. He glanced at me briefly before directing all of his attention to his wife, which described exactly how he'd looked at me every day since our ill-advised interaction, to put it lightly.

I couldn't blame him, and didn't; what had I expected? This avoidance was the best way to keep what happened from being discovered, as well as ensuring it never happened again. Still, I had to admit that I found it unpleasant, but I couldn't imagine any course by which our relationship was repaired.

"Nebt-Het was just agreeing to travel to the great house with me so we can get a few days on solid ground. We are in desperate need of respite." Auset looked over her husband's shoulder before turning her attention back to me. "We were hoping you would be open to making that work with the schedule."

Ausar nodded and looked away. "I see no reason why you two can't miss the first day or two of our stop in Abdju. It is our next stop. But we are destined for home directly after, are you sure you don't want to hold out until the tour is truly complete?"

Auset stood, satisfied. "I'm sure, I really need a day. Let's head out after dinner, senet." It was then she frowned and took my wrist, examining my face intently. "Beloved, you look positively ghastly, are you alright? I can't believe how pale you've become, let me get you below deck," she said, grabbing my elbow without giving me a moment to respond.

I didn't pull away but I didn't let her drag me off either. "The last thing I need is to add claustrophobia to my nausea and insomnia. Please, Auset, just take me home."

In a flash we were in my apartment at the great house, the courtyard doors wide open, a welcomed heavy wind cleansing the space and covering us. I sighed audibly, holding back tears of joy, flinging myself onto the bed and landing uncomfortably without caring.

"Should I leave you here? Are you going directly to sleep or do you want to get a bite to eat first?"

I could not imagine taking her up on that offer. "No, I do not intend to move from this bed right now, but I would like to eat something later." I rolled over so I could face her before she left. "If you could, please send an attendee to wake me right before dinner."

Auset nodded and left in silence, leaving me to my gratitude. No longer subject to the tyranny of travel, my body settled quickly, relieving me of much discomfort almost immediately. I sighed and sat up just as a flash burst before me; Setesh had followed us home.

"Ausar told me you came here. I suppose you just couldn't take it anymore."

He sat on the bed next to me and I slumped my body into his. "Auset said she needed a day to rest and I thought, if she gets a vacation, I want one too." I glanced up at him sheepishly. "Explaining it makes me sound rather bratty."

"That was plenty bratty," Setesh mumbled with a chuckle, "you should have just said you needed respite. You were miserable, and I was miserable watching you be miserable."

I smiled. "Will you stay for dinner tonight?"

He didn't answer right away; I knew I was wrong to have asked. Our responsibilities are to the realm first - none of us can put duty aside for personal sentiment. Still, I hoped he would, just this once.

Setesh cleared his throat. "Just through dinner. I can't stay longer than that, you know." A moment passed. "I'm not sure I should even stay that long."

I looked up at him, still unwilling to relinquish him completely. "I appreciate that you will, for me."

Before the room could descend into silence, there was a knock at the door. An attendee poked her head into the room cautiously. "Naswt Biti has arrived as well, and he is staying for dinner. He's asked everyone to gather at the regular time."

Setesh nodded, and she disappeared. I felt myself shiver, and he instinctively pulled me close, as if body heat was what I needed. The evening I was looking forward to had crumbled away. I closed my eyes as if to make time stand still, a power I did not possess.

As usual, no one was there when I walked into the hall for dinner. I thought to go into the kitchen and check on the meal being prepared, but I quickly decided against it. The attendees are more than capable, I told myself, seeking any available excuse to avoid upsetting my senses again.

Just as I prepared to sit, Ausar walked in, hesitating briefly as he realized we were alone. I remained standing until he made his way to his chair and we sat simultaneously, taking peeks of one another that we hoped would go unnoticed.

"I must apologize for the way I've treated you lately," he eventually began, his eyes fixed upon the table before him. I took the opportunity to look at him directly while he continued to avoid my glance. "I haven't known what else to do. I feel as if-"

"You owe me no apology, Naswt Biti," I cut him off, looking away just as his gaze left the table. "You owe your time and attention to your people. You have not mistreated me in the least."

I looked back to Ausar, and this time he did not look away. The silence around us deepened; my heart skipped a beat. "Nebt-Het," he began, as if to plead with me, and I would have let him if not for the merciful interruption of our spouses walking in together, a rare and slightly welcome sight.

I cleared my throat and made to stand, but Auset stopped

me. "No need to be so formal senet, especially when I know you are not feeling well. Perhaps your afternoon rest had done you some good?"

I smiled graciously. "Tu, it has made a world of difference. I was just thanking Naswt for his generous decision. I should be ready tomorrow to finish our grand tour."

Setesh took my hand. "A tour I suspect will be your first and last, at least if you have to travel by ship." We both smiled; he was right about that. "The unpredictable nature of the water seems to oppose you entirely."

"I am immensely grateful to be on solid ground," I answered, looking at my husband lovingly. He kissed my knuckles just as the attendees began to bring out the food.

It only took a few moments for the meal to be fully spread out before us, and my siblings did not hesitate. I watched each of them as they began to eat; none of them were shy about demonstrating the fullness of their need. I smiled and took a deep breath, trying to gather the fortitude to dive in. I too was starving, but there was no way I would get down - or keep down - a single bite of food.

I looked at the plate in front of me and cringed. My mouth watered and my stomach flipped. I closed my eyes and took a deep breath, which included the heavy aroma of the cuisine before me, and the possibility of an eruption heightened.

I opened my eyes and looked across the table at my sister, who was studying me watchfully. I smiled. "I'm going to retire to my room, if no one has any objections."

"Are you alright?" Ausar asked, clearing his throat, Auset's eyes penetrating in their stare towards me. I was so unnerved by her attention, I almost couldn't respond.

"Tu, I'm fine," I finally stuttered, looking away. I turned my eyes to Setesh. "It appears I simply did not rest as well as I'd thought. I will eat later."

I pushed my chair out and stood, nodding towards Ausar, then Auset. I looked down to Setesh, who was looking at me curiously. He nodded. "I will ask the attendee if they can store your plate without it spoiling. Send someone for me if you need anything."

I touched his shoulder, grateful, and smiled, then walked from the room as slowly as I could stand, to avoid drawing suspicion. Once in the hall, I began to rush to my chambers, to deal with my pangs of nausea privately.

I sank onto the bed in relief after throwing the courtyard doors open. The cool breeze swept into the room, billowing over me. When I started feeling better, I stretched my limbs out across the reeds as far as I could before shrinking my form back into a tight ball. I don't know when I decided to try to sleep, but just as I began to succumb to the feeling, I heard a throat clearing behind me. I turned to find Auset standing in the doorway between the bedroom and the sitting room.

I sat up, surprised. "You didn't need to check on me."

She pulled the door closed behind her. "I know, but I thought we should talk."

"Sure, of course," I told her, frowning. I motioned for her to join me on the bed, but she didn't move from her place. "What's going on, what's wrong?"

Auset hesitated, and then took a reluctant step towards me. "You are with child."

I looked up at her and found her stare just as penetrating as it had been at dinner. "How could you know that?" I asked, sliding my legs towards the edge of the bed and placing my feet on the ground.

"That is why you didn't eat tonight, and why you have been so sick during our tour? It is not the water that is affecting you, it is your pregnancy."

I nodded and kept my eyes upon her. "You saw the

symptoms, from all the work we've done. I should have known you would recognize it."

Auset shook her head and looked away. "There is only one reason why you would not share this joyous news with me." She paused and closed her eyes. "It is because there is bad news that comes along with it."

I inhaled sharply. Ausar could not have told her, I thought to myself, which means she is speculating. I tried to remain calm. "Why would you think this is joyous news? Being with child when I was not hoping to be is news I have not wanted to share."

"Perhaps you are not happy about it," my sister responded quietly, "but that is not why you didn't tell me."

"Why do you think I didn't tell you?"

Auset closed her eyes and sat on the ground, letting the silence stir around us for a few moments. When it was clear I was not going to budge, she sighed. "Ever since we returned from Anu and he left that night to find you..." She looked up at me, unwilling to hide the hurt. "How could I not notice my husband sneaking out of our bed? You both thought you were being discreet but it was so obvious, and I knew it was just a matter of time..."

Her voice trailed off as she looked away again. Now that she had been so direct, to deny her accusation would require a level of dishonesty that I was not prepared to assume. I sighed, holding back tears. "Auset -"

"No excuses, Nebt-Het. I have to accept this situation but I'm not going to listen to your attempts to make it okay." We looked at each other, letting the tension linger in our hesitation. "I haven't spoken to my husband about this yet, or yours, but we will need to do so very soon, before you begin to show."

I closed my eyes, wanting this to be an illusion, wanting the image of my sister to be conjured by my immense guilt, a simpler consequence of my shame. I sighed once more; I knew she would still be there when I opened my eyes.

"If it's all the same to you, I'd like to consult Seba before we go to our husbands," I told her firmly, knowing I had no power in this scenario but choosing to assert myself anyway. I looked down at her, and found her looking up at me. She nodded.

"Fine, we can do that. Tomorrow, first thing."

The door cracked open, and Setesh entered nervously, not knowing what he was interrupting. Auset stood. "I'm glad you're feeling better," she said to me, before nodding at my husband and leaving quickly. I reached out my hand to him and he clutched it tightly.

"Do you need anything?" he asked, looking for an explanation from me that I was unready to give. I tried to ease his concern with a smile, but I knew it didn't work.

"No, I'm fine; just lay down with me before you go." I pulled him down to the bed and folded my body inward once more. Setesh wrapped himself around me and kissed the back of my neck without asking what he didn't want to know, and it didn't take long before I drifted to sleep.

My siblings departed the great house shortly before the sun had reached its apex. I stayed behind, leaving them to complete the tour without me. Auset and I had already consulted with Djehuty and knew how we would proceed as soon as they returned from the final leg of the trip.

Setesh had been exceptionally attentive before leaving, reminding me of the early days of our marriage. "Are you sure you will be okay here, alone?" he'd asked, holding my face delicately, and searching my features for any sign that I would need him or the company of others.

I'd grabbed his hands gently and smiled to reassure him. "I have been here alone on many occasions," I said. "You must go, and I will stay."

He kissed me and dispersed so quickly and so close together, it felt as if I had been touched by nothing more than a light breeze. I had mixed feelings about being left alone, but I knew that staying behind was for the best, and the people of the land would not miss me in the least.

A few days after they'd gone, I woke to find Seshat standing over me, waiting for my afternoon nap to end. I sat up abruptly; she reached out her hand and I took it instinctively. In a blink we were home, the space fashioned as it had been on the day of our wedding, a hall filled with light, stretching out into forever.

I looked to her for answers, but she was gone. I tried to leave to no avail; I then tried to transform the surroundings in some way, but at this too I failed. I sighed and sat down, resigning myself to being stuck there, waiting for the reason to reveal itself.

"You don't have enough energy to do what you are trying to do," my great-grandfather's voice filled the space soundly, causing the sensation of the walls shaking. Of course, I knew the movement was only my perception, but it still caused me to shudder. "No need to stand, formalities are not necessary."

He sat beside me, keeping his eyes fixed on the nothingness spread before us. He did not move or speak for a while, until finally I could wait no longer. "What am I doing here?" I asked, the annoyance in my tone clear and unrestricted.

Ra chuckled. "You are here because I wanted you here." He shifted so that he could look down at me while still facing forward. "Your next question will be, why did I want you here. And I think you have some idea of why that is."

I didn't respond. "I was stubborn once. I did not embrace the future that was meant for me, meant for all of us. We both know how that turned out." He paused again. "You must know that you have already done what you were supposed to do."

I rolled my eyes and looked away, not wanting the Great Father to witness such insolence. "You say that only to ease my burden," I mumbled, unappreciative and not consoled in the least. "What I have done is wrong. I do not deserve your generosity."

Ra chuckled again and faced me. I turned towards him in response, keeping my eyes low, not meeting his gaze. "Even the worst of us enjoys my generosity," he responded contemplatively.

We sat there in silence for a bit, until he began to speak once more. "What does it behoove you to stay angry with yourself? Will you find the secret to changing the past this way? Will it improve your character?"

I sighed and conceded. "As always you speak wisdom Yit-Eah, but it is much too soon for me to behave as if what I've done was acceptable. How else can I be sure that I have learned my lesson, if not to remain angry and unforgiving?"

He chuckled once more, infinitely amused by my pain. "How else indeed."

"Do you believe Setesh will ever forgive me, or Auset?" I whispered, feeling in that moment that their embrace would give me permission to forgive myself.

"I believe that they will become who they were meant to, as will you. You can choose to embrace that truth, for better or worse, or you can fight it. I remind you that it is your choice."

He stood and gathered his heavy robes around him, his posture casting a shadow deep and long. I looked into his eyes for but a moment and I knew I'd seen eternity. "You have become more accustomed to the earth plane, and weighted by its fetters. You will carry your child for the same term as the women do. You will experience all that they do, and you will not have the strength to return here on your own until after you have given birth. The sage will be ever near, and through him you will see me. It is you who will turn your face to the heavens in the days to come."

The Great Father dispersed and left me to my wounds. I had just enough strength to travel home on my own, but he was right, my body was no longer my own. I felt an unnatural stirring within me, and I thought to be happy, but would not be.

My siblings would be gone for two more weeks. When they returned I would have to hide my showing for a day or two, but I knew we would not have much time before everything would be revealed, either from protruding evidence, or purposeful honesty. A few times during the wait I called out to Auset, hoping she would hear me and visit, and we could assist each other with preparing for the moment to come, but she either did not or would not hear me. My calls went unanswered and I was left to myself. I had been in the per eah without my siblings many times, but this was the first time I was ever alone.

He leaned in to kiss me, and I turned my head, giving him my cheek. Setesh hesitated before pecking me, softly and quickly. I turned from him; if he hugged me or reached out in any way, that would be the end of my secret and I could not let him find out that way.

"You seem distant," he stated the obvious. I sighed and gave him my back.

"I just feel drained, is all," I mumbled, just loudly enough for him to hear me. "If it's okay with you, I would like to stay down the hall for the night."

He didn't respond or object, so I exited. I felt terrible at leaving his side like that when being in his presence was all I wanted at that moment, but I wasn't ready. Auset and I had a plan, and I had to stick to it. I owed it to her not to go against my word.

Dinner was tense; in fact the next three days were impossible. I avoided everyone as much as possible, and at mealtime I entered last and stayed the longest. I had already begun to loosen the waist on my garments, but the men saw me so infrequently that they had no time to notice.

Auset noticed, however, and finally she was ready to move forward. After the third dinner, we waited in the sitting room of her apartment; Auset on a stool along the back wall, and I in an armchair near the bedroom door. Neither of us stood when Ausar came in, causing him to look at both of us suspiciously. He closed the door behind him tightly as he interpreted the tension of the room.

"You told her?" he asked me calmly, looking at Auset.

Auset cleared her throat. "She didn't have to."

Ausar looked at me, surprised. I didn't look away or hide my face; the time for shame had passed. He nodded and steadied himself. "Okay. What does this mean, then, that both of you are here?"

I looked to Auset, who was glaring at her husband. "Are you not even going to say you're sorry?" she asked him, blood boiling.

He sat in the armchair that was furthest away from where we were sitting. I was impressed by how well he was keeping his composure. "Perhaps you and I should discuss this without Nebt-Het?"

Auset scoffed. "There is no need for secrets between us now."

"I am certain you two need to speak without me," I interjected, seeing the direction this was going, "but for now, let me say what I need to say and then I will go."

My sister looked back to me, which oddly had a calming effect upon her. She rose from the stool where she had been waiting and moved to sit in the armchair next to me. I looked across the room at Ausar, who was hiding his nerves, keeping his breath steady.

"I am going to tell Setesh tonight that I am with child," I started, releasing both of their gazes and keeping my eyes averted to the floor. "The problem with that is, Setesh is infertile. We have known that he could not impregnate me for a very long time. So he will know..."

"...he will know that you have been with someone else," Ausar finished for me, mumbling. He fell back into his chair, composure broken.

I blinked and looked to Auset, who, despite her anger, was responding to her husband's distress with compassion. Her eyes were filling with tears. I reached out for her hand, and she responded in kind.

"There is no way to get around telling him about what happened between us." I looked back to him, still holding my sister's hand. "I know what this will do to him, but the evidence is already visible, and there is not a chance that I can keep it a secret much longer."

Ausar nodded without speaking. Once more I looked at Auset, hoping she would speak, but she didn't. They were staring at one another in a way they had never before. I let go of her hand and exited the sitting room, entering the hall, taking a deep breath. I stood there for as long as I could before I set off to find Setesh. No matter how long I delayed, I would never be prepared for this conversation.

I found him in our courtyard, bathing meditatively. I stood there silently as long as I could before coughing to let him know I was there. Once he'd opened his eyes, he smiled at me and wordlessly motioned for me to join him. I shook my head no, choosing instead to sit cross-legged along the opposite edge of the pool. I kept my eyes on him, and watched as he sat up, knowing to prepare for something bad, not knowing it would be the worst. I almost didn't speak, but eventually, it poured out. I am pregnant, I said. With your brother's child, I said.

Setesh didn't look angry, but content. It was as if he had expected it, or had known all along, and was just thankful that I had chosen to be honest. This response rattled me. I had steeled myself for a verbal beating, and Setesh barely batted an eye. I let the silence settle in.

Setesh nodded and looked away from me. "I suppose congratulations are in order," he started, his voice sounding even and genuine. "Our kingdom will have an heir."

I frowned, confused. "I am not his wife, you know that's not how it works," I said, tilting my head. "Don't you have something you want to say, to me?"

He shook his head and slumped back into the pool. "Do you want me to be happy for you?" I still couldn't detect any sarcasm in his tone. "I thought you were okay with never having children. If I knew you were not, we could have discussed it; you didn't have to go behind my back. Still, if you are getting what you want, then good for you."

"I didn't want a child. I don't - I, I didn't do this for a child," I cried out in response. This was worse than being yelled at.

He looked back to me. Finally I could see an emotion, not the anger I was expecting, but disappointment instead. Hurt. I almost collapsed under its weight. "Then why did you do this?" he whispered, when I would have given anything to hear him shout. "Why would you do this?"

I looked down to avoid his stare. It was an appropriate yet impossible question. Because you are unreasonable? Because you are too sensitive? Because you fight all the time, with me and with everyone? Because you left me here? Except I couldn't say any of those things, because he wasn't the one who had done this.

I was.

I couldn't hold back my tears any longer, and Setesh got out of the pool and left me to them, on the ground, unable to move. My body curled itself up into a ball as I wept, guttural sounds emitting from me, rattling my spirit. There were so many things I could have tried to say, but the answer that would have mattered was the thing I couldn't say. That Setesh and I had suffered from the same insecurities, and yet he had taken the higher path, the harder path. That I had looked for validation in every place except myself. That he had never betrayed any of us, despite our frustrations with his attitude, arrogance, anger. That I had betrayed him and broken my promise. That I had failed.

I couldn't begin to say how long I'd lain there, but eventually, I cried myself to sleep. When I woke, I was no longer in our courtyard, but was in our bed, the air thick and hard to breath. I cried into the night, and no one came to disturb me, or stop me. When finally light began to blanket me, I knew I had to rise.

After bathing I slipped into the hallway as quietly as I could, looking to gauge the atmosphere of the house from a distance before making my presence known. The hallways were completely empty; it appeared that not a single attendee was on duty, an oddity. I walked towards the great hall, where the presence of a commotion began to disturb me; I could hear my husband's voice.

"This is the first child to be born to our generation, brother," I could hear Setesh say, with a convincing pleasantness to his tone, causing me to frown. "Of course I forgive you, and congratulate you, for this is such a momentous occasion."

I stepped into the threshold and was quickly taken aback by the sight. Setesh was standing next to Ausar, who was beginning to smile in acceptance of the generous words of forgiveness from his brother. Across the room Auset was being hugged by our mother, with Seshat by her side, and Djehuty in another corner speaking in hushed tones with our grandmother, Tefnut; their faces lit up as they noticed me at the door. Tefnut rushed to me and enveloped me in her arms, her soft tears blanketing my forehead.

"Your mother and I cannot stay for long but we could not resist an opportunity to congratulate you, our daughter," Tefnut whispered into my ear. She released me and stepped back to take me in once more, realizing that I was already showing, reaching down to touch my pregnant belly as though a curiosity. "What a wonder that you are to be mother to a god, and while fully incarnate. It is a miracle."

Auset and Nut had made their way over to me, and Seshat and Djehuty had moved closer to where my brothers talked. I didn't know how to respond, so I didn't, allowing them to fawn over me until a loud clap silenced the room; an announcement.

"I must insist that we celebrate this unexpected and wonderful development," Setesh called out, his voice light and joyous. I shook my head emphatically, ready to object. "My brother has agreed to allow me to plan a festival in his honor, to celebrate the coming of his firstborn."

Auset's face beamed, but her eyes were hard as iron. "What a wonderful idea," she said to the group, her calm exterior serving as confirmation for all.

I turned to Auset, reaching for her arm so I could have a word with her, but my mother interceded with a tight hug and three kisses to my cheek. I smiled as I thought she expected me to, and when she pulled away I glanced to the side for my sister, who had gone without a word. Tefnut and Nut took me by my hands and led me into the courtyard, and we sat in the garden while they shared stories of motherhood, although I must confess to not hearing a single one, my mind so fully occupied with the idea of celebrating an occasion that was not a blessing in the least.

I heard a knock at the door to the apartment. "Please, let yourself in," I said to whomever it was, hoping that I would not have to rise from my bed of reeds.

Setesh came in carefully, as if he thought I would kick him out once I knew it was him. "The attendees told me that you moved all of your things down here," he said delicately.

"I had no opportunity to tell you myself, as you have been with Ausar all day, discussing plans for the festival. Besides," I added, likely sounding rather testy, "I did not find it prudent to continue to sleep in my marital bed while carrying the child of another."

He nodded without coming in further, standing near the door as if only a guest. "You did not need to do that for my sake. I am not angry with you, and I don't want you gone."

I shook my head. "You should be angry, and you should want me gone." I looked up at him, searching his features for a sign. "Why do you want to throw a festival?"

Setesh sighed and looked around for an armchair; finding one, he took a seat and stretched his limbs wide. "Do you remember how hard it was to respect him in the beginning? When he was fumbling around, making mistake after mistake, unsure of every decision?"

I smiled and looked away. "Yes, I remember. You were so angry; you thought he should know everything all at once. You couldn't believe he didn't know what he was doing."

"And you were so patient with me. You kept telling me to let him get his bearing, and to support him, and to remember the importance of unity." Setesh chuckled. "I never thought your words would be applicable to a scenario such as this, but here we are."

I sighed. "So you are doing this for show, then? A show of unity? Are you truly angry then? Please, you can be honest with me, I am your wife."

"Are you? Because in the moment when you should have proved that, you instead gave yourself to another," he hissed at me, finally letting his anger sneak out. His eyes lit with fire and his frown darkened the entire room, causing me to tremble. He exhaled sharply, trying to pull his emotions back in. "I am doing this because I truly believe you are sorry - you are BOTH sorry - and I am hoping that I will find a way to forgive you. I desperately want to forgive you."

I looked down into my lap. "To know that you want to forgive me means everything right now. I do not know if you will be able to, but I appreciate that you will try." I looked across the room, hoping to influence him with direct eye contact. "And I will do whatever I can to make that easier for you, but please, do not have this celebration. I can't go through with that, I just... this is humiliating enough for all of us, we can do without the public spectacle." I couldn't tell if my pleas were making any impact upon him; he'd averted his eyes away from me and instead focused on the floor, hunched over with his elbows on his knees. "Husband, please hear me. Don't you understand that this is a mistake? What we did was a mistake, it was wrong and it is not worthy of celebrating."

"You will do what I ask you to do? What you must do to earn my forgiveness?"

I shook my head. "You are going to say that I must do this or I will never earn it. I know you will. Setesh, there must be something else I can do."

He looked up at me, his countenance sinister and cold.

"There will be plenty more for you to do. You will do all of those things, and this as well."

Setesh stood and walked over to the bed until his frame hovered above mine with an imposing sense of dominance. "Tomorrow the attendees will move all of your things back to our apartment, and if you are to sleep anywhere outside of our bed for the remainder of your pregnancy, you will ask my permission first. You will take no more night walks and you will be with me whenever I request your presence."

"You can't be serious!" I objected, my voice betraying my surprise, and my fear.

"I can be and I am." He turned to exit, but stopped at the door. "It has been hard to have me as a husband, and now you have made it hard to have you as a wife."

The great room was filled to bursting, and the commotion loud and happy, with smiles covering every face but three.

Even Ausar had relaxed completely into the festival, shaking hands with all those in attendance, and receiving every congratulations with warmth and gratitude. He walked into the room wearing the double crown, leopard skin draped atop his left shoulder, thick gold cuffs glittering from each wrist. Ausar was the picture of confidence and pride, leaving Auset and myself at the front alone to feign our excitement. Auset wore her crown and usekh without flinching, her chin stoic and face steeled, firm. She looked lovely in her royal blue, lovely and miserable.

I watched the room carefully, trying not to look nervous but certain that my apprehension was apparent on my face. I was not used to being placed as the equal to Hmt Naswu, and my place across from her upon the dais felt unnatural and unearned. It did not help that I wasn't sure who these people were that Setesh had invited; none of the other Ntru were there, not even Seba or Seshat. After a while I assumed that our guests were important persons from throughout the kingdom - generals and governors and priests, men and women who were appointed as leaders in their region or nome. They must be here to extend their congratulations on behalf of their people, I reasoned, but still suspicious, for I had participated in our recent tour, and did not remember meeting any of these people in all that time.

I had no choice but to let it go. I instead turned my attention to my siblings, wishing that any one of them would look upon me with a friendly glance, but Auset refused to peek in my direction, and Ausar was too busy conferring with his adoring fans. I was not given an opportunity to ask Ausar to change his mind at any point during the weeks of planning, as Setesh was true to his word and refused to let me out of his sight. I'd even hoped Auset would try to stop this from happening, but she never once objected in any of the discussions. I'd entered the hall tonight feeling marginalized and insignificant, even though mine was the belly bearing the child of honor.

I glanced over to my far right, where Auset was sitting in her place as our Queen. Setesh knelt before her and whispered something which caused her to frown. She appeared to whisper back before he stood and spoke again. Her face was clearly pained, but she did not rise immediately; instead she took her time, standing carefully to not draw attention to herself, and then quietly making her way towards the door. I stood to follow her, but Setesh quickly crossed the dais and placed his hand on my shoulder.

"You cannot leave yet, dearest sister," he hissed, pushing me back into my seat. "I am almost ready to present Naswt Biti with his gift."

"What did you say to her?" I whispered back angrily, my attention placed firmly on the door.

He let go of my shoulder and walked around to the front of my seat. "Nothing that she has not already said to herself." Setesh called the room to attention, and everyone fell silent. "Can I compel Naswt Biti to take his place beside the mother of his child?"

Ausar ascended the dais and sat in his throne, placed center stage. "Perhaps we should not start without our Hmt Naswu. Do you know where she has gone off to?"

Setesh blinked. "She was not feeling well, and said she needed a moment. I can send someone after her if you like." He turned and motioned for an attendee, but Ausar stopped him quickly. "No, she will return when she is able. We can proceed without her."

I thought I noticed the hint of a smile in the creases around Setesh's eyes, but it came and went so quickly that I decided that I must have been mistaken. I looked at Ausar who was beaming, looking upon my weight with pride.

"Before I present your gift to you, Naswt Biti, I would like for you to preside over a contest." Setesh waved his hand, and in marched at least ten attendees, carrying a heavy and elaborate chest on their shoulders. They placed it down upon a large table in the center of the room, and all of the eyes in the room grew in wonder, including my own. The chest was made of a dark, rich wood, decorated with gemstones from across the kingdom, including emeralds and lapis lazuli, and gold. It shone brightly and demanded everyone's attention, which it immediately had.

Setesh cleared his throat. "Whoever can fit within this chest exactly shall be the winner of this beautiful prize. Anyone here is eligible to try, just climb in, one at a time, and you must fit the dimensions perfectly - not too large, or too small, or too short, or too tall. Is there anyone who is interested in taking home this chest designed by me, commander of the armies of the two lands?"

Ausar sat up in his seat and watched as guest after guest tried and failed to fit the dimensions of the chest. Even a few of our attendees tried to climb in, to no avail; it appeared that no one would meet the qualifications as put forth by our commander.

The energy in the room appeared to be waning, as no one had won or even came close to winning. Just then Ausar stood. "You said anyone here is eligible to try, correct?"

Setesh hesitated. "Yes, anyone here, but Naswt Biti -"

"I am here, and I would like to try to win this chest for myself." Ausar began to make his way down from the dais and towards the center of the room.

Setesh attempted to stop him once more. "Naswt Biti, don't you think it makes more sense for someone who is not of the royal house to be gifted with this lovely chest? One of the people should be allowed to take this home."

I realized then that something was wrong, and stood as quickly as a pregnant woman could, which created the opportunity for me to make my second realization - I was surrounded by guards, three men from the corps who faithfully served their commander, and they were armed. I remembered the words of Ra, and knew how powerless I was to disperse, to run, to find my sister. Yet Ausar was oblivious to all of this, and Setesh had him right where he wanted him.

Ausar smiled at Setesh and patted him on the shoulder. "You said yourself that anyone here can try. If I am the winner I will happily give the chest away but I have the right to compete as does anyone else here."

Setesh obliged our king. "As you wish, Naswt Biti." He stepped out of the way and allowed Ausar to climb into the chest. Ausar stretched out his limbs comfortably, finding that the chest fit his every dimension exactly.

"Ausar, get out of the chest!" I shouted, giving the guards a reason to restrain me, their pull gentle and their grip tight and convincing. But it was too late; even if he had heard me, he certainly didn't heed my words.

"I fit exactly! I am the winner of the contest, and the chest is mine!" Ausar cried out excitedly, one moment before the lid of the chest fell upon him, trapping him within.

"And it shall be yours forever!" Setesh snarled, binding the edges of the chest with heka, sealing it completely so that no air could get in and no one could get out. I could hold myself back no longer and began to push against the men restraining me, a searing, high pitched shriek ringing in my ears as it tumbled out of me, over and over. I fell back into my seat as he nodded to the men in the room and they gathered around to carry the coffin off to parts unknown.

Setesh then approached me, eyes red with fire. "Nice try to warn him, but you were too late."

I tried to stand, but the guards' hands on my shoulders kept me seated. "Where are they taking him?"

Setesh snickered and sat in the throne beside me - Ausar's throne. "My men are going to throw the chest into the river, and without the ability to disperse or air to breathe, his physical form will die."

It took me a moment to respond to that most incredulous plan. "Are you serious? What are you doing, you can't do that!"

"Why can't I?" he threw at me angrily, continuing to snarl. "If this were not meant to happen don't you think someone would be here to stop it?" When I didn't speak right away, he continued. "Your precious Naswt Biti violated the laws of Maat. He committed adultery. He lied to all of us, all of his people, even to you. He lusted for his brother's wife and held covetous desires. He has made himself unfit to rule, so I am restoring the balance. "How can the people live in righteousness if their leaders refuse to do so?"

I blinked and scoffed. "Your words are noble, but your intentions are not. You want me to believe that you did this for the good of the kingdom? Why did you not simply hold a council meeting, ask the Ntru to remove Ausar from the throne? You chose to kill him to get revenge. You chose to indulge your own anger."

He turned to look at me. "You should be grateful my anger is directed at him and not you."

"Is that a threat?" I asked, fully taken aback. "Setesh, are you threatening me?"

Setesh stood. "That was not a threat, but this is." He stepped closer to me, once again hovering over me, succeeding in inspiring a sense of intimidation and alarm. "Only the power of Ra can undo the heka that I have done. If you conspire with your sister in any way, trying to get Ra to interfere, it will cost you, and your child." He turned to walk away. "I mean it, Nebt-Het. Stay out of it."

The room was plenty empty now, but the guards had not left my side, even as Setesh began to exit. "You can tell your men to back down," I called out to him. He stopped and turned around to answer me, this time his tone calm and even, and light. "Consider them your personal bodyguards for the time being. They will be with you day and night to make sure nothing happens to you. Your safety is most important to me."

"Now it is you who lie to me. And who will trap you in a chest and throw you into the river?"

Setesh smiled and left without another word. The three guards did not move until I made to stand. One of them kindly offered his arm to assist me to my feet, and they kept but a short distance behind me as I made my way down the hall, towards our apartment.

"Dua for the escort; I am surely safe here," I turned to tell them as I began to enter the sitting room.

The one in charge shook his head. "One of us will guard the door to the sitting room, but he will stand guard in the courtyard and I will be at the bedroom door. You must let us in."

I smiled. "So I am to have no privacy then."

The one assigned to the courtyard, the same one who had offered me his arm, looked away. "We will try to be as discreet as we can, but we cannot leave you unattended for even a moment."

I nodded and complied, having very little choice. I quickly decided I would sleep in what I was wearing when I entered the bedroom and found Auset laying upon my bed, looking as though she had cried herself to sleep. Whatever Setesh had told her was clearly meant to upset her and cause her to leave. I wanted to wake her, but what could I say with all of these men around? They would surely report any of my behavior to their leader.

The man in charge reached down to wake Auset, and I stopped him. "I'm sure you know she is no threat to me. She is already asleep, and she is still our Queen. You will treat her with respect."

He hesitated, but acquiesced. I lay beside her and took one of her hands in mine; imaging the agony she would be in when she wakes in the morning to find her husband gone. I didn't think I would sleep at all, but soon enough I found my thoughts drifting away.

I woke to find that my sister had not left, but was standing out in the courtyard, gazing at the mid-morning sun. She heard me rise and looked back in my direction, her expression puzzled and uneasy.

"Is there any reason why you have guards in your apartment? Are we in danger, what happened after I left the celebration last night?" Auset asked as she stepped into the bedroom, her tone filled with naive concern.

I tried to smile to avoid giving the guards a reason to feel alarmed. "Setesh is so worried about my pregnancy," I lied, hoping to sound convincing. "He figured I might go into labor when no one is around, so he came up with this plan to make sure I am never alone. Silly, right?" I added quickly, trying to sound lighthearted, but hoping this would be clue enough to my twin that something was off.

It was, and I saw the frown set in around her eyes, even as her lips and cheeks smiled in amusement. "Silly indeed," she added, in what was undoubtedly the last time the word would be used to describe my husband. Auset took my hand and led me into the courtyard, keeping enough space between us that our words would be easily heard. "I am not ready to leave your side yet, senet. Will you take a quick swim with me?"

I frowned but nodded, not knowing why she wanted to swim, but choosing to follow her lead. She turned away so that I could disrobe, and motioned to the guard to do the same. He obliged her immediately, and once I was securely under water, she did the same.

I smiled at Auset as she settled in on the opposite side of the pool. "This is actually quite soothing. I feel much lighter, surprisingly."

She nodded. "I thought you might." We fell silent, partly from enjoying the soak, and partly in an effort to proceed with care. Auset spoke first. "I am realizing that I am not as rested as I once thought. I want you to tell me all about last night but let me just enjoy the quiet for a little while longer."

"Gladly." We went quiet again, but this time I closed my eyes and leaned back on the edge of the pool. If the guard thought we were just napping, he wouldn't think to disturb us.

It wasn't long before I felt her light knocking on the door of my consciousness, and I relaxed enough to let her in. "Tell me the real reason why you have guards," Auset began immediately, not wasting any time.

I sighed deeply, and spat out the truth without hesitation. "Setesh thought to keep the guards around me to stop me from telling you what happened last night. He threatened my life if I interfere. He threatened my child's life."

I could hear Auset gasp from across the pool, but I needed to concentrate to keep from breaking the mental connection. Her thoughts started rushing in, panicked. "What did he do? Where is my husband? What happened, Nebt-Het?"

"You need to calm down, because if you react wildly I don't know what these men will try to do to either of us. Can you promise me you will stay calm?"

It was a ridiculous question; I figured as soon as I told her, there was no chance she would stay calm, but she had to try. Auset steadied her breathing and waited for me to continue.

"Last night was a trick, senet. Setesh took out his revenge on Ausar. He trapped him in a chest and had men from the army throw his body into the river." I paused for a moment to take a deep breath. "I don't know what condition his body is in, but I don't think he had enough air to live for very long in there. I, I... I think..."

There was silence between us, but Auset had not overreacted, and that was good. After a moment's pause she spoke again. "Why wouldn't Ausar just disperse out of the chest? I know we're all a bit weaker from living here for so long but he couldn't be that powerless."

I swallowed nervously. "Setesh sealed the chest with heka.

He said only the power of Ra is strong enough to break the seal."

She retreated entirely from my mind, pulling herself out of our connection. I opened my eyes to see her across from me, the tears welling up and beginning to spill out over her cheeks. Still, she didn't cry out. Instead, Auset dunked herself under to mask the water on her face, and stayed under for as long as she could. I sat motionless, waiting for her to reappear; she came up from under the water at the same time as Setesh found us out in the courtyard.

"There you are," Setesh said casually. "We have been looking for you all morning; I had no idea where you'd gotten to."

She wasn't ready to speak, so I thought to buy her some time. "I would think you would do a better job of reporting to your commander," I said to the guard nearest me, who was just realizing that perhaps he'd made a mistake. I then turned my attention back to Setesh. "Auset has been here all night. I suppose this means you were not here last night at all?"

He smirked at me. "No, I have been up planning my coronation ceremony." Auset looked up at him, her face betraying both her anger and surprise. "I'm sure my dear wife has found some way to tell you what's happened already. Your special twin sister connection is no secret to me." Setesh turned then to his guards. "Tell the others they are dismissed for now, but to be available this afternoon to answer for this. I cannot wait to hear why my wife was not alone when I specifically instructed you three to ensure she had no guests or visitors."

The guard looked scared for only a moment, and he glanced down at me before exiting. I knew I had taken advantage of his kindness, but Setesh would see it as weakness, and punish them accordingly. Still, I wasn't apologetic - Auset would have found out eventually, and this had to be the way.

The three of us were alone, and Setesh squatted at the edge

of the pool, continuing to smirk at the two of us. Auset wasn't a hostage there, she had enough strength to disperse out if she wanted to, but for whatever reason, she wouldn't leave me alone with him. I have to admit how grateful I was for her presence.

"I know you threatened my sister and our child's life if she told me what happened," Auset began, asserting her queenly authority as she had grown into doing. My eyebrows shot up, impressed by how bold and direct she had been.

Setesh shrugged casually. "She is safe as long as you and her do not attempt to leave the per eah or call on any of the other Ntru. I'm sure she told you there's nothing either of you can do anyway."

Auset looked at me directly and nodded. "I want you to promise me that she will be safe and her child will be safe no matter what. In return, I will sit next to you at your coronation and endorse you as our Naswt Biti."

"Auset, no," I interjected immediately. "You can't do that." I tried to stop her, but she held up her hand at me, and I stopped. She had a plan.

"No, Nebt-Het. I want Setesh to promise your safety and the safety of your child for as long as the boat of Ra sails across the body of Nut. If he can promise me this, I will endorse him in return."

Setesh stood suspiciously. "Why would you bargain that? You care that much of the safety of the woman who slept with your husband and their illegitimate child?'

Auset looked at him and brazenly stood, baring her entire self to us. "Ausar lied to me. He lied to all of us. No one can blame you for what you've done." She got out of the pool and grabbed the nearest cloth, covering herself while keeping her back to Setesh. "I understand that my sister is also wrong, but her child is innocent. You will promise me that they will be safe, or I will stand against you." She turned back to look at him, her eyes fierce and fiery. "You know that you cannot be Naswt Biti without my support. I AM Queen. And you also know that you cannot force me to give it. This is the only way, Setesh. Promise me."

He hesitated, and looked back at me as I sat there silently, desperately afraid to speak. I wanted so badly for him to reject her offer, for her and me to take a stand against him, to fight this. But Setesh had his eye on the throne, and Auset was ready to gift it to him with an ease that would be impossible for him to reject. "I accept your offer. I promise that I will not ever put Nebt-Het's life in danger, or the life of her child. As long as the sun rises and sets, they will be safe."

I exhaled what I'm sure he interpreted as a sigh of relief. "Don't get so excited, dearest sister," Setesh called over his shoulder as he made his exit. "I wouldn't start looking forward to a life of ease and comfort if I were you."

Neither of us moved until we heard him exit into the hall outside of the sitting room. I stood and began to get out of the pool. "Stay here, in the courtyard," Auset instructed me, in her queen tone. I nodded and began to dress as she dispersed. After a few minutes, she returned, taking my hand and pulling me into the bedroom. "I wanted to make sure we were fully alone. There are no guards, and Setesh is in the open field, meeting with his troops."

I closed the courtyard doors behind me. "What are you doing? You can't endorse him! If you do this, you legitimize everything he's done. Auset, what are you thinking?"

"I'm thinking that Setesh is not as smart as he thinks he is. I need him to feel safe, like he's beaten us, so I can sneak out and get Ausar back."

I shook my head, confused. "Didn't you hear me? He said only Ra can reverse the seal."

Auset smiled. "No, he said only the power of Ra. Our Great Father is not the only holder of his magic anymore."

I blinked, realizing what she was referring to. "You think you can reverse it, using his secret name?"

She nodded. "I know I can." Auset sat in an armchair and I sat on the bed facing her, anxious to hear this plan of hers. "I'm going to get him back, Nebt-Het. After the coronation, Setesh will feel like he's won, and he won't mind in the least that we're missing. He'll think there's nothing we can do to stop him; he won't even bother to look for us. We can go and find Ausar and give my husband the ceremony that he deserves, and then we will find a way to end the reign of Setesh."

I hesitated. "Not we, Auset. You."

That wasn't the response she was expecting. "You need to go with me, Nebt-Het. I'm going to need your help."

I sighed heavily. "I can't leave like this, Auset. I can't."

My sister stood and moved closer to me, and I could see her anger bubbling to the surface. "So sleeping with my husband is something you can do, but when I ask you to help me make it right, you CAN'T?"

"I am perfectly clear about who is responsible for all of this. I just can't go with you."

She scoffed and turned away from me, her head shaking back and forth wildly. When she finally looked back at me, her eyes were wide and she pointed at me furiously. "You got my husband killed, Nebt-Het. I will never, EVER, forgive you for that."

I looked up at her in disbelief. "But you forgive him? How is that right? He lied to you just like I did, he broke your trust, but you forgive him and not me?"

"We are twins, we look exactly alike. He probably didn't even know what he was doing, but you did." Auset didn't move from her spot, and her voice rang steadily with conviction. "What did you do, wear my colors? Put on my oils? What did you do, Nebt-Het, how did you trick my husband?"

I kept my eyes on her, returning her piercing stare with one of my own. It was my turn to be filled with rage. "You know *exactly* what happened and you know I did none of those things."

My sister looked away, crossing her arms over her chest. "You're right, I'm sorry," she said, starting to calm down. "I don't mean to be irrational, I am just so... angry."

"And you have every right to be, senet. You are right to demand me to go with you, I owe you that much, I owe you more than that, but you have to know that I can't."

She looked back to me and sat on the ground in front of me, shaking her head back and forth, trying to comprehend the situation. "Do you really think if you stay here, Setesh is going to forgive you?"

I chuckled and looked away. "No, my husband will dangle the carrot of forgiveness in front of me for a million years, always keeping it just out of my reach. There is not a single thing I can do to earn it. He will never grant it and I can never earn it, I know."

Auset looked to me just as I was looking back to her. "It really is because of the baby, then? You really think staying here is the best thing for your child, with Setesh angry with you? He's only going to get worse, Nebt-Het. You know how he is, and he's going to be completely unreasonable now." She slid across the floor closer to me, and reached for my hand. I took hers in mind, keeping the grip light. "You really think we can trust that promise of his?"

I smiled, but even without seeing myself I knew it probably wasn't convincing. "Setesh isn't going to hurt me, at least not physically. He'll keep his promise in the most creative of ways." I swallowed and frowned, not wanting to look her in the eye any longer. "You can't do what you need to do with me tagging along, Auset. I am too heavy, I can't disperse and I can't run. You are taking a risk assuming he won't come after us, a risk I don't want you to have to take, a risk that lessens if you leave me here. He might let you go, but he will chase me to the ends of the universe, I am sure of that. Besides, you'll have to take a ship if you take me with you, and if you take a ship, he will catch you. He will catch us both."

Auset sighed heavily, and I continued. "You have to get Ausar back. What we did was wrong, but you're right, he deserves better than this. We can't just let Setesh throw his body into the river, and you are the only one who can do something about it."

"I just, I wish I didn't have to do this alone," she mumbled, and I looked down to see her staring at the ground, looking genuinely afraid for the first time in centuries. As pregnant as I was, I needed to be down there with her, and so I slipped off the bed onto the floor and pulled her into my arms.

She didn't cry, but she did relax once in my embrace. Her head rested on my shoulder, and I touched my chin to her crown, my arms around her shoulders. We sat like that for a while.

"We've never been separated like this before," she said eventually, without moving. I didn't let her go either; I wasn't ready to.

"No, not like this. But Auset, I think this is the only way."

"I think you are right." She began to pull herself out of my lap, and I let her go, reluctantly. She sat up next to me and sighed. "I am going to leave right after his coronation, and I don't know how long I will be gone."

I nodded. "You will be gone however long it takes."

Auset looked at me somberly. "Promise me you won't tell Setesh where I've gone. Can you distract him and give me a head start? He may come after me but I want to have a chance."

"I won't tell him where you're headed, and I won't tell him that you are able to reverse the heka. I'll do what I can, anything I can, to keep him off your scent."

"I will come back as soon as I have him, Nebt-Het. As soon as I have his body, I will return, and we will perform the ceremony and leave this place together, for good."

I smiled. "I will wait for you, sister, I swear it."

Ka- Spirit

The air was thick and balmy on the eve that Setesh was initiated as Naswt Biti, humid and difficult to breathe. The room looked as it had during the first coronation we attended, with red in place of the blue fabrics of prior. Auset did not participate, as only her presence in all of her royal finery was required to assuage the concerns of the populace. She sat on her throne atop of the dais as witness and endorsement, barely flinching throughout the ceremony. Her baldness was the only sign that she was in mourning, as Auset had cut off her hair the day after Ausar was killed, and for now there would be no confusing sister for sister.

I thought I would be allowed to miss the occasion, but attendance was my obligation as a member of the royal house. I dressed plainly and kept myself out of sight, standing to the side while I watched the priests take my husband through the sacred rite.

Setesh had filled the room with supporters, men from the warrior corps whose families had followed his leadership for generations, men who had inherited the spirit of combat from their fathers and their fathers' fathers. Their energy was cold and stifling, which only made it harder for Auset and I to pretend to smile.

We thought we were to have dinner alone that night, presuming that Setesh would continue to celebrate well into the evening, but we had no such luck. Shortly after sitting down, he came striding into the room, bringing with him a heavy gust of wind and two bodyguards. They stood post at the door while he deliberately headed for his seat at the head of the table. Auset and I looked at each other and stood, reluctantly, for our new King.

"Don't look so glum, ladies," Setesh said sarcastically, sitting with as much flourish as his austere sensibility could muster. "Today is a joyous day, and we should be celebrating together, as a family." He grinned at me, the curl of his lips sinister, before returning his expression to the scowl that I was most used to.

Auset sat first, and I waddled behind her slowly. "We are certainly pleased that the kingdom will have clear and decisive leadership," Auset responded evenly. "The people need to know whose direction to follow, and now they have their guide."

Setesh relaxed even further, hearing her sensible words. It had been easier than I'd thought to convince Setesh that we were defeated, with Auset offering a few strategically placed words to soothe his ego and me sulking, feigning defeat. He relished the sight of my displeasure and found comfort in what he assumed was the sentiment that he shared with Auset - their triumph over the two who had betrayed them.

The attendees began to bring out the food, which no longer caused me any sickness, but instead I found myself snacking constantly, craving the sweetness of figs and the sharp taste of onions - always together. It was odd enough to cause Auset to look at me suspiciously, and as with most things concerning my pregnancy, Setesh was rudely fascinated by it.

"I am surprised you made it to the coronation," he started, breaking the silence after we'd settled into our meal. "The attendees tell me you are sleeping all the time."

I swallowed hard and looked at him. "I rested this morning before the ceremony. I made sure someone woke me in time."

He rolled his eyes and mumbled, "It wouldn't have mattered

if you were there or not, really." Setesh shrugged his shoulders and looked at Auset to see if she would condone or condemn him. She hesitated for a moment, eventually choosing to smile. "I agree that it would not have affected the outcome of the ceremony."

I shook my head and looked away, tired of this conversation. "Exactly, Auset," Setesh responded, sitting up straighter and turning his attention to her. "You are exactly right. What can she do? Nothing. You are so right."

"If it is okay with you, I will excuse myself," I said as I began to stand, the process taking much longer than it used to.

Setesh watched me before responding, directing his words at Auset. "This is the spectacle that your husband found so irresistible. You should be ashamed that he was willing to betray you for that," Setesh spat out mockingly. I froze, surprised, but true to form, our sister took it in stride.

"I imagine that he is regretting that choice, wherever he is now," Auset responded sincerely, looking across at me. I sighed; even though I knew she was pacifying our brother, it didn't stop my feelings from being hurt.

Finally Setesh answered my request, waving his hand at me dismissively. "Go, get out of my sight."

I nodded at him, then Auset, before fleeing the room, his laughter loud and resonant against my back. I took a deep breath and headed to my sister's apartment, where I was going to prepare for her departure.

Immediately upon entering I began to sort through the two large trunks in her bedroom, filling one with only clothing of Ausar, and the other with her attire. I closed both trunks and looked out into the hallway for an attendee, calling Kasna down to me. "Hmt Naswu asked me to get rid of her husband's things," I told her, pointing at the trunk holding the clothing of our former King. "Please see to it that this trunk makes its way down to the temple, perhaps there are things they would like to preserve."

She looked at me nervously, but nodded. I touched her hand lightly before she turned away. "Please let me know as soon as this is done, and if you can tell me when I am with Naswt, that would be most preferred."

"Should I let him know what I am doing now, or wait until it is done?" Kasna asked cautiously. I smiled; she was the right one for the job.

"Don't disturb him until it is complete. I appreciate your thoughtfulness on this matter." She nodded her understanding, then left to make the arrangements. I said a quick prayer of gratitude that she was in the right place at the right time before heading towards the dock, hoping to find the ship that Auset preferred to travel in when touring the countryside. Thankfully it was there, all of the pieces of our plan fitting together like magic.

One of the men on board went to fetch the shipmaster for me, so I wouldn't have to climb the awkward rope ladder. He came out quickly, surprised that it was I who summoned him.

"Hmt Naswu is planning to leave late tonight for a vacation in the lower land," I told him, hoping to be forgiven of my little lie. "She would like for you to take her, if your ship is not destined for other harbors."

The shipcaptain smiled proudly and broadened his chest. "I will have everything ready for her departure. It won't take me long, she can come here as soon as she's ready."

I nodded. "Please send someone to the per eah to pick up her trunk as soon as possible, dua, and she will be bringing a few attendees along with her."

He nodded his consent, and I made my way back to the house, going in the direction of my apartment to rest and avoid drawing suspicion upon me, happening upon my sister in the hall.

"There you are," Auset started breathlessly, as if she had been running. "Is everything set then?"

I motioned to her to keep her voice down, and took her by the hand, leading her into the sitting room of my quarters. "I think so; I'm just waiting to hear the final word. But everything is in motion."

Auset peeked back into the hall, then once into the bedroom, to make sure we were alone. "I might not get another chance to say goodbye," she whispered, taking both of my hands into hers. "Are you sure you don't want to come with me?" she pleaded, and I almost felt it was for her more than it would be for me.

I nodded. "I'm sure. You have to go, Auset."

She nodded back. "Okay. I will send word to you when I return. As soon as I get back."

I nodded again, and smiled. We looked at each other for a moment longer before hugging tightly. I knew we had nothing to be nervous about; we had worked out every single detail and gone over it many times in our minds. All she had to do was leave.

She pulled back and looked at me once more, taking in my sight, before heading down to her quarters, where she would sit until it was time for her ship to depart. I stepped out into the hallway, looking to find Setesh. I needed to be with him when the attendee returned from the Temple.

It wasn't long before I spotted him sauntering through the house, enjoying his first night as Naswt Biti. He saw me watching him and smiled, coming over to join me outside of our apartment.

"You never believed this moment would ever come to pass," he started, his tone joking, but I frowned, not sure of his intention. "No, I suppose I did not," I answered, keeping my eyes on him. "But then again, so many things have happened that I never believed would," I added thoughtfully.

Setesh nodded and leaned against the wall next to me. I almost stepped away, surprised by how close he'd gotten. "I actually owe you a debt of gratitude, you know," he told me, true sincerity in every word, confusing me further.

"You don't think I slept with Ausar so you could become Naswt Biti, do you?"

He chuckled. "No, not on purpose, and I can't imagine that you meant to get yourself pregnant, yet here we are. You did what you did and, as a result, I am now King. I don't think I would be if it were not for you. I am grateful."

I nodded. "I suppose you are welcome, then."

"When are you going to deliver yourself of that child?" his voice filled with frustration. "You are making me tired watching you be tired."

I smiled at him, this moment causing me to relax. "I am experiencing a full earth term pregnancy," I reminded him, "so I must wait until my waters flow."

Setesh looked away, his face pained by thoughts of my child. I wanted to touch or kiss him, but that part of who we were was long gone. I lowered my head, guilty of what we had lost. Neither of us spoke or moved until we heard someone clear a throat in front of us.

"Excuse me, Seret," Kasna spoke cautiously, keeping one eye on Setesh, "the trunk that you asked me to move, it has been delivered."

I nodded. "And it was the trunk with Ausar's things, correct?"

She looked nervous, as she probably had not stopped to check what was in the trunk, but had only followed my orders. "Tu, it was the trunk that you and Hmt wanted disposed of."

I frowned; I didn't want her to dispose of it, but only to deliver it to the Temple. I tilted my head and looked at her for a moment longer, not ready to dismiss her yet.

"I did with the trunk exactly as you commanded of me, Seret," Kasna asserted, giving me her full attention. I understood then; she was not sure if I wanted Setesh to know where the trunk had gone, so she was dancing around that detail.

I smiled and made a mental note to reward her for her excellent attention to this matter. "Dua, you are dismissed for the evening." She curtseyed and backed away as was the custom before turning to head to her home for the night.

Setesh had listened quietly to the exchange, but it had certainly piqued his interest. I moved to enter our apartment and he followed me with a slew of questions. "So, Auset decided to get rid of Ausar's things?"

"Tu, she thought it was time."

"And they're no longer here?"

"As of this evening, his trunk has been removed from the per eah."

"ALL of his clothing? ALL of his garb?"

I smiled. "Tu, all of it."

"She had them thrown out, disposed of?"

I hesitated. I could tell him the truth, which had been our plan, or I could lie, which might buy Auset additional favor when he discovered that she'd moved out. "I think she intended to have his things destroyed, you know, anything that didn't belong to the realm," I said cautiously, slowly. "She didn't speak to you about it first?"

"No," Setesh mumbled, sitting in one of the armchairs. "When did she pack up his things?"

I hesitated again. "She asked me to do it, and I packed everything after dinner. She said she couldn't bear to look at it," I added, which really was true. Auset had practically cried at the suggestion of moving his clothing and garb out of the great house, but she relented when she realized how it would support her departure.

I looked over at him, and he was nodding, taking it all in. "I hope I didn't do something I should not have," I said quickly, wanting to gauge his reaction. "It really seemed like the best thing, so that both she and our kingdom can move on."

Setesh looked up at me solemnly. "For once you've done something right." I wanted to roll my eyes, but I resisted the urge. "I will have to speak with her in the morning about a new title. It doesn't make sense to call her the wife of the King unless she plans to become my wife. We shall see how that goes."

I couldn't let that get to me, even though that was the intention. "Is it okay if I retire? I am in desperate need of rest."

He nodded, and I curtseyed and moved into the bedroom, closing the door behind me. I knew there was no chance Setesh would sleep here tonight; he and I had not shared a bed since before the party. I had asked him to let me move out permanently on multiple occasions, which he vehemently refused each and every time. I also had no idea where he was resting his head, but I was in no position to demand that information, or to behave as if his decision was an affront to our marriage.

With the doors to the sitting room shut behind me, I cracked the doors to the open courtyard, letting in a chilly, soft breeze. I stood there for a few moments, breathing deeply, before fully retiring, still clothed, expecting an abrupt disturbance first thing in the morning.

I woke suddenly the next morning, hot air spewing in from the west, the dry desert wind coating the walls of my sleeping quarters. Setesh must not have realized that Auset was gone, or else how had I been allowed to sleep to the middle of the morning?

I quickly accepted my good fortune and disrobed, deciding to take a long bath before heading for a meal. I no longer had any responsibilities on the council, and there was no need for my involvement with household duties, so with Setesh in charge I officially had no place where I needed to be.

The water running from the Hapi into my underground pool was warmer than usual, causing the baby in my womb to move around anxiously for a moment before settling low, a less than comfortable resting place but one I had grown accustomed to. I rubbed my belly in the spot where I thought I would feel the baby's head, in what I hoped was a soothing motion. It was actually more relaxing for me than I'd expected, and I sighed deeply and leaned back against the edge of the pool lazily.

After a luxurious soak, I rose from the pool to get dressed and discern the mood of the per eah, hoping to gauge from the attitudes of the attendees what energy the Naswt was giving off today. In an oversized white caftan, I stepped out into the hall and headed straight for the kitchen, crossing paths with smiling attendees who were performing their duties calmly and even-paced.

I could hear Setesh speaking before I even crossed the threshold to the kitchen. Surprised by the idea that he would be engaged in casual discussion with the help, I peered around the frame of the door, hoping not to be seen. He was there with his new commander, a general who had risen quickly through the ranks and had clearly made quite an impression. I decided to make my presence known so I could look at his face better; I was very certain he was one who'd attended that awful festival and his appointment was likely a reward for participating in mutiny.

"There you are, dear wife," Setesh's voice rang out in a light hearted tone that immediately unsettled me. I slowed my walk into the room and curtseyed to him, obeying protocol since we were not the only ones in the room.

"Had you been looking for me, Naswt?" I hoped my question sounded casual but I suspected that my nerves were very clear.

He shrugged and looked away. "No, I don't think I would have any trouble finding you if that were my wish." Setesh waved at his general and the man bowed and exited, leaving us alone in the kitchen. I looked around at the shelves filled with jars and bags of grain strewn along the edge of the walls before fixing my gaze on my husband, who was watching me purposefully. His stare caused me to shift with discomfort but I didn't move my eyes from his.

"Your sister's left the great house," he announced casually, without moving. My eyebrows went up, but other than this, I refused to twitch.

"Did she tell you she was leaving?" I asked, hoping not to betray her, or myself.

He smiled softly and it did not leave his face as fast as I was accustomed to. "No, she did not, but she told you." When I didn't respond, he resumed his regular scowl. "Don't try to deny it. I know you were the one who spoke to the ship captain last night."

I nodded. "I did help her make the arrangements."

"So then," Setesh asked, taking one large, commanding step towards me, "why didn't you tell me?"

My heart began to beat faster, but still I made not only sudden movement. "I wrongly assumed she would discuss it with you first. I saw no reason why I should be the one to report her movements to you."

He stepped in even closer, and I could feel his breath on my cheek. "Where did she go?" he whispered down at me, causing my breath to quicken. I tried to step back, but he grabbed my forearms and held me in place.

"She, she... she -"

Setesh tightened his grip. "Tell me."

I took a deep breath. "She said she can't stand to be here without her husband. She doesn't want to be here when I give birth, she doesn't want to see..." He let me go and turned away from me, beginning to pace the room. I continued the story that I had rehearsed over and over for just this moment. "Auset didn't want you to know how upset she has been. She said that neither of us deserve her tears but she's been so heartbroken. She wanted to get away, so she went to Inbu Hedj and intends to stay there for a few weeks to recover."

His tone was still even, and low. "Are you sure that's where she went?"

I sighed in relief; he believed me. "I told her that she should take a ship to prove to you that she is not trying to go behind your back to the Ntru. That's when she asked me to make the arrangements. I really had no idea that she wasn't going to tell you her plan to leave."

He turned back to face me, and tilted his head in mock surprise. "Why are you so pale, wife? You look positively frightened."

I looked away. "My child was stirring Naswt, I hope you understand."

"I appreciate that you told me what you know - and you did tell me everything you know, correct?"

I closed my eyes. "Tu, everything."

"I appreciate that." I looked to Setesh again, and he was leaning against the far wall, directing his dark stare at me once more. "Next time, you'll tell me what you know as soon as you know it and if you hear from her at all, you will report it directly to me, or I will resume having guards follow you around."

I nodded in understanding and turned to leave. "One more question, Nebt-Het," he called out to me, and I stopped. "How jealous are you that she left and you cannot?"

I couldn't bear to turn and see the smirk of victory across his face, but I had to. I looked back to ask, "So you're not going after her, to bring her back to the per eah?"

Setesh rolled his eyes at me. "Why would I go after her?"

I hesitated and stepped deeper into the kitchen. "Well, because you told us not to leave without your permission, and she did."

He scoffed. "I no longer care what she does." He pointed at me and grinned. "You, on the other hand, you are going to stay right here, by my side, where you belong."

I truly did feel defeated in that moment, and I looked down and away, which only served to boost his sense of triumph. He laughed viciously and I took that as my opportunity to leave the kitchen as I was no longer hungry. Once in the hall I started to cry tears of sorrow, and joy.

The next two months passed by quickly. Setesh found himself handling the intricate details of running a nation, which appeared to be more than he had anticipated. After suspecting that I was in contact with Auset behind his back, he'd ordered two guards not to let me out of their sight ever, but after a while they had nothing to report, so he allowed them to stand down. He'd eventually moved all of his things into the apartment previously occupied by Ausar and Auset, since it was the largest one in the great house, and left me to have my space exclusively. I had only time on my hands, preparing to give birth shortly. I knew my time had to be coming soon.

He'd been so busy; we'd shared very few meals in that time, which I had mixed feelings about. I stopped expecting him to join me for dinner, and he never stayed for breakfast long, only leaving enough time to ask about how I was feeling. His genuine tone and look of concern aroused in me the hope that perhaps he really was coming around to forgiving me.

I came to breakfast early one morning, hoping that the extra time would give us an opportunity to talk. He was not alone when I entered, but he quickly ended his informal meeting and joined me at the table. It still felt odd to see him in the seat Ausar had occupied for over five hundred years; odd to not have him sitting next to me.

Setesh cleared his throat. "You're up early."

I smiled at him. "We never get to talk anymore. I thought we could."

His features softened, and he nodded. "How are you feeling?"

"I should be delivering very soon, any day now I think," I answered, beaming. He smiled back at me warmly as I touched my belly. He sighed.

"I wish I had been more reasonable back when all of this first started," he told me, looking away. "I told you I would try to forgive you, but I don't think I have."

I hesitated. "You need time, I understand. I never expected that you would forgive me in an instant."

"No, I mean," he started, and stopped. "I have not tried."

We fell silent, not looking at each other. "I have been avoiding you recently," he finally mumbled, still evading my glance, his hands balling into fists on the table as he spoke. "Every time I see you I just get so... angry. I feel consumed by it and all I want to do is make you hurt the way you have made me hurt."

He looked back at me and the shadows in his face saddened me. "I can understand that," I mumbled back, not knowing what else to say.

Setesh shook his head. "I wish I could promise you that I will be kinder, but I know that I cannot. I still love you, Nebt-Het, but the truth is, I hate you too." He sat up straighter and uncurled his hands. "I don't know what to do about that, so perhaps it is best that we don't spend any time together. As little as possible."

I closed my eyes, but that didn't stop the tears from running. I decided to change the subject. "Are you okay, Naswt, with everything? Is there anything that I can do to help you lead our kingdom?"

He stood, pushing his chair out behind him with a heavy force. "I will send word to you if there is an assignment you can fulfill," he responded coldly, his voice pained and sharp. "First deliver yourself of that burden, and then we shall see."

I took a deep breath and nodded, then looked up at him. He was staring out to the door of the room, avoiding me, but not leaving either. He stood there, letting the silence settle in the room, and he broke it softly, with a mumble that I almost didn't hear.

"I just don't, I still don't understand why."

I looked away. "He..." I hesitated and swallowed. The words were crawling up my throat, piercing me over and over. "He saw me when I needed to be seen."

I should have said something more, but I didn't. I couldn't, even though he was still there, as if waiting for me to try. I had nothing. He finally left without another word.

I gave birth two days later, my heart heavy with the regret that I had ruined everything with one unfortunate choice. I was alone when my water began to flow, and I knew it was time and I knew what to do. I tried to deliver alone, but the pain overwhelmed me and my screams rang out. The space around me filled with women who held my hands and wiped my brow, who held me up and helped me to maintain my balance upon the birthing bricks, who shouted with joy and rang bells to celebrate the arrival of my son. I cried when I was delivered of him, as I could feel the magic seeping back into my being, finally feeling like myself again.

I fell back onto the bed and allowed the midwives to clean him and drape him, not reaching out for him, not being the one to comfort him. At some point I drifted into a numbing sleep and when I awoke, my son was resting quietly against my breast. I placed a hand on his head and cried for him, until he woke with a start and began crying for himself.

Djehuty and Seshat were waiting for me in the sitting room on the morning of my son's fifth day. I had just finished feeding him from my breast and was still clutching his tiny frame, wanting to protect him from threats that had not yet presented themselves. Seshat stood as I stepped into the room; I had not thought to expect them but I should have.

"Congratulations are in order," Seshat whispered, a smile crawling across her face as she stared at the peaceful face of my son. I smiled at her politely and passed the baby to her without hesitation, and she held him gently, cooing.

Djehuty glanced over at her before directing his attention to me. "We don't have to travel to do this," he said in a reassuring tone, but I shook my head no quickly, ready for the recharging experience of home.

"Just give me a moment to prepare," I insisted, stepping out into to hallway before he could object. I ran out into the large exterior courtyard, where I suspected to find Setesh training a new company of warriors. He was sweating profusely as he easily bested a young warrior in a light sparring match. One of his men on the side saw me sprinting towards them and whistled to Setesh.

My husband glanced at me before nodding to the man who'd whistled, letting him know to take over temporarily. Setesh then turned his attention to me. "Why are you interrupting me?" he asked in a tone that masked the harshness of the words.

"Seshat is here to take me to the naming ceremony. I did not want to leave without discussing it with you."

He relaxed at this and looked away. "You have my permission. Go, home and back. No detours."

I nodded and curtseyed before turning to leave. "Let me know as soon as you are back," he added before running off to rejoin his troops. I sighed and hurried back indoors.

"I'm ready," I told Djehuty confidently, and he took my hand. Seshat dispersed first, holding my quiet son in her arms, and we followed close behind. She was beside me when I arrived, my son mysteriously asleep as if under a spell. I kept my eyes on his unchanging face, grateful and fascinated by his simple embrace of stillness as the light began to invade.

I returned to the great house alone, holding my son, whispering his name over and over, chanting it for him alone. Anpu, Anpu, Anpu.

It wasn't long before I heard a knock at the door. Reluctantly I placed my son down to continue his rest. I was not worried; I knew the travel would strengthen him, especially since he had been born in the physical world and not in the ethereal, as had I and my siblings. I took my attention from him to see who was waiting for me in the sitting room.

One of our newer attendees was there, a young woman who chose to follow in the footsteps of her mother and serve the royal house. She stood when I stepped into the sitting room, twisting her fingers around themselves as she nodded her head in respect. I smiled. "Is everything okay?"

"Tu Seret, I was just checking to see if you were back yet. Naswt Biti sent me to check," she clarified, glancing up at me to see if that was okay. She shifted her weight from one foot to another and looked away, biting her lip.

"You can let him know I am here. I just arrived." I stepped closer to her and placed my hand on her shoulder, trying to reassure her. "You don't have to be so nervous, you know."

She sighed and dropped her hands to her sides. "I apologize, I don't mean to be. I haven't been able to get over watching you in labor. I was so afraid. I didn't think you would live."

I squinted, trying to remember. "You were holding my hand?"

Resha blushed, glad that her contribution was recognized. "Tu. I came in the room, and Kasna was standing behind you, supporting your back, and you had such a wild look in your eyes... I did not know what else to do. I just grabbed your hand, and you squeezed so hard. It was terrifying."

Now it was my turn to look away. "I certainly did not mean to scare you so. Now I must apologize to you."

She looked up into my face, finally relaxing. "I was so surprised to see Naswt Biti waiting in the sitting room, listening to you give birth. Kasna said he was there first, before anyone else arrived."

I hesitated. "He was there?"

Her eyes widened. "I did not mean, perhaps I should not have said... my apologies, Seret, I thought you knew."

"No, I..." I turned away from her, digesting the new information. "You did nothing wrong. Thank you for telling me that."

We were both silent for a moment. "I will head directly back to Naswt Biti and let him know you've returned."

"Yes, please do," I told her, and heard the door open and

close behind me, and Anpu began to whimper from the other room, beckoning me to his side. I walked in and scooped him into my arms, trying to lull him back to rest. He quieted quickly, but kept his gaze firm upon my face, looking up at me with a discomforting seriousness.

Another knock came from the outside door, but this time I was unwilling to put down my son. I took him with me to greet my visitor, opening the hall door to find Setesh waiting in the hall, patiently. Neither of us spoke or moved for several moments; I finally stepped back and gave him the space he needed to enter. It was not like he needed my permission to come inside, but I appreciated that he waited to receive it.

"Is everything okay with him?" he asked impatiently, slumping onto the bed that we once shared. I chose to sit across the room, in one of the far armchairs.

"He is fine. It was his first jump. You remember what the first jump was like."

Setesh smiled wistfully. "I do, surprisingly."

I hesitated. "His name is Anpu. He who is to guide." He nodded and kept his attention focused on the door to the outside courtyard. I couldn't hold back any longer. "Was there anything else you needed, Naswt? Did you have any questions for me, any concerns I can address?"

He stood. "No. I wanted to know if you had heard from your sister. Have you?"

"No," I answered quickly, and honestly.

He began to make his way to the door, but I stood and spoke, stopping him in his tracks. "Why did you come here, when you'd already asked Resha to confirm that I had arrived?" When he didn't answer right away, I continued my line of questioning. "Why were you in the sitting room on the night of my delivery, and why didn't you tell me you were here? And why are you even speaking to me after you told me to stay away from you? What is going on?"

His shoulders slumped forward, and he hung his head. I stepped closer to him, close enough to whisper softly, wanting to restrain my threatening tone. "Tell me, husband. Please."

Setesh turned back to face me, his face stoic and dark. Cold. "Refrain from referring to me as your husband. I am Naswt Biti to you, nothing more."

His distance was so immediate, it caught me entirely unaware. I stepped back and nodded, not sure how else to respond. Setesh stepped towards me, closing the gap that I had just created. I moved once more and he matched it, each step more threatening than the last. Anpu began to whimper once more, his cries muffled, as if afraid to increase his volume.

"I was here when he was being delivered because you commanded the attention of the entire home, and to ignore you is to make a nation aware of my weakness. I did not tell you because I was not here for your comfort, nor was I concerned for your well-being. I told you not to disturb me but you did so anyway. You interrupted me in front of the warriors as if your authority is equal to mine. I am speaking to you because you are a resident of the great house and I enjoy the privilege of ruling said house, and you would do well not to lose sight of my generosity."

I took a deep breath. "Send us away, then. Send me to live anywhere you decide and be rid of me for good."

He rolled his eyes and looked away. "Why should I make things easier for you? What have you done to deserve that?"

"Perhaps nothing," I started, "but it is clear that my presence here does not make things easier for you."

"And that is what I aim to change, starting right now," Setesh told me, turning on his heels to begin pacing the room. "You are not going anywhere, so you can get that idea out of your head now."

"But why, Setesh? That is what I cannot understand," I pleaded with him, finally laying down my son. "You say you do not care for me any longer, but you refuse to let me go. I no longer believe you. You keep me here because you want me here."

"I keep you here because I need you here. Need is not want."

I sighed once more and sat on the bed, keeping my attention focused on Anpu. "I don't understand why you think you need me here. Because we are married, you need to keep up appearances? Because Auset is gone? Because of my son?"

"Because ALL of those things, Nebt-Het!" Setesh shouted at me, the undertone of his voice hinting at a growl. His eyes bulged with red for just a moment before he reasserted his composure, no longer pacing the room. "I am not the one who has done things that require justification. I have the luxury of never being required to answer to you ever again, and I will no longer tolerate your questioning me."

Anpu began to cry louder now, his tiny fists swinging in the air directly above him. He was distressed, and I moved to pick him up once more. "Leave him where he is," Setesh ordered me, and what was previously just a hint of a growl had completely matured. I looked at him, and he was deathly serious, his eyes burning with anger as he waited for me to defy him. I looked over at my son with compassion, but for both of our sakes, I did not move.

"What do you propose I do to make things easier for you?" I whispered, looking at him directly, eye to eye.

He took a deep breath and resumed pacing. "I need you here because you are the only person who remains from the previous council. With Auset gone, it appears that I do not have the support of the Neteru. You are the only thing that stops the dissent from spreading throughout the kingdom."

He sighed deeply before continuing. "I do not want you here.

I asked you to stay away from me and I meant it. But you cannot leave, not until I have further established my rule and quelled any concerns about my legitimacy as King. Do you understand?"

I looked away. "Yes, I do."

He grew quiet while continuing to pace, the only sound in the room were the wails of my child. I sighed. "I had no idea that you were dealing with dissenters. I thought Auset eliminated any chances of that by legitimizing your claim to the throne."

Setesh finally stopped moving, and I turned back to face him, noticing for the first time the lines that had formed beneath his eyes, the creases in his forehead.

"The whispers began in the distant edges of the realm, once the rumor that the Neteru have abandoned me had time to travel." He sat once more, this time in the armchair where I once sat. "It has only been a few months since I became Naswt Biti. It is still early enough for the ambitious and foolish to think they can usurp my throne – perhaps follow my own example."

I studied his face compassionately. "You will need to tour the countryside then, with your troops. Display your strength and secure your borders. The warriors will not turn from their commander, and that has always been your asset."

He shook his head. "There is so much that needs to be done here. It would take so much for me to travel, more than it used to."

I smiled. "More than when your only concern was the troops?"

Setesh chuckled and looked at me. "Yes. Yes, that is right."

"Let me help you, Naswt," I stressed, leaning forward to hold his attention. "I have experience with these things. I can help you figure this all out."

He looked away and closed his eyes, the damaged part of his spirit against accepting my assistance in any way. Still, he needed me. "Fine. Yes, I will let you help. First we will need to figure out what things I need to be informed of daily, and what things are less urgent. Then we can begin to prepare my journey."

I took a deep breath. "I will come to the council meeting in two days to present my thoughts. This way, your new councilors will see me in support of you; it will boost their confidence."

Setesh looked at me. "Fine. That will do."

Anpu had begun to quiet down on his own, crying himself to sleep. I still had not moved towards him, and as Setesh motioned that I could attend to my son, I decided to let him fuss for a few moments longer, to give Setesh my undivided attention.

"I appreciate that you will trust me to assist you, Naswt. It, I... it is a great honor."

He stood, and I rose also in respect, bowing my head to him. He turned to walk out and I followed him, walking to the outside door as he made his way into the hall.

"If you speak to Auset," Setesh began, then stopped. I frowned, not knowing what to expect. "If you speak to her, let her know it was not my intention to be cruel to her," he finished, his gaze penetrating and direct. "Her husband deserved what he got. She did not. I hope that her grief does not consume her, and she is able to... I hope that she understands."

My stomach twisted into knots. I did not believe that a time would come that Auset would ever understand what he did, but I could not say that. I smiled and prayed that it looked real. "If I speak to her, I will let her know."

He nodded and walked away, deliberately. I dropped my

head against the door frame, the anxiety overwhelming me, before remembering my crying child and rushing back into the bedroom to be at his side. He no longer seemed to need me, but I needed him. After feeding him, I held him to my chest and rocked us both to sleep.

I woke suddenly, gasping as if from a night terror. Auset had returned. I could hear her calling me on the wind which flowed in from the courtyard like a whisper on a distant ear. I looked to my right and saw Anpu undisturbed, and I sighed in relief. We celebrated the first anniversary of his birth just a few weeks ago, and he had matured to sleeping soundly through the night.

I looked at him once more to make sure he was okay before stepping out into the courtyard. Once outside, her whispers grew louder until it seemed as if she were standing right next to me, speaking directly into my ear. I breathed deeply and patiently, listening.

"Senet, we are almost ready. I will make the arrangements and we will hold his ceremony on the night of the waning moon. I will tell you where soon."

"We should not speak like this," I whispered back, hoping she could hear. "Open your thoughts to me, I have so much to say."

I closed my eyes and waited to see the door open to me, stepping into it to find my sister standing in the center, back erect and strong. I felt an overwhelming urge to curtsey to her, and so I did, despite never really caring about that protocol when she was actually Queen.

"You did not need to do that," she whispered to me, still keeping her voice low as if afraid to be discovered. We both knew no one could hear us here.

I smiled. "I know, I am just so glad to see you." She opened her arms to me and I took her hands, walking into her hug slowly, our embrace tight and warm.

"I have been working with Setesh for a while now," I began quickly, wanting to tell her everything I could in whatever time we had. "It is in a small advisory capacity. We do not speak often and it is usually in front of others when they can see that he has not been entirely abandoned by the Neteru." When she did not respond, I continued. "He has expressed remorse for how his actions may have hurt you. He wanted to look for you a few months back, so that he could speak to you and hopefully aid in your process of grieving and acceptance."

She looked away. "Did he send anyone after me?"

"No, of course not. And he does not know the true reason why you left." I searched her face to try to gauge what she was feeling. "He still believes it is because living here was too painful."

Auset looked back at me. "I have been gone so long," she murmured, "so much appears to have changed."

I sighed. "So much has changed with you as well."

"I was a servant, waiting for the right time to reveal myself and reclaim my husband's body." She turned her back to me and I knew it was to stop me from seeing her tears. "I find that I feel so differently about everything now. I cannot possibly continue to be angry with Setesh for what he did."

Stepping towards her, I interjected, "Perhaps you need to tell him what you are planning to do, instead of doing it behind his back. So much has changed, senet; none of us are in the place where we were when you left."

She looked back to me, her face composed. "Has he forgiven you yet?"

I was taken aback. "Not entirely, no..."

"And has he been kind to your son? To my husband's son?"

I looked away. "He has not been unkind, if that's what you mean."

"No, I am not asking if he is cruel. I am asking if he is kind." Auset gave me her back once more. "I am not going to take the chance that Setesh will try to stop me. I have a plan and I will see it through to the end. You have to decide if you will be part of it or not."

I sighed, frustrated. "Of course I intend to be a part of it. I just wanted you to know what you've missed."

Auset glanced back at me over her shoulder. "I appreciate that." She hesitated for a moment. "What is his name, your son?"

I paused. "Anpu. He who is to guide."

She kept her glance straight ahead, her posture pensive and elegant. I waited for her to respond. "I cannot tell you where I am hiding, nor can I say where Ausar is. It is not that I do not trust you, but I do believe that Setesh will force you to share what you know if he believes you know something. You cannot share what you do not know."

I nodded. "I understand."

Auset turned back to me and threw her arms around me, enveloping me in one of her consuming, loving hugs. I tried to respond in kind; I had missed her more than I knew.

"I cannot wait to meet our son," she whispered in my ear before pulling back and looking into my face. "I cannot wait until the three of us can leave this place, together."

I smiled reluctantly. I was not sure I would be able to leave, partly because I was not sure Setesh would allow it, and partly because I was not sure I wanted to leave anymore. But I did not share either thought with my sister. "Let us first provide your husband with the ceremony he deserves."

She nodded and pulled away from me, and I turned to leave

her consciousness. "Nebt-Het," she called out to me, her voice shaky, and I turned to look at her once more.

Auset swallowed, but she continued without faltering. "I hope that you know I forgive you. I was not present for you as I should have been. I was too busy being Queen, enjoying both the responsibilities and the perks." She took one small step towards me. "You did not say so, but I know now that my absence contributed to your choice to seek comfort elsewhere. I truly hope you will forgive me for not being there for you when you were in need."

I felt my body shiver, and knew that my own tears were not far behind. I wanted to reach out to her, but back in the bedroom, Anpu had begun to stir. I needed to return. "I do forgive you, Auset. You promised you would return for me, and you have. I just want to look to our future."

She smiled and tilted her head. "Your son will call for you. Go to him."

I nodded and relaxed, the first beads making their way down my cheeks. "You will hold him soon."

I took a deep breath and felt my lungs gasp for air; I was back in my body, leaning against the stone wall in my courtyard. The tears that had begun to fall continued, and I took a few moments to inhale the dry dawn air before walking into the bedroom and greeting my growing son. He stood as he saw me approach him, his hands grasping for something to support his legs as they wobbled beneath him. I reached out my hand and he took it quickly, inching closer to me with the bright grin of achievement overwhelming his features.

I smiled at him and knelt when he'd made it to my side, choosing to pick him up and kiss his slender cheeks. Anpu nestled his face into my shoulder and grew quiet again in the comfort of my arms. I sighed in relief.

"Where is she?" I heard coming up from behind me, and as I turned to face the shouting, the doors to the per eah swung open, and Setesh came rushing out. He looked around until he spotted me, sitting in the garden at the edge of the outer courtyard, watching Resha play with Anpu. Setesh ordered his men to stand down, but they did not leave, instead choosing to stand guard at the entrance of the great house while their leader approached me, his steps large and his form imposing.

"You LIED to me," he began, without explanation. I glanced down at the two of them, sitting in the dirt. Resha looked at me, fear beginning to cross her features; Anpu kept his attention on the dirt, kneading it relentlessly with his hands.

"What are you talking about?" I asked as I stood, completely confused. Setesh scoffed, insulted by my response, and his body doubled over in anger. When he straightened, it was as if he had grown another six inches. His frame loomed over mine, and as he closed the space between us, I found myself inhaling sharply.

"You know what I am referring to. You lied to me about your sister. You lied to me about why she left here and where she was going. You helped her to betray me."

My frown deepened; I wanted to ask how he knew, but I also wanted to deny it altogether, swear I had no idea. My hesitation gave me away. Resha had already picked up Anpu, who was squealing his displeasure as she inched the two of them away. His cries pulled attention from me to them, and Setesh glanced in their direction before focusing on me, fists balled, breathing fiery and sharp. Resha turned and ran towards the village, I assumed towards her own home. I looked at my husband; his eyes were a bright, frightening red.

I swallowed. "Naswt, I don't know what you are thinking -"

"I don't know what *you* are thinking, Nebt-Het," he interrupted, his tone low and even. I was grateful that he was no longer shouting, but I could barely look at him, the shadows in his face causing me to shiver. "You and your sister plotted behind my back. You deliberately lied to me, AGAIN. You must know that to plot against Naswt Biti is to commit an act of treason."

He smirked, but it was not from amusement. I tried to step backwards, but was flush against the garden edge, the foot-high wall of rocks digging into my shins. "That is not, you are not... what happened, Naswt? Tell me what happened."

"I FOUND HIS BODY!" he shouted with a growl. "I found the coffin on the river's edge this morning. How foolish you two were to think I would not recognize the chest that I designed myself, which I'd worked on for weeks."

He stopped ranting to look at me, taking a step backwards. "No, you did not know it was there," he reasoned, no longer shouting. "You would have tried to stop me from hunting this morning if you had known. So perhaps you did not plot against me?"

I had stopped being afraid for myself. "Setesh, what did you do?"

The corners of his mouth turned upwards in a sinister grin. "I opened the chest, and tore his body limb from limb. I scattered the pieces far and wide."

I gasped. "Where is Auset?"

He shrugged and chuckled, his red eyes affixed to mine. "I did not see her, I only heard her wail. She knows what she's done, and she knows how I feel about it." Setesh straightened up and resumed his scowl. "When are you going to learn, Nebt-Het? This is a new world now, and I. Rule. It. Know your place, or -"

"Or what, Setesh? Or you will kill me too?" I asked, cutting him off. "You have made me a prisoner in my own home. You have taken everything away from me!"

"You deserve worse than what I've done to you." He turned away from me, finally releasing his hands, which had been clenched so tight that they had begun to go pale. "I would be well within my right to kill you, and Auset, for what you have done."

I shook my head. "You cannot just decide that on your own, you have to take your grievance to the council."

He spun around back to me. "You mean MY council? With MY councilors, the ones whom I appointed and are extremely loyal to ME?"

"No, Setesh. I mean the council of the Neteru."

He lunged so quickly that it caused me to gasp, closing my eyes and hunching my shoulders. When a blow did not come I opened my eyes once more and he grabbed my wrist, pulling me into the great house at such a force and speed that I could barely keep up. My feet dragged against the rough dirt floors as I used my free hand to try to wrestle away from him.

He opened the door to my apartment and continued into the bedroom, throwing me onto the bed with all of his might. I landed with a heavy bounce, followed by a hard thud. It made me dizzy, and I dropped my head to the mat, hoping to regain my composure.

Setesh began to pace the room. "Call your sister here," he ordered me without looking in my direction.

"So you can do what?"

"Who are you to question me? I gave you an order!"

I shook my head. "No. I will not."

Setesh gave out a loud growl and I shrank back on the mat. "Call her here NOW!"

"NO!" I shouted back, matching his intensity as best as I could. "If you want her, you go get her yourself!"

His men rushed into the room, alerted by all of the screams. "Are you okay, Naswt Biti?" one of them asked him as they entered.

Setesh punched the wall, and the print of his fist caused a large crack to travel the stone wall. "Stay here with her. Do not let her out of your sight and stop her from dispersing if she tries to leave."

Hesitatingly, the warrior asked, "how are we supposed to do that?"

Setesh rolled his eyes and turned to me, first spreading his arms to full length before slamming his palms together and directing a pyramid shaped light into my direction. "Just don't let her out of this room. Not into the sitting room, and not into the courtyard. And do not let anyone else in either."

I jumped off the bed and began to rush towards him, causing two of his men to restrain me back into place. "My SON is out there, Setesh," I shouted at his back, "my SON!"

Setesh turned back to me. "You think I care about that boy? You'd better hope she brings him back eventually."

I screamed, falling to the ground beneath me. The warriors who had restrained me stepped back as Setesh left us alone, ignoring all of my cries. I continued to scream and cry from my spot on the floor beside the bed, until the sun had fallen beneath the edge of the world and night had overcome us.

Eventually I crawled from the floor onto the bed, resting my head down, trying to compose myself, but I could not have been there for longer than a moment before all three warriors collapsed, as if fainting. I sat up abruptly as the courtyard doors burst open dramatically and Auset's dark blue mist floated in.

"Sister, don't!" I whispered to her, trying to protect her from the heka Setesh had cast, but she emerged from the mist and reached out her hand to me.

"Take my hand," she ordered me gently, and in my despair I

couldn't even begin to argue with her. I reached out and grabbed her, and in an instant we were on the deck of a ship, headed towards the lower lands. I turned to face my sister and saw her holding Anpu on her lap as he bounced playfully, giggling.

I stepped towards them, incredulous. "How did you... Auset?"

She smiled at me modestly. "I learned how to harness my gift while I was away." Auset looked at Anpu and smiled larger, her face bright and happy. "I have learned how to do a great many things."

I sighed and tried to smile. "You two have met."

"I followed Setesh back to the house; I knew he was going to come after you," she responded, her eyes still affixed to my son's happy visage. "When the girl ran off with your son, I followed her and convinced her to give him to me." Auset looked up at me, eyebrow raised in amusement. "It certainly was not easy. She was determined to protect him. Luckily, her mother recognized me and told her it was safe."

I sighed in relief, then frowned. "Perhaps we should take her with us. I would not want Setesh to harm her or her family."

Auset glanced back, over her shoulder. "She is below deck with her mother now."

I nodded. "It seems you have thought of everything."

She tilted her head at me. "I knew we had to act quickly. We did not have time to discuss a plan. Don't be cross with me, sister. We are all safe."

I took a deep breath, crossing the ship to sit beside my family. "Where are we going now?"

Auset looked at me. "We are going to find my husband."

Mes – Birth

"Are you serious?"

Auset nodded without flinching. "Absolutely," she confirmed, her voice resolute. "I set out to perform the rite to send him off properly and that is what I still intend to do."

I shook my head, surprised. "Setesh told me he scattered the pieces of his body. What you are trying to do is impossible."

Smiling, she looked away. "Nothing is impossible." We sat in silence for a few moments, Anpu pushing himself off her lap and standing in front of us, trying to walk on the rocking ship. "The ship will dock soon to find a safe haven for the girl and her mother. You are welcome to stay with them, or even to return home if that is what you'd like," Auset finally told me, matter-of-factly.

I frowned. "I'm not leaving you. I am just…" I took a deep breath and sighed. How could I tell her she was being unreasonable in her grief?

"I'm not, though," she answered me, before I'd even let the words out. "This is not my grief talking, only my sense of what is right. There are so many things that we have done wrong, it is past time that we got something right."

I could not disagree with her, and I did not focus on the fact that she had just read my mind without the ceremonious entry that was usually required. Instead, I contemplated the task ahead of us, trying to discern how we would get through such an onerous task, and was there even anything I could actually do to help?

My eyes drifted across the boat, finally landing on my son, who had tottered close to the ship's edge. Auset and I both stood, watching him as he let out a scream, pointing awkwardly at the river. I ran over and scooped him into my arms, and Auset looked out over the edge of the boat, trying to see what had upset him so. He mumbled nonsense in my ear before screaming once more, and in an instant Auset had dispersed to the spot that Anpu had focused on.

When she returned, she was holding a head. Ausar's head.

Anpu reached out to touch it, and Auset brought it closer to him, close enough that he could touch his tiny hand to his father's forehead. My stomach tightened into knots. After a moment, Anpu let go and dropped his head to my shoulder, drifting immediately to sleep.

Auset smiled knowingly. Nothing was impossible. "He who is to guide," she reminded me, causing me to look down at my son in wonder. "He is going to show us where to go."

Resha and her mother clung tightly to one another as they departed the ship, looking around cautiously as if expecting a threat to attack at any moment. I continued to nurse Anpu while Auset tried to assure the pair that they would be safe.

"Are you sure we will not be in trouble? I have abandoned my post," I could hear Resha whisper, not convinced that she would be free of the charge of treason against the King. Auset nodded reassuringly, and when she touched the girl's forehead, Resha was instantly calmed.

"I promise you that you and your mother will be safe here." Auset looked at Resha's mother for a moment, touching her forehead in exactly the same way. The mother relaxed and lightened her grip on her daughter. "Stay in the shadows for a few weeks. Keep yourselves out of sight, and do your best to blend in. No harm will come to you," Auset promised, taking a step back now that the two were calmer, convinced. Resha's mother took a deep breath and smiled, curtseying to Auset, which cued Resha to do the same.

I stepped closer to where they were standing. "Are you sure you will have somewhere to stay in the city?"

Resha's mother nodded, continuing to smile. "Yes, I have a brother who built a home here to be close to the family of his wife; we should be able to blend in among them just fine."

"We will use different names," Resha added, watching Anpu rest at my breast longingly. "At least in the beginning."

I nodded and looked at Auset, who met my glance. She nodded at me before turning back to them.

"Go now while you have the cover of night to protect you. Tell no one what you have seen or who you have been with."

Resha took her mother's hand and they cloaked their heads and faces before rushing off towards the village, into the night. Auset and I turned back to the ship, and both of us began exhaling heavy breaths which carried the name of our grandfather towards the sails. In this way we were able to manipulate the wind and push the ship offshore, sending it up the river without passengers or crew.

Auset walked over to me, standing at my left. I secured Anpu with my right arm so that I could reach my hand down to take my sister's. Auset squeezed my palm before reciting the heka. "May our feet land on solid ground. May our path be unobstructed. May our way lay plain before us. May we be hidden in plain sight. May we reach our destination."

We recited it again and again, four times in total, before I released her hand from mine. I took Anpu from my breast and wrapped him to my body with a long, soft fabric. He was asleep, content and unaware, as I preferred it, and although he was getting bigger every day, he was still too small for me to leave him to walk with us on his own. I knew I would need to carry him for much of our journey, but I was prepared to do whatever it would take.

Auset reached a hand out towards the desert in the west, which seemed so far from this side of the river. We waited for a moment until the scorpions emerged from the water, having risked the travel from the west bank to the east, where we stood. There were seven in total, and without a word they moved into a clear formation, with three before us, one on each side, and two behind.

Auset stepped towards the north, the scorpions moving in perfect rhythm with her. I stayed at her side, safe within the boundary that they had set. I was not sure if she had a destination in mind, but we both knew we had to start moving.

After a long stretch of walking without rest, Auset stopped and touched my shoulder. "Let me hold the child," she whispered, staring straight ahead. The sun was beginning to rise to our right and I knew I would benefit from the reprise. Still, I hesitated.

"I don't want to burden you," I whispered back, and she shushed me gently, as a mother would, and reached out her hands to me, not allowing room for me to deny her request. I began to unwrap the fabric from my body, loosening Anpu from my chest. Auset caught him in her arms and began to gently wake him. I frowned, afraid that he would cry out at his rest being disturbed, but he woke peacefully and smiled up at his aunt, who beamed at seeing his bright face and round cheeks. I felt the soft embers of jealousy smolder within me, watching the way their eyes connected, but I swallowed it quickly, knowing that it was silly for me to be so possessive over a moment. Auset placed Anpu on the ground before her and he stood without wobbling, looking around as if surveying the countryside, gauging our location, discerning.

"We were never like this," Auset murmured to me without looking away from my son. "I feel like we were born with our magic, but here he is, having to figure it all out."

I frowned. "He has not demonstrated any connection like we used to. Besides what happened on the ship, I have not seen any evidence that he is more than just a baby."

Auset looked at me as if I was being ridiculous. "Of course he is more than just a baby, Nebt-Het." She paused for a minute, looking down at Anpu. "Have you even tried to show him how to disperse, or anything?"

I scoffed and looked away. "He is much too young for that."

"He is millions of years old." I looked at Auset, her face somber and taut. "He is one of us."

I sighed, not knowing how to respond to that. I wanted to point out that I had been completely alone for the last year, taking care of my child with no assistance from her or anyone. But perhaps there were things I should have known, as a mother, as his mother. Clearly she could see what I had not.

Anpu took two steps towards the river, hesitating before screaming out and pointing towards the distant west. Auset tilted her head in the direction of his finger before dispersing out to see what he was directing her to. She returned a few moments later, completely empty handed.

"Anpu," she began to ask, kneeling in front of him, "what are you trying to show me? Is there something there?"

He nodded and giggled, and took her hand before reaching up for mine. Once between us both he used our arms as leverage to jump up and down excitedly, amusing himself with the little game he'd created.

Auset shook her head and looked at me. "No, I know something is there, it has to be," she mumbled, not sure what to do next. I shook my head, not really knowing either, with Anpu continuing to tug on our arms, flopping around between us gleefully.

Suddenly he stopped moving, and in the next moment we were on the west bank, the expansive desert spanning out ahead of us. Anpu let go of our hands and pointed once more, this time without screaming. We both frowned and knelt, trying to understand his message.

"Are you telling us we need to search the desert?" I asked softly, putting my hand on his head reassuringly, trying not to look surprised or concerned that he had brought us both here with such speed and ease. Anpu responded by falling backwards, letting his legs out from under him, his face squeezed up with frustration.

Auset frowned and stood. "This would be so much easier if he could just talk," she sighed amusingly, but the words must have sparked inspiration in her, because she quickly fell to the ground and pulled Anpu into her lap, forcing his eyes to meet hers.

"Relax," she told him softly, and he closed his eyes, and after a moment, she closed hers. I sat there waiting, amazed and confused.

Anpu did not open his eyes; he instead drifted off to sleep. Auset stood and gathered him into her arms. "He can open his thoughts to me; he must have gotten it from you. But the magic, it takes so much out of him. Even this little bit is too much."

I could hardly wait for her to continue. "What did he tell you?"

"Setesh has scouts nearby on the east bank. He moved us west to avoid them. We need to hide for the day and begin again later tonight, when they've been convinced that we are not in the area."

My eyebrows rose, as I was genuinely impressed. "He was able to sense them like that?"

Auset shook her head. "It's so odd, I mean, because he does not have the same abilities like we did, like we do, since he was born here. But your son is powerful, senet. We would do well not to underestimate him."

I smiled, proud, wanting to wake him and see what he would do next. "Since he's so young this process might take longer than it would if he were older, fully able to access his power, but he's limited in what he can do in this form," Auset told me with a sigh. I looked up at her; I could see how this was taking its toll on her emotionally. She missed Ausar, and had spent so much time away from him, away from home, constantly on the run. But I could see other things too; her determination and resilience shone through like the sun between cracks of a stone wall.

"He's never been home, except for his naming ceremony," I offered, wondering aloud if that might help. "Should we jump home for the day, come back in the evening?"

Auset and I looked at each other, both considering what that would mean for our journey, knowing that cosmic time is vastly different from earth time. Still, it appealed to her to give us all a recharge by leaving this realm. Without a word, she nodded and knelt, shuffling my son to her left arm and grabbing a handful of sand with her right. She blew the sand over the scorpions to cover them before dispersing, with me following close behind.

It was not until we'd found the first forearm that Auset got the idea to build a monument to her husband in each location where his body was found. Anpu and I journeyed home while she jumped from village to village, instructing the temple keepers to erect a site to memorialize the first Naswt Biti. In truth, Auset had no power to demand such a thing, but the people loved her, sympathized with her, disliked their new King, and no one hesitated to follow her orders. The first eight locations were built at the same time, which I imagine confused and infuriated Setesh to no end. The next memorials were to be built one at a time, as we located the additional portions of Ausar, growing closer and closer to making him whole again.

Anpu grew quickly from the brief moments we spent hiding from Setesh at home, the astral energy maturing him in increments that would have taken longer on land. Even though it had only been about six months of searching, his physical features placed him around seven years old, and he'd grown to better understand his spiritual abilities. There was no way we would have accomplished as much as we did without him.

Finally, in search of the final piece of Ausar, Anpu pointed us towards the great lake in the south. Auset used heka to fashion a small boat of papyrus and we boarded, guarded by the scorpions, and began the long trip up river. As days passed and we ascended into the upper lands, I could see Anpu get quieter and less playful, a sign that he was struggling to detect his father's body.

Finally we were at the lake, and still we had no clue as to where we should look next. We abandoned the boat and began to walk around the lake's edge, following Anpu as he strained to guide us.

"Are we in the right place, sweet child?" Auset asked him patiently, hoping to encourage him to admit defeat, but he could not, or would not.

He shook his head and frowned deeper. "No, it's here, I know it is here, I just..." he exclaimed, darting in and out of bushes, trying to understand why he struggled so. I looked at my sister, whose pained face betrayed her gentle voice; she was worried that he would not be able to find it, and we would have no luck finding it on our own.

We circled the lake twice before Anpu began leading us back down the river, abandoning the lake altogether. Finally Anpu pointed. "There, it's there," he shouted, relieved and pleased with himself. Auset rushed to the place where he pointed and found a rather long fish flopping on the riverbank, recently shored and dying.

Auset stood there for a moment, and I watched her back stiffen. "Anpu, are you sure? There is nothing here but a fish," she asked him, trying to remain calm.

He walked over and stood next to her. "That's it. That's the final piece."

Anpu's voice was so young and innocent, it was impossible to be angry with him, but I knew my sister would be upset. "Anpu, come here and stand by me," I called to him, and he ran back to my side. Auset picked up the fish and began to chant over it, and it glowed with a soft green light for a moment, but as the life drained from the animal, so did the light.

She turned back to us, devastated. "The fish. It... ate my husband."

I shook my head and stepped towards her. "No, well, I mean... it only ate a piece of him..."

"Can't you get the piece out of the fish?" Anpu asked from behind me. My eyebrows shot up, hoping that perhaps that was an option, but Auset shook her head.

"I think I could, if the fish were still alive, but not now. It's gone for good." Auset sunk to the ground and held the fish in her lap, cradling it tenderly, her breaths heavy and filled with sorrow. "We needed that piece."

I watched her for a moment before turning back to my son. "Anpu, do you want to play in the trees a bit while we talk?" He nodded and ran off, and I went to sit next to my sister. "We have all of him, except his... member... I think we can still do the ceremony, Auset."

She nodded. "You're right, and I should have been prepared for this to happen." Auset looked at me and smiled. "We can always replace it with something, for the ceremony. We have everything else we need."

I touched her shoulder. "Are you sure you're okay, senet? What is troubling you?"

"You would not understand," Auset answered, brushing me off. I tried not to be offended, but I could not help but to take her words personally.

"You could at least try to help me to understand," I told her, and she met my words with a deep sigh before sitting up and meeting me straight in the eye.

"I thought I needed his member so that I may bear him a son."

She was right; I did not understand. I sat back and frowned. "Auset, he cannot possibly have the ability to physically impregnate you while he is... no longer alive in the physical form, with or without the... flesh. Why would you think that if you had it, you could change that?"

Auset scoffed and stood, brushing off the moss from her back and legs. "I knew you would judge me, but you have to know that everything I am trying to do is because I have to do it."

"Why do you think you have to?"

"It is destiny, Nebt-Het, it is meant to be." She shrugged with a frustrated smile and sighed once more. "I cannot fight it and neither can you. I cannot avoid it and neither can you. I have the fortune, or misfortune, of knowing how this story will end. I have the vision of millions of years. I am playing my part and whether you know it or not, like it or not, so are you."

I shook my head and stood as well. "That makes it sound like we have no choices of our own to make, Auset, and I do not agree with that. We can always choose. We can always decide."

"I am trying to tell you that we have already decided."

It was my turn now to sigh and look away. "When did you decide that you wanted to have a child of your own?"

Auset hesitated. "So many times, Nebt-Het. Every birth we attended, I knew I wanted a child. When I saw you experiencing the sickness, I knew, and watching your belly grow larger with the seed of my husband, I knew." She turned back to face me, her eyes pleading for my understanding. "When I realized that I had gained this vision, I spent so much time harnessing that gift just to see my future with a child. And now I know why it had to be this way, and I am finally ready for him, for my son."

I knew she was telling the truth; the way Auset gazed upon every new life brought forth into this world let me know that she longed for one of her own. The way she beamed at Anpu and treated him with such love and kindness tugged at my own conscience, and I knew she would make a wonderful mother, the best mother. Still, I could not wrap my head around what she was hoping to do. It was like me to be realistic, and her to feel that the universe had no limits.

"So how will this work, exactly?" I asked, trying to be supportive, turning back to face her.

She smiled, relieved. "I'm not sure, actually, I -"

"I thought you said you had the vision," I interjected, my frustration rushing back. "Can't you see what we are supposed to do next?"

"Nebt-Het, I... it doesn't work that way," she responded, ignoring my tone and thoughtfully dancing between the shrubbery. "I can see it, but I still have to know it, like, know what it takes. I still have to harness and focus and channel to make the vision manifest." Auset stopped dancing and tilted her head, trying to describe the indescribable. "I know we can do it, and we will do it, because I see us doing it, but we still must take the journey from here to there."

I wanted to roll my eyes but I knew that would not help. "What *do* you know?" I mumbled, hoping I could refrain from interjecting for once.

My sister paused and resumed her thoughtful dance. "I will have to recreate his member somehow, so that there is a physical medium for his energy to manifest through. But other than that, I'm not entirely sure. I mean," she giggled, looking to see if Anpu was in earshot and lowering her tone, "I certainly do not want to make love to his body in front of you and our son."

I smiled apprehensively, feeling my cheeks redden. "I appreciate that consideration," I told her, causing her to giggle once more. She had not completely lost her youthfulness, but it had been so long since I'd known this side of her. I took her hand and squeezed it. "I know you will figure it out. In the meantime, we have to find a place where we can set up and do this."

"I already have a place," she told me, pointing towards the horizon. "There are mountains east of this lake. The ceremony takes place there, of that much I am sure."

I nodded and took a deep breath. "Anpu," I called out to him, beckoning my son back to my side. He emerged from the bush, face brown with dirt, grinning. I frowned, preparing to scold him, but Auset stepped in before I could get a word out.

"You appear as if you have had a tremendous time out there," Auset said to him, reaching for his hand. He clasped hers excitedly, and began rambling on about his adventure as she led us to our fateful destination, with me following closely behind. I wanted to ask her why we did not just jump there, instead of spending the afternoon walking, but I decided that she must have had a reason, and instead tried to relax into the experience.

Auset walked us straight into the mountain, directly into a

large cavern shaped at the base, between the largest of rocks. Anpu curled up into a corner to rest while Auset began to prepare, moving stones into place so that she could lay the form of Ausar, putting each piece into place one by one slowly, tenderly. I stepped outside to give her a moment alone with him, wondering how she must be feeling to finally see him like this, all together for the first time in years.

"Nebt-Het, I am ready for you," I could hear her calling out to my consciousness, her thoughts carried on the crisp breeze. I sighed and entered the cavern, finding that Auset had lit the space with tiny orbs of light that hovered around the body of her husband. Ausar lay there, still and cold, but something in his countenance appeared present. I wanted to reach out and touch his face, but I could not bring myself to do it in front of his wife.

I took a deep breath. "What do you need me to do?" I asked her in the same way she had called me forth, and in this way she guided me into place, at his head, with her standing guard at his feet. She sent the words that I was to say into my mind, and when I was ready, Auset woke my son and asked him to stand in the center, at the torso of his father, and he received his instructions nervously but anxious to do his part, ready.

Auset began to call for him, calling for her beloved to return to her, crying out loud and so strongly that it caused us both to weep, and as we stood before the body of our King, her lamentations were driven from her, verse by verse, as if compelled by force. I called out to him in turn, imploring him to bring himself to us, to show his face to his sisters, the two ladies, and it was as if I had been taken over by a spirit greater than myself, the magnitude of my cries weakening my body, and I could no longer stand, falling dramatically to my knees.

Our energy began to revive Ausar, but only marginally. His heart did not beat, but the flesh of his face shone from within, a bright green orb of light all that remained of the man that had once been. The phallus that Auset had created stiffened and reached for the heavens. We stopped chanting, and I watched my sister close her eyes, but she did not mount him physically. Instead Auset used her magic to hover above him, floating ethereally long enough for the green orb to leave his body completely and make its way into her.

The body was rendered lifeless, with nothing of his essence remaining. Anpu began to wrap it in linen, saying the invocations that would completely detach the soul of Ausar from the vessel that he would no longer use. When the body was fully draped, Anpu touched one hand to the center of the body's chest; the other hand rested on the forehead. He closed his eyes and took a few deep breaths before his eyes shot open and he looked to Auset for guidance, disturbed and confused.

She tried to smile and look calm. "Take your time, do not panic," Auset encouraged him, her voice soft and loving. Anpu nodded and closed his eyes once more, and this time, when his eyes opened, he was smiling, successful. "I think I did it right," he said loudly, breaking the tranquility of the moment. Auset grinned and I sighed in relief.

"Are you okay, sweet child?" Auset asked him, reaching her hand out to him. He took it and together they walked from around the table to the front of the cavern. I stayed where I was, near the bier, leaning against the wall.

He appeared to nod. "Tu, I'm okay. Can we go to the other world now?"

She glanced at me. "You should come with us," Auset instructed, rather than asked, holding out her hand. I was astonished by how strong she was, even after all the energy we'd just expended. I pulled myself up and walked over to her, taking her fingers gingerly, gratefully letting her take us home.

We could not stay home, for it was now her turn to bear a child in the physical realm, and Anpu longed to return to the land of his birth. It was strange to hear him call this land home; Auset and I had lived here for hundreds of years, and it would never be home for us. But Anpu had a different connection with the physical world, and we understood that it was our responsibility to nurture that. We found a quiet place between the mountain and the river where we could settle, and with a quick cloaking spell, we settled in for an almost languid existence. For the first time in centuries we were not teaching, birthing babies, attending council meetings, throwing festivals or trekking mercilessly along the Hapi. We were just two women. Two mothers.

My unreasonable emotions continued as Auset grew in her pregnancy. The nausea that plagued me barely affected her, and she seemed immune to the exhaustion, the night sweats, the discomfort. Instead, Auset had the glow of motherhood, her aura radiant and strong, and every day she was more attractive than the day before. Where I rarely had the desire to participate in an entire day when I was with child, Auset spent her mornings in the dirt, nurturing our garden, and her afternoons playing with Anpu, inventing new ways to amuse the quickly growing boy.

I came in one evening after reinforcing the cloaking spell to find the two of them sitting in the main room, Anpu listening intently to Auset as she shared stories of our life in the per eah, what it was like in days long past. He laughed softly as she painted the picture of his father struggling to hold his head high with the weight of the double crown upon it at the end of a long festival; the redness on her face when she would to slip into council meetings late; a memory of my shock when we watched a woman give birth for the first time. Anpu was enthralled and he sat still through the entire journey of our memories, and at the end Auset leaned into him and whispered, "I cannot wait until you and your brother are making your own memories in the great house."

I stiffened and inhaled sharply. I had no intention of allowing my son to get tangled into that world. "Anpu, are you tired? It has been a long day and tomorrow awaits."

Anpu sighed and stood, stretching his limbs. "**Gerh nfr**," he told Auset, hugging her tightly before exiting to his personal space for rest. Auset stood and I turned to face her boldly.

"Do NOT put those thoughts in MY son's head."

Auset looked at me, surprised. "How else is he supposed to be prepared? Our sons are the next generation; it is their birthright to rule as we once did."

I shook my head emphatically. "Your son is the heir of his father, entitled to the legacy of his father. My son -"

"Is his brother. Ausar is his father also. Anpu will support his brother as Setesh once supported his." Auset paused for a moment. "You know what I mean."

"Is this another conversation about destiny that you and I are going to have?" I asked her, knowing already what the answer would be. "Anpu is too young to have decided what he's going to choose in twenty years."

Auset scoffed. "Just because you are choosing to be short-sighted does not mean that I have to be."

I rolled my eyes. "How can you be? You have the *vision*."

Neither of us spoke for a few moments. "That responsibility is what ruined our lives, Auset. Everything fell apart and I am not willing for you to set Anpu up for disappointment and failure."

Auset looked at me with squinted eyes and flared nostrils. "That *responsibility* is the only reason why Anpu is here. You would not even have a son if it had not been for that responsibility, so excuse me if I refuse to see it as the worst thing that has ever happened to us."

I sighed. "That is not what I meant and you know it."

"I only know what you said," Auset responded, clenching her jaw. "If you want to punish yourself for all eternity that is your right, but Anpu and I, and my son, we do not have to join you."

I closed my eyes. "I just want him to have the best life he can."

Auset sighed. "Do you not think that Mwt and Yit wanted that for us as well?"

I did not respond to her, I could not. Instead I turned away, taking deep breaths, wanting to enter the night and take a walk to clear my head.

"They are going to be successful," I heard her call out behind me. "Heru will defeat Setesh and reclaim the inheritance that is his."

"But why does Anpu need to be a part of that?" I asked her, turning back to face her. "Why do you insist on including my son in your son's destiny?"

Auset shook her head. "That is not what I am doing. Anpu has a path of his own."

Quiet fell between us once more, and I motioned towards the other room. "We should stop talking about this tonight, I do not want to upset him."

Auset nodded in agreement, but she threw one more comment at me as I turned to exit. "I understand what you are afraid of," she started, pausing briefly before finishing, "but I really hope you grow to see that you have nothing to fear."

I smiled and tried to keep calm. "I have asked you not to invade my thoughts like that."

"You leave me no choice."

"You had a choice," I reminded her, but stopped myself from

going further. The words that I swallowed made my stomach turn, causing me to shudder as they echoed in the hollow of my frame. Silence settled in once more, but I did not continue my walk towards the door.

I turned back to Auset, who had made her way to the ground, gingerly caressing her protruding belly. Her eyes were wet, although her cheeks were still dry. I knew she hated fighting with me, when all we had were each other.

"Ausar would be very impressed with you," I whispered, stepping towards her.

She looked up at me and gave me a confused smile. "Why do you say that?"

"I remember once, he told me that he was not sure you would ever... fight, for him... he had this odd belief that perhaps my marriage was superior because of all the... chaos..." I let my voice trail off, and turned my eyes towards the wall, remembering.

Auset chuckled softly. "I had the same idea once." I looked at her, astonished, and she glanced at my expression sheepishly before explaining. "I used to imagine what it was like, to scream at one another from across the room, throwing things and slamming doors, and then... and then making up. It sounds ridiculous now but I wanted to have a real fight with my husband."

"You and Ausar argued sometimes," I reminded her.

"Ausar and I disagreed, but you and Setesh fought. There was such a profound difference, I had this mistaken belief that it meant maybe something was missing." Auset paused for a moment. "He got the idea from me I think, one night. I tried to pick a fight with him and he refused to engage. We laid in bed with our backs to each other. 'A man should have passion for his wife,' I hissed at him, or something like that. I was so annoyed with him. Then a few years later, you were with child.

Then we really did have something to fight over."

I sat next to her, closely. "But you didn't fight then, not over that."

Auset looked away. "No, we didn't. At some point I'd realized that I was being immature to compare my marriage to yours. I was choosing not to see all of the imperfections in your union, choosing to idealize those brief moments, rather than considering what it was truly like to be married to a man like him." She turned to face me, and although her expression was resolute I could see in her eyes that she'd felt sorry for me. "You and Setesh were not fighting *for* each other, you were fighting *with* each other, and that wasn't really what I wanted, not truly. So, I chose to forgive him, and you, and to focus on strengthening our union and getting us back to where we used to be." She looked over my shoulder, a wistful look crossing her face as the memories crossed past her mind's eye. "We spent that time rediscovering one another; rediscovering our love for one another. I never appreciated him as much as I did then."

I let her thoughts drift off, not wanting to interrupt them, not knowing what to say. It felt like another lifetime ago. We'd behaved like such children. I still felt ashamed of what I had done; even with her forgiveness, even with the blessing of my lovely son, I still felt like I should have known better, been better, and this conversation, once meant to make her feel better, was steadily increasing my burden of guilt. I sighed.

"Why did we do this to ourselves?" I mumbled to myself mindlessly, not intending for Auset to venture an answer.

She scoffed. "Why indeed, senet. Why did we fall short, why did we do absurd things? Because we are not what we wish to be, not yet at least, and we will never be, until we do the absurd thing, because that is what we choose, and it is... *absurd*, but it just... is. It just is."

I had not needed her to say that aloud, but it only propelled my thoughts faster to hear her confirm what was spinning throughout my consciousness. Perhaps Auset had chosen not to fight precisely because she knew those weeks would be the last of her husband's earthly existence. Or perhaps she had just chosen to appreciate it as such. Not to waste a single moment more wishing she could be or do or have something other than what was meant for her. Ausar had been meant for her. We'd always known it, and no matter how absurd things got, the fact remained.

And Setesh had been meant for me. And Auset had allowed her moment to shape her, and she was better for it. And I had to decide how I would respond, how I would choose. But maybe I already had.

Auset delivered her child, and five days later she traveled home to receive his name. When she returned I was behind the house lying in the grass, gazing directly at Aten, and she sat by my side, taking my hand, causing me to sit up.

"His name is Heru," she whispered to me, smiling brightly, tears of joy coating her cheeks. "He is the dawn of a new day."

I shivered as I heard those words cross her lips. "What does that mean?"

Auset squinted at me, trying not to allow her joy any disturbance. "It means he is going to take the realm back from Setesh. Heru is going to take his rightful place as the heir of his father's legacy."

I nodded and tried to smile. "Yes, he will."

"What's wrong?" she asked me, her smile erasing completely from her face.

"Nothing, Auset; I am fine." I stood and began to make my way into the house, with Auset following quickly behind.

"Nebt-Het, tell me, please," she pleaded with me, grabbing my arm and turning me to face her. "Please do not make me feel like I have to read your thoughts again."

I took a deep breath. "I can't stay here, Auset."

The room fell quiet. "And where will you and Anpu go?"

"No," I said, shaking my head. "He is going to stay here with you and Heru."

Auset titled her head. "So... you're going to abandon your son? Why would you want to do this?"

"Want is not a part of the equation," I whispered, looking away. "The simplest explanation is that I believe it to be the best course of action, for all of us."

She looked at me wearily, the joyous occasion of naming her son now marred by this. "What is the less simple explanation, then?"

I paused again. "I know that it is the right thing to do," I said, which was true in its own way. "I do not know if I can explain why. I just know I have to go."

"You should at least try harder to explain."

I signed. "Auset, please."

My sister shook her head. "What do you think you have to gain?"

I looked away from her. "I have a lot to gain, we all do." I met her in the eye and held my resolve. "You will not need to worry about me. I know I will be fine."

"You don't know that."

"I DO know that."

We both held our stance for a moment before Anpu ran into the room. "The baby, he's crying," he told Auset, looking up at her as if I was not even in the room. She leaned down and kissed his crown. "I will be there in a moment, sweet child." Anpu beamed up at her before rushing back to Heru's side.

Auset looked back to me and gasped slightly. "Is THAT why

you are leaving? Are you angry because I love your son? Because he loves me?"

I rolled my eyes. "Don't be ridiculous, Auset. You are supposed to love him, and he you. We are all family. Why would that make me angry?"

Auset softened and tilted her head. "You think I should be angry at you still, that I should be unable to stand the sight of my husband's child, born of my sister." She shook her head and stepped towards me. "You must see that I have forgiven you, and now it is turn for you to forgive yourself."

I turned away from her, giving her my back and walking closer to the window, the three room cottage feeling smaller than ever. "This is not about forgiveness. I am only thinking about what is smart, and I know that our children will be better off if I am not here."

"I don't think that makes any sense, but if you really think that's what you should do, I will support you, senet." I felt my sister's hand rest on my shoulder and I sighed in relief. I did not want to leave after a fight.

I turned back to look at her. "I truly do. This place is not my place. I don't belong here."

"You are family, Nebt-Het. You belong wherever your family is."

I nodded. "I know that, Auset."

Auset sighed. "Well, if you are determined, I will come up with a way for us to send word to one another, so you will always know where to find us if you decide to come visit, or come home."

I frowned. "You think you will have cause to leave this place, to move around and hide?"

"No, actually I don't." Auset shrugged and looked away. "But I... maybe I do not know everything."

"Don't you, though?" I whispered, trying to stop myself from crying. "If this is not the right thing, can you not just tell me that I am destined to stay, to be with my son, our sons?"

Auset fumbled to find an answer, but there was not one available. If Heru and Anpu had the destiny that she believed them to have, I would only be in the way, doubting and fearful, holding them back. I knew she was listening to my thoughts without my consent, but she said nothing, nor did she continue her attempts to talk me out of it. We both stood there, avoiding each other's face, thinking about the days to come, until neither of us could avoid the infant's cries any longer. I followed her into the small room that our sons would share and watched Auset as she fed Heru, and I knew I could not stay. They each had their destiny, and I had mine.

It would have been easy to disperse home, leave this world behind and find comfort in the sheltered shadows of eternity. I could have chosen to hide there, perhaps I should have. But the chance to travel the realm unencumbered was too appealing for me to resist.

I stripped myself of anything that would identify me, anything that would tie me to the royal family, and left our tiny house before dawn, before Anpu would awaken and ask me the questions I couldn't bear to answer. I walked along the bank of the Hapi, gathering water and nourishment as I went, stopping only to greet Ra when the sun reached its apex. The sun was midway through its journey to the west when I came upon a ship willing to board a passenger. I was not worried about being recognized, but I recited a quick heka that would make me unrecognizable to all but the Neteru before brazenly standing at the fore of the ship as it began to push northward through the beloved lands.

Our countryside was beautiful in a way that I had never realized before. The great inundation was beginning to subside and I could see villagers working diligently along the edge of the water, clearing the irrigation pipes to ensure that the flow would remain uninterrupted. Crocodiles snapped their lethal jaws from time to time, but the men were attentive, and none fell prey to the threat, at least none that I witnessed and for that I was grateful.

As the sky grew darker the edge of the river became abandoned as the villagers returned home for the evening, to their families. We kept sailing for a while, until the darkness was too bleak and continuing too dangerous, but I could not bring myself to abandon ship, and instead enjoyed the night air while the shipcaptain and his crew dined and rested. Alone, I explored the ship, reciting heka for protection and safe travels, naming each part of the ship to strengthen it as I went.

That morning, before the sun had fully risen, we had begun moving north once more, and each day we sailed further, and each night we stopped, which provided me an opportunity to explore. I had been to some of these places once before, but the experience felt new. Some of the places we stopped were vast and heavily populated, and others were just a few families, enjoying their isolation. I knew I was being oddly intrusive but I could not help but to peek into windows, watch mothers kiss their sons good night, watch fathers light fires, watch the family make offerings to Bes. I performed heka over the homes where their prayers and offerings were plenty, hoping that my gift would make up for my spying.

The ship made its final stop in the large city of Anu, and I thanked the captain for allowing me safe passage before disappearing into the morning bustle. The riverbank was boisterous with fishermen beginning to celebrate the plentiful bounty, but that was nothing compared to the city center, where farmers and herders were making their way to the temple to make offerings to ensure that their fields and beasts would produce. Many of the herders brought live animals with them, and young children were amusing themselves by chasing the chickens around, to the displeasure of all. I giggled as one particularly inquisitive child looked under the bottom of each hen for eggs, causing the birds to squeak their disapproval.

I knew I would not be allowed to enter the inner sanctum of the temple, not while disguised, so I walked around to the back wall, where other pilgrims were placing their ears against the stone and whispering their petitions, hoping to hear a blessing fall from the lips of Atum-Ra, hoping to be heard in turn. I did not want to stand out, so I too turned my face and pressed my ear against the wall, closing my eyes to ask that this land, and its people, continue to experience joy and abundance. I thanked the Great Father in advance for answering my prayer, and when I opened my eyes, I gasped in surprise by how close Setesh was standing to me.

"I have to admit, I did not expect to capture you so easily," Setesh mumbled, stepping in closer, causing the hair on my neck began to stand. I turned and pressed my back against the Temple wall to the sound of a menacingly familiar snicker. "And if you are here, your sister and son must be very close by. Tell me, where are they?"

I took a deep breath. "Actually, they are both rather far from here, I… I left them weeks ago."

He gripped my bicep tightly and continued to mutter into my ear. "What kind of mother abandons her son? It is so like you to fail at everything."

I smiled and looked up at his face. "Not everything; apparently I am still rather good at causing your blood to boil."

Setesh looked away. "What standard, if that is what you consider to be a talent."

"Is there another who might rival me? Is there any who can infuriate Naswt Biti so?"

Setesh clenched his jaw tightly, and balled his fists at his side. I touched the fingers on his right hand softly, barely perceptible at first, allowing my touch to drift across the back of his hand, his wrist, his forearm and bicep, landing gently on his chest. He responded as I knew he would; the man, my husband, was still in there, somewhere.

"I will not be convinced to treat you as any less of the traitor that you are," Setesh growled hungrily, the resonance of his tone exciting me.

"I have not asked you to," I whispered, surprising myself.

I had not planned to become his prisoner today, or any day for that matter, but somehow I was ready for this. Somehow I knew this was supposed to be. I lifted my wrists as if granting him permission and he grinned, excited.

He motioned for two of his guards to come over, and they bound my wrists before stepping back. Setesh led me by the binding to the front of the temple, where the guards called the people to attention; the center fell quiet and the people cowered.

"Remove the disguise," Setesh ordered me, and I said the heka that would allow my true self to be seen once more. Gasps rang out around the crowd, and a few turned their face from me, not wanting the bad luck of letting their eyes fall upon a traitor.

Setesh looked at me as he spoke to the people. "This woman is an enemy of your King, a traitor of this great realm. She has now been taken prisoner and will be returned to the per eah to await her punishment." He turned to the crowd. "Let this be a lesson to all those who would oppose me. There is no one who is above Naswt Biti. All are subjects under the mercy of his law."

"But she is a daughter of Ra!" one brave soul cried out, and my heart sank, hoping that whoever it was would go without being seen or caught. But that was not to be. The guards grabbed him by his shoulders and threw him to the ground, kicking his sides to force him to remain face down in the dust. They looked back at Setesh, waiting for his word on what should be done.

Setesh looked at me. "What do you think I should do with him?" he asked, clearly enjoying his moment of power. His grin was evil, sinister. I almost did not recognize this person before me.

"Bring him with us to the per eah, and decide there," I said calmly, knowing Setesh would never risk it. I could free him at the first opportunity, and I would.

Setesh waved to his guards to release the man, and they did, returning to my side and beginning to lead me through Anu, up and down each narrow passageway, parading me, the traitor, for all to see. The people turned their backs to me, pulling their children out of my path, grabbing tiny amulets of Bes for protection. I wanted to cry, but I could not, not while anyone could see my face, not with Setesh so near.

When it became clear that the parade had its intended impact, Setesh sent his guards to the dock and took me by the arm, jumping us back to the grand courtyard of the per eah. His grin was evil, sinister. Setesh spat at the ground near my feet and widened his stance, his hands on his waist. "I thought I would have to drag you back kicking and screaming."

I looked towards the great house; attendees were gathering at windows and along the river's edge, and guards came forward at the entrance to await for orders from their King. "I do not have to be here if I do not want to be," I told him, looking him straight in the eye. "You cannot make me do anything."

Setesh rolled his eyes. "You place too much faith in your

magic."

"If I remember correctly, you once placed too little faith in it."

He stepped towards me, the rage bubbling just below the surface. I felt his breath against my cheek and I closed my eyes, struggling to keep my own breath steady and even. "What is your game, woman?" Setesh snarled at me, his tone low and chilling. "What kind of trick is this?"

I inhaled deeply. "You captured me, Setesh. Do you think I walked into your entourage on purpose?"

He stepped back and raised his chin, fully in his power. Setesh had embraced his darkness, and it terrified me. He motioned to the guards at the door, but I began walking towards the guards of my own accord.

"She is a daughter of Ra," he reminded the guard, stopping him from leading me out to the village for arrest. "Take her into the great house. She will live as a prisoner here." The guard nodded and continued to escort me to the apartment that I knew too well.

Little had changed inside of my chambers, despite having been gone for much more than a year and taking nothing with me when I'd left. My trunks still lined the far wall and the bed was clean, dressed in fresh reeds. The doors to the bathing courtyard were closed, and the sitting room had been emptied of all furniture. I took my hand back from the guard and sat on the bed, and Setesh dismissed him, leaving us alone.

"Perhaps you did know I was returning," I said, tilting my head curiously, "or else why is my space so readily prepared for my arrival?'

Setesh smirked at me, closing the door behind him. "Tomorrow morning you will meet the person who I have assigned as the house manager. Your concerns will be directed to him and if he deems it necessary, he will report them to me. I will address you only if and when I choose to. You will not come to me ever."

Setesh stopped to look at me, and I simply nodded my consent. He continued. "You will have no visitors and you will not travel. You will not sit in on council meetings and you will only attend ceremonies at my request. You will eat here unless I require you at meals. You will give no orders to the house attendees and will receive no benefits or privileges."

"As you wish," I said calmly, undisturbed.

"You know, I'm curious," Setesh said, frowning. "Why don't you just leave here?"

I paused, not sure what he meant. "I thought I was under arrest?"

Setesh smirked briefly. "Leave Kemet. I will let you go, but only if you promise me that you will never return to this land. Ever. Not as long as I rule, which I intend to, for a VERY long time."

"And where am I supposed to go?"

He rolled his eyes. "Home. To the swamp you love. To be with Heru-Ur, or... Ausar," he mumbled angrily, his face darkening at the thought. "Somewhere else. Anywhere else."

When I did not answer right away, Setesh continued. "You are a traitor. Your freedom is a constant reminder of my failure, and I cannot, I WILL not, allow you to roam freely, to encourage other traitors to oppose me, or to think that I can be challenged. There will be punishment for your presence." Setesh shrugged casually. "Or, you could just leave for good. And I never have to see your face again."

I diverted my glance to the ground and thought quickly. What happens if I stay - what happens if I go?

My thoughts rested on Auset, preparing her son to oppose Setesh and reclaim his father's kingdom. And I knew then that I could not leave.

"I cannot make that decision so rashly," I answered somewhat honestly. "Can I not think on it for a while?"

Setesh opened the door to the sitting room, his frown a deep expression of annoyance. "Since you cannot think, you will stay here. Perhaps you can be useful from time to time."

Without another word he stormed out, slamming the doors behind him. I had expected him to seal the room, to use heka to try to bind my own abilities, but for whatever reason he did not, which was all I needed in order to remain in communication with Auset and the children. I sighed in relief and disrobed, immediately in need of a long bath.

That night, a hawk landed in my courtyard, a bright golden light seemingly tied around its leg, as if a ribbon. I pulled at the light and it unraveled, releasing the message. I could barely hear the whispers of my sister, so I brought the ribbon of light to my ear, allowing it to sing to me of my family, of all that had happened, of all I had missed.

Once their message was complete, I held the light to my lips and whispered my response, confirming that I was safe, letting them know that my return had been successful, from my perspective at least. I knew Auset would want to know why I had let Setesh bring me here, why I would choose to stay, and as much as I wanted to tell her of my plan, I also knew she would try to stop me.

Finished, I blew on the light, causing it to fasten itself once more to the hawk, and the hawk immediately flew off, taking my love to them. I woke the next day hoping that it would bring another message, knowing that it may be weeks before Auset saw fit to send word again, knowing that every morning I would find myself rising with hope, and knowing that this was the first time I had felt such optimism in a very long time.

"You shouldn't be here." The voice coming from behind me startling; I was expecting to be alone, as I had seen only three people since I'd arrived four months ago, and the house manager was not due to deliver my dinner until later in the evening. I turned to find it was my brother, Heru-Ur, causing me to gasp. It had been centuries since I had seen him, spoken to him.

"How did you know I was here?" I asked him honestly, feeling as if in a dream.

"Auset told me," he confessed, looking away, his expression cautious and alert. "I wanted to meet our sons," he added hesitatingly, under his breath.

I diverted my gaze to the opposite direction. "Then you have met my reasons for being here," I asserted, firmly.

He scoffed. "I don't believe that." I looked back at him, his face harder, older. "Tell me the truth, why are you really here?"

"I have told you," I insisted. Heru-Ur shook his head in disbelief.

"He can't be saved, Nebt-Het. You cannot save him."

I sighed and collapsed onto the edge of the bed. I understood why my brother thought this to be my motivation, but I wasn't ready to correct his perception, not yet. "Perhaps you are right. Perhaps I cannot save him, but that doesn't mean he can't be saved."

Heru-Ur rolled his eyes, stepping closer to me. "What makes you think he is even seeking redemption? He does not believe he has done anything wrong."

"That is not true," I insisted. "He knows right from wrong."

"Does he? Do you?" my brother asked me, sitting beside me, taking my hand. "It is very honorable for you to believe in him the way you do, but what if you are wrong and he is lost, completely?"

I pulled my hand away. "I can't believe I am hearing this coming from you."

He sighed. "I know that all things are possible, sister, but this is most unlikely. I am realistic about how this will end; I don't think you are."

I shifted to face him. "What does it mean, Heru, for me to give up on him just because he made mistakes? I made mistakes too. Are you and Auset going to give up on me?"

Heru-Ur shook his head. "It's not the same and you know it. Everything that he has done -"

"He did because of me!" I blurted out, needing to hear this truth acknowledged between us, stumbling across my confession. "If I had not made the decision to... none of this would have happened if I had just..."

"So are you here to punish yourself then? Because that is not what any of us want. Your son to grow up without his mother? Is that what you want?"

I grew quiet then. "Perhaps I AM just here to punish myself, to sit in the misery of the monster that I created."

Heru-Ur took my hand again. "You did not make him a monster. He had this inside him all along."

"Still," I continued, speaking truthfully, "I opened the way for it to emerge. I have to live with that fact for all eternity: that my choices brought us here."

He sighed. "Auset said you would not be convinced to return to her."

I looked away. "That is not the only reason why I am here," I mumbled, my first time admitting this out loud. "I really am here because of the children. Auset could have told you that I needed to leave our sons in her care. This was the best way for that to happen." This was not the entire truth, but it was all that I could tell him now.

"Not to come here, though," Heru-Ur told me. "You could

have gone home, gone anywhere. You did not have to come here. You don't have to STAY here."

He tilted his head, trying to force me to meet his eyes, so I did. "No, I have to," I asserted. "There is nowhere else."

This time, it was he who released my hand. "So you will not come with me, then."

"I wish I could," I told him, meaning it genuinely, "but if I leave now, I will never be able to forgive myself. I started something here and I must see it through."

Heru-Ur stood, and I followed suit, taking in the sight of him, the wisdom that ran through his hair, the experiences that told his story dancing in his eyes. I longed to hear that story, but not now. Not here.

"I know I don't have long," he acknowledged, and I smiled.

"You took a great risk coming here," I told him. He smiled back at me before looking at the door. We knew Setesh was approaching from the hall.

"Be careful, dearest sister," he whispered as he dispersed, his visit now just a memory. Even before his light had completely cleared the room, the door burst open and Setesh entered, his tight grip around the base of a large mace.

"Who was that?" he snarled at me, and I knew he could not be cajoled out of it. "Who came here after I told you not to have visitors?"

I sat down, needing to gain my bearings. "I cannot control the Neteru, Naswt. I sent him away as quickly as I could. I did not mean to disobey your charge."

He dropped the mace to the floor and crossed the room in two steps, gripping me tightly around the neck and lifting my frame into the air with one hand. My body began to gasp for air as I struggled to resist the natural inclination to disperse.

"Who. Was. It?"

"Your brother," I managed to squeeze out between gasps,

and Setesh dropped me onto the bed unceremoniously. I coughed a few times while I caught my breath.

"What did Heru-Ur want?"

I cleared my throat. "He wanted to take me away from here."

Setesh narrowed his eyes suspiciously. "Then why are you still here?"

I sat up straight, regaining my composure. "Because I choose to be."

This was only the third time he had been here since I'd arrived. The first two times appeared random, as if he was simply confirming that I had not violated the terms of my stay, and Setesh had paid me no attention during his examination. This time, he studied me as if a curiosity; angrily fascinated with my insistence.

"I have no intention of forgiving you."

I swallowed. "Tu, I am aware."

Setesh nodded. "Do you want me to admit that I was wrong?"

My eyebrows raised. "Were you?" I asked, instead of stepping into the trap that he'd presented.

"Not one bit."

I nodded and looked away; no good would come from my pursuit of that. "I come here seeking nothing from you," I told him, which was true in its way.

Setesh, however, saw right through me. "You are after something, and while I do not know what it is, I will find out, and I will punish you for your dishonesty."

The guard stepped in just then, earning my gratitude. "Naswt Biti, I have received word from the lower land," he told Setesh, falling to one knee. "The border is lost. The warriors were forced to retreat further inland."

Setesh nodded at him, and he rose and exited. "I am not done with you," he turned his attention back to me, his growl sending chills throughout my form.

I took a deep breath. "I will be here when you return."

He snatched his mace from the floor and stormed out, leaving me to question how much ground had been lost since my departure. I waited anxiously for the house manager to arrive with my meal, ready to interrogate him, to discover how easy it would be to get information from him.

Khetnu stepped in cautiously, knowing that I would be expecting him, but showing respect to my personal space. "Seret," he said with a flourish, finding me sitting on the bed, facing him as he entered. Khetnu carried a tray of food atop a stool, and he stepped closer to put the stool near my feet. "If it is okay with you, I will just leave this here..."

Before he could place everything down, I stood. "Are you terribly busy? I was hoping for your company while I dined." I motioned that we should step into the sitting room, and Khetnu hesitated, but indulged me. I grabbed one of the armchairs and carried it into the sitting room, and after Khetnu placed the stool before me, he went back and fetched one for himself.

I watched as he set himself up to face me, the short, round man who had been my only real guest for months. He wore baggy brown pants, so large that he needed a rope to keep them in place. The rope was covered by a long grey tunic, and the way his clothing seemed to swallow him whole only served to make him look older than he was. His hair had begun to thin on the top, but his face bore no sign of strain or aging.

Khetnu did not have the frame or talents of a warrior, which had brought some disappointment to his family, having descended from a long line of champions. Still, he had a heart for service, and made the decision to work in the per eah to make up for the skills that he lacked. I hated knowing that I was about to betray his kindness, but I did not feel that I had much choice.

"Were you in a rush to get back? If Naswt Biti has assigned

you to a particular charge, you should not keep him waiting," I started, and watched as he fidgeted and glanced at the door.

"No, Seret," Khetnu tried to assure me, "you are my top priority. I would never disrespect your request by abandoning you or my post."

I smiled and took a tiny bite of an overripe plum. "I appreciate that. You are the only one here who even acknowledges my presence."

Khetnu looked away once more, but the fidgeting had subsided. "Naswt Biti has charged the household to ignore you completely, and most here are much too afraid to disobey."

I frowned. "It is not as if he is terrorizing anyone, is he?"

Khetnu shook his head casually, shifting lower into his seat. "No, no," he admitted, "but he is quick to temper. It... frightens most, even the men."

"And you? Are you afraid of him?"

Khetnu smiled mischievously. "Not frightened, but I do proceed with caution."

I smiled back and continued to enjoy my meal. "I suppose part of why I am not allowed to interact with any of you is because I am not afraid of him at all." I looked at Khetnu straight, to give him the impression of fearlessness, and when I did not flinch, he nodded in approval.

"What are some of the stories that are told about him?" I asked casually, looking down at the tray. When Khetnu did not answer right away, I frowned. "Oh now," I said, "There must be something that is being whispered in the corners."

Khetnu glanced over his shoulder, as if concerned that the wall might be listening. "Actually, most of the gossip is about his new policies, all of the changes. One of the women in the kitchen was surprised recently by her husband's sister, who fled here with her family from the lower lands after an uprising near the border." He looked around again nervously. "Everyone who has family in the north has been trying to get word to them, make sure they are still alive."

I stopped eating and sat up. "Is her family okay, the woman in the kitchen?"

He sighed. "Yes, hers is, but some have not been so lucky." Khetnu frowned and tilted his head. "You have no idea what has been going on?"

"No," I said, "but I would appreciate it greatly if you would share with me what you know." Khetnu looked afraid, but his eyes met mine and he did not look away. I sighed. "Please Khetnu, I care about what is happening to our people."

He looked at me, relieved. "I thought you already knew, and just didn't care. It is much worse than anyone here will admit. The stories that flood in from travelers are just awful, and Naswt Biti acts as if it is not so bad. But the realm has descended into chaos."

***

The next morning I left the room for the first time, ignoring the whispers of the attendees in the hall who immediately scurried to find safe haven, away from the battle that both they and I anticipated would result. Dramatically I pushed open the heavy doors to the great hall, interrupting the council meeting, masking the degree of my dread with poise.

"Have you lost your mind?" Setesh shouted at me from the head of the table, jumping to his feet as soon as he saw my face. "You have no right -"

"I HAVE right," I interrupted him, shouting back, matching his intensity. "I am a daughter of Ra and I WILL be heard by you."

I did not approach any closer, and he did not move towards me. Our impasse lasted but a moment before Setesh looked up and down the table at his advisors. "GET. OUT."

Not a single one of them hesitated, and the guards exited last, closing the doors behind them. It was then that I started to make my way from the back of the room to where Setesh stood, waiting for me to explain myself. "Have you really put the warriors in charge of travel, the temples, cities - everything? So you hold your control by having your men threaten and arrest and kill." I slammed a fist against the table and tried to puff out my chest. "Is this what you call proper leadership? Because if so, your standard is left wanting."

"Your little show has amused me," Setesh responded, smirking at me calmly, "but I do not know how much patience I have left."

I scoffed and crossed my arms over my chest. "Admit it, Setesh. You are making terrible decisions and it is causing the men to question you. That is why our people in the north have begun to revolt. The warrior corps is stretched by having to scatter men all along the countryside, and you do not have enough men in the places where they are actually needed."

His arms were around my biceps then, and he pushed me against the wall violently, throwing me off balance. "That. Is. ENOUGH."

I tried to push him off me, but he only shook me harder, gripped my arms tighter. "This is not your nation to destroy!"

"YES IT IS!" he screamed directly into my face, causing me to go deathly still. I closed my eyes and let him shake me for a moment longer before he released me completely, putting space between us. I leaned backwards into the wall, listening as he continued his rant. "No one else has come here to tell me I am making mistakes. NO ONE. Not Djehuty, not Seshat. Not Ra. NO ONE. And here you come, telling me how to be a leader. A King. You know nothing about leadership. I AM a King. I am THE King. You cannot tell me how to be what I am. I will do this my way and you are powerless to stop me, and you will not interfere into my affairs again."

I realized I was panting a bit, staring at him directly, unafraid. He met my stare, and I saw that he was panting as well. I lowered my chin and my lip quivered. He did not look away.

"You will lose this kingdom if you do not change your course of action, Naswt Biti. You will not be able to call yourself the King for much longer."

I meant that as a genuine warning, and Setesh closed his eyes, incensed by having to admit how right I was. When his eyes opened again, the glow of rage had been replaced by the embers of desire, and while that had not been my intention, I lacked the motivation to discourage it.

I walked to him and kissed him deeply, feeling his resistance melt away as he rid me of my clothing. Soon he pushed me away and turned me around, pressing me against the wall, punishing me with each thrust. His fingers wrapped around my throat, slightly less severely than before, and I surprised myself by responding eagerly to the violence. He finished, and stepped back, and I crumbled to the floor beneath me, spent.

Setesh cleared his throat, and looked as if to speak, but decided against it, instead leaving me there to gather myself and return to my quarters, without looking back to the table, where the mace that he so often gripped was resting. I glanced at it nervously before heading to my room, walking so the guards would see me and monitor my position. When I finally sank into the bathing pool in my courtyard, I recognized the familiarity of the emotion coursing through me. Stopping the tears was beyond my capability.

I could not take it back though; I could not take anything back. I closed my eyes and tried to find myself. How did I get here? I barely recognized me, throwing myself at him like that, after the way he'd spoken to me, treated me. I wasn't entirely clear why I was here at all. What if my entire plan was completely misguided? I slid under the water; maybe I should just go home and stay there until Heru was of age. I could feel myself wanting to sigh deeply. That wasn't the answer. I started something that I had to finish.

I came up and closed my eyes, and took the satisfying breath my lungs had desired. Tears continued to fall across my cheeks, mixing with the bathwater effortlessly. I was so far from where I ever thought I would be, but now was not the time to worry about that. I had taken time to contemplate my state that I did not have.

I reluctantly pulled myself from the pool and let the water drip from my body for just a moment before dispersing quickly into the great room, grabbing the mace from the table, and returning just as quickly to the bedroom as I'd left. The mace was heavier than I'd expected it to be, which caused me to wonder briefly about how strong Setesh really was, his ability to wave this around without struggle deepening my sense of anxiety and urgency.

Examining it from top to bottom, I held the top in my right hand and the base in my left; once I removed my hands entirely from the weapon, it floated gently in front of me, and I kept my hands level beneath it, palms facing upward, creating a soft gray aura around it. There was no response to this, as the mace was not enchanted, and I breathed a sigh of relief. The gray smoke then began to wrap itself around the mace, as if it were strips of linen, preparing the mace for burial. I looked to the door quickly before whispering heka:

"I am She, the evening boat of Ra, the lady of watchfulness, the great power in the place of Ausar, Auset, and Heru. One of the great nine enchants this weapon, no longer effective for he who wields it. The holder shall find his malice turned to compassion; anger to understanding; resentment to forgiveness. No longer shall this be used in rage against the children of the Great Father. The Unseen One who is known and unknown to all conceals what He chooses not to reveal."

I took a deep breath as the mace seemed to soak the gray smoke into itself, and once the immersion was complete I gripped the base again. I could not discern any difference from how it felt in my hands before, so I quickly jumped the mace back to the great hall, leaving it in the place where I had found it, where I knew Setesh would come to look for it, if he had not already noticed it missing. My energy gathered back in the pool in my apartment's courtyard, and I slid under the water once more, to wait.

Sa – Protection

I did not leave the per eah then, even though it would have been understandable if I had gone, welcomed even. At the time, it felt like abandoning the realm that I had helped to build, the structure that I had supported for centuries. I believed it needed me, and despite being unwanted by its current leadership, I could not find it in myself to leave. I could not watch the world crumble around me and do nothing, and there was nowhere else that I would have preferred to be.

It feels wrong to admit that, knowing that my son was in the world, growing every day, becoming who he is without me. I should have immediately wanted to return to his side, but the realm was just as much mine as he was. Anpu was in good hands, and Kemet was not. I often felt that perhaps I'd made the wrong choice, but as I have come to learn, you make the choices you feel are best in the moment that you are making them, and you live yourself into the consequences. I am certain that he wouldn't be who he is if I had not become who I am.

The next year in the per eah was easier once the spell was cast, and its effect on Setesh was quick and noticeable. Within a week I found myself back at the table during council meetings, needed because once more I was the only one besides him with any experience running a nation. But the uprisings continued, particularly in the far flung regions of our beloved lands, where the touch of our Naswt Biti was so imperceptible that it was believed to be non-existent.

"You will not come with me." Setesh spoke after dismissing

his counselors from the room. It was a question that sounded like an order. He stood with his back to me, staring out the large window to the east as darkness slowly crept across the sky.

I sighed. "You do not need me to." I stood, staying where I was, the seat Djehuty used to occupy, near the door. "This journey is to show you as the loving father to your people, their guide, their source of strength and inspiration; while reinforcing that Naswt Biti is he who will bring the flail across their naked backs should they fail to listen. You have done too much flailing and not enough... loving."

Setesh nodded, but still did not turn to face me. I stood there, waiting for him to dismiss me, patiently, silently. Finally he responded.

"I will make this tour of goodwill," he mumbled softly, "I will take one of the priests with me, but I will not leave you in charge while I am gone."

I swallowed. "I had not expected that you would."

Setesh finally turned to face me. "I will appoint someone who I trust, someone who no longer serves in the corps, to be my eyes and ears. And you will report to him, and assist him in every way."

"As you wish, Naswt."

"And Khetnu? Are you satisfied with having him by your side?"

I hesitated. "Khetnu serves at the pleasure of the King, and his function gives him authority over the entire royal house. He is not my attendant personally."

Setesh smirked, but it was gentle, teasing. "Do you trust him?"

"Yes," I answered honestly, taking a deep breath. "Khetnu is a good man."

Setesh nodded. "He will remain here and make sure your

needs are met in my absence. You are dismissed."

I curtseyed and left the room without speaking again. Setesh would spend considerable time across the realm, and I would be here, alone, again. But this time, I was not dismayed by the prospect, only grateful for my freedom, and for the truce that my heka had cast.

Again I could have left, anytime during the two year span that Naswt Biti was away from the great house, but still I stayed behind. It had not taken long for me to convince the King's Eyes and Ears that I could be trusted, and despite his many years of leading warriors, he was humble enough to recognize and heed my advice. The attendees restored their sense of respect towards me, curtseying in the halls when I passed and standing when I entered the room. Not confined to my apartment, I participated in the harvest festival and in the celebration of the annual inundation, and it was so familiar, my old self was coming back into being. And while that had been my intention, it was not what I wanted.

Setesh returned to little celebration; his journey had also failed to accomplish its purpose despite the apparent softening in his personality. I took that as an opportunity to retreat from making public appearances, pulling back from council meetings and taking meals alone in my suite, under no threat or coercion. I needed to try and figure out what I was doing wrong.

A knock at my door pulled me out of my thoughts and back to the present. "You may enter," I shouted, and Khetnu peeked his head around the edge of the door before stepping fully into my bedroom.

"It is only me, Seret," he announced himself unnecessarily, making an informal bow before coming closer to the bed. I had been laid across it lazily, but in his presence I began to sit up.

"Is there something I can help you with?" I asked when, after a few moments, Khetnu had not spoken.

He cleared his throat. "Tu, my apologies, I just wanted to see if you were planning to take dinner in your room again tonight, or if perhaps we could draw you out to join Naswt Biti for a meal?"

I frowned and sat up straighter. "Has he requested my presence?"

Khetnu hesitated and averted his eyes. "Naswt Biti simply asked me to inquire, Seret."

I looked at our house manager closely, trying to read his expression, but I remained unclear as to his intention. "I will join him if I am summoned. If not, I will respect his rule for me and stay here."

Khetnu nodded and bowed once more, but did not move towards the door. I watched him struggle with what to do next. "Is there something else?"

"Tem, my lady," he started, "I just wanted to make sure that everything is okay. You had such interest in the state of the realm just a few weeks ago, but it seems now that you have turned your back on such matters. Is there something troubling you?"

I kept my attention on him, and he did not look away this time. "Please do not interpret my solitude as forsaking the people. I am here should I be of need. I simply have other matters that I must attend to."

Khetnu sighed. "I understand. May I come to you, then, if there are matters that require your attention?"

"Of course," I reassured him. "Is there something immediate that you believe I should be concerned with?"

"Tem, Seret," Khetnu tried to reassure me, but I was not convinced. Still, I did not push further, and allowed him to depart without another word. I was tempted to allow him to pull me back into the thick of things, but if I were to trace my troubles to a single source, I knew it was my failure to be satisfied with the place that I had been given. My ambition and lack of faith had caused me to betray my husband, devastate my sister, abandon my son. My challenges were not external as they may have been for others. Instead, I was my own challenge.

As difficult as it proved to ignore the reports from across the realm and not offer my counsel, I wanted desperately to rebalance the scales by staying out of it. I ignored the voice of doubt that told me to stop being so extreme, that Setesh needed me, that I was important and valuable and wise. The impulse within that urged me to seek distinction began to quiet itself, and outside of taking my moonlit walks, I settled in to the comfort of being unseen and unheard.

Another year passed before an impossibly familiar dread began to creep into my being, this time completely unrelated to anything that had happened in my life or in the great house. This time I knew I was being summoned, and I knew not to ignore it.

"Welcome home," Djehuty spoke grandly as my energy reformed and I opened my eyes. Usually Seshat would be the one to greet us, so to see Seba directly caused my eyebrows to rise.

"I hope I did not keep you waiting," I said, not knowing what else to say.

Djehuty gestured to his left, and long, narrow benches manifested for us to sit upon. We could look directly at one another as we spoke, which made this occasion all the more significant. In his regal purple robes, Djehuty seemed older than ever before, his dark eyes heavy with compassion and his lips turned down in a thin, emotionless frown.

After a brief silence, I cleared my throat. "Is something wrong?"

Djehuty nodded. "Yes, there is."

I swallowed, as the prospect of what he was not asking me to do began to make me nervous. "Things appear to be smooth, for now. Setesh is no longer terrorizing the attendees. The house is calmer, at ease."

"That may be true," Djehuty acknowledged, "but."

He stopped speaking so abruptly, it was all I could do to take a deep breath. "Okay," I accepted, shifting my weight gently, and pausing for a moment. "Okay."

Djehuty smiled and raised an eyebrow. "Okay."

I shook my head. "I don't understand."

"You do, you just do not want to." Djehuty stood and stretched his legs a bit, beginning to pace the room thoughtfully. "You want to stay in the house, endure no conflict. Experience no more of your husband's animosity."

I looked away. "He's asked me not to call him that."

"I am aware."

I looked back to Djehuty, who'd turned to face me, still smiling. His knowing look was reassuring, but annoying. "If I must do this, then I want to come home after it's done, for good."

Djehuty smiled broader, and returned to his seat on the bench. "No, you will not come home. You will stay in the great house until you are called."

"Called? For what?"

Djehuty shrugged. "When you are needed."

An insufficient answer, but I knew I'd get no more from him. I sighed. "So you and Ra intend to torture me then?"

"You intend to torture yourself," Djehuty reminded me, crossing his arms over his chest. "You are the one who chose to go there and stay. So stay."

I closed my eyes. "I don't need to stay there, Seba."

"Don't you?"

I sighed once more. "What if I'm wrong? What if this isn't what I am supposed to be doing?"

I heard Djehuty chuckle warmly, and I looked at him. His eyes twinkled with warmth, reflecting the light of the night sky. "What if indeed."

We sat there silently, I with my illusions of what to come, and he with his patient and quiet wisdom. I knew I could not refuse what I was being told, for Djehuty spoke as the mouth of the Great Father, and to deny this would be to defy the highest authority.

"What happens after I lift the heka?" I mumbled gently.

Djehuty cleared his throat. "Everything that is meant to."

I could not help but to despise his answer. "You can't be more direct?"

He looked away, no longer smiling. "No. I cannot."

I sighed once more, and nodded, closing my eyes to make the jump home, landing in my bedroom right as the sun had begun to embrace the western horizon. Khetnu would be arriving soon with a meal, but I was not hungry; I had been completely recharged by the few short moments spent in the ethers.

The knock came to my bedroom door, and Khetnu entered silently. I looked up at him and nodded, and he bowed before starting to exit, as quietly as he'd come.

"Before you go," I called to him, causing his back to stiffen, "is Naswt Biti having his dinner in the great hall? Is he even here today?"

Khetnu frowned and looked at me curiously. "Naswt Biti is at dinner presently, and I believe he is alone. Are you planning to join him? I am happy to take your things to the great hall, if you'd like me to."

I shook my head. "No, no," I answered quickly, "I will take it myself. Dua."

He nodded and took his leave, and I sighed, turning my back

on the food laid out before me without a second glance. Taking a deep breath, I jumped myself to the room where Setesh ate, because if I'd walked down the hall, I might have turned back before getting there.

Setesh sat up when he realized it was me. "Look who has come out of hiding," he mumbled, his frown softening.

I began to walk towards him, but stopped. My plan had been to distract him long enough to take possession of the mace, but something about that didn't feel right. Despite how angry and intolerable Setesh might become, I had to make an effort to do the right thing.

"I have come to ask you for your mace," I told him plainly, looking him directly in the eye.

Setesh tilted his head, curious. "Why would you need it?"

I paused, but did not look away. "To lift the binding spell that I placed upon it."

"A binding spell," he repeated, his tone full of wonder. Setesh looked away for a moment, in admiration of my work. "Why would you want to lift it now?" he asked as his lips curled into a snarl. I felt my insides shudder. "Do you believe that I am fully tamed? Or do you prefer me at my worst?"

"Neither," I admitted, "I believe it was a mistake to try to bind you in the first place."

That was partly true, even though I had not come to that conclusion on my own. Still, I was willing to own my error, and I waited to see what the consequences would be. Setesh studied me as I stood there under his disapproving and bitter glare.

Eventually, he shrugged. "It is in my bedroom," he grumbled, returning back to his meal. I waited a moment for him to speak once more, but when it appeared he would not, I turned to make my exit.

"Wife," Setesh growled derisively, "you should stay there and wait for me."

I spun around to face him. "Why would I want to do that?"

"I don't recall asking you what you wanted."

Setesh still did not look away from his food, and I became angry at the primal instinct eager to obey him. "You cannot decide I am your wife again just because you... need something."

Setesh glanced up at me. "Isn't that what you've wanted all along? Isn't that why you're here?"

I took a deep breath. "Why can't we talk here? What do you have to say that is so private?"

"Can you not for once respect me and DO AS I'VE ASKED?"

His shout caused the table and chairs to shiver in tandem, and I too felt a chill fall across the room. I closed my eyes and spun around once more, leaving without another word. I walked down the hallway to his apartment, entered the bedroom, and found the mace, resting in a treasured spot along the east wall. It took me only a moment to pull the gray mist from the weapon and release it altogether, and by the time I was finished I knew I would wait for him there.

I did not have to wait for long, thankfully. "Is it done?" he asked as he walked into the room, flinging himself upon the bed with abandon.

I nodded. "Tu, it's done."

Setesh looked at me as I sat across the room in one of the armchairs, keeping my back straight and feet firmly planted upon the floor. He reached down to the corner and picked up the mace, holding it in his left hand, eyeing me cautiously. "It does feel different," he mumbled.

"It does not," I spat out quickly. "You did not detect the spell before, and thus you cannot be aware of its absence."

"What makes you think I did not know about the spell?"

I rolled my eyes. "What did you summon me here to

discuss?"

Setesh sat up, then stood, walking over to me, his grip on the mace tight. I stiffened my back even more. "What reason would you have for a binding spell, since you are clearly not afraid of me?"

"Setesh, please," I whispered, not wanting to look up at him. I knew that he was trying to break me, and I believed then that he would win.

He began to pound one end of the mace into his right hand, as his left continued to grip to the long, heavy handle. Each thud caused me to wince, despite my effort to appear unaffected. I shut my eyes tight; yet steadying my nerves became more and more challenging.

Right then I could hear the words of Djehuty echoing through my frame, and I tried desperately to hold them in this moment. Before one can master a realm, one must first master the self.

I took a deep breath, and stood, opening my eyes. The thud stopped, and Setesh matched my stare, waiting to see what I would say, or do. I chose to do nothing, just hold my stance.

"It was an honor to be allowed to have a say in my kingdom, despite everything you have done to betray me," Setesh grumbled softly.

I swallowed. "Yes it was."

"Then why did you abandon your position?"

I blinked, and my gaze landed upon his chest. "To cease being one seeking distinction."

"You will not abandon me. You owe me that."

I looked back up at him, his stare sharp and cold. "No. I will not."

Setesh looked away, and took a small step back. I wanted to breathe a sigh of relief, but I knew we were not done. "Your spell afforded you certain liberties that you did not deserve.

This is yet another example of you betraying me for your own benefit without giving any real thought to how your actions affect me or anyone else."

My eyes fell to the floor. "You know that wasn't my intention," I whispered.

"Intention or not," Setesh paused for a moment, "everything that has happened to you, and everything that will happen to you, is the consequence you must bear. I will not allow you to believe that you have gotten away with what you've done."

"I don't believe that."

"Good." I looked up to see him turn away from me and begin making his way to the courtyard. "You will continue to take meals alone, stay indoors, and keep away from the attendees and guards. I will come to you in private if and when I believe that you can be of service to me. You will not ever refuse me."

I shook my head, although he could not see. "I will not refuse any reasonable request that you make of me, Naswt Biti. But I cannot say that a time will not arise when I will see fit..."

My words trailed off as Setesh turned back to look at me. I knew better than to play with fire. I waited silently for him to speak, or scream, or attack. I could see by the width of his chest and tension in his arms that any of the above were viable options.

"Get out," he whispered, and I immediately obliged.

For the first time, I chose to follow the rules. Khetnu became my only visitor again for an entire year, and he was unable to stay every day, as his time was full with managing the great house. I was forced to make peace with being in the background, forgotten, unseen. The one thing I had always feared was coming true, and I had no choice but to accept it, and I was finally willing to.

I settled in to this life of quiet solitude not to make Setesh happy, but to experience what was intended for me all along. I began to experience the physical plane without the burden of ambition, without needing to make myself important, without wondering what else I could or should be doing. I chose to appreciate what I was doing, even if that was nothing, which it very often was. I let go of myself entirely, and I felt more like myself than I'd ever felt in this form.

Setesh finally came to check on me. He found me leaning against the outer wall of my apartment's small courtyard, as I was during most nights, looking to the horizon.

"Khetnu tells me that you have not left this room."

I turned to face him, and noticed the worn and tired lines in his face. "I have barely left this spot, except to eat and sleep." I motioned to the floor, and he sat on the ground, crossing his legs under him. I did the same. "I was not expecting you."

Setesh looked into the starry night. "The temple at Hebenu needs a new high priest, since the elder priest has fallen very ill. It will not be long before he leaves this world." He stopped briefly, and I waited for him to continue. "He has a son, who is old enough and learned, and who has been made to believe that he will take his father's place. He also has a prized student whom he has groomed for many years. A man that many say is wise and whose words heal the spirit." Setesh looked down to the ground, purposely avoiding my face, but did not continue.

I cleared my throat. "Perhaps there is a way to give them both something that they want." When Setesh did not speak, I continued. "It is possible they only *believe* they want the same thing. Perhaps if they were made aware that there are other options, they may realize their hearts' true desires."

Setesh nodded, stood, and walked out. So it began with us, that he would drop in once a week and share a thought, and I would speak to it, and he would leave without another word. This became our routine for five years, until one day I dared to break the pattern.

"When was the last time you've been home?" I asked, right as Setesh began making his way towards the door. The question stopped him, but he did not face me.

"I cannot recall the time," he admitted gravely, "it seems like it was a lifetime ago."

I took a deep breath. "You should go and recharge. You must keep your strength if you are to continue to be an effective leader."

Setesh looked at me. "Are you implying that I am losing my effectiveness?"

"**Tem.** Only that you can be better if you go."

He looked away. "You don't get to tell me what I need."

To that I did not respond, and he left without another word, this time choosing not to return for over a month. I made no effort to offer more than what was asked of me, and our weekly sessions resumed.

Soon after, I could tell he had taken my advice and gone home, for the strain in his eyes had been lifted, and his skin had been revitalized. "Is there something you want?" he asked me, emotionless, without warmth or genuine concern.

"Yes, actually," I admitted, "I do miss taking walks at night. I would like to stroll through the village, with your permission."

He nodded. "I will grant you that, as long as you remain where my guards can see you. If you intend to change your course or alter your location, you must make me aware of it first."

I nodded my consent. He didn't begin to exit, and his hesitation caused me to speak. "I can see you are reenergized. Is it safe to assume that you've traveled home?"

"Tu."

I smiled. "I'm glad. You look well."

Setesh turned and looked at me, and for the first time in a long time, I found myself seeing my husband. It took me completely by surprise, and I felt my cheeks redden. "I think I will retire for the evening, Naswt Biti. I thank you for stopping in to see me."

A darkness passed over his features quickly. "Gerh nfr," he mumbled, and left.

I took my first walk in many years the next night, and enjoyed it thoroughly. There were a wealth of guards roaming throughout, at least a few of them tasked with reporting my movements, but I did not mind the supervision. The opportunity to see life flourish was my primary concern. I walked every night, except for those when Setesh came to see me, never getting tired of being bathed by the light of the moon.

Not much changed over the next three years. Setesh continued to visit once a week, less for advice and more for company. Most nights we did not even speak, just sat in the courtyard and enjoyed the night. Eventually I learned to retire to bed and leave him to his meditations, but after finding him asleep in an armchair near my bed on two separate occasions, I began to invite him to stay whenever it was clear he had no interest in going. I looked forward to spending these nights with my husband, and I understood from this that I should have focused on what I had all along, instead of concerning myself with what I didn't.

Still, nothing is meant to last forever. On the night that changed everything, I dispersed from the great house to the outskirts of the village and began my regular walk along the center path. I noticed quickly that several of the guards were not posted in their normal spots, and I wondered why I had been left to wander unobserved, not naive enough to believe that it was because Setesh had extended his trust.

I came back to the apartment to investigate, stepping into the hallway cautiously, hearing the loud voices cascading down the hallway, inching closer to hear without making my presence known. I could not make out the words of whoever was in the room with him, but I could hear his voice reverberate to where I crouched, eavesdropping.

"Are you saying you THINK he has an heir, or you KNOW?" There was a hesitation, a stretch of silence that apparently went on longer than Setesh wanted, then a loud thud and the sound of a chair breaking against the wall. "Are you telling me that there are citizens taking up arms against MY WARRIORS based on a RUMOR?"

I dispersed back to my bedroom immediately, stepping into the courtyard and locking the doors behind me. Taking a deep breath, I pulled up a dark green ball of light from my center and whispered into it, "He knows." A hawk flew down and landed on the wall, and I wrapped the light around his claw before he took off once more, headed towards Auset and our sons. I sighed in relief, which lasted only a second, as I turned to find Setesh banging on my courtyard door.

I knew he would break it if he had to, so I walked around the pool's edge back to the door and unlocked it voluntarily, then held my hands up in a defensive positive, expecting him to throttle me for information. He stepped into the courtyard and instead began to walk around the pool in the other direction, away from me. I sighed again, another short lived relief.

"You knew about this, didn't you?" Setesh asked me, his tone deceptively calm, but with all of my experience, I knew of the violence that lay underneath.

"Tu," I answered simply, not wanting to pretend that I had no idea what he was referring to, not wanting to lie anymore.

He nodded and looked down. "And you know where they are?"

I hesitated. "I know where they were," I answered honestly, believing that Auset would move as soon as she got my message, and any information I provided him would be useless.

Setesh looked at me. "When was the last time you heard from her?"

"A week ago."

"How old is he?"

He began to approach me, and I backed into the courtyard wall. "Setesh, please."

"Answer my question. How old is he?"

I shook my head. "He is just a boy, barely a man."

Setesh chuckled. "Well, which is it? Just a boy or barely a man?"

I didn't answer, and when he got close, I dispersed to the other side of the pool. He spun to face me, his eyes lit and his lips curled. "Is your son with them? Is that why you did not bring him back here with you?"

I nodded, for it was all I could manage in the moment. Setesh began to walk towards the courtyard doors, and I hoped for a minute that he was done questioning me, but I should have known better. He dispersed to where I stood and grabbed my arms so quickly that I did not realize I was taking him with me when I jumped. We landed in the open field, to the west of the per eah, and he dropped my arms forcefully, causing me to fall into the desert sand. I looked up at him, towering over me.

"Is he coming for me here? Is he going to try to take the realm from me?"

I blinked. "No, not... not yet."

"Not yet," he mumbled, turning away. "So, eventually."

I took a deep breath, trying to steel myself. "Yes, eventually."

Setesh knelt in front of me. "And is that why you are here? To help them? To hide them from me?"

"No," I answered him honestly, picking myself up enough to

look at him directly. "Auset is more powerful than you or I. She does not need my help to hide from you, or to protect her sons from you. You want to believe that I have betrayed you again, but I have not."

"I don't believe you," he mumbled, standing and looking away.

I stood also, amazed by what I was seeing. "You DO believe me. That is why you are afraid. You are afraid that the sons of Ausar will have a claim to this realm and it will threaten your hold over the people, over their hearts," I declared, beginning to shout these truths at his back, daring him to refuse them. "You are afraid that this rumor will erode the legitimacy of your Kingship; that you will turn out to be a temporary placeholder until the real King takes his rightful place. You are afraid of a child. And you should be."

Setesh laughed a roaring howl that spun the winds around us and shook the sky. "You are simply trying to get a rise from me, woman, but I am not in the mood for you today." He turned back to face me. "I am not pleased that you did not share this information with me, when I distinctly remember ordering you to tell me everything you knew."

I did not answer, and he studied my face for a moment, waiting to see if I would speak. When I refused, he shrugged. "And how exactly is this child going to remove me from the throne?"

I frowned. "That is not important right now, Setesh."

"And why not?" he asked me, amused.

"Because he is not coming for you today. Nor tomorrow, nor the next day." I stepped closer to him so that I could see him more clearly. "For now, you are still Naswt Biti, and you will be for the foreseeable future."

His face was even, steadied, and while he did not look angry, he also did not look worried. I tried not to blink, holding my own against him. After a moment, Setesh nodded and turned to face the great house in the distance. "You do not think I should find them."

I swallowed. "I do not think you *will* find them. And you will waste your energy on a thankless, impossible task, when there is much that needs to be done here, right now."

His hand was swift, and I found myself falling to the sand before even knowing that I had been hit, his knuckles against my lip drawing blood. I looked up, his countenance menacing, his lips curled in a sinister grin. "You take too many liberties with your speech," he said, a bitter lightness in his tone. "You eat because I allow it. You live because I allow it. You stay because I ALLOW IT."

I closed my eyes. "I hope I will not need to remind you of this again." I sighed and nodded. He grabbed my arm and pulled me to my feet. "When we return to the per eah, you will show me on a map where they were -"

"I cannot do that, Naswt." I spoke without hesitation, resolved. "Punish me if you must but I am not going to reveal to you their location."

"I intend to." He jumped us to the far end of the village, to the dark, unkempt cottage that was used to hold those who violated the law. The guards stood upon seeing us, and one of them quickly turned to open the locked door. Setesh threw me inside, and I looked around to find I was alone, the door locked firmly behind me. I expected he would then use heka to bind me to my new home, but he did not, instead charging the guards to hold me there before returning to the per eah.

I did not understand why he would not seal this place, and thought it to be a trap somehow, so I settled in along the back wall of the cottage to try to figure out what exactly could be his plan. At some point I found myself awakened by the sun peeking in through the narrow windows, and a loud banging at the door. I did not even remember succumbing to the sleep, but before I could stand, the door crept open carefully and Khetnu stepped inside holding a jug of water and a bowl of bread and fruit.

"I was sent to bring you a meal, Seret," he announced respectfully, despite the significant reduction in my status. "I apologize for not being able to present this to you in a more suitable environment," he added quickly, looking around nervously at the condition of the room.

I smiled. "No, this is fine, I appreciate that you made your way here to tend to me."

I gave him permission to sit, and took the jug from him, as I was more parched than hungry. The quick gulp caused a small sting as I recalled where my lip had been cut the night before. I put the jug down and brought my hand to my face, causing Khetnu to tilt his head in concern.

"Are you alright, Seret?" he asked, examining my features. "Have the guards been cruel to you during your time here?"

"No, no," I assured him, brushing off his concern. "I am fine. You will need to return to the great house soon. I will be quick."

Khetnu tried to smile and take in his surroundings. "I am sure Naswt Biti will not leave you here for long. He spent much time preparing me to come here to tend to you this morning, expressing grave concern to your condition. I am sure you will be back in the great house yourself in no time."

I looked away. "You are quite the optimist, Khetnu." After a moment of silence, I added, "I am content to stay here as long as it is needed. Naswt Biti will allow me to return when he deems it appropriate."

"I'm sure there is something you can do to speed the process along," he nudged gently, trying to be casual. "You are his sister, and his wife. He cannot want to keep you here like this."

I smiled. "Unfortunately my current state is not of my doing, and thus changing it is not up to me."

Khetnu looked confused, and continued to watch as I ate, slowly. "If you have committed no crime, then why has he locked you away here? Surely it is a mistake; he cannot be so cruel to his own flesh."

I frowned. "Are you truly this naive, or are you being facetious?" After the words poured out of me, I realized how harsh they sounded. "Forgive me, Khetnu. I did not mean to offend."

He stood and wiped off the dirt from his legs. "You did not offend. You are right in a way. I am aware of how hard Naswt Biti is. Yet I cannot fathom being such a way with one's own family, is all. I would think that you would be held in his heart as an exception."

I looked up at him once more and smiled. "Surely you have heard what I have done to earn his disregard. I am no innocent."

He paused and glanced out of the window. "I have heard that you have birthed the son of your husband's brother, the son of the great King Ausar. I was young when you were with child, and not yet in service of the great house. But I have heard."

I focused my attention back to the bowl before me, but it was not long before I realized that Khetnu had not pulled his attention away from the window. It was then that I felt the warming sensation in my core, and I heard the soft cry of a falcon. I knew the bird was hovering above the cottage, waiting for an opportunity to come down and deliver a message from Auset.

I stood and touched his shoulder, pulling his attention away from the sky. "You should get back to your responsibilities. I appreciate the time you have spent here with me today."

He shrugged casually and did not move towards the door. "I can stay a little longer, Seret. I am not yet needed at my post."

I smiled in understanding. "Naswt Biti sent you here, did he not?"

His eyes shot up in surprise. "Only to make sure you were well nourished, Seret! He was concerned for your well-being; even though he is angry, he does not want -"

"Stop, Khetnu," I interrupted, shaking my head. "You and I both know that is not true. He sent you here to see if you could encourage me to reveal the information that he seeks."

Khetnu looked at me for a few minutes, his eyes wide, before sighing deeply and dropping his shoulders and gaze. He looked down at the floor as if ashamed, but when he brought his eyes back up to mine, I could see that truly, it was fear.

"My son is in the warrior corps," he began, explaining to me quietly. "Naswt Biti said that if I return without learning where Auset is, he will make sure my son never returns to his family."

I took a deep breath and nodded before reaching my hand out of the thin slot in the wall. The falcon descended and I felt the ribbon slip off his claw and rest between my fingers. I pulled my hand back inside and listened to the message, then clapped my hands together four times, scattering the light and sending the falcon back to his place in the heavens.

Turning to Khetnu, I began to give him what he needed to hear to keep his family safe. "Tell Setesh that I received a message from Auset while you were here. Tell him that Auset and our sons were settled in the south, but now she has decided to move them to a village in the north, where they can live among the people and get to know the land that they will one day rule. Let him know that the message did not say which village; only that it is in the lower lands. Assure him that I scattered the message in front of your eyes and did not send word back to her. Do you think you can do that?"

He nodded, and sighed in relief. "Is that truly where Auset has taken your son?" Khetnu asked, his voice sounding so innocent that I wanted to believe that he had no ulterior motive for asking. Still, I did not trust him to keep the truth from Setesh when under pressure, and so I lied, hardly the worst of my sins to date.

"I would not let you deliver a false message when it would cost you so much." I stepped closer to him, hoping he would be convinced by a genuine gaze. "I am sorry that this has compromised the life of your son, but I promise I have given you what you need to keep him safe."

Khetnu was convinced, and his arms tensed up for a moment, as if he was struggling with the desire to hug me. Instead, he knelt to pick up the jug and bowl before bowing to me formally, his eyes watering. "Thank you," he said, his voice soft. "I am sorry that you had to compromise your family to protect mine."

"You have nothing to apologize for," I assured him, and he turned and exited the cottage without another word. I was there for a little while longer before one of the guards opened the door and stepped inside. "You have been asked to return to the per eah," he announced dramatically, expecting me to step past him and begin the long walk back. Instead, I dispersed back to my apartment, immediately disrobing for a long bath.

I knew Setesh would likely find the small house where Auset had been hiding with the boys, but even if I had given up their true location, he would never find them. I believed in the potency of her magic, and her ability to cloak their identities as needed. I hoped that Anpu was stronger now, able to sense danger well before it approached, able to guide them to safety and conserve his abilities. I knew that Heru was older, his own abilities and strengths being defined. I was not worried for them at all, surprising myself by embracing a genuine sense of faith.

Khetnu came in to bring my night meal, smiling from ear to

ear. "Naswt Biti has guaranteed the well-being of my son for the information I provided him earlier," he shared with me as he placed my food down on a small tray. "He could not believe that I actually saw you receive a message. He was very pleased."

"I am so glad that it all worked out so well," I told him, and I meant it.

"Naswt Biti traveled to the south this afternoon, doing that light thing," he continued, "and he found that little house that you told me about, but you were right, they were gone. But he found clues that they had been there until recently, so he was satisfied for now. He ordered warriors to begin looking for them in the north, and I think he is going to follow them in a few days."

I drank from the jug and nodded. "Probably sooner than that."

"The generals are concerned about the warriors leaving their positions in the north to search for Auset. They think it is essential that the border be held with high reinforcements, but Naswt Biti does not care. He is determined."

I nodded again, this time not responding. Khetnu continued to assail me with the details of the day until I finished eating. I placed the jug onto the tray and smiled.

"Will you let me know who he decides to leave in charge here, in his absence? Assuming you hear something, I mean." I smiled at him innocently, and he grinned back.

"Tu, Seret, of course I will." Khetnu collected everything that he'd brought in with him and began to make his exit, but something stopped him. "Do you know what they say about you? The parents of the village, they feed a fear of you, to keep their children well behaved."

My eyebrows rose in shock. "Fear? Of me?"

Khetnu hesitated. "They say you come in the shadows of

night to release the Ba of a man while he sleeps. They say you are the mother of the eternal night; that you decide when the time is right to send us to the west." He swallowed and averted his eyes. "The children are told never to look upon your face, and the villagers have begun to fear when you stroll by their homes. I just thought you should know that."

I wanted to laugh, but I could see the hints of truth in his eyes and I knew that even he was feeling a bit cautious in my presence. "I suppose it is my fault," I admitted, "I have locked myself in this house for many years. It is only natural for one to become superstitious, but Khetnu, you have nothing to fear."

He appeared to relax a bit, and smiled. "I hope I did not upset you by sharing this with you. I just thought you should know."

"The people will be most relieved," I responded, "for I suspect that was my final night outside of these walls for a very long time."

I was once more confined to my bedroom, this time with no visits from Setesh to anticipate. That is not say he stopped checking in on me; only that the pleasant comfort that we had come to afford one another had gone for good. Instead I was faced with the challenge of enduring his wrath, which grew steadily with each passing year. He and I both knew that the coming of Heru drew near, and it only made him angrier, desperate to eliminate the largest threat to his rule, unable to focus on any other thing.

My only true comfort lied in watching Khetnu gracefully age, despite the increasingly infrequent occasions when he was able to stay and sit with me. I never asked if Setesh had told him to stop being kind to me, but I suspected that he knew his actions might be met with punishment. I hope they never were.

Setesh no longer restricted his visits to the evenings, instead choosing a more irregular schedule, which kept me on constant alert. He was especially harsh in the mornings, and as he left my bedroom, his maniacal laughter would shake the doors in their frames, and I would burst into unwanted sobs. I would never let him see me break, but that did not mean I was not broken.

Khetnu found me one early afternoon, my body curled around itself, trying to give the comfort I could seek in no other place. I had long stopped crying, but I couldn't bring myself to rise and face the day. Defeated, I felt his hand rest upon my shoulder. It was difficult but I rolled over to face him, and he smiled.

"Seret, you must eat something," he told me gently, sitting on the bed next to me. "I cannot allow you to starve yourself."

I tried to smile back. "Dua for your concern, but I will not wither away if I miss a single meal."

Khetnu frowned. "From the look of the trays I collected yesterday, you have missed more than one meal." He paused and glanced out the courtyard doors. "I will not leave until you eat something."

I knew he meant it, so I pulled myself up and took a deep breath. "Is there any news from the south?"

"He has not found your sister's son, if that is what you mean." Khetnu looked at me, his frown lines deepening. "That does not mean he has ceased his search. On the contrary, he has dedicated more of the warrior corps towards seeking Auset. The rebellions continue to go unaddressed."

I sighed. "And the trade routes?"

Khetnu shook his head. "Littered with thieves, as I told you before. Many tradesmen have chosen not to sell their wares outside of their home city, because it is not safe to travel between the two lands."

I closed my eyes. Without tradesmen from the south bringing their wares to the north, and vice versa, many would be left without the resources they needed to properly preserve food and water for the inundation season. Not securing the routes of passage was a dire mistake, but I could do nothing about it, and Setesh would care of nothing but Heru. "What about the temple at Iunet? You mentioned before that it had been raided by rebels from a neighboring town."

"Abandoned completely by the priests. It was not safe for them to stay there. Even the gold has been stripped from the shrine, the precious stones... or so I have been told."

I nodded and looked at him, and he placed the tray across my lap. "I suppose this means there will be no harvest festival this year."

Khetnu smiled wistfully. "There is not much to celebrate."

I took a small bite of an especially sweet honey cake; Khetnu knew these were my favorite, and sure to entice me. As I nibbled, I could see him examining my face and neck closely. "You'll find no marks today," I reassured him, "words only bruise the spirit, not the flesh."

I continued to eat while Khetnu watched me, sitting closely without speaking. I did not want to talk either, but I greatly appreciated his company.

When I finished, he lifted the tray from my lap and stood, ready to take his leave. I slipped my legs over the side of the bed, and with my back to my guest, I began to stretch.

"Seret, I... I have heard that you can do the light thing just like Naswt Biti can."

I hesitated. "Yes, I can."

I stood and turned to face him, and saw him looking at me curiously. "So, you are not trapped here; why would you stay if you could leave at any time?"

I blinked a few times, struggling to receive the question.

"One day soon a son of Ausar will come to reclaim the land that rightly belongs to him. I used to hope that when he got here, he found there was a land still worth claiming. I used to hope that I could give that to him."

He shook his head. "You endure much for the sake of others. What if it is too much?"

I turned away from him, looking out into the courtyard. "What is too much?"

"Do you truly believe that Auset and her son will successfully overthrow Naswt Biti and retake the kingdom?"

I heard the voice of the Great Father, and decided that his words were most poignant in this moment. "I believe that we will each become who we are meant to become."

Ab – Heart

Twenty years after I'd left them to their destiny, the son of Auset stepped into my bedroom from the courtyard. He said not a word, but I knew him by the sight of him. I took a deep breath, and examined his features with wide eyes. He was the image of my brother, the elder Heru, with a similar build and height, and just enough in his eyes to let me know that he was indeed the son of Ausar. I wanted to step closer, touch his face, but I barely knew him at all. Instead I smiled and closed the door tightly behind me.

"Mwt says it is almost time," Heru spoke first, looking at me directly, his dark eyes piercing into me. I kept his gaze affixed to mine and nodded. "She says you are to come with me."

I nodded again before looking back at the door behind me. "Now," he added, without ceremony or softness. This was not a suggestion, but I had not wanted to refuse. I found myself nostalgic for this house which had kept me, which I had kept, for hundreds of years, even with all of its painful memories and wretched fights, even though I had not departed from it yet. I could not imagine ever returning. Without looking at him I took his hand, and he sped me off to the south, to the place where I had last laid eyes on my family.

Auset came out from the house, but she did not rush to embrace me as she would have in our youth. Instead she let me look her over, making sure she was still my mirror image. In so many ways I could see my face in hers, but I knew that we had lost the thing that had once made us indistinguishable. We had given it up for something greater. It was now I who wished her arms around me, but I refrained and instead continued to smile at her and her son.

"I did not know if you would come," she began, speaking softly, taking a gingerly step towards me.

I chuckled. "It was not as if your son had given me much of an option."

She looked at him and grinned. "I did not mean for you to force her," Auset told him playfully, and he shyly looked away. "But you did not feel forced," she added, turning back to me.

"Not at all," I confirmed, and that was true. "It was time," I added, and that was also true.

"You could have left at any time," Heru interjected, his anger slightly tempered. "Why did you not return to us on your own?"

It was not the first time I had been asked the question, and would not be the last. On a few occasions, I had been known to ask myself that. I could not explain it to him, however; I knew it would never make sense. "I was where I was meant to be. That is what is most important."

Auset nodded and finally approached, taking my hands in hers. "You at least tried to assist Setesh with managing the realm," she said, which was more like a question.

"I did try, which is unfortunately not worth much." I let her lead me into the house, to the place where we had last argued. "I am saddened by the current state of our kingdom, as I am sure you are."

Heru hung back a bit, listening but trying not to intrude. Auset pulled me to sit across from her on the floor, and I passively fell into place. "It will be just a few more days before Heru initiates the battle with Setesh," Auset told me, looking over my shoulder to her son as she revealed his plans. "We are waiting for the final confirmation from Djehuty."

I nodded, processing quietly. I had not seen Seba or his wife Seshat in years. "I take it that he is well?"

"Tu. I would say that he has asked about you but, he has not... well I mean, he has not asked me about you. I can only assume that he has checked in on you over the years, I imagine that it has been rather frequently."

"I believe that," I whispered, smiling. "It is I who have been disconnected. I have not been home for many years."

Auset's eyebrows rose. "No, you have not. I can only imagine how drained you must be from not having the opportunity to recharge."

"I have not needed it," I told her, looking away. "I have barely used magic since I returned to the per eah. It is Setesh who is constantly squandering his strength, even when he has been warned against it."

"Who would warn him against such a thing?" Heru asked from behind me.

I turned to look at him. "I would."

"Why wouldn't you want to see him weakened? That will make it easier for me to defeat him."

I spun completely around so that I could face Heru entirely. "Because that also made it easier for him to destroy the realm that your father built. I did not want him strong. I wanted Kemet strong. A strong nation needs a strong leader."

Heru took a deep breath. "Still..."

"Setesh is not going to be easy for you to defeat, no matter how long it has been since he has traveled home," I responded, choosing not to dance around the truth. "He has had centuries of experience, not only with this body, but with this realm. Your father never bested Setesh in a match, and Heru-Ur had a hard time against him as well. Setesh has been to war and commanded armies, and he has been preparing for you for seven years."

Heru looked over my shoulder at Auset, who had not said a word. I turned back to face her. "I am not on his side, not in the least. I will play whatever role it is that I am meant to play to ensure victory for Heru, without hesitation and without complaint. But I have seen Setesh fight, I have been on the receiving end of his fist and I know what he can do. If we go into this believing that there is an easy way, we will lose."

Auset looked over my shoulder to her son, and I could see her imploring her son to listen to my caution with her eyes. But Heru was young, and destined to make the errors of youth. I could feel him standing, and I looked back to see him.

"I appreciate what you have said to me, but I too have been preparing for him. And you have not yet seen what I am capable of."

I nodded, resignation washing over me. "I look forward to the opportunity. Will you be training again before the day comes? I can take you to your opponent's preferred training location; perhaps that will give you some additional insight, if you are interested."

Heru's features softened and I could see him looking forward to it even before he answered. "Tomorrow, then, so we can do it before Djehuty sends word."

I smiled and nodded. He nodded at his mother before leaving us alone. I turned back to Auset, who was beaming at me lovingly.

"I needed you to say those words to him. He has heard them from me so often, I do not think he listens anymore."

I shook my head. "It is not as if he has listened to me, but I am happy to be of service."

Auset frowned and grabbed my hands again, wrapping my fingers around hers. "You said that Setesh has hit you, when? Why? Are you okay?"

I looked away from her, wanting to pull my hands back as well. "It does not matter. It is all over now."

The room fell silent, and I felt my sister trying to invade my thoughts to learn the things that I had not shared. But I was prepared for her, and would not let her in.

"Your gift has gotten stronger in my absence," I mumbled, glancing back at her sideways.

Auset grinned. "Apparently not strong enough."

I sighed and looked around the room wistfully. "Should I assume from his absence that he had not wanted to see me?"

There was a long hesitation before Auset let go of my hands and stood. I was not expecting such a strong reaction, but as soon as I looked up at her, I understood. "He wasn't... Anpu was not ready to greet you. I -"

"No, you do not need to explain. It is I who abandoned him. He does not owe me a receptive welcome."

Auset wiped her hands against her legs. "It is not as if you abandoned him entirely or left him without care. He was with me."

"Still," I added resolutely, "he was not with me."

My sister turned and looked out of the window, mostly to keep herself busy I felt, not really because she needed to watch the afternoon sun. "When he hears that Setesh was violent, and that you protected him, he will understand."

I smiled and stood. "That is optimistic of you, senet, but I am sure you have already told him everything, and if I have done irreparable damage to our relationship, then I will accept the consequences of my choice."

Auset turned back to me. "It was worth it, then? Leaving your son here, losing him? Leaving me? It was all worth it?"

I nodded. "It was what I needed to do." We lingered again for a moment in silence before I looked around. The room felt much smaller than it had when our sons were younger, many moons prior. "I should not stay here tonight but will return in the morning. Is that okay?"

"Will you go back to the per eah?"

I shook my head. "Actually, I think I will go home."

No one was there when I landed, which was just fine with me. It gave me the opportunity to take in the sensation of lightness, of being outside of my body for the first time in over a decade. My form felt as if it were charged, and every step I took over the perceived surface sent streams of light surging through me. I found myself changing the space as my mind drifted through the memories of all of us being here, laughing, learning, preparing for marriage, for a life away from everything we'd ever known. I could see it, I could still feel it, yet it belonged to a person who was no longer me. In the timeline of my mind, it was centuries ago, but to this place, to home, it has just happened a moment ago.

I hoped to visit and depart without incident, not sure if I wanted to see anyone, and the others stayed away, although I could tell that my mother was longing to leave her post and be at my side. I knew there would be plenty of time for that, but not now. I threw myself back through the ethers, towards the tiny house to meet Heru, ready to take him to the desert, to test his endurance.

I stepped into the main room and found him there, waiting. "Are you ready?" I asked patiently, holding out my hand to him. He nodded and crossed the room, taking my hand.

I looked over his shoulder to Auset. "Will you come with us?"

Auset looked nervous for just a moment, then smiled, letting her concerns pass unvoiced. "No. You two can go without me. Perhaps I will join you later."

I took another jump, pulling Heru along with me, a simpler task than it would have been had I not chosen to recharge. When we landed he let go of my hand and scanned the open terrain, the desert being a much different place than the forest where he'd grown up.

"Why is this his favorite place to train?" Heru asked without looking at me. I smiled, knowing it was not personal; how could it be?

"Setesh told me once that this is one of the harshest places to live in this realm," I shared with him, having to recall the weeks after our wedding that we spent learning to love one another. I took a deep breath. "The climate here, the dry heat, the overbearing sun. There are few places to get respite here, no shade, no water, no comforts. It is more draining to one's energy than any other spot and if you can last here, you can last anywhere."

Heru nodded and looked at me. "What type of things did he like to do here?"

I smiled. "He ran, a lot. He would go through the forms, over and over again, the next time faster than the one before it. All of the things you probably learned, just, everything is harder here, in a difficult climate."

Heru nodded again, scanning once again. "Are you going to stay with me while I work out?"

That felt like an odd question, and I looked away. "I was looking forward to seeing how ready you are to defeat my husband. But I can understand if you do not want the company."

He frowned. "I apologize, I did not mean that you could not stay. It's just; it is odd to have you here instead of hearing about you, to actually see you." Heru looked at me once more. "I remember you caring for me, when I first came forth into this realm. The memories are scattered and vague, but I remember that you were there."

"Yes, I was there."

Heru steadied himself, and began to move through the first of the forms, slowly and with great ease, but I could tell that he was surprised that he began to sweat even after giving such little effort. "Why do you still call him your husband?"

I hesitated. It was a fair question. "Because he is, even if it is only a technicality." I paused before adding, "I imagine Auset still refers to your father as her husband."

Heru smiled. "Yes, she does." He continued for a moment, reminding me more of his father by how measured he was, every sweep of his foot and press of his palm calculated, with purpose. "Do you miss him?"

I frowned. "Do I miss Setesh?"

"No, do you miss my father?"

Again he had caught me off guard. "I suppose I do, in a way, but surely not the way that your mother misses him."

That answer appeared to satisfy him. As he sped up I could see that he was beginning to struggle, the sun moving through the sky and becoming oppressive. But he did not want me to know that he struggled, and he pushed through the tremors in his legs. As I watched him, I could see why Auset was nervous for him, but she knew that he must be as ready as he could be, or else I would not be here.

After the sun had climbed a fair way into the sky, Heru took a break. I'd stood the entire time, but when he collapsed, I followed him on to the hard ground. "I appreciate that you brought me here," he said sincerely. I nodded without speaking, and he continued. "Will you be disappointed if I do not win? Is there a part of you that wants to see him succeed?"

I quickly shook my head. "No, not anymore. Setesh has had his time, and now it is yours. I will be upset if you do not win, but I do not believe you are being sent into a battle that you are destined to lose."

He nodded. "You have not asked me about Anpu. Did you ask Mwt about him last night, after I left you two alone?"

How inquisitive you are, I thought to myself, remembering how similar his mother had been in her youth. "We spoke of him, yes."

"Are you anxious to see him again?"

"In my own way, yes." I looked down at the ground between us. "But I will not force him to see me. I will wait until he is ready."

Heru scooted closer to me. "Can I tell you something?" he asked, launching into his statement without waiting for me to answer. "If you wait, Anpu will assume that it is because you are not ready. You should approach him and let him know you miss him. If you tell him you want to see him, then he will realize that he wants to see you." He leaned back and shrugged. "That is what I think, anyway."

I smiled, appreciative of the advice. "You know him a bit better than I do," I said, looking back up at him. He smiled and looked to the ground, and I could see in his expression how close they had become, as brothers.

"Has your mother ever told you how much you look like your namesake?" I asked him as I stood, wanting to give him time to continue working out without audience.

His grin deepened. "She has told me that many times. Personally, I don't see it," he shrugged again, looking away.

I giggled, knowing that feeling. "I will let Auset know that you are still here. You will be okay to get back by yourself, yes?"

"Of course."

I nodded before leaving him to head back to the house. It was empty when I stepped inside, but I did not leave. Instead I began to tidy up, as was my nature. It could not have been easy having two boys to clean after, I thought to myself, imagining what our sons must have been like when younger.

"Mwt," Anpu said from behind me, and I spun quickly to face him. He was standing in the threshold, deciding if he should step in or not. I moved towards him tenderly.

"Please, come in." The brief inquisition from Heru had shaken me, but I would not turn him away, if he were ready to talk. I had no interest in waiting.

Anpu was thin, but he had clearly spent much time training and sparring alongside his brother, which made his frame very similar to that of his father. Still, in his face, all I could see was me, his eyes dark and deep, and his cheekbones strong, defined. I closed my eyes at the thought that he also looked like the woman who raised him, but when I opened them, I knew that this was my son and mine alone.

"I had not realized you would be back yet, from training with Heru," he started, not knowing where else to begin.

"I just got back," I answered before gesturing for him to sit. How like me to give him permission to sit in his own home, I quickly thought, but brushed it aside to focus on him. "I am happy that I was here, to have a chance to see you."

Anpu nodded and examined my features. "I had expected that you would visit, over the years." His tone was not accusatory, just factual. I had anticipated some anger, but instead I was greeted with a version of acceptance that felt like nonchalance.

"I will not lie to you," I responded, deciding that he was old enough to know the truth. "I could have visited; I had a great deal of freedom, for a prisoner."

He frowned. "But you chose not to."

"Yes I did." Those words were hard to swallow. "It was easier for me that way, although perhaps it was not easier for you."

Anpu looked towards the door. "It was hard, at first. I missed you. But I settled in fine. After a while, I was thankful you did not take me with you. I enjoyed having a brother, and being able to travel between realms, meet my father and connect with the other Neteru. I would not have been able to do that if you had not left me here."

"No, you would not have." I hesitated for a moment. "What

do you remember, from your time at the per eah?"

His back stiffened. "The most distinct memory I have is the feeling that you were afraid. I remember feeling like you were hiding me. I remember that he threatened you."

Anpu stopped speaking, and I did not know what to say yet, so I let the silence settle in around us. He cleared his throat and continued. "You were trying to keep me safe, I think, by cooperating."

"I was trying to accomplish much," I admitted, "and yes, your safety was an important part of that."

"He never tried to hurt me though, not that I remember."

I nodded. "It is very possible that he never would have tried to hurt you. I only knew that I would do anything I could to prevent having to find out."

The room grew quiet once more, and I looked back into the face of my son, who appeared to be processing everything, perhaps trying to remember more, think of new questions. "Auset told me that he hurt you," he shared, meeting my gaze.

"Setesh and I... we did not always get along."

"Do you still love him?"

I hesitated. "Yes, in my own way," I answered, repeating words from earlier, both times sharing what was true. "He is still my brother, he is one of the Neteru. He is my husband."

"Is that why you returned to him, out of love?" Anpu asked, and again I was forced to defend the choice that I had made.

This time, I tried to be more direct. "I returned to the per eah because I love you, Anpu, and because I love myself. I am not sure if you can understand this, but it had very little to do with him in the way that I think you believe it did."

"It is very difficult to believe that you chose to be where he was because you love me," he challenged me gently. "Did you think you could repair things between you? I do not understand what you sought to accomplish."

I sat up a bit straighter, and noticed he was doing the same. His mannerisms were mine, his posture, his tones. I felt the tears welling up as I observed this reflection of myself, the man he had become without me.

"The past is already done, there was never anything I could do about that, and I never thought of it as returning to him, not like that. But I did leave you, because I understood that the future would one day be the present, and each of us needed to be prepared for the part we must play." I paused and lowered my eyes, needing to choose my words with care. "It was about respecting your place in the world, and finding mine."

He did not respond right away, so I was not sure if he would press me further, or if he would move on. He chose the latter. "Auset has told us everything about you, or so I feel," he started before pausing again. As I waited for him to continue I was more convinced that he was me, watching him calculate his thoughts. "She has told us a lot, but I do not know what you know about us, or really, about me. Do you want to know anything, about the time that we've spent apart?"

I inhaled sharply. "I would like to know everything," I whispered, ready to settle in for a lengthy tale.

He appeared as if ready to begin, but something stopped him. I waited, unsure if he were anticipating my questions or deciding where to start. I sat patiently until he closed his eyes and I felt him knocking on the door of my mind; I opened it and allowed his visions to become mine. There the terrain was laid out brilliantly, and we began to hover above it, observing the movements of the land below.

"Heru and I have determined that this is an acceptable border, or perimeter, around the house. Every day I review the border and assess any changes that have occurred from one day to the next. I assess if those changes are natural, or unnatural. I calculate what could have caused those changes, and Auset assists me with this if I cannot figure it out on my own. In this way we know what is approaching, what to be prepared for."

He glanced at me and continued. "By the pattern of the waves upon the shore I can tell if ships approach. I can see if men have walked the ground and how long it will take them to get to the house. I am showing you what will happen tomorrow if all things continue in their current course. That is what I have learned to do, with the help of Mwt, or Auset, I mean."

I found it difficult to respond as I marveled in the emotions that came over me, seeing him fully grown, complete in his power. "It is fine if you call her Mwt," I whispered, "do not worry that you will offend me."

He took my hand and led me to the ground in his vision, and I could see undefined light forms standing in front of the house, talking rapidly. "It will not be long before Djehuty returns with news, so this is my vision of him giving the word to Heru and Mwt, and you and me. I have not projected what will happen beyond that, but when Djehuty gives the word, more will become clear."

I nodded and looked at him, but still I remained silent. "I know that you did not want me to have the life that you had, but Heru will need me, and I have grown to know that this is my place."

I squeezed his hand. "I have grown to know it as well."

"Still, you do not want it."

I sighed and smiled. "Does it matter what I want?" I asked sincerely, not hiding my truth. "You are your own being. You will be who you are meant to."

Anpu looked at me, his expression even and emotionless. "I have come to appreciate that you left me here. You did me a great service. It was a most unselfish thing to do."

I felt vulnerable under his gaze, yet unafraid. "No, it was the most selfish thing I have ever done. And I am grateful that you do not hate me for it, even if you cannot love me, or will not."

He looked down and dropped my hand, and the connection between us was broken abruptly. I opened my eyes and found my son, his vulnerable self finally displayed, the inner conflict that I'd expected all along. I reached out for him, quickly and without thinking, and he pulled away entirely, standing and crossing to the opposite side of the room, turning his back to me before I could get to my feet.

I took a step towards him and stopped. Again I waited. He was a stranger to me, and I did not know what else to do. Finally he spoke. "You are here now." Anpu dispersed and left me to myself, and I had no way to follow him, for I had no idea where he'd go. I sunk back to the floor and pulled my legs to my chest, wrapping my arms around them, breathing deeply and turning my face to the heavens.

I spent the night at home once more, this time answering my mother when she called out, allowing her to join me. She arrived and did not hesitate to throw her arms around me, and I fell into them, relieved to have someone else hold me up for once.

We sat together silently for a while. I did not want to speak, and she did not push me. I feared that when we finally began to talk, I would have to answer the same questions that everyone else had thrown at me, and I was exhausted of having to explain myself. Instead, when I pulled my head from her shoulder, she placed her hands on my cheeks and looked deeply into my face.

"My, you have grown," Nut exclaimed, causing me to smile. I looked down and felt myself blushing in an oddly youthful way.

"Dua," I whispered, not knowing how else to respond.

Nut sighed and released me, but kept her warm gaze affixed. "Every time one of you comes, I never feel it is for long enough," she shared with me. "That is the curse of being a mother. You must release when all you truly want to do is never let go."

I looked away again, wanting to say something, opening my mouth to prepare for what would come. Instead my head shook in confirmation, silence being the truest response.

Nut touched my shoulder lightly, continuing to beam her unconditional love in my direction. "You should get back," she urged me gently; "you must tend to your responsibilities, and I to mine."

I took her hand and kissed it, a look of wonder crossing my face as I met her stare. "Dutiful as ever, mother."

She nodded, and this time it was her whose lips parted but released no sound. It was the first time I felt mature around her, as if I was no longer her baby, and the feeling was disappointing and empowering, all at once.

I stood first, and watched as her energy dissipated, in magically reluctant form. Once Nut was gone, I took a deep breath, then closed my eyes and returned to the small house, hoping to meet everyone as they rose for the day.

Instead, Auset was already outside, tending the small plot right beneath the front window, long fabric draped over her head, blocking my view of her face. I knelt beside her and watched her for a moment as she purposefully ignored me and threw all of her attention to this work.

Frowning, I looked around. "Where are our sons?"

"Anpu has gone to check the perimeter, I suspect, although there is not much need for that anymore," she mumbled, still not looking to me.

"What happened, has Djehuty come?"

"No," Auset said, and this time she stopped working and

sighed worriedly. "Heru left this morning, before any of us had risen."

I hesitated. "Left?"

She sighed. "He's gone to the per eah. He decided he was ready, and he would not wait any longer."

Auset resumed her dig into the earth, and I sat back on my heels, processing the new information. I wanted to ask her more, but she was clearly not receptive, having hung her head lower and completely turned away from me. I stood and looked away from the house just as Anpu was coming through the trees, approaching stealthily.

I looked at him and motioned to Auset, and he nodded. We entered the house together and stepped into one of the back rooms, where it would be harder for Auset to overhear us unless she wanted to.

"What happened?" I asked, without qualifying what I'd meant.

"Heru... he, he decided not to wait any longer."

I arched an eyebrow. "It was just that simple, then?"

Anpu looked around nervously, as if unwilling to divulge any of the details. "He was boastful yesterday, when he came back from, wherever it was you took him." He paused and I tilted my head, waiting to see if this was yet another thing that would be blamed on me. "He just seemed, fired up. I knew he was getting impatient, but he just wouldn't wait any longer."

I nodded and sighed. "Perhaps I should not have taken him there. It was not my intention for him to become overconfident."

"You didn't do that," Anpu admitted, looking at me, his back a little slumped. "Heru was already leaning in that direction. It's my fault actually, that I did not account for this possibility."

I straightened my back, which prompted him to do the same. "We will have to support his choice, come what may. What did

Auset say about it this morning?"

Again, he paused, and his shoulder slumped ever so slightly. "She didn't say anything, really. She just got up and went straight for the garden. But," he added, lowering his voice, "I don't think she thinks he can win."

I nodded. "And what do you think?"

He took a deep breath, and I could see him playing different scenarios in his mind. "I think his victory is unlikely. The timing is off, and his approach was wrong. But he has been preparing for a long time. Maybe he will surprise us."

"No," I mumbled, looking away, "I would not expect that."

A noise behind me prompted me to look back into the main room, where Auset and Djehuty had entered. I stepped in and Anpu followed me cautiously, although he stood far enough back that it seemed like he was not really with us.

"I appreciate that the three of you want to fix this, but there is nothing to be fixed," Djehuty told us matter-of-factly, to which I nodded. He motioned for us to sit, and Auset and I did; Anpu chose to lean against the wall behind me. "Heru did exactly what I expected him to do."

I cleared my throat. "I don't understand. If this was the plan, then why were we waiting for you to return?"

Djehuty smiled mischievously. "I did not say this was the plan. I said this is what I expected."

Auset shook her head. "You knew he would grow impatient. You knew he would be anxious for revenge."

"So did you, even if you did not want to face it." Djehuty continued to stand, pacing the room slowly, reminding me of one of our torturous classes. "Heru is young; it is time for him to make his mistakes. He has been sheltered for a long time by his mother. He has to become a man."

"Those mistakes cannot come at the expense of his life," Auset challenged Djehuty, her fiery eyes glaring up at him.

I frowned. "His life is not in danger, senet; you are being dramatic."

"Am I?" she whispered, upset, as any mother would be.

"You are feeling, and not seeing," Djehuty answered her, tapping her shoulder lightly. "Take a deep breath and then tell me what you see."

Auset closed her eyes, trying to do what Djehuty was urging. It seemed even after all this time there were yet more lessons for us to learn. But even as she was able to stop herself from crying, she still continued to frown, her vision blocked by her worry for Heru.

"I, I can't" she finally whispered, and another tear made its way down her face. I reached out and took her hand, and she smiled weakly at me.

Djehuty shrugged. "Let us see what comes of this. In a few days, he will either return, or we will go to him. There is nothing to be done until then."

Anpu knelt beside Auset, and she leaned into him, letting go of my hand. I sat back for a moment, then stood and smiled at Djehuty, who, I realized, had been watching me. He motioned for me to follow him outside, so I did.

"You don't seem to be as affected as everyone else," he started, his back to me.

I cleared my throat. "I don't know him very well," I admitted, keeping my voice low. "I am empathetic, for my sister's sake..."

"Be honest, then," Djehuty requested, turning to face me. "What do you think?"

"I don't have the same gift as Auset," I reminded him, frowning. "I cannot see the future, or anything like that."

Djehuty shrugged. "You may not see, but you still know."

I shook my head, trying to understand, not knowing how to respond. Djehuty looked at me curiously and smiled.

"You know Setesh very well. What would you anticipate to

be his first move?"

I blinked a few times. "He, he... he would make sure he keeps the upper hand."

"And how would he do that?"

"He would pick the place... and he would go on the defensive, so he could observe his opponent, see if he could find any weaknesses..."

Djehuty nodded. "What do you think would be Heru's first move?"

I took a deep breath. "Well he's young, and being impulsive... he would be aggressive, and assertive. Heru would go on the offensive; he would do exactly what Setesh wants him to do."

My sister's hand touched my shoulder, causing me to jump; I had not realized she had come outside behind me. "Then what?" she asked cautiously.

"Then... I... Auset, you are the one who should be telling me." I knew I sounded harsh, but I did not want the pressure of telling her that her son would lose. "This is your strong suit, not mine. You cannot fall short just because you're upset."

She looked at me, surprised for but a moment. "You're right," Auset admitted with a sigh. "I should have seen this coming. I have not been myself. I have not been focused."

I looked at Anpu, who appeared to be a bit annoyed with me for upsetting his mother. Auset would not look at any of us, and instead began to wander off towards the nearby trees.

I ignored the scowl being thrown in my direction and followed her. "It is no use to scold yourself, or for me to scold you," I told her gently, touching her shoulder when she finally stopped moving. "But you do need to calm down and prepare for what comes next."

Auset turned back to me and nodded before looking at Djehuty. "I will take a trip home, to recharge. When I return, if Heru is not back, we will go to the battlefield and view his progress."

Djehuty smiled. "That is a sound course of action." He reached out his hand, and Auset placed hers in his. Djehuty nodded at me before jumping them both to the ethers, and I turned to look at my son, whose face no longer betrayed any irritation.

"I assume it is acceptable for me to stay here with you until she returns?"

He nodded without looking at me, and turned to enter the house. I sighed, and let my thoughts drift back to the words Djehuty spoke to me earlier. I may not see, but I can know, and I could, if only I would let myself.

It was long past time for me to acknowledge the fact that I was not, and had never been, a failure. Flaws in my character had been exposed, and there'd been many moments where I allowed my judgment to lapse, but that did not discount the more numerous occasions when I proved myself a smart counselor, a patient wife, a supportive sister. Truly, I had been everything that I could be at that time, and now, in this different time, I could be more. I was more.

The air was thick and heavy, so I knew we were not arriving to witness victory of any kind. Instead the hot desert wind whipped across my face, burning my lips and punishing my eyes. I breathed a sigh of relief that Auset had warned me to cover my head, and pulled the green fabric around my shoulders and over the lower part of my face.

The red lands were at their worst today, and it pained my feet to walk across the rough desert sand. I knew we were close, the sound of lightning crashing with every attack, every thrown punch, every kick.

Auset stuck out her arm, and Anpu and I stopped walking. "There," she pointed ahead of us, and when I squinted all I could see were two bright red balls of fire, angrily dancing around each other, on the ground and in the air. One appeared to be chasing the other, and the longer I watched, the better I was able to make out their forms. The light of Setesh shone brighter, and loomed slightly larger, and as I could make out his face I knew that he had hardly broken a sweat at all.

Three days at home had done wonders for Auset, who'd returned complete in her power, her nervous energy released and the puffy redness gone from her eyes. We spent one final day at the house before coming to see what was happening, listening to Auset as she tapped into her gift of sight. She had been vague about what we would happen upon when we arrived here, but I had no doubt that she was much clearer than when she had left.

She'd arrived in the middle of the morning. I was inside, keeping myself busy, and Anpu was outside, doing the same. We had spoken very little since she had departed. I assumed it was because he did not want to talk, although I suspected that he believed to be doing me the favor. Nevertheless, we had not avoided each other, but found a rhythmic coexistence that did not require much chatter. The silence, which would have made a younger Auset impatient, seemed to be calming to my sister, who relaxed into a stillness that was difficult to penetrate.

"Is he smiling?" Anpu asked incredulously, stepping out from the left side of Auset to look at me with wildness in his eyes. I nodded reluctantly and looked at Auset, and we formed a bit of a circle as we realized what was happening.

Her face was serene; she was neither disturbed nor elated. "Heru will not win today. We will need to take him home very soon."

I turned back to face the warriors as they continued to crash into one another, over and over without respite. I took a few steps forward, with Anpu and Auset matching my every move. I could see that Heru was struggling under the harsh conditions of the desert wind, but it was here that Setesh would thrive.

"You were right that Setesh would bring him here," Auset said. "Heru should not have agreed to come."

"But he did, because he thought the desert was no real challenge."

Auset placed her hand on my shoulder. "He did because he thought he was ready to win. It is the folly of youth that has made him bold. Our brother is about to teach him a most necessary lesson."

Anpu interrupted, "But he will not kill him, or hurt him too badly?" his voice cracking with genuine concern. Auset and I both smiled to reassure him.

"No, Setesh will not," I said, then looked to Auset to see if she wanted to speak. She motioned for me to continue. "He believes himself above reproach, certainly above defeat. He does not take Heru to be a true challenge. He won't harm him."

Auset nodded again to reassure Anpu once more that his brother would be safe. I reached down and took her hand, squeezing it. She had been terrified a few days prior that Heru would not come home alive. Now she knew the future, and in her wisdom she would allow it to happen.

Heru fell from the sky, landing on the ground with a heavy thud that caused Anpu and I to step back. I covered my eyes for a moment, and when I pulled my hand away I could see him completely embodied, the sheen of his light dulled by exhaustion. He stood and tried not to pant, but it was no use. He was worn, his clothing torn and covered in dust, and his face slightly bruised, but not as bad as his pride. Heru stood and turned away from us, not wanting to look any of us in the eye. Auset raised her chin and steeled her backbone, and Anpu and I did the same.

Setesh landed a few yards away from Heru, and they resumed a slower hand-to-hand combat on the ground. I could tell that Setesh was toying with his younger opponent, taunting him as he would a warrior being trained for the corps. I clenched my jaw; it pained me to watch this play out. In the moment I wished this could have been resolved differently, without this level of embarrassment. Why didn't Auset step in; why didn't Ra?

Finally Setesh laughed, and it echoed across the field. Heru leaned to strike him once more, but Setesh stepped to the side and the blow missed its target altogether. Setesh kicked Heru on the backside and laughed again, louder, making sure that we heard him as he tormented the son of Ausar.

This time, Heru was prepared, and he lashed out just as Setesh was letting down his guard. Heru took the elder warrior by surprise, who had thought the younger fighter was down and defeated. Setesh quickly scrambled, attempting to gain the upper hand, and just when I thought perhaps this fight would go a different way, Setesh knelt to the ground and threw a handful of dung into his opponent's eye.

Heru screamed, and Setesh laughed once more. Heru continued to scream, and fell to one knee, hands covering his face. Even in knowing what was coming, Auset still gasped in pain, and took two steps towards her son. I reached out and grabbed her arm, stopping her from treating Heru like a child.

Heru stopped screaming, and after a moment, he lifted his head up. His right eye had gone undamaged, but he was scarred and blinded in his left. He closed both of his eyes and stood, balling his fists as if he wanted to continue the fight, but Setesh would not indulge him.

"It does not make me strong to slaughter a three legged lamb," Setesh called out to Heru, his tone mocking as he feigned a position of mercy. "I am lord of the red lands, and powerful is my mighty arm, as you have learned this day."

Heru opened his mouth as if to speak, but decided against it, and instead used what was left of his strength to disperse away from the battlefield, decidedly giving the victory to Setesh. Auset left immediately, following her son; Anpu moved as if he would go as well, but stopped as he noticed Setesh turning and walking confidently in our direction.

"We should go now," he mumbled to me, reaching for my hand.

I looked at my son. "You can go. I will be behind you in just a moment."

Anpu hesitated, but he did not leave. Instead, he stood straight up behind me, as if ready to defend me against any threat.

Setesh chuckled. "And you think I would go from such a fight to hitting a defenseless woman?" He looked at Anpu with pity. "There is no need to worry. I will not hurt your mother."

Anpu did not move, and did not speak. I moved closer to my husband. "You know this is not over."

Setesh shrugged, his scowl one of nonchalance. "I am available to continue tormenting Heru, if that is what you wish. He cannot defeat me. He will not."

Auset reappeared at my left, and stepped between Setesh and I. "You have done nothing this day except ensure your own defeat."

I stepped back, and Setesh glowered menacingly, his eyes dark. Auset was not affected, however; her expression motionless and determined. "I should have ripped you to shreds as I did your husband," he growled at her, so close that I thought she could feel his breath on her cheek. "You are pathetic and weak, giving your forgiveness when all they offered was betrayal and deceit. I thought you were a queen, but it turns out you are a fool."

Auset leaned in and kissed her brother's cheek, examining his features lovingly. "All of the riches, the land, the men at your command." She stepped back and tilted her head. "You are still not the better man."

Setesh looked at me, his deep breaths betraying the fire that raged within. When I searched his eyes, all I could find was the eternal inferno eating him alive, and I knew that my face betrayed the pity I felt for him. He stepped towards me, threateningly, and by instinct I stiffened and took a deep breath, but when my eyes opened, I was back at the small house, my son's arms tight around my shoulder.

He held me for a tiny moment before releasing his grip. I exhaled a sound of relief. "He said he would not hurt you, but I didn't believe him," Anpu explained unnecessarily. I nodded and looked at him, grateful.

We stepped into the house to find Djehuty there, and we instinctively kept our distance, hovering near the doorway as Djehuty continued his ritual, not stopping to acknowledge our presence at all. Heru was sitting, his shoulders slumped over and his body entirely at rest; Djehuty walked in a circle, creating a seal around Heru that contained the greatest of his healing power. Auset returned, and immediately began to channel a stream of light from her heart to her son, whispering heka that filled the room with song. I took a deep breath and closed my eyes, calming my thoughts of worry to avoid interfering with the work being done.

Finally Djehuty stepped back, and Auset stopped her chanting. Heru began to disappear, one tiny crystal of light at a time, until his entire form was gone. I stepped into the room and looked at Djehuty, who was nodding in approval.

"I have sent him home," he explained casually, not appearing worried at all. "There are a few things left to teach him before he can resume battle. But today's lesson was invaluable. Heru needed that before he could accept what I have to give."

I nodded, and Djehuty sped off behind him. Anpu came out from behind me, and approached Auset.

"Couldn't you have stopped this from happening? How did you not know that it would end this way?"

I looked at my son, surprised by how bold he was being with Auset, but I saw myself in his outburst, my very reflection. I'd had the very same thought on the battlefield, but I did not say so, for here, in the calm, I knew the reason.

Auset shook her head and reached out to calm him, but he stayed outside of her reach. "I know this is difficult, it may be hard to understand but -"

"You could easily capture Setesh, force him to stand before the Neteru, stand judgment for his crimes," Anpu continued, beginning to pace. I stayed back, allowing him to let off steam. "I don't see why this had to happen. What if it is worse next time? What if Heru cannot win?"

Auset sighed; she did not want to fight with him, but she would. "Heru could not win yesterday, he was a child, just as you are a child, or at least you are being one now." That quieted Anpu, but still he smoldered under the surface. "This was for his own good, and for yours as well. You must trust that Djehuty and I know what we are doing."

Anpu took a deep breath. "Even though you keep secrets from us? Even though you send us out to fulfill our destiny with only half of the information that we need to be successful, we should just trust you?" He shook his head emphatically. "You must understand how difficult it is to extend that trust when I have seen my brother blinded by your silence."

Auset looked at me. "Yes I do, actually." I blushed and looked away; faced with how impetuous I must have sounded years ago. "You should go home to be with him. Djehuty will surely have some wisdom to impart upon you as well. Go, and perhaps you will get the answers you seek."

Anpu did not hesitate, rushing from the room in a quick flurry, leaving his mothers behind. I looked at Auset and did not speak.

"Do you see now? Do you finally see?" she pleaded with me, tears rushing to her eyes, causing my tears to flow as well. I tilted my head and tried to smile, finding myself unable to speak, yet my face was painfully uncooperative. She doubled over as the moisture began to run down her cheeks, the sorrow and doubt that she had shed rushing back. I turned and looked out of the window, and when I closed my eyes, I knew the wisdom of millions of years.

Maat – Order

"I know I should not have been so impulsive," Heru told us boldly, having gained a century's worth of wisdom in only a few short days.

I looked at his face closely, searching for a sign of the damage that had once been inflicted, but could find none. Instead, it felt as if his sight were improved; his gaze penetrating and his focus intense. Even his voice seemed deeper, although I knew that to be an illusion. Physically he was exactly as he had been before, but Heru was forever changed.

"So what is your strategy; what is the next step?" Auset asked him calmly, sounding not like a mother at all, but a commander, a leader. She was pacing the room with Heru standing directly in the center, and I against the back wall. The blue fabrics that she wore whirled around him but he did not move, nor did he allow himself to become distracted.

"I will draw him to me this time. I will manipulate him, which will anger him." Heru cleared his throat confidently. "The angry do not act with care or thought."

Auset nodded, but the look on her face was skeptical. I tilted my head, watching her watch him. "What do you know that you can use against him?"

Heru looked at me, gauging how I would feel about his answer. I straightened my head. "She is his soft spot," he answered, not moving his eyes from me.

I frowned at his curious choice of words. "Perhaps it is more apt to refer to me as a trigger."

Heru nodded. "Yes, a trigger. You are a trigger for him."

"What else?" I asked, knowing these answers better than Auset.

He frowned. "Will I need more?"

I nodded without moving from my place along the wall. "Setesh will know that you are trying to make him angry. It will not be so easy as to just mention my name."

Auset glanced at me, then looked back at Heru. "What else can you use against him?"

Heru looked down at the ground, searching his thoughts. "He has lost ground in the rebellions. Warriors have abandoned the corps since he has been leader."

"More personal than that," I told him, stepping forward. "Remind him of his impotency, his inability to father children. Mention Anpu. Mention that he was never good enough to be Naswt Biti, that he was a mere subject under the rule of Ausar."

Heru glanced at his mother. "Don't you think that is cruel?"

"Yes, I do," I told him, firming my stance. "That is why it will work." I took another step towards Heru, forcing him to give me his attention. "It is cruel to hit one where it hurts, and I respect that you do not want to be cruel, but Setesh will not be so... generous." I turned away and began to return to my original place. "This is war, Heru. He will not be nice and he will not be fair, and you must be prepared to use all of the weapons at your disposal."

I faced him once more, and he was searching his mother's face for approval. Auset gave it, and she looked to me. "You will not need to lie, exaggerate, or be vicious," I told him. "You will only need to speak what you know; speak truth, and he will be bent to your command."

Heru nodded. I was not sure if he could do it, when the time would come, as I knew it would. Still, I ducked out of the room and joined Anpu in the back, who appeared to be in deep meditation. I sat beside him and he opened his eyes.

"What is different now?" I asked him, not looking at him.

Anpu cleared his throat. "Heru is less anxious, so he will be better able to maintain his center throughout the battle. Setesh is now the arrogant one. He has unwittingly given Heru the upper hand."

I touched his shoulder, this time turning my face to his. "And what is different about you now?"

He smiled. "Not much, and everything," Anpu mumbled, causing me to smile. He too had been greatly changed, and I was grateful for it, even though I did not deserve it. I raised my hand to his crown and touched his thick, dark locs with my fingers, before tracing my fingers lovingly across his cheek.

"I can never say how much I missed you," I whispered to him, saddened by thinking of everything that I had failed to witness by being absent.

Anpu shook his head to silence me. "You do not need to," he whispered back, and I felt forgiven, or at least understood. He took my hand and kissed it, then clutched it in his lap tightly. "You are here now."

Those words were gentler this time, but the moment passed quickly. "It is time," Auset called out from behind us, and we both rushed to our feet and back into the front room to join her and Heru, finding Djehuty had come as well.

Djehuty looked at each of us in turn, a somber expression crossing his visage. "It is time," he announced dramatically, as was his way.

I looked to Heru, who met my glance and nodded. I smiled in return. Anpu stepped to him and took his arm, and they shook hands as men before hugging tightly, as brothers. No sooner had Anpu released him than Auset bound him into her embrace, her arms wrapped around his broad frame tightly.

She pulled back a little to take in his features, then kissed each of his cheeks twice, finally releasing him entirely.

Heru turned to Djehuty. "Am I to go alone then?"

Djehuty nodded. "Tu. The others will join you when the time comes."

Heru nodded his response, and then left without additional delay. Djehuty followed, presumably to return home, leaving the three of us alone to wait once more.

Anpu glanced at each of his mothers. "I will make sure no one is coming for us, although I do not believe we are in any danger."

Auset smiled at him. "Better to be safe. Go." He left through the front door, a much less dramatic exit. I looked at my sister.

"Taunting Setesh," she began, her face curling up in annoyance, "is that why he hit you?"

I should have known that she would not let that rest. I sighed. "I was never trying to taunt him. But I did choose to stand up for myself, and at times, violence was the consequence for that choice. There were times when Setesh wanted me to suffer, and I did."

Auset did not respond, so I sat upon the ground, to continue telling her of our time apart. "Once he found out that Heru was coming, he became insufferable. He insulted me often for leaving Anpu behind," I confessed to her, unable to look her in the eye. "He would accuse me of being a terrible mother, betraying my son as I had betrayed him." Auset sat across from me and reached for my hand, taking it in hers. My eyes began to spill over and my body hunched low. "He called me a failure, a weak and unnecessary creature, and it was all I could do to not believe him."

I started to weep, and Auset slid closer and took me into her lap. "I spent my days convincing myself that I had not made a horrible mistake, desperate for word from you to reassure me that our sons were safe and well. I spent every moment justifying why I had chosen to stay, asking myself if it was worth it."

I took a deep breath, finally able to stop my tears from flowing. "There was not a day that passed when I did not wish I could be with him," I whispered into her shoulder, closing my eyes and sighing.

Auset traced her hands along the top of my head softly, to comfort me, and waited a few moments before asking, "Which him?"

I opened my eyes and sat up, looking at her in disbelief. "You must know I do not mean Ausar," I responded, not knowing what else she could mean.

She laughed, gently nudging me. "I know that," she teased, and her eyes showed me she meant it. I exhaled in relief, glad that the moment was lighter. "No, I... I know that you still love your husband, senet," Auset continued seriously, "and I wonder if you wish it could be as it used to be before."

I looked at my sister, and I could see her own longing in her eyes. Although Auset would be able to visit her husband whenever she returned to the cosmos, he would never again be able to join her here, and for now, her presence was required in this realm, forcing them apart for vast stretches of time.

"I do not know how you survive each moment without him," I told her honestly, and we clutched each other's hands and leaned into one another, shoulder pressing against shoulder. "Neither do I," she whispered.

"To answer your question, however, I meant my son," I told her, pulling back and sitting up straight. "Setesh will never again be the man I remember him to be. In fact I am not sure he was ever truly that man. He was never meant to be."

Auset nodded and watched me closely. "He did try," she admitted wistfully, remembering.

"Tu, he did," I mumbled gently, "but it always came back to this."

We let the silence settle in around us, choosing not to say what did not need to be said. Finally Auset released my hands so that she could stand, holding out her arms to help me to my feet.

"The past is the past, dearest sister," she said without a hint of sarcasm. "Come and help me tend to the garden, while we wait for news from Heru."

As before, it was four days before we traveled to the battlefield, but this time we did not find ourselves in the middle of an angry, hot desert. Instead, we were on a gentle grassy plain, a long stretch of land that spanned between two mountains; quiet and secluded, yet open and airy. I turned my head up to the heavens and thought I could feel Heru-Ur nearby, knowing this was just the sort of place that he would choose to frequent.

The air was much cooler here, easier to breathe, which would make the warriors more evenly matched. I could make them out on the opposite side of the plain, jumping through the air at the speed of light, Setesh emitting a deep, bloody red from his form, and Heru shining brightly, a warmer, golden red.

Auset stepped out from between Anpu and I, watching as Heru struck Setesh with no blind aggression, more carefully calculating his opponent's next move and preparing for it, protecting himself. It was Setesh who fought wildly, growling and grunting with each blow, becoming angrier every time he missed the young warrior.

"He looks as if he wants to kill him," Anpu said, stunned, and he was right. I had never seen Setesh so inflamed, and it had clearly caused him to lose all sensibility. None of his moves appeared to follow reason; he seemed to be lashing out angrily, anxious to end the battle, to end Heru.

Anpu and I followed Auset as she cautiously walked closer to their match, watching as Heru struck Setesh across his face in a series of blows that brought him to his knees. Setesh dropped his hands to the ground and conjured a spear, using it to swipe at the legs of his challenger, but Heru jumped in time and kicked Setesh in the chest, pushing him backwards. Setesh rolled into a standing position and spat, seeing that Heru had also conjured a spear of his own.

"You are just like your father," Setesh cried out to Heru. "He has always thought himself my better. But it is I who protected this kingdom for hundreds of years. It is I! And I NEVER got the respect I was due."

Heru spat at the feet of his father's brother. "You had your chance to prove your worth, and instead of being a great leader you brought ruin to our land. It is YOU who has fallen short, not I and not my father. He was a great man, and you are his shadow."

"I am a great king!" Setesh shouted, and the earth trembled. I shivered and clutched my robes around me, and Anpu reached out to take my hand. "You are a child, speaking of things you do not know. Allow me to teach you a lesson!"

He flung his spear at Heru aimlessly, and Heru was able to duck him, stepping backwards casually. Setesh continued to press forward, not caring that his effort received little response, just hoping to cause hurt or draw blood, unable to focus.

Heru looked as if he would go on taunting Setesh, but decided against it and instead began to strike back, inexplicably pushing Setesh in the other direction. Heru punched him with the fist gripping the spear, and when Setesh threw his arms back in defense, Heru ducked to the ground, kicking the legs out from under the distracted fighter. Setesh landed on his back with a terrible thud, the surprise causing him to drop his sword. When he made his way to his knees, he was stopped by the two spears crossed on either side of his neck.

"Enough!"

The loud cry of his mother was enough to prevent Heru from striking the final, fatal blow to the neck of our brother, my husband. I exhaled loudly, feeling a stunning sense of relief and realizing that my eyes had filled with tears. Auset was right; this had been enough.

She walked up until she was standing slightly behind Heru, placing her reassuring hand on his shoulder. "You cannot take his life into your hands. I will not allow you to violate Maat in this way."

Heru gave a stern and defiant look to his mother over his shoulder, then looked across the field to Anpu, then back down to Setesh. "He killed our father, your husband. He violated everything that we hold sacred. He cannot be allowed another opportunity to destroy everything that has been established."

Auset shook her head, frowning and removing her hand from him. "And who will you be, once you've committed this act of vengeance?" she asked, taking the few short steps around him to stand behind Setesh, facing Heru, forcing him to see the wisdom of her mercy. "What will you become, if you are allowed to indulge in your wrath, as he once did?"

"Mwt, you must understand -"

"Enough, my son," she said in a much gentler tone. "His fate is not yours to decide."

Heru hesitated before reluctantly lowering the weapons to his side, but before Setesh could take advantage of his freedom, Auset bound him to her using a thin slip of papyrus, so fully charged by her magic that he couldn't break free. Setesh struggled against it briefly before accepting the inevitability of his capture.

Auset grabbed Setesh by his shoulders, then, without a word, disappeared in a flash. Heru turned to Anpu and I, making his way over to meet us. I smiled nervously, wiping my eyes and summoning the strength we'd all need to face the Great Father.

"Come, I will take you," I said, reaching out for his hand. He took my hand tenderly and looked away, breathing deeply. I looked to my left and took my son's hand once more, and he clutched mine with a determined resolve. In an instant we were separated from our earthly forms and arriving at home, where I was certain Ra was waiting for us, expectant.

We landed a few feet behind Auset, who kept Setesh bound and on his knees in front of her. Heru left my side to stand next to his mother, and Djehuty appeared facing us, at what seemed to be the front.

"They are here," Djehuty called out, and one by one I began to see the faces of the Neteru emerge from the darkness.

Our parents, Nut and Geb, the keepers of heaven and earth.

Shu and Tefnut, our grandparents, twins of wind and water.

Neith, grandmother of the Neteru, self-created one.

Atum, the elder statesman, finisher of the world.

Ptah, the master craftsman, he who answers prayers.

Bastet, protectress of home, family, and joy.

Seshat, wife of Djehuty, knower of secrets.

Kheper, the rising sun, the bringer into being.

Serket, she who causes the throat to breathe.

Khnum, the potter who creates things from himself.

Heru-Ur and Ausar, my brothers; one the great falcon, the other, the great King.

They were there, and all of the others, their forms materializing before us, to witness the reckoning. I tightened my grip around my son's hand, grateful that I would not have to stand alone.

Ra stepped out from the center, making long and deliberate strides to where Auset and Heru stood. He looked magnificent as ever, gold beams of light spiraling up his mighty frame like silks blowing in the wind. Ra motioned to Auset to release Setesh from the heka that kept him immobile; when she did, Setesh stood and attempted to return to the physical realm, with no success.

"No one is leaving until the proceedings are complete," Ra announced, mostly to Setesh, but loudly enough for all of us to hear. "It is time for this matter to be heard by all."

Auset looked at Heru, nodding for him to step forward. "Great Father," Heru started nervously, "I am the rightful heir to the kingdom of my father. It is I who should be given dominion over the beloved lands. I have inherited it, and with my defeat of Setesh I have earned it."

Setesh was less humble in his appeal. "Ausar forfeited his right to be sovereign when he fathered a child with my wife," he reminded, his tone snide and dismissive. "He violated the laws of Maat and he had no embodied son at the time, which meant kingship was rightly granted to me."

"What of your older brother, Heru-Ur?" Tefnut called out, "Was he not considered or consulted in the transferral of leadership?"

Heru-Ur cleared his throat. "I willingly relinquish any claim one may believe I have over the realm. I have no desire to rule. I am here only as a witness."

Tefnut seemed to be nodding her understanding. Setesh continued, feeling ever confident. "My fight with Heru is not reason for me to be displaced from the throne at this time."

"No, but your mismanagement of the realm is," Heru challenged, roused by seeing Setesh express such certainty. "You have lost favor with the people, and you have lost ground.

Your policies have practically ruined everything that we have worked for!"

Setesh began to clench his fists, the anger beginning to boil. "And you think you can do better? You are nothing but a child! I cannot believe we are even entertaining this discussion."

Heru looked to the Neteru. "I know I can do better. My mother was Great Royal Wife for hundreds of years, and she is one of great power and wisdom. My father was Naswt Biti, and I have not only his counsel, but the guidance of our seba Djehuty. I also have my brother, Anpu, who can serve as a counselor to me as well." He turned his attention to Ra. "I will allow myself to be guided and taught. I will learn from my father's mistakes and from the mistakes of Setesh. I do not take this responsibility lightly. I have been preparing every day of my incarnation for this."

Setesh scoffed. "So your only qualification is that others can help you? What does that say for what you can do? Nothing. I have been leading this kingdom on my own!"

"You had help," Heru reminded him dryly, and I smiled, grateful to be thought of.

That only made Setesh angrier. "I had traitors surrounding me! Betrayed by my own family! Deserted! Disrespected! And I still managed to rule. I found a way to break down all obstacles in my path. What can you do when you are faced with challenge? Run to your mother for help?"

"All obstacles except me." Heru stepped towards Setesh. "You LOST our battle! That is proof that you do not have what it takes to be Naswt Biti."

"YOU lost the first round," Setesh reminded him, moving in closer. "Now seems like a good time for a deciding match."

Heru closed the last inch of space between them. "Fine with me."

"Not fine with me," Ra told them, his voice amused with their tiny show of aggression. "You are not here to finish beating each other. You are here so that we may decide."

"I am afraid that neither of them really appears to understand the charge of being a sovereign leader," Atum spoke, his voice heavy with age and wisdom. He stepped forward from where he stood, a soft gleam radiating from his dark bald crown. "Both are being rather childish."

Serket stepped up with raised eyebrows, making her thin face appear even longer. "I agree," she added, "and I do not find either of their claims to be compelling."

Geb looked at Setesh. "My youngest son has wanted the opportunity to rule since he was born. He has always had a zest for leadership, a strong desire for it." He took a deep breath, and looked at Ra, apologetic. "But skill does not always accompany desire, nor wisdom."

Setesh seemed taken aback. "Is my own father saying that he does not think I am up for the task?" He sounded sincerely hurt.

"I am saying that you have the passion that one would want in their leader," Geb responding, imploring Setesh to understand. "But I am sure you have learned by now, passion is not enough."

Setesh looked away, unable to respond.

"Does no one believe that Setesh can do it?" Bastet said sweetly, in her calming purr-like voice. "He is an experienced warrior, and military leader, with talents that are essential if we are to retake the cities that were lost and reunite the two lands."

"And what happens if we give Setesh the tools to succeed? If he is better supported, perhaps he can turn everything around," Tefnut quickly added optimistically.

"For my part," Neith called out, surveying the room with an almost imperceptible squint, "I recommend that Heru be awarded the throne. I am prepared to cause the sky to *crash* to the earth if he is not."

Ra looked across the room at his mother and smiled. "Thank you for that, Mwt; your recommendation has been received." He turned his attention to Ptah and Khnum, neither of whom had chimed in. "I am interested in hearing your thoughts, my brothers."

Ptah glanced at the two contenders with a cautious smile. "I trust that whatever decision made will be in the best interests of all involved."

"Surely you have some thought you can voice," Neith prodded.

Ptah hesitated, finding it hard to stay silent at her insistence. "Should not this decision be made by those who know them best? Perhaps only the nine should have a say in this, and not us all." Khnum did not speak, but nodded his agreement.

Djehuty shook his head. "I fear that each of the nine have their own selfish motivations," he acknowledged. "Having all of us here to make this decision will ensure accountability to Divine order."

There was a brief pause before Ausar cleared his throat. "May I say something?" he asked, leaving our mother's side to stand closer to Ra and Djehuty.

Ra nodded. "Please do."

Ausar turned to address Setesh "I made quite a few mistakes with you, brother, but the one that matters most is probably not what you think it is." He paused and took a deep breath. "I made you feel that your contribution was unappreciated by not giving you the recognition that you needed. If I was truly the great King that everyone said I was, I would have given you the accolades that you desired. More than anything else that happened, I am most apologetic for how I mishandled you, and our relationship. When you pretended not to be angry, I should have known better, and I would have, if I had paid more attention to you, if I knew you as well I should have. I have apologized to you for quite a few things in the past, but not that. Not the most important thing."

Setesh looked confused at hearing these words, but also angry and not wanting to stop being angry, as if his heart was telling him he should stop, but he couldn't. He unclenched his fists and dropped his head, stepping back. My compassion overflowed; I could not stop myself from responding, and as I stepped towards him, Anpu let my hand go.

But Setesh did not turn to me. Instead, he looked at Auset, who reached her hand out to him, and then to Ausar, who smiled and nodded. There you are, I thought. Nut began to cry, and Geb wrapped his arm around her, letting her lean into him.

Setesh stepped closer to Auset, allowing her hand to rest upon his forearm, before turning to face the Great Father. "The decision is not mine to make," he mumbled humbly.

"No, it is not," Ra gently reminded us all, and motioned for Setesh to return to his place next to Heru at the front. I returned to where Anpu stood and took his hand again, and he squeezed it, which I was not expecting. "Has anyone else anything more to say?"

No one answered him. "Well then," he responded, mostly for himself. I looked to the back of Auset and knew that she was looking longingly at her husband, who was standing once more with our parents, and I hoped they would have time later to reconnect.

"I find in my head that I agree with Atum and Serket. There has been little done to prove that the realm is safe under either of you. But," Ra continued, looking directly at Setesh, "Heru has not had an opportunity to fail, whereas you have had your chance, Setesh, and you have not done the best job with what you have been given." He turned away from Setesh and faced the Neteru, pacing the room slowly. "To be fair, it has been a very short period of time. We've each made mistakes, and improved, yet Setesh has not been given enough time to show that he can improve, or will, or cannot, or will not."

Djehuty cleared his throat. "Each of us has the capacity to transform, as you well know."

Ra nodded. "I do. But for some of us, transformation does not happen easily." He turned back to look at Heru, then Setesh. "Nor does it always happen by what we do ourselves; most often, it requires the guidance of others."

He took a deep breath, still keeping his focus on Setesh. "What has concerned me most is your inability to forgive, which is a key component to your ability to lead. You have been in your earthly form for hundreds of years, and that heaviness may be contributing to the issue, so I'd like you to stay here for a while, spend some time with me before taking a new post governing lands that will need to be developed to the west."

Setesh nodded. Ra looked at Heru. "You are the rightful successor to your father's post, but more importantly, you have the support of some very key advisors. I am not sure if you alone are ready, but with Auset, Anpu, and Djehuty at your side, I will give you the chance to be the King that you say you will become."

Heru turned to Auset, and I could see he was beaming, as was Ausar, looking at his son proudly. Even Anpu had a hard time hiding his excitement, for Heru and for himself.

Ra turned to face the Neteru. "I believe we have come to the end. You are each free to depart, or stay, at your own will."

Many of them began to leave, but our parents stayed behind, to embrace Setesh, speaking to him quietly on the side. Anpu looked at me and I nodded, and he left my side to go hug his brother, and be embraced by their mother and father.

I looked at them, relieved at how everything had come together, and hardly noticed Ra making his way over to where I stood. "Take a walk with me," he said, less of a request and more of a loving demand. I turned to follow him and he took me back to the place of our last conversation, the long room not feeling as empty or as quiet as it once did.

"You seem to have reconciled things nicely with Anpu," Ra observed, motioning for me to sit. I did, and he sat next to me, leaning in such a way as to be facing me. I did the same, to look at him in kind.

"He has been receptive after the week he spent here with Djehuty," I admitted, nodding. "It wasn't until I saw him again that I really understood that he may not forgive me."

"But he has, or he is trying to."

I smiled and looked over his shoulder. "Yes, he is. So am I."

Ra tilted his head, forcing me to look him in the eye. "Are you? Or have you?"

I smiled again, and turned my attention to my lap. "I have. Or at least, I thought I had."

"And what is causing you to second guess yourself?"

I looked up, towards the front of the room. "Old habit."

Ra nodded and sat up straighter, not responding for a few moments. "How about me? Have you forgiven me?"

I looked at him. I wanted to be surprised by his question, but I wasn't. "I must admit that it has been a long time since I have given it much thought."

"But you have given it some thought."

I hesitated. "I was never sure if there was something I should be forgiving you for."

"But you were angry."

"Yes, I was angry," I admitted, "but I was never sure if my anger was justified."

Ra shrugged. "What if it was justified?"

I shook my head and shifted uncomfortably in my seat. "It's not as if you did anything wrong to me."

"Perhaps it is okay to be angry when someone does nothing to you."

"That sounds irrational," I charged.

"Perhaps anger is irrational," Ra responded, and to that I had no answer. I looked down at my feet again, uncomfortable with how immature this discussion had made me feel.

When Ra did not speak, I looked up and turned back to him. "The truth is that I was not irrational," I told him, for the first time being honest with the Great Father. "It was your charge to give each of us guidance, and when the time came I did not receive what I needed from you, or Djehuty. You left me out there for decades, for centuries. And when we needed you, where were you? Why didn't you interfere; why did you not say something?"

It was his turn to shift in his seat. "Should I have?"

I looked at him incredulously. "YES!"

Ra smiled at me. "And where would Anpu be, if I had? Or Heru? Or you?"

His question threw me off, but only slightly. "You and I both know it did not have to happen that way." I exhaled deeply, resigned. "Except it did, didn't it?"

I sighed again and leaned over, resting my elbows on my knees and my chin in my palms. "This way was so painful, so terrifying, I cannot help but to wish we could have avoided some of that."

"And yet this was the course you chose, for yourself and for everyone else."

I looked at him. "I did not choose to marry Setesh."

Ra shrugged once more. "You chose how to respond."

I sat back once more, crossing my feet at the ankle. "And I did the best that I could, which never really felt like enough. I just wanted to know that I was doing what I was *supposed* to be doing - what you wanted me to be doing."

He touched my shoulder reassuringly. "You are always doing what you are supposed to be doing, my darling girl. Always."

I felt myself crying. "I was so angry with myself," I told him, knowing he already knew but still needing him to hear me.

"You were just angry enough," he said. "Angry enough to try to be better. Angry enough to make better decisions, to make the right ones." Ra moved around again to sit a little closer to me, his arm stretched across the back of the bench. "You were forced to transform by the moment you were in, and you accepted that, with little complaint and little hesitation, if I remember correctly. You did not wait to be asked, and you did not wait to be told. You played the part that you were meant to play, and you did so with great bravery."

I poked out my lower lip a bit. "Thank you," I mumbled, not wanting to show how satisfying that was.

Ra chuckled. "So now, explain to me why you stayed in the per eah instead of coming home all those years ago."

"You know why," I sighed, reluctantly.

"I'd like to hear you say it."

I sighed once more. "Because I..." I stopped again, closing my eyes. "Because I made a choice."

Ra nodded and stood, causing me to look up at him. "As we each must. As we each do."

I shook my head. "Wisdom is very easy to learn and very difficult to practice."

"Now you've got it." He began to walk towards the back of the room, and I stood, turning to address him one last time.

"You knew, didn't you?" I asked, causing him to stop. Ra kept his back to me as I continued, "You knew about the snake; you knew Auset was there the whole time."

Ra turned and looked at me once more, smiling calmly. "Who among us can escape the consequences of their choices?"

We looked at each other for a moment longer, and I smiled,

nodding. Ra waved his right hand and Setesh appeared, standing stoically and alert. We both looked at Ra, confused, who turned his attention to Setesh. "I will summon you to my side in the solar barque once you have finished saying goodbye." He dispersed, and it was quick and bright, and when he'd gone, the room became a dark, empty space.

Setesh looked at me without moving. "I don't know how to stop being angry with you," he admitted softly. "I expected so much better from you."

"And I from you," I told him, which raised his eyebrows in surprise. "We both fell short. I wish we had known how to handle it better."

"What did you expect from me that I did not give you?"

I looked away and closed my eyes. "It's too late to hash out every detail." I looked back to him, wanting to never fight with him again. "There were so many things that you did not do, that you couldn't do, and that wasn't *my* fault, but it wasn't your fault either, not really, it was just -"

"My choice," he mumbled, cutting me off. "It was my choice."

I sighed and looked off into the distance. "We stopped being married long before Anpu was conceived."

He sighed. "Yes we did." We looked at each other once more. "I wish we'd handled that fact very differently."

"It happened," I whispered, "the way it was meant to."

Setesh frowned, the contemplative version. "I have to go."

"I know." I looked down at my feet for a moment. "I wish I had loved you enough."

He nodded. "I wish I had loved you enough."

I nodded, and took in the sight of him once more, my husband.

Setesh left without another word, dispersing in a slow and steady jolt. I took a deep breath, and wrapped my arms around myself, comfortable letting the silence and the darkness sink in.

"Are you sure everything is okay out there?" Auset shouted at me from the small courtyard on the opposite side of her bedroom. I sighed and smiled, amused by her motherly worry.

"I am sure, senet. Or perhaps I should call you Great Mother."

Auset stepped into the bedroom and looked at me with a girlish smirk. She looked lovely, her dark blue dress long and loose, with a shimmer that gleamed as the fabric moved with the breeze. Auset had chosen not to let her hair grow back, and it suited her, the cropped style that was once her husband's. She was wearing her lapis lazuli usekh around her neck and shoulders, and had just finished tying the dark red knot to her waist. I watched as she affixed the earrings of amethyst, then dropped her arms to her side, letting me look her over. I nodded my approval and approached her, carrying her Ankh and shuti on a small gold pillow.

She took the pillow from my hands and placed it on the bed, then threw her arms around me joyously. I hugged her in return, our affection for one another finding its happy medium.

Auset sighed before releasing me, then took an opportunity to look me up and down. I was wearing a matching rich green dress, and while my usekh did not feature the gleam of lapis, bright emeralds were placed similarly along my collar. There were so many reasons why today felt differently than the first coronation we'd attended, or even the second, and it was different, in all of the important ways.

Auset smiled and nodded. "I can only do this with you on my side," she said. I appreciated that she remembered, but it was no longer true.

"You CAN do this without me," I said, taking her hand, "but I am grateful that you will not have to."

"I am too."

She followed me as I led her into the hallway, and we walked side by side towards the great room, where I knew every seat was taken, every space filled.

We stepped in together, and everyone in the room stood and faced the aisle. There was only one gold throne on the dais, and it glimmered like something out of a dream. Auset and I took a deep breath, inhaling the sweet scent of lotus before marching somberly to the front of the room, each of our guests bowing to us as we took our place before the dais to wait for the land's next King.

An attendee stepped forward and handed Auset a large heavy book; she would hold it primarily for show, since she knew all of its contents by memory. I looked behind me at the trays that the attendees held with the adornments for Heru, checking one final time that everything needed was there. I nodded to Auset, who nodded to the back of the room, and Heru began to make his way down the center aisle.

Heru had never looked stronger, his eyes steeled and his shoulders calm and confident. Each step he took seemed both light and loud. His presence was known. He reached the front and knelt upon the leopard skin, as had his father, and stretched his arms out, palms facing the heavens. Heru flinched for just a moment, but took a deep breath and kept calm. I knew he was ready.

Auset took her time reciting the sacred passage, allowing the levity of the day to sink in. Heru did not look fazed or afraid, however; he simply waited patiently until his mother had finished. Then she looked down at him, and I stepped in closer.

"Who are you to this land?" Auset asked him.

He took a deep breath. "I am its father, its protector, its defender. I am he who guarantees security at all times, in all places. I cover this land with my shield and I guard it with my life. Without rest, without ease, without ceasing." I leaned in and wrapped the solid gold cuffs around his wrists and biceps, and he flexed slightly, and they fit perfectly.

"What will you do for this land?"

"Give all that is demanded at me, at all times, in all ways. Every drop of blood that flows through this body belongs to these beloved lands." I knelt at his side and tied the dark red knot around his waist.

"Who are you for your people?"

"A keeper of righteousness, an establisher of harmony, an espouser of truth, and an enforcer of justice. I am a symbol of Divinity, the jewel of the Hapi, the perfection of many incarnations." I snapped the usekh into place, the broad collar draping elegantly around his chest and shoulders.

"What will you do for your people?"

"I will govern with the full authority granted me by the Neteru. I will choose when to rule with compassion and when to show no mercy. I will respect the gravity of these choices and take responsibility for all that happens under my domain." I handed him the Heq and Naqqaqa, and he gripped them so tightly I thought they might break.

"Where is your domain?"

"The land of Nekhbet, the land of the flowering lotus, the land of the sedge." I picked up the Hedjet, both hands around its base, and slid it firmly onto his crown.

"Where is your domain?" Auset asked once more, firmer than before.

Heru swallowed. "The land of Wadjet, the land of the papyrus plant, the land of the bee." The Deshret was harder to slip on, but Heru did not move until I had it firmly in place.

As they had with his father, the crowd began to dance and chant even before Heru had gotten to his feet and he could not wait to face the people, his people. Heru held the Heq and

Naqqaqa tightly as he thumped his chest and joined the men in their stomping and roaring. He ascended the dais and took his place before his throne, the crowd growing louder as he got closer to his destination. Heru looked down to Auset, who nodded at him to quiet the crowd, and he did, before sitting atop the throne of his father and mother.

Auset looked at me and I could tell that we were giving one another the same broad grin, not caring that it was hurting our faces. She tilted her head at me and the butterflies began in my stomach. I looked down the aisle and saw my son making his way to the front, the black Nemmes around his head and shoulders, his posture impeccable. I lifted my chin and he nodded at me before looking up to the new Naswt Biti and performing the proper greeting, the Nedj Hra Heberber. Everyone in the room stood and followed suit, bowing to Heru, the first acknowledgement of his ascension to the throne.

"I have learned quite a bit in preparing myself for this charge, and one point that I have found most resonant is that wisdom cannot only come from self. There are times when even I will need to look to others, for they may see clearly when my vision is blurry." Heru looked down at Anpu. "I am fortunate to have a brother who has a sense of right and wrong, who thinks and sees clearly, who takes his time before passing judgment and who is ready, willing, and able to give his talents, time, and energy to this realm."

Heru stood and nodded to Anpu, and Anpu dropped to one knee. "It is my honor to appoint you to the role of **Djati**, my foremost council, second in command throughout the kingdom only to me, Naswt Biti."

Anpu called out, "It is MY honor to serve you, Naswt Biti, to serve the people, to give my life to these beloved lands. I pledge to uphold the faith that you have placed in me by wielding the power that you have granted me with wisdom, caution, and respect."

Heru turned to the throne before beginning to descend the dais. Once on the ground, he touched Anpu on the shoulder, and Anpu stood, and Heru placed a large golden Ankh in his left hand. They looked as if they wanted to hug, but protocol demanded a different sense of propriety, so instead they shook hands firmly before turning to their adoring public. The room was once again filled with the sounds of a joyful celebration, and I felt a few wayward tears making their way down my face, my grin brighter than ever.

Anpu and Heru climbed the dais together, and Heru sat once more while Anpu stood slightly behind the throne, to its left. I stayed before the dais, and my sister stepped out into the aisle to give the closing Dwa, taking a deep breath.

"Praise be to Amen Ra. I make hymns in His name; I give Him praise to the heights of heaven and to the ends of the earth. I tell of His majesty and might to those who sail downstream and those who sail upstream. Stand in awe of Him. Declare Him to your son and daughter, to the great and the small. Declare Him to generation after generation who are not yet born. Declare Him to the fish in the deep and to the birds in the sky. Declare Him to the ignorant and to the wise. Stand in awe of Him."

Auset paused for a long time, allowing each person in the room to bask in the moment and experience the sentimentality of the ceremony and the prayer. I found myself breathing deeply, inhaling the essence of the moment so that I could hold it forever.

"I found Amen Ra came when I called to Him," Auset began to finish the prayer in a clear and resonant tone. "He gave me His hand and I found my heart strong and full of joy. And all I did succeeded."

Amen Maat, I whispered, then crossed my arms over my chest. I exhaled deeply, grateful that we had gotten through the day, and hopefully anticipating the many days before us that remained.

GLOSSARY

Ab en NTR – the will of God; the Divine mind

Abdju – one of the oldest cities of the ancient world, known to many as Abydos

Amen-Ra - the unseen and seen forces behind all of Creation; the culmination of the Divine essence (omnipresence) and the Divine power (omnipotence)

Amen Maat – May harmony be established

Ankh – called the key of life; embodies the masculine, the feminine, and their sacred union

Apep – the embodiment of chaos and darkness; said to attack the solar barque daily and is thus considered the enemy of Ra

Aten – the physical sun disc

Deshret - red crown

Djati - head of a company of statesmen and high officials who counsel the King

Dua - to express thanks and gratitude

Dwa - to praise; to uplift in worship

E m htp - I come in peace and satisfaction

Gerh Nfr – Good Night

Hapi - Nile River

Hebenu – ancient city located on the site of modern-day Kom el-Ahmar

Hedjet - white crown

Heq - crook carried by the King, represents sovereign authority

Het NTR – house of God; place of worship and spiritual enlightenment

Hmt Naswu – Royal Wife

Inbu Hedj – large city of the ancient world, later called Menefer and eventually known as Memphis

Isfet – chaos, imbalance, disorder, and injustice; the principles championed by Apep

Iunet – famous temple complex of Dendera

KMT/Kemet – Ancient Egypt

Maakheru - true of thought, word, and deed

Maat - truth, justice, righteousness, and harmonious balance; the virtues and morals that serve as the foundation of Kemety spiritual principles and cultural tradition

Medu NTR - words of God; divine speech

Meskhenet - birth house; your fate as related to the conditions upon which you entered the world (for example, your zodiac sign is part of your Meskhenet)

Mwt - mother

Naqqaqa - flail carried by the king; represents the responsibility of wielding great power

Naswt Biti - ancient name for pharaoh; was given to the King who unified Upper and Lower Kemet. Means "he of the sedge and the bee"

Nedj Hra Heberber – to pay homage to one (royals, high priests, ranking officials) by bowing

Nemmes - crown worn on the heads of royalty, most commonly recognized from the bust of Tutankhamen

NTR/Neter - everything we can perceive and everything we cannot perceive; considered in common vernacular to be akin to God

NTRU/Neteru - attributes of NTR that exist to maintain life as we know it; understanding these attributes aid our ability to relate to self, others, and the world around us; considered in common vernacular to be deities or gods and goddesses

Per eah – great house

Seba - teacher

Sekhem – personal power; the kundalini force

Sen – brother

Senet – sister

Seret – a title used by a woman of royalty

Shem e m htp - I go in peace and satisfaction

Ta Meri - the beloved land; another name for Kemet

Tem - no

TepRa – the divine utterance from the highest authority; known in colloquial speech as oracle

Tu - yes

Urat – cobra that sits upon the brow as a representation of the kundalini force

Usekh - broad collar

Waset – ancient city known today as Thebes, which was located within the modern city of Luxor

Yit - father

Yit Eah - great father

ACKNOWLEDGEMENTS

To my mom, Lenore, and my father, Henry, who allowed me to deepen my love for literature even at the expense of my vision and sleep pattern.

To Isaac, Katrina, Bryant, Hannah, Tashika, Twana, Breanna, Aaliyah, Daviana, and Royce, for teaching me that unconditional love is always accompanied by immeasurable aggravation.

To Mentu Ra for helping me stay committed to my health. To Maaka'ra for bringing me cake.

To Raven Seshat Sat'Heru of Ab Seshat Marketing Services for managing to do such beautiful typesetting work and simultaneously prove how disciplined you truly can be.

To Sa-Nekhet en Asut Menta (Qupid Art) of Konscious Creations for bringing imagination to life for the cover design, and surprising me with a rewarding flyer.

To my beta readers, Sekhem Ra, Huron, and Karen, for your feedback; it allowed me to get necessary perspective on this journey and improve on the perfect.

To Heru Seed (Robert Gay) of Tehuti Films for not hesitating to set up a photo shoot for one most reluctant model.

To Heseti Ra Kheper (Kraig Murphy) of Kemotion Visuals for never ceasing to lend your website building expertise.

To Khisa for reading the cosmos to help me plan the book release, and an invaluable friendship.

To Mwt Shepset Sharrur TepRamutab and Nu Aset Temple.
To Kajara Nia Yaa NebtHet and Ra Sekhi Arts Temple.
To the Serudj Tawi Ketem.

To the Temple of Anu. My tribe, my flesh, my being.
To Hem NTR Naswt Biti Ra Sankhu Kheper.

Made in the USA
Middletown, DE
06 April 2016